JOHN BUNYAN.

THE

PILGRIM'S PROGRESS

FROM THIS WORLD

TO THAT WHICH IS TO COME.

DELIVERED UNDER

THE SIMILITUDE OF A DREAM.

By John Bunyan.

THE TEXT DIVIDED INTO CHAPTERS; WITH AN INTRODUCTION; INDEX; NOTES, CHIEFLY SELECTED FROM BUNYAN'S OWN WRITINGS; AND A SKETCH OF THE AUTHOR'S LIFE.

BY STEPHEN B. WICKENS.

For here have we no continuing city, but we seek one to come.
Hebrews, xiii, 14.

TWENTY-FIFTH THOUSAND.

New-York:
PUBLISHED BY CARLTON & PHILLIPS,
200 MULBERRY-STREET.
1854.

BIOGRAPHICAL SKETCH.

The author of the Pilgrim's Progress was born at Elstow, a small village near Bedford, England, in 1628. His father, who was very poor, was a tinker, and brought up his sons, of whom he had several, to the same business, but of none of them is anything known except the subject of this notice.

Bunyan records with gratitude that his parents, notwithstanding their poverty, sent him to school, "to learn to read and write, the which," he adds, "I also attained according to the rate of other poor men's children, though to my shame I confess, I did soon forget that little I learnt, even almost utterly." Associating with wicked companions he was early initiated into profaneness, and, impelled by the natural energy of his character, he soon became a sort of ring-leader in all kinds of boyish vice and ungodliness. "From a child," he says, "I had but few equals for cursing, lying, and blaspheming the name of God; yea, so settled and rooted was I in these things, that they became as a second nature to me."

But he was not suffered to pursue his vicious career without some checks of conscience, and warnings of the awful consequence of such a course of life. "Even in my childhood," he says, "the Lord did scare and affrighten me with fearful dreams. For often, after I have spent the day in sin, I have in my bed been greatly afflicted, while asleep, with the apprehensions of devils and wicked spirits, who still, as I then thought, laboured to draw me away with them, of which I could never be rid. Also I should at these years be greatly afflicted and troubled with the thoughts of the fearful torments of hell-fire, &c. These things, I say, when I was but a child, did so distress my soul, that then, in the midst of my childish sports and vanities, amidst my vain companions, I was often much cast down and afflicted in my mind therewith, yet I could not let go my sins." The effect of these dreams was but slight and transient; and when after awhile they left him, and his apprehensions of future punishment wore off, he gave loose to the reins of his vicious propensities, and followed after sin more greedily than ever.

When about seventeen years old, the civil war then raging in England, he enlisted as a soldier in the parliamentary army. He was present at the siege of Leicester, where on one occasion he was drawn out to stand as sentinel, but another, offering himself, was sent in his place and soon after killed at his post. Twice also during his youth Bunyan was providentially preserved when in imminent danger of drowning. These mercies made little impression at the time, but were afterward remembered with thanksgiving.

Soon after quitting the army, and when only about nineteen years of age, by the advice of friends who thought it might have some effect in restraining his vicious course, he married; "and my mercy was," he says, "to light upon a wife whose father was counted godly. We came together as poor as poor might be, not having so much household stuff as a dish or spoon betwixt us both; yet this she had for her part, *The Plain Man's Pathway to Heaven*, and *The Practice of Piety*, which her father had left her when he died. In these two books I would sometimes read with her, wherein I also found some things that were somewhat pleasing to me; but all this while I met with no conviction. She would also be often a telling me of what a godly man her father was, and how he would reprove and correct vice, both in his house and among his neighbours; and what a strict and holy life he lived, both in word and deed."

The reading of these books, and the admonitions of his wife, he tells us, begot in him "some desire to reform his vicious life, and fall in very eagerly with the religion of the times; to wit, to go to church twice a day, and that too with the foremost, and there very devoutly say and sing as others did ·" yet still he felt no convictions of guilt, and could not give up his sins. Some time after, he was shamed out of his habit of profane swearing by a severe and unexpected reproof from a woman of notoriously bad character. He also began to take delight in reading some parts of the Bible, which led to further reformation in his outward conduct. His neighbours were amazed at this change "from prodigious profaneness to something like a moral life," and began to commend him as a religious man; "yet," he says, "I was but a painted hypocrite. I was proud of my godliness, and thought I pleased God as well as any man in England."

From this self-righteous delusion he was awakened by hearing a few pious females converse on the subject of religion. Their talk was about a new birth—the work of God in their hearts—how they were convinced of their miserable state by nature—how God had visited their souls with his love in Christ Jesus—with what promises they had been comforted and supported against the temptations of the devil, &c. "At this," says Bunyan, "I felt my own heart began to shake, and mistrust my condition to be naught; for I saw that in all my thoughts about religion and salvation the new birth did never enter into my mind; neither knew I the comfort of the word and promise, nor the deceitfulness and treachery of my own wicked heart. . . I was greatly affected with their words, both because by them I was convinced that I wanted the true tokens of a truly godly man, and also because by them I was convinced of the happy and blessed condition of him that was such an one."

He was now, to use his own language, "in a flame to find the way to heaven and glory;" so intent was his mind on spiritual and eternal things, that "neither pleasures, nor profits, nor persuasions, nor threats, could make it let go its hold; it would then," he says, "have been as difficult for me to have taken my mind from heaven to earth, as I have found it often since to get it again from earth to heaven."

Having then but little knowledge in divine things, he was much perplexed by the numerous errors which were abroad in the land, especially those taught by a vile set of Antinomians called Ranters. Distrusting his own wisdom, he wisely sought that "which is from above," and betook himself to hearty prayer in this manner:—"O Lord, I am a fool, and not able to know the truth from error: Lord, leave me not to my own blindness, either to approve of or condemn this doctrine; if it be of God, let me not despise it; if it be of the devil, let me not embrace it. Lord, I lay my soul in this matter only at thy foot, let me not be deceived, I humbly beseech thee." Such a prayer, offered in sincerity and faith, could not be denied. "Blessed be God," he continues, "who put it into my heart to cry to him to be kept and directed; for I have since seen even the effects of that prayer, in his preserving me, not only from Ranting errors, but from those also that have sprung up since."

The limits of this brief sketch will not allow us to enter into a relation of the fierce and distressing conflicts and temptations through which he passed before he entered into the liberty of the children of God. Difficulties about election, fears lest he had outlived the day of grace, misconceptions of passages of Scripture, (especially Heb. xii, 16, 17,) and blasphemous suggestions of the enemy of souls, so harassed and distracted him that for the space of two years, with a few brief interruptions, he was almost in a state of despair. But at length this passed over, and "the Sun of righteousness" arose upon his soul "with healing in his wings." "Now," says he, "did my chains fall off my legs indeed; I was loosed from my afflictions and irons; my temptations also fled away; so that from that time those dreadful scriptures of God left off to trouble me. Now went I also home rejoicing, for the grace and love of God."

After he had been taken out of the horrible pit and miry clay of despair, and his feet set upon the rock Christ Jesus, he united himself with the Baptist church at Bedford. This was 1655, when he was about twenty-seven years of age. His conversion exercised a beneficial influence on some of those who had been his companions in sin. He says, "When God made me sigh they would hearken, and inquiringly say, 'What is the matter with John?' When I went to seek the bread of life, some of them would follow, and the rest be put in a muse at home. Yea, almost the whole town, at first, at times, would go out to hear at the place where I found good; yea, young and old for awhile had some reformation on them: also some of them, perceiving that God had mercy upon me, came crying to him for mercy to."

He had not long been connected with the church, when he was desired by some of the most pious and judicious members to take a more prominent part in their religious exercises, by occasionally speaking a word of exhortation to the people. This, at first, his modesty and a feeling of unfitness for the work induced him to decline; but his brethren, being convinced from his promptness in prayer, his wonderful acquaintance with the Scriptures, and his readiness of utterance, that he possessed gifts which might and ought to be used for the edification of the church, continued their entreaties, until, though with much diffidence, he consented to their request, and "did twice," he tells us, "at two several assemblies, (but in private,) discover his gift among them; at which they not only seemed to be, but did solemnly protest, as in the sight of the great God, they were both affected and comforted; and gave thanks to the Father of mercies for the grace bestowed on him." At length, being encouraged thereto by a sense of duty, by the approbation of those who heard him, and by the continued desires of the church, he was, with seven others, after solemn prayer and fasting, "more particularly called forth and appointed to a more ordinary and public preaching of the word." His commission was similar to that of a local preacher among the Methodists; for he continued to exercise his vocation as a tinker, while he preached the gospel, "without charge," in the country round about. As a preacher he soon became eminently successful and popular, and the people flocked by hundreds, from all parts, to hear him. But he cared little for the applause of men, being never satisfied unless he saw some good effect from his preaching. "If I were fruitless," he says, "it mattered not who commended; but if I were fruitful, I cared not who did condemn." So greatly did he rejoice over his spiritual children, that he reckoned himself as possessing great treasures in every place where he had been instrumental in the conversion of souls. In the exercise of his ministry his practice was to get into the "darkest" places in the neighbourhood; "not," he says, "because he could not endure the light, but because he found his spirit lean most after awakening and converting work." Like Paul, too, he preferred "to preach the gospel where Christ was not named," lest he "should build upon another man's foundation."

In 1660, Charles II. being restored to the throne, episcopacy was once more established by law, and no other form of religion tolerated; and the old penal laws against Dissenters were restored and enforced, and new ones enacted. In the persecution which followed, Bunyan had the honour of being one of the first victims. On the 12th of November, 1660, he went to preach at a village called Samsell, in Bedfordshire; but just as he had commenced the services he was arrested and taken to prison. Here he lay till the quarter-sessions of the county, which were held at Bedford in January, 1661, when he was indicted for having "devilishly and perniciously abstained from coming to church," and with being "a common upholder of unlawful meetings and conventicles." In a conversation with the justices he admitted that he had held meetings for prayer and exhortation; and this being taken as a confession of the indictment, he was remanded back to prison, and threatened that if he did not in three months agree to conform to the established church, and leave off preaching, he should be banished the kingdom. The latter part of the sentence was never attempted to be carried into effect, but for twelve long years he was kept a prisoner in the common jail. During this confinement he was graciously sustained by the consolations of the Spirit; though at times he was much cast down with thoughts of the destitution of his wife and four children, one of whom was blind. He employed himself during his imprisonment in making tagged laces for the support of his family, and in writing religious books, especially the First Part of the Pilgrim's Progress, and his autobiography, entitled Grace Abounding to the Chief of Sinners. The circulation of these books has been productive of far more good than he could have effected by his preaching, had he been at liberty; so that the malice of his persecutors was overruled by God, to "the furtherance of the gospel."

The Lord gave him such favour in the sight of the keeper that for a time he was allowed to go in and out almost as he pleased, so that he could frequently be with his family, and sometimes in the night he would visit the little flocks to whom he had been accustomed to dispense the word of life. His frequent absence from the prison came at length to the ears of some persecuting prelates, who sent down an officer to talk with the jailer on the subject; and, in order to find him out, he was to arrive there in the middle of the night. Bunyan was at home that night with his family, but so restless that he could not sleep: he therefore told his wife that he must return immediately. He did so; and the jailer blamed him for coming in at so unseasonable an hour. Early in the morning the messenger came, and said, "Are all the prisoners safe?" "Yes." "Is John Bunyan safe?" "Yes." "Let me see him." He was called, appeared, and all was well. After the messenger left, the jailer said to Bunyan, "Well, you may go out again when you think proper; for you know when to return better than I can tell you." During the last seven years, however, his confinement was very rigid.

In October, 1671, while yet in prison, he was elected one of the pastors of the Baptist church at Bedford, of which he was a member; and this office he held for sixteen years after his release, which took place in the latter part of 1672 He did not, however, confine his labours to the town of Bedford. It was his custom two or three times a year to take an extensive tour in "the region round about;" and once a year he paid a visit to London, where his reputation was so great that the place in which he preached would no contain half the people that came to hear him.

It was during one of his annual visits to the metropolis, that his useful labours were brought to a close, his last sermon being preached there in July, 1688, from John i, 3. The occasion of his death was as follows:—A young man, a neighbour of Bunyan, falling under the displeasure of his father, who threatened to disinherit him, applied to Bunyan to act as mediator in his behalf. The good man, though labouring under bodily indisposition, readily undertook the task, and went to Reading for that purpose. Having happily succeeded in effecting a reconciliation, he set out on horseback on his return to London, a distance of thirty-seven miles. The day proved rainy, and he arrived wet and late at the house of the friend with whom he lodged. His exposure brought on a violent fever, which in ten days terminated his laborious and eventful life. He fell asleep in Jesus on the 31st August, 1688, aged sixty years.

"Servant of God, well done!
Rest from thy loved employ;
The battle's fought, the victory won,
Enter thy Master's joy."

INTRODUCTION.

We question whether the whole range of English literature comprises another book that has obtained a celebrity so great and a circulation so wide, or that has been the source of so much pleasure and profit to its readers, as the Pilgrim's Progress—a work which, in view of its extraordinary merits and the disadvantages under which it was composed, may well be regarded as one of the most extraordinary productions of human genius.

The First Part of the work, as is well known, was written while Bunyan was confined in Bedford jail, "a prisoner for the word of God and the testimony of Jesus." The manner and occasion of its composition are related by the author in the Apology with which it is introduced to the reader, from which it appears that it was not the result of any preconceived design, the first idea of the work suddenly occurring to him when he was engaged on and had nearly completed another book on a somewhat similar subject—"the way and race of saints." The idea being too good to be lost, he "set it down," and one thought introducing another, and these again beginning to "multiply," he concluded to "divert" his "vacant seasons" in carrying out the plan thus spontaneously suggested to his mind. This he did without the least thought of publication, or indeed any other inducement than the pleasure he experienced in the performance.

> "Thus I set pen to paper with delight,
> And quickly had my thoughts in black and white:
> For having now my method by the end,
> Still as I pull'd it came; and so I penn'd
> It down; until at last it came to be,
> For length and breadth, the bigness which you see."

"When the general idea was once started, we can easily believe that with a rapidity of forethought and combination beyond the power of slower faculties to comprehend, the whole road from the field where Christian meets Evangelist to the gates of the Celestial City would be opened in perspective, its main divisions would be marked, and the grand events in the journey of the Pilgrim fixed by the author, almost without a conscious effort of the imagination at the time. . . . Everything connected with the Pilgrim's Progress, of human infirmity or religious experience, had been intensely and unremittingly 'the burden of the Lord' laid upon the author's spirit, even from his youth upward;* and when, in the course of composing another book, the plan of this crossed his thought, it was accomplished *necessarily*, we may say, in the easy and spontaneous manner which he himself has stated."—*Montgomery.*

The work being finished, the author not unnaturally supposed that what had afforded himself so much gratification might, if published, be interesting and useful to others also; and he therefore sought advice of his friends on the subject.

"Some said, *John, print it;* others said, *Not so;*
Some said, *It might do good;* others said, *No.*"

Finding his counsellors thus divided in opinion, he at length concluded to give the casting vote in his own favour, and test the soundness of their advice by sending the work to the press, leaving it for the public to settle the question, "which advised for the best." The objections which the author states and answers in his Apology are doubtless the same as were urged by those of his friends who would have dissuaded him from publishing.

* In the preface to his Holy War, he says of this part of the Pilgrim, "It came *from mine own heart*," &c. That much of it (especially Hopeful's account of his conversion) is a transcript of his own experience, there can be no doubt. Some striking parallel passages from the Pilgrim and Grace Abounding are given in the Life of Bunyan, pp. 268, 269; and the number might be greatly increased

It was long a matter of doubt in what year the Pilgrim first appeared, no copy of the original edition being known to be in existence; but it was commonly supposed, that as it was written during the period of the author's imprisonment, it must have been published if not before, at least soon after, his release. This opinion, however, was shown to be erroneous by Mr. Philip, who, in his Life of Bunyan, gives a chronological list of his writings, drawn up and published in 1691 by Charles Doe, a cotemporary and friend of the dreamer, who entitled it, "A Catalogue-Table of Mr. Bunyan's Books, and their succession in publishing; most according to his own reckoning." In this list "The Pilgrim's Progress, First Part," is placed, without any date, between "The Strait Gate," published in 1676, and "Come and Welcome," which appeared in 1678, showing that it must have been originally published in one of those years or in the intermediate one. But the matter has recently been put beyond doubt or conjecture by the discovery, in fine preservation, of a copy of the *First* edition, "Printed for Nath. Ponder, at the Peacock in the Poultrey, near Cornhill. 1678." It is a 12mo. volume of two hundred and fifty-three pages, and in a bookseller's catalogue of that day is advertised, "price, bound, 1*s.* 6*d.*" The title-page presents the same words and order of arrangement as have so long been familiar to all classes of readers; with the remarkable distinction, found in all the older editions, that the word DREAM is made the prominent feature, being in much larger type than any other word in the page.

Mr. Pocock of London, to whose Bibliographical Notice we are indebted for these and several other particulars, was allowed by the proprietor to examine this rare and interesting volume, and collate it with subsequent editions. The result of this comparison shows, that the author afterward greatly enlarged and improved his work by adding to his original conceptions several new scenes and characters.

The following passages were all inserted subsequently to the first edition.

1. Christian's discovery of his distress to his wife and children, from "In this plight," to "what shall I do to be saved?" See pages 46, 47, of this edition.

2. His meeting with Mr. Worldly Wiseman, and its consequences, and the second meeting with Evangelist, from "Now as Christian was walking solitary by himself," to "Mr. Worldly Wiseman's counsel."—Pp. 59–69.

3. Christian's relation to Goodwill of the cause of his delay.—Pp. 72, 73.

4. His discourse with Charity at the house Beautiful, from "Then said Charity," to "thou hast delivered thy soul from their blood."—Pp. 110–112.

5. The four lines of verse on Christian's leaving the palace.—P. 118.

6. The appearance of Evangelist to Christian and Faithful before they came to Vanity Fair, from "Now when they had got almost to the end of this wilderness," to "as unto a faithful Creator."—Pp. 159–161.

7. The subsequent reference to Evangelist.—P. 168.

8. The account of Mr. By-ends' rich kindred.—P. 178.

9. Mr. By-ends' conversation with his three friends, &c., from "Now I saw in my dream," to "the flames of a devouring fire!"—Pp. 180–187.

10. The account of the "old monument," from "Now I saw," to "remember Lot's wife."—Pp. 189–192.

11. The whole account of Giant Despair's wife, ending with, "I will search them in the morning."—Pp. 199–204.

12. The meeting of the pilgrims, after passing the river, by the king's trumpeters, from, "There came out also," to "they came up to the gate."—Pp. 267, 268.

The work is introduced as usual by The Author's Apology, and ends with the lines entitled The Conclusion, both of which are exactly the same as in the later editions.

The only other variation to be noticed is, that in this *first* edition several of the songs are inserted without the words which now connect them with the narrative. The addition of these connecting words was no improvement to the book, for by them the author's reflections are sometimes strangely put into the mouths of the pilgrims. Examples of this may be found on pages 158, 228, 233: in the last instance Bunyan had put in the margin, opposite his rhymes, these words, "The Dreamer's Note," which, with singular inconsistency, he retained after inserting the line which appropriates them to Christian.

Such was the favour with which the work was at once received, that a "*Second* Edition, with Additions," containing two hundred and seventy-six pages, was issued in the same year as the first. There is a copy of it in the British Museum, and another in the Bodleian Library at Oxford.

To the *third* edition was prefixed an engraved frontispiece, containing in the foreground a portrait of "the author dreaming," with a lion watching in a den beneath, (probably designed as an emblem of the author's imprisonment,) while in the back ground is seen the pilgrim, "with a book in his hand and a great burden on his back," wending his way from the City of Destruction to "the wicket-gate." It was, for the time it was published, quite a respectable engraving.* We cannot ascertain that any copy of this edition has been discovered.

The *fourth* edition, "with additions," appeared in 1680. It contained two hundred and eighty-eight pages. The popularity of the work was at this time so great as to ex-

* A very curious variation of this portrait was published in 1684 as the frontispiece to the first edition of the Second Part of the Dream, beautifully engraven by Sturt. In this Part the author's figure is brought down to the lowest line of the picture, the den and lion being omitted. Above him, Christiana, Mercy, and the four children are travelling from Destruction to the wicket-gate, near which stands the dragon-dog, with the enemy's castle on the other side.—*Pocock.*

cite the cupidity of certain knavish booksellers, who now began to issue spurious editions, as we learn from the following statement printed on the back of the portrait-frontispiece prefixed to the fourth genuine edition:

"*Advertisement from the Bookseller.* The *Pilgrim's Progress*, having sold several Impressions, and with good Acceptation among the People (there are some malicious men of our profession of lewd principles, hating honesty, and Coveting other men's rights, and which we call *Land Pirates*, one of this society is called *Thomas Bradyll* a Printer, who I found Actually Printing my book for himself, and five more of his Confederates,) but in truth he hath so abominably and basely falcified the true Copie, and changed the Notes, that they have abused the Author in the sense, and the Proprietor of his right, (and if it doth steal abroad, they put a cheat upon the people.) You may distinguish it thus, The Notes are Printed in Long Primer, a base old letter almost worn out, hardly to be read, and such is the Book itself. Whereas the true Copie is Printed in a Leigable fair Character, and Brevier Notes as it alwaies has been, this Fourth Edition hath, as the third had, The Author's Picture before the Title, and hath more then 22 passages of Additions, pertinently placed quite thorow the Book, which the Counterfeit hath not. *N. Ponder.*"

The *fifth* edition, "with additions," was also published in 1680. In addition to the portrait it contained a whole-page wood-cut of the martyrdom of Faithful, with four lines of verse beneath. This was the first edition that contained any illustration besides the portrait. On the back of the frontispiece was the following advertisement announcing the publication of several additional illustrations engraved on copper, which were sold separately, for one shilling.

"The Pilgrim's Progress having found good acceptation among the people, to the carrying off the fourth impression, which had many additions more than any preceding: and the publisher, observing that many persons desired to have it illustrated with Pictures, hath endeavoured to gratifie them therein: and besides those that are ordinarily printed to this fifth impression, hath provided Thirteen copper-cuts, curiously engraven, for such as desire them."

The *eighth* edition, published in 1682, contained a portrait similar to the preceding ones, but not so well executed;

also wood-cuts of Faithful's martyrdom, the Castle of Giant Despair, and the Pilgrims carried upon clouds to the Celestial City, with verses beneath each cut. No additions were made to the work after this, though the words, "with additions," were continued on the title-page for several years.

The *tenth* edition, published in 1685, is advertised in Dunton's Catalogue for that year at one shilling. In this edition the cut of Doubting Castle is omitted; and the author's name is spelled BVNIAN in the title-page. On the back of the title is an advertisement of the *Second* Part of the Pilgrim's Progress, price also one shilling, published in the preceding year.

In 1692 appeared the *thirteenth* edition, containing fourteen new wood-cuts, rude enough both in design and execution, though superior to the former ones. They were probably most of them copied from the "copper-cuts," published in 1680.

To each of these cuts in the old editions were attached four lines of indifferent but characteristic verse, which were retained as established parts of the pictures so long as the original designs were copied and republished, which they continued to be for more than a century; as we have seen them all in an edition not more than fifty years old. These verses having no connection with the narrative, except as appendages to the cuts by which it was illustrated, they are rarely found in modern editions; but as it was our desire to include all that Bunyan published as a part of the work, we have added them in those cases where we have given cuts of the subjects to which they refer; the remainder, with a list of the old illustrations, will be found below.

The *first* cut represented Evangelist meeting Christian, having in his hand a scroll, with the words, "Fly from the wrath to come." The verse will be found on p. 48.

The *second* represents Evangelist meeting Christian when the latter, having gone out of the way by advice of Mr.

Worldly-Wiseman, is alarmed lest Mount Sinai should fall on his head.

When Christians unto carnal men give ear,
Out of their way they go, and pay for't dear;
For Master *Worldly-Wiseman* can but show
A saint the way to bondage and to woe.

The *third* cut represents Christian knocking at the Wicket-gate. See p. 70.

The *fourth* represents him arrayed in the fine robe given him by the "shining ones." His burden is falling into the sepulchre, and his old rags are lying about; but strangely enough, no cross is to be seen.

Who's this? The Pilgrim. How! 'tis very true,
Old things are past away; all's become new.
Strange! he's another man, upon my word:
They be fine feathers that make a fine bird.

In the *fifth* cut, Christian is sitting in the arbour on the top of the Hill Difficulty; beneath are Formalist and Hy pocrisy losing their way, to whom the lines refer:

Shall they who wrong begin, yet rightly end?
Shall they at all have safety for their friend?
No, no; in headstrong manner they set out,
And headlong will they fall at last, no doubt.

The *sixth* represents him passing the lions after ascending the hill.

Difficulty is behind, Fear is before;
Tho' he's got on the hill, the lions roar.
A Christian man is never long at ease,
When one fright's gone, another doth him seize.

In the *seventh* cut Christian, clad in armour, is descend. ing from the palace into the Valley of Humiliation. The verse under it is a repetition of one in the text. See p. 118.

The *eighth* represents Christian's battle with Apollyon.

A more unequal match can hardly be;
Christian must fight an angel; but you see
The valiant man, by handling sword and shield,
Doth make him, tho' a dragon, quit the field.

In the *ninth* he is seen passing the Valley of the Shadow of Death. See page 126.

The subject of the *tenth* cut is the trial of Faithful before Lord Hategood.

> Now *Faithful* play the man, speak for thy God;
> Fear not the wicked's malice nor their rod:
> Speak boldly man, the truth is on thy side,
> Die for it, and to death in triumph ride.

Under the *eleventh* cut, which represents Faithful being burnt at the stake, and also ascending to heaven in a chariot of flame, are these lines:—

> Brave *Faithful!* bravely done in word and deed.
> Judge, witnesses, and jury, have, instead
> Of overcoming thee, but shown their rage;
> When they are dead thou'lt live from age to age.

In the *twelfth* picture Christian and Hopeful are seen shut up in Doubting Castle, while the Giant is keeping watch before the door with a club in his hand. The cut and the lines are given on the next page.

The *thirteenth* cut represents the shepherds entertaining the pilgrims on the Delectable Mountains.

> Mountains Delectable they now ascend,
> Where shepherds be, which to them do commend
> Alluring things, and things that cautions are;
> Pilgrims are steady kept by faith and fear.

In the *fourteenth*, and last, we see Christian and Hopeful passing the River of Death, with two angels standing on the shore to receive them.

> Now, now, look how the holy pilgrims ride,
> Clouds are their chariots, angels are their guide!
> Who would not here for Him all hazards run
> That thus provides for his when this world's done?

The original cut, to which these lines were adapted, represented the pilgrims ascending on a cloud to the Celestial City.

As a specimen of the grotesque and barbarous style, in which the artists of Bunyan's own day were wont to illus-

The Pilgrims now, to gratifie the Flesh,
Will seek its ease: but Oh! how they afresh
Do thereby plunge themselves new griefs into!
Who seek to please the Flesh, themselves undo.

trate his matchless parable, we give on the opposite page a fac-simile of one of the cuts in the edition of 1682.

The preceding notice will be understood to refer only to the First Part of Bunyan's allegory. The success of that and other works of our author gave rise to a host of imitations and impositions. In allusion to these he says, in the ntroduction to his Second Part,

——" Some have of late, to counterfeit
My Pilgrim, to their own my title set;
Yea, others, half my name, and title too,
Have stitched to their books to make them do."

It was not uncommon in those days for authors to put their initials only in the titles of their books, and the fraud alluded to in the third line consisted in putting Bunyan's initials to books which he did not write, in order to impose them on the public as his. Bunyan's publisher makes a similar complaint in an advertisement to one of his tracts; he says, " This author having published many books which have gone off very well, there are certain ballad-sellers about Newgate and London Bridge, who have put the two first letters of this author's name and his effigies to their rhymes and ridiculous books, suggesting to the world as if they were his.* Now know, that this author publisheth his name at large to all his books, and what you shall see otherwise he disowns."

* The following is a specimen of this species of fraud: " *The Saints' Triumph; or the Glory of the Saints with Jesus Christ.* By B. Printed by J. Millett for J. Blaze, at the Looking-Glass on London Bridge. 1688." The title contained also a rude wood-cut portrait of Bunyan, which, with the initial, B, occasioned the work to be ascribed to him. In this or some similar way several other books were imposed upon the world as the works of Bunyan, and so successfully that two of them—*Heart's Ease in Heart's Troubles,* and *The World to Come: or Visions of Heaven and Hell*—have even been reprinted as his, both in England and in this country, within the last five years; yet no person at all acquainted with the style of our author could fail to detect the imposture by reading a single page.

In the lines which conclude the First Part, Bunyan had suggested the probability of his dreaming "yet another dream;" and this it was, probably, that led some of these knavish book-makers and sellers to "counterfeit the Pilgrim and his name," and thus palm off their own trash as the genuine productions of the Dreamer himself. Of these dishonest imitations, Dr. Southey says, "Only one of them has fallen in my way, for it is by accident only that books of this perishable kind, which have no merit of their own to preserve them, are to be met with: and this, though entitled 'The Second Part of the Pilgrim's Progress,' has no other relation to the First than its title, which was probably a trick of the publishers. These interlopers may very likely have given Bunyan an additional inducement to prepare a Second Part himself."

The genuine Second Part of the Pilgrim—"wherein is set forth, the manner of the setting out of Christian's wife and children, their dangerous journey, and safe arrival at the desired country"—was published in 1684. On the back of the title-page was the following notice: "I appoint Mr. Nathaniel Ponder, but no other, to print this book, John Bunyan, January 1, 1684." It was a volume of two hundred and twenty-four pages, and contained, in the way of illustration, besides the frontispiece described in the note on page 15, another engraving by the same artist representing the demolition of Doubting Castle, with the usual verse beneath. (See page 428.) Dr. Southey tells us that "no additions or alterations were made in this part, although the author lived more than four years after its publication." It reached a sixth edition in 1693.

The two parts of Bunyan's allegory, which were originally published and for many years continued as separate, distinct volumes, have now for probably a century been uniformly printed as one book. The *thirtieth* edition, published in 1750, must certainly have contained both parts, being an 8vo. volume. It was "Printed for W. Johnstone in Ludgate street;" and "adorned with curious sculptures by J. Sturt." These "sculptures" are said to be truly "curious," perspective being entirely discarded throughout all of them, and the figures clad in grotesque dresses, and placed in strangely contorted positions. In most, probably all, of the old editions the headings of the pages throughout are in Black Letter, and the marginal references and notes, which are very numerous, in *italic*, as are also all the proper names, quotations from Scripture, and poetry, giving the volume a very singular appearance.

As editions multiplied, and the book, increasing in fame and circulation, gradually worked its way from the more humble to what are called the higher classes of society, an improvement in its typographical and mechanical execution, and in the style of its illustration, followed as a matter of course. An edition was published in 1796 (by T. Heptinstall of Fleet Street) which not only exceeded all that went before, but also those which followed it for some years. It is a handsome royal 8vo. volume, printed on fine paper with an ample margin, and embellished with a portrait and eight very superior copper-plate engravings, some of them from the elegant designs of the late T. Stothard, R. A. At the close is a "Key" to the work, occupying thirty-two pages. Within the last few years, however, many handsomer and much more richly illustrated editions have issued from the London press, which have been the means of introducing the work "among classes of persons who a century ago would not have touched it without perfumed gloves, lest they should be soiled by vulgarity or bitten by Puritanism."

The astonishing spread of the English language has carried Bunyan's Pilgrim with it, and made it a household book in every quarter of the globe. But its progress and usefulness have not been confined within the limits of its author's native tongue. Even before the publication of the Second

Part, the First had not only acquired an extensive circulation in Great Britain, and in the colony of New-England, (whither it was carried by Puritan emigrants,) but had also been translated into French, Dutch, Irish, and Gaelic, a fact to which the author refers with a feeling of honest gratification in the introduction to the Second Part. (Page 277.) A Dutch edition was printed at "*Utrecht* by *Jan van Paddenburgh,* 1684," with wood-cut illustrations far superior both in design and execution to those in any of the early English editions. It was very soon (before 1691) translated into the Welsh language, "and established itself as second in estimation to the Holy Scriptures throughout the principality."

"Bunyan could little have supposed that his book would ever be adapted for sale among the Romanists. Whether this was done in the earliest French translation I do not know; but in the second there is no Giant Pope. This contains only the First Part, but promises the Second, should it be well received. The First Part, under the title of *le Pelerinage d'un nommé Chretien,* forms one of the volumes of the *Petite Bibliotheque du Catholique,* and bears in the title-page a glorified head of the Virgin. A Portuguese translation, (of the First Part only,) in like manner cut down to the opinions of the public for which it was designed, was published in 1782."—*Southey.* It is said that a copy of the Pilgrim in elegant binding is preserved in the Vatican at Rome.—*Ivimey.*

Not only has the Pilgrim been rendered into almost every European tongue, but it has also found its way into lands of which perhaps its author never heard, whose inhabitants can now read in their own tongue the story of "his setting out, his dangerous journey, and safe arrival at the desired country." It has been translated into the modern Greek, Armenian, Arabic, Tamul, Malay, Burmese, Malagassy, (or the language of Madagascar,) and even into Chinese.

More recently it has had the honor of being rendered into Hebrew, for the benefit of the Jew, for whom it must possess a peculiar charm for its numerous citations out of those original Scriptures, with which he has been familiar from childhood; and it will be read with even greater delight by that growing population of Hebrew Christians, (as yet unassociated to any great extent,) for whom a literature is becoming absolutely necessary.—*Jewish Chronicle.*

We cannot ascertain when the Pilgrim's Progress was first reprinted in this country. Charles Doe, writing in 1691, only three years after Bunyan's death, tells us it had then been printed in New-England.* A writer in the Christian Review, (vol. iv, p. 418,) says, "The earliest American edition we have seen is the ***sixteenth.*** It was 'Printed by John Draper for Charles Harrison over against the *Brazen Head* in *Cornhil* Boston N. E. M,DCCXLIV.' It is adorned with wood-cuts, which, though rude, are expressive." A writer in the Boston Weekly Magazine says he has examined the *seventeenth* edition, printed and published in the same year by the same persons. He has also seen a copy of the *fifty-seventh* edition, dated only about twenty-five years later, and some time before the revolution.

The allegory or parable was in ancient times a favourite mode of communicating instruction. And not without reason; for by it truth has often, before the individual was aware, effected a lodgment in the heart which pride, prejudice, or self-interest had fortified against every kind of direct assault. It is also a source of pleasure, in the exercise it gives to the mind in discovering its meaning, and tracing out the resemblance between the sign and the thing signified; so that it affords entertainment and instruction at the same time. Our blessed Lord often adopted this method of teaching; and his parables "obtained a hearing

* He says, it "hath been printed in France, Holland, New-England, and in Welsh; and about a hundred thousand in England."

from those who would not bear his 'hard sayings:' and still these divine allegories—the parable of the prodigal son, for instance—have charms for readers who never take home to their own bosoms their spiritual import."

It is a characteristic, however, of nearly all *extended* allegories that they soon become wearisome and tedious, so that the reader is apt to desire the end long before he reaches it. The Pilgrim's Progress is almost the only one of any length that has attained a lasting popularity; and this is doubtless owing in no small degree to the fact that, though written "under the smilitude of a dream," there is, as Mr. Montgomery observes, "very little of pure allegory in it, and very few abstract qualities or passions are personified;" it is indeed a skilful combination of the allegorical, dramatic, and narrative, in which the author, while he has retained all the advantage of the allegory, has succeeded in investing his parable with the interest of a real story. Whether we regard it as a metaphorical delineation of Christian experience, or as a mere romance describing scenes of strange adventure, we accompany the hero of the story with untiring interest through all the successive stages of his journey, from his first setting out on his perilous enterprise till the ringing of the bells welcomes his safe arrival at the Celestial City. Such is the spell under which the author holds us, so thoroughly life-like the manner in which the scenes and actors are presented to us, that we seem to be rather spectators and auditors than mere readers; the Slough of Despond, Doubting Castle, the Delectable Mountains, and the River without a bridge, are places, which, for the time being, have in our imagination a real and tangible existence; "we know the straight and narrow path, as well as we know a road in which we have gone backward and forward a hundred times;" and our feelings and sympathies are enlisted in behalf of the pilgrims as though we had a personal interest in the success of their undertaking

One great attraction of the work (and indeed a prominent source of Bunyan's power both as a preacher and a writer) is found in the abundant and skilful employment of Scripture language and imagery; a feature in which our author excels almost every other writer with whom we are acquainted, and "which lends to his fancy a richness and a charm it would not otherwise possess." He was thoroughly acquainted with the *letter* and baptized with the *spirit* of the Bible. When suffering the pangs of a guilty conscience, hanging as it were over the flaming gulf, and as yet ignorant of the way of salvation, he had searched the sacred volume with the deepest interest—poring over its hallowed pages with the agonizing earnestness of a man who felt that life or death depended on the result—if perchance he might find some ray of light to shine in upon the darkness in which his soul was enveloped, some gleam of hope to chase away the despair that was swallowing him up. And in after life, when he had found that for which his soul panted, he continued with unabated interest his communings with the word of God, making it the man of his counsel, the rule of his life, and the companion of his happiest hours. His intense study of the Bible made him in a great measure what he was. That holy book was the source of his inspiration, the model on which he unconsciously formed his homely yet pure and nervous style, and the storehouse whence he drew his metaphors, his arguments, and his illustrations. He that loves the Bible cannot but admire the Pilgrim's Progress.

A rigid inspection may discover some minor incongruities in the allegory, and discrepancies in the conduct of the story; but they are such as can detract nothing from the general merit or usefulness of the work. Some of them, indeed, were unavoidable; and few would be detected by any except those who have acquired what Dr. Southey terms "the ill habit of always reading critically."

The Second Part has been sometimes, but most unjustly, depreciated as unworthy of the First. It may not, perhaps, contain any single passages equal in power and sublimity to the description of Christian's battle with Apollyon, and his passing through the Valley of the Shadow of Death, or in which the allegory is so admirably sustained as in the account of the capture and imprisonment of the pilgrims by Giant Despair. But if there be in it less to astonish and surprise the reader, there is quite as much or more that is calculated to delight and instruct; and few, if any, who have accompanied Christian to the Celestial City, will feel any abatement of interest in travelling the same road with Christiana and her companions. The author has in this Part drawn less from his own personal experience, but he has given us more of the fruits of his observation and acquaintance with the world.

The Second Part is even more abundant in incident than the First, and the characters are much more numerous and equally well supported. "The author's knowledge of human nature is unexhausted; his vein flows more freely the oftener it is opened. In the pilgrimage of Christian and his successive companions, Faithful and Hopeful, he portrayed personal and solitary experience, or only bosom fellowship between believers. In the journey of Christiana and her family, gradually increasing to a goodly troop, he seems to have had in view to illustrate the communion of saints, and the advantages of church membership. Though each individual is strikingly dissimilar from all the rest, they harmoniously agree to walk by the same rule, and mind the same thing. It is delightful to travel in such a company, and hear them not only tell their several histories, but discourse of the adventures of others who have gone before; so that to the last stage in the Enchanted Ground, when they find Stand-fast on his knees, there is a perpetual change of captivating anecdote and biography.

"Among the characters which so eminently enliven and adorn this part of the Pilgrim's Progress, *Mercy* is the most lovely; and though of the utmost simplicity, it would be difficult, among the most finished portraits of womanly excellence by our first poets, to parallel this in delicacy and truth of drawing and coloring. *Great-Heart*, *Old Honest*, and *Valiant-for-truth*, are all heroes, yet each has a personal identity, and acts as neither of the others would have done in similar circumstances. *Fearing*, *Feeble-mind*, *Ready-to-halt*, and *Dependency*, are of one family—brothers, yet sufficiently distinguished to be known individually. Even *Gaius* and *Mnason*, the two hosts at whose houses the pilgrims are entertained, are neither ciphers nor tallies they resemble each other in nothing but hospitality. This fine discrimination, which runs through all our author's characters, whether of men or women, might alone entitle John Bunyan to be ranked in a high class among writers of original genius."—*Montgomery.*

It is a peculiar and distinguishing merit of Bunyan's allegory that it seems to possess an almost equal attraction for readers of all ages, classes, and characters. Those who are too simple to comprehend its spiritual meaning, or who have no sympathy with the author's spirit and design, yet love to dwell upon the visions of his creative fancy. It is alike the wonder and admiration of

——"marvelling childhood, blooming youth,
Ripe manhood, silver-tress'd and serious age."

Not only does the "man *approve*" that which "charmed the boy," but his interest in its pages actually increases with advancing years. "The very things which are 'milk for babes,' are 'strong meat' to the same persons when they become men. What is admired as *history* in childhood, is admired as *mystery* in youth: what is admired as *ingenuity* in manhood, is loved as *experience* in old age. In *childhood* we sit, as it were, on Christian's knee, listening to the tale of his hair-breadth escapes. In *youth* we join him upon his perilous journey, to obtain directions for our own intended pilgrimage in the narrow way. Before *manhood* is matured, we know experimentally that the Slough of Despond and Doubting Castle are no fictions. And even in *old age*, Christians are more than ever convinced of the heights, and depths, and breadths, and lengths of Bunyan's spiritual wisdom. The faltering tongue of decrepitude utters, as sage maxims, the very things that it had lisped as amusing narrative; and we gravely utter as *counsel* to the young, what we prattled, as *curious*, to our parents. The same thing never has been said, nor can be said, of any other uninspired author. He is the rainbow of experience, fascinating for ever."—*Philip.*

By those who sit in the critic's chair, and claim to be the dispensers of literary fame, the Pilgrim was at first either entirely overlooked as unworthy of notice, or despised as the offspring of ignorance and enthusiasm. But these days and opinions have for ever passed away. Some of the most distinguished writers of modern times have delighted to record their sense of its surpassing excellence, and have added their notes of admiration to the applause of the multitude. Dr. Johnson who hated, as he said, to read books through, characterized this as one of the two or three works which the reader wished longer. Byron, Wordsworth, Southey, Montgomery, Walter Scott, and Macaulay, have all borne honourable testimony to its literary merits. Cowper's high commendation is often quoted and well known. The poet Coleridge says, "This wonderful work is one of the few books which may be read over repeatedly at different times, and each time with a new and different pleasure. I read it once as a theologian, (and let me assure you there is great theological acumen in the work,) once with devotional feelings, and once as a poet. . . . I know of no book, the Bible excepted, as above all comparison, which I, according to my judgment and experience, could so safely recommend as teaching and enforcing the whole saving truth, according to the mind that was in Christ Jesus, as the Pilgrim's Progress. It is, in my opinion, incomparably the best *summma theologiæ evangelicæ* ever produced by a writer not miraculously inspired." The late celebrated Dr. Arnold, writing to a friend on the subject of "the old divines," observes, "As it is, I hold John Bunyan to have been a man of incomparably greater genius than any of them, and to have given a far truer and more edifying picture of Christianity. His Pilgrim's Progress seems to be a *complete reflection of Scripture*, with none of the rubbish of the theologians mixed up with it." His biographer adds in a note: "His admiration of the Pilgrim's Progress was very great: 'I cannot trust myself,' he used to say, 'to read the account of Christian going up to the Celestial City, after his passage through the River of Death.' And when, in one of the foreign tours of his later years, he had read it through again after a long interval, 'I have always,' said he, 'been struck by its piety: I am now struck equally, or even more, by its profound wisdom.'"*

The following striking incident is related in the biography of the late William Maginn, LL. D., who was one of the most finished scholars and popular writers of modern times. His mind was a storehouse of learning, from which, at a moment's warning, he could draw forth exuberant riches; but, alas, he became a slave to intemperance, made a shipwreck of his reputation, and died in abject poverty. He was one day attending the funeral of a literary friend and boon companion, at Bunhill fields, and as soon as the ceremony was over he said to the grave-digger:—"Grave-digger, show me the tomb of John Bunyan." The grave-digger led the way, and was followed by Maginn, who appeared particularly thoughtful. As they approached the place, the

* Life of Thomas Arnold, D.D., late Head-master of Rugby School, and Regius Professor of History in the University of Oxford.—P. 296.

doctor turned to a friend who accompanied him, and, tapping him on the shoulder, said, quietly,—"Tread lightly." So unusual a remark, coming from one who never exhibited any particle of the pathetic, either in his manner or conversation, attracted the attention of his companion. Maginn bent over the grave for some time in melancholy mood, and seemed unconscious of any one's presence. The bright sunshine poured around him. No more illustrious mourner ever stood beside that grave. At length he seemed moved, and turning away he exclaimed in deep and solemn tones, "Sleep on, thou Prince of Dreamers." In less than a year, he also slept the sleep of death, and O! how blessed for him, if, even at that late hour, he had learned to imitate the humble faith of that illustrious dreamer, and had followed his Pilgrim to the Celestial City!—*Presbyterian.*

But the commendations which the learned and the great have bestowed on his work would be esteemed by John Bunyan as nothing worth in comparison with the tokens of Divine approval furnished in the multitudes who, by the blessing of God, have been guided by it from the City of Destruction into the straight and narrow way "that leadeth to life," and who will be as stars in the crown of his rejoicing "long as eternal ages roll." More than a century and a half have passed away since death set the seal of silence on his lips, and stilled the voice that was wont so eloquently and successfully to enforce the claims of the gospel of salvation, and plead with men to be reconciled with God; yet through his Pilgrim he still continues to preach, and preach effectively too, pointing countless thousands the way to brighter worlds, and alluring them to walk therein; nor is it likely that his influence will cease or diminish till time shall be no more.

As specimens of its usefulness we give the following instances, which have lately met our eye in the public prints:—

A family in one of our Western settlements having been converted by means of the Pilgrim's Progress, loaned it to their neighbours until whole households were awakened by its perusal, and four persons professed to have passed from death unto life. The work of awakening and conversion is still going on in the settlement.—*American Messenger.*

A few months since a Baptist minister in Dutchess county, N. Y., sold a copy of the Pilgrim to a sister who had recently joined his church. Her husband read it, and by the blessing of God it was the means of his conversion. He was led to think seriously that he had not yet passed through the "Wicket-gate," and to feel the infinite importance of personal religion. The result was, that he found peace with the Saviour, came before the church, related his experience, and was received for baptism.—*New-York Recorder.*

It is sometimes made to supply in a measure the lack of a living ministry:—A gentleman in Faircastle, Va., gave a copy of the Pilgrim to a resident of the same county, who lived in a very destitute neighbourhood. When he returned home he read portions of the book to his neighbours, and they were so deeply interested in its contents, that they assembled at his house to hear him read it chapter by chapter.—*Am. Mess.*

If such fruits are produced from a few copies of the work, which are yet doing good service, what a harvest of souls may be expected from the myriads that have been and are being scattered in every quarter of the earth; and what encouragement is furnished to the friends of religion to aid in extending its circulation and consequent usefulness!

In preparing the present edition great pains have been taken to insure accuracy in the text; for which purpose it has been collated with the best London editions, which were corrected from copies published during the author's life-time.

The original work abounded with references to Scripture passages, many of which were found to have but little connection with the subject in hand, for which reason they are in some editions entirely omitted. We have carefully examined all the texts referred to, and dropped only such as were irrelevant or unnecessary, while many of the most im portant are given in full at the bottom of the page; thus superseding the necessity of turning to the Bible for them.

The division of the work into chapters of moderate length, and embracing subjects that are complete in themselves, will be found a convenience to the reader, by furnishing appropriate stopping places; while the Index will be a grea assistance in finding particular passages to which he may wish to refer.

Of the Notes, which are chiefly of a practical character, a large portion have been selected from Bunyan's own writings. We are aware that some, especially those who read the book merely for the sake of the story, or, as Bunyan expresses it, "play with the *outside* of the dream," object to annotations altogether, deeming them an incumbrance. Such persons can easily pass them over. Others, however, in whom a desire of edification is mingled with admiration of literary excellence, may not esteem it a profitless interruption to have their attention occasionally diverted from the shadow to the reality, from the parable to the spiritual lesson it was designed to teach.

We will now no longer detain the reader with these disjointed observations, but introduce him at once to the work itself, earnestly hoping he may so profit by its perusal that when his earthly pilgrimage shall terminate, he may obtain an abundant entrance into the everlasting kingdom of our Lord Jesus Christ, and eternally rejoice in the reality and possession of that glory, of which the wondrous dreamer has here presented us so bright a vision.

S. B. W

New-York, August, 1845.

THE

PILGRIM'S PROGRESS

FROM

THIS WORLD TO THAT WHICH IS TO COME

DELIVERED UNDER THE SIMILITUDE OF A DREAM

PART I.

WHEREIN ARE DESCRIBED THE MANNER OF HIS SETTING OUT;
HIS DANGEROUS JOURNEY; AND SAFE ARRIVAL
AT THE DESIRED COUNTRY.

I have used similitudes. Hosea xii. 10

THE

AUTHOR'S APOLOGY FOR HIS BOOK

When at the first I took my pen in hand
Thus for to write, I did not understand
That I at all should make a little book
In such a mode; nay, I had undertook
To make another; which, when almost done,
Before I was aware I this begun.

And thus it was: I writing of the way
And race of saints, in this our gospel day,
Fell suddenly into an allegory
About their journey, and the way to glory,
In more than twenty things which I set down
This done, I twenty more had in my crown;
And they again began to multiply,
Like sparks that from the coals of fire do fly.
Nay, then, thought I, if that you breed so fast
I'll put you by yourselves, lest you at last
Should prove *ad infinitum*, and eat out
The book that I already am about.
Well, so I did; but yet I did not think
To snow to all the world my pen and ink
In such a mode; I only thought to make
I knew not what: nor did I undertake
Thereby to please my neighbour; no, not I;
I did it my own self to gratify.

Neither did I but vacant seasons spend
In this my scribble: nor did I intend
But to divert myself, in doing this,
From worser thoughts, which make me do amiss.
Thus I set pen to paper with delight,
And quickly had my thoughts in black and white.

For having now my method by the end,
Still as I pull'd, it came; and so I penn'd
It down: until it came at last to be,
For length and breadth, the bigness which you see.

Well, when I had thus put my ends together,
I show'd them others, that I might see whether
They would condemn them, or them justify:
And some said, Let them live; some, Let them die;
Some said, John, print it; others said, Not so;
Some said, It might do good; others said, No

Now was I in a strait, and did not see
Which was the best thing to be done by me:
At last I thought, Since ye are thus divided,
I print it will; and so the case decided.

For, thought I, some I see would have it done
Though others in that channel do not run:
To prove, then, who advised for the best,
Thus I thought fit to put it to the test.

I further thought, if now I did deny
Those that would have it, thus to gratify;
I did not know, but hinder them I might
Of that which would to them be great delight.
For those which were not for its coming forth,
I said to them, Offend you I am loth:
Yet since your brethren pleased with it be
Forbear to judge, till you do further see.

If that thou wilt not read, let it alone;
Some love the meat, some love to pick the bone.
Yea, that I might them better palliate,
I did too with them thus expostulate:

May I not write in such a style as this?
In such a method too, and yet not miss
My end—thy good? Why may it not be done?
Dark clouds bring waters when the bright bring none;
Yea, dark or bright, if they their silver drops
Cause to descend, the earth, by yielding crops,

Gives praise to both, and carpeth not at either,
But treasures up the fruit they yield together;
Yea, so commixes both, that in their fruit
None can distinguish this from that; they suit
Her well when hungry; but if she be full,
She spews out both, and makes their blessing null.

You see the ways the fisherman doth take
To catch the fish; what engines doth he make!
Behold how he engageth all his wits;
Also his snares, lines, angles, hooks and nets;
Yet fish there be, that neither hook nor line,
Nor snare, nor net, nor engine can make thine:
They must be groped for, and be tickled too,
Or they will not be catch'd whate'er you do.

How does the fowler seek to catch his game
By divers means! all which one cannot name:
His guns, his nets, his lime-twigs, light, and bell:
He creeps, he goes, he stands; yea, who can tell
Of all his postures? Yet there's none of these
Will make him master of what fowls he please,
Yea, he must pipe and whistle, to catch *this;*
Yet if he does so, *that* bird he will miss.
If that a pearl may in a toad's head dwell,
And may be found too in an oyster-shell;
If things that promise nothing do contain
What better is than gold; who will disdain,
That have an inkling of it, there to look,
That they may find it? Now my little book,
(Though void of all these paintings that may make
It with this or the other man to take,)
Is not without those things that do excel
What do in brave, but empty notions dwell.

"Well, yet I am not fully satisfied
That this your book will stand when soundly tried."

Why, what's the matter? "It is dark." What though
"But it is feigned." What of that? I trow

Some men by feigned words, as dark as mine,
Make truth to spangle, and its rays to shine.
"But they want solidness." Speak, man, thy mind.
"They drown the weak; metaphors make us blind."

Solidity, indeed, becomes the pen
Of him that writeth things divine to men:
But must I needs want solidness, because
By metaphors I speak? Were not God's laws,
His gospel laws, in olden time held forth
By types, shadows, and metaphors? Yet loth
Will any sober man be to find fault
With them, lest he be found for to assault
The highest wisdom! No, he rather stoops,
And seeks to find out what by pins and loops,
By calves and sheep, by heifers and by rams
By birds and herbs, and by the blood of lambs,
God speaketh to him; and happy is he
That finds the light and grace that in them be.

Be not too forward therefore to conclude
That I want solidness—that I am rude:
All things solid in show not solid be;
All things in parable despise not we,
Lest things most hurtful lightly we receive,
And things that good are of our souls bereave.
My dark and cloudy words they do but hold
The truth, as cabinets inclose the gold.

The prophets used much by metaphors
To set forth truth: yea, whoso considers
Christ, his apostles too, shall plainly see
That truths to this day in such mantles be.

Am I afraid to say, that holy writ,
Which for its style and phrase puts down all wit,
Is everywhere so full of all these things,
Dark figures, allegories? Yet there springs
From that same book, that lustre, and those rays
Of light, that turn our darkest nights to days.

Come, let my carper to his life now look,
And find there darker lines than in my book
He findeth any; yea, and let him know,
That in his best things there are worse lines too.

May we but stand before impartial men
To his poor one I durst adventure ten,
That they will take my meaning in these lines
Far better than his lies in silver shrines.
Come, truth, although in swaddling clothes, I find
Informs the judgment, rectifies the mind;
Pleases the understanding, makes the will
Submit, the memory too it doth fill
With what doth our imagination please;
Likewise it tends our troubles to appease.

Sound words, I know, Timothy is to use,
And old wives' fables he is to refuse;
But yet grave Paul him nowhere doth forbid
The use of parables; in which lay hid
That gold, those pearls, and precious stones that were
Worth digging for, and that with greatest care.

Let me add one word more. O man of God
Art thou offended? Dost thou wish I had
Put forth my matter in another dress?
Or that I had in things been more express?
Three things let me propound; then I submit
To those that are my betters, as is fit:

1. I find not that I am denied the use
Of this my method, so I no abuse
Put on the words, things, readers, or be rude
In handling figure or similitude,
In application; but all that I may
Seek the advance of truth this or that way.
Denied did I say? Nay, I have leave,
(Example too, and that from them that have
God better pleased, by their words or ways,
Than any man that breatheth now-a-days,)

Thus to express my mind, thus to declare
Things unto thee that excellentest are.

2. I find that men as high as trees will write
Dialogue-wise; yet no man doth them slight
For writing so: indeed if they abuse
Truth, cursed be they, and the craft they use
To that intent; but yet let truth be free
To make her sallies upon thee and me,
Which way it pleases God: for who knows how
Better than he that taught us first to plough,
To guide our minds and pens for his design?
And he makes base things usher in divine.

3. I find that holy writ, in many places,
Hath semblance with this method, where the cases
Do call for one thing, to set forth another:
Use it I may then, and yet nothing smother
Truth's golden beams: nay, by this method may
Make it cast forth its rays as light as day.

And now, before I do put up my pen,
I'll show the profit of my book; and then
Commit both thee and it unto that hand
That pulls the strong down, and makes weak ones stand

This book it chalketh out before thine eyes
The man that seeks the everlasting prize:
It shows you whence he comes, whither he goes;
What he leaves undone; also what he does:
It also shows you how he runs and runs
Till he unto the gate of glory comes.
It shows, too, who set out for life amain,
As if the lasting crown they would obtain:
Here also you may see the reason why
They lose their labour, and like fools do die.

This book will make a traveller of thee,
If by its counsel thou wilt ruled be;
It will direct thee to the holy land,
If thou wilt its directions understand:

Yea, it will make the slothful active be ;
The blind also delightful things to see.

Art thou for something rare and profitable ?
Or wouldst thou see a truth within a fable ?
Art thou forgetful ? Wouldest thou remember
From New-Year's-day to the last of December ?
Then read my fancies ; they will stick like burs,
And may be, to the helpless, comforters.

This book is writ in such a dialect
As may the minds of listless men affect :
It seems a novelty, and yet contains
Nothing but sound and honest gospel strains.

Wouldst thou divert thyself from melancholy ?
Wouldst thou be pleasant, yet be far from folly ?
Wouldst thou read riddles, and their explanation ?
Or else be drowned in thy contemplation ?
Dost thou love picking meat ? Or wouldst thou see
A man i' the clouds, and hear him speak to thee ?
Wouldst thou be in a dream and yet not sleep ?
Or wouldst thou in a moment laugh and weep ?
Wouldst thou lose thyself and catch no harm,
And find thyself again without a charm ?
Wouldst read thyself, and read thou knowst not what,
And yet know whether thou art blest or not,
By reading the same lines ? O then come hither,
And lay my book, thy head, and heart together.

JOHN BUNYAN.

THE AUTHOR DREAMING.

THE

PILGRIM'S PROGRESS.

CHAPTER I.

Christian, feeling his burden, and alarmed at his danger, flees from the City of Destruction—Is met by Evangelist, who directs him to the Wicket-gate—Obstinate and Pliable go after Christian, to fetch him back—Christian persuades Pliable to go with him—They fall into the Slough of Despond—Pliable, discouraged, returns home—Christian, assisted by Help, gets out of the Slough on the side next the gate.

S I walked through the wilderness of this world, I lighted on a certain place where was a den,[1] and laid me down in that place to sleep; and as I slept, I dreamed a dream. I dreamed, and behold, I saw a man clothed with rags, (Isa. lxiv, 6,) standing in a certain place, with his face from his own house, (Luke xiv, 33,) a book in his hand, and a burden upon his back.[2] I looked, and saw him open the book, and read therein; and as

[1] Bedford jail, in which Bunyan was twelve years a prisoner for conscience' sake, and where he wrote his Pilgrim's Progress, and several other works. Speaking of the clearness of spiritual vision with which he was favoured while in prison, he says, "I never had in all my life so great an *inlet* into the word of God as now."

[2] The "great burden upon his back" is designed to represent the oppression of a guilty conscience. The Psalmist makes use of the same figure: "For mine iniquities are gone over my head; as a heavy burden they are too heavy for me." Psalm xxxviii, 4

he read he wept and trembled; and not being able longer to contain, he brake out with a lamentable cry, saying, "What shall I do?"[3] Acts xvi, 30.

In this plight, therefore, he went home and restrained himself as long as he could, that his wife and children should not perceive his distress; but he could not be silent long, because that his trouble increased. Wherefore at length he brake his mind to his wife and children; and thus he began to talk to them: "O my dear wife," said he, "and you the children of my bowels, I, your dear friend, am in myself undone by reason of a burden that lieth hard upon me; moreover, I am certainly informed that this our city [the world] will be burnt with fire from heaven; in which fearful overthrow, both myself, with thee my wife, and you my sweet babes, shall miserably come to ruin, except (the which yet I see not) some way of escape *can* be found whereby we may be delivered." At this his relations were sore amazed; not for that they believed that what he had said to them was true, but because they thought that some phrensy distemper had got into his head; therefore, it drawing toward night, and they hoping that sleep might settle his brains, with all haste they got him to bed. But the night was as troublesome to him as the day; wherefore, instead of sleeping, he spent it in sighs and tears. So when the morning was come, they would know how he did. He told them, "Worse and worse:" he also set to talking to them again; but they began to be hardened. They also thought to drive

[3] Reader, was this ever your case? Did you ever see your sins, and feel the burden of them, so as to cry out in the anguish of your soul, What must I do to be saved? If not, you are yet carnal, dead in your sins, lying in the arms of the wicked one.—*Mason's Notes.*

away his distemper by harsh and surly carriage to him: sometimes they would deride, sometimes they would chide, and sometimes they would quite neglect him. Wherefore he began to retire himself to his chamber to pray for and pity them, and also to condole his own misery; he would also walk solitarily in the fields, sometimes reading, and sometimes praying: and tnus for some days he spent his time.[4]

Now I saw, upon a time, when he was walking in the fields, that he was (as he was wont) reading in his book, and greatly distressed in his mind; and as he read, he burst out, as he had done before, crying, "What shall I do to be saved?"[5]

[4] There are some poor sinners in the world that plainly see a change, a mighty change, in their neighbours and relations that are coming to Christ; but being ignorant, they attribute this change to other causes, as melancholy, sitting alone, going to too many sermons, too much studying and musing on what they hear, etc.; and, therefore, they advise them to leave off reading, going to sermons, the company of sober people, and to be merry, and busy themselves in the things of the world. But come, poor ignorant sinner, let me deal with thee. It seems thou art turned counsellor for Satan: I tell thee, thou knowest not what thou dost. What! count convictions for sin, mourning for sin, and repentance for sin, *melancholy!* Poor, ignorant sinner! can't thou judge no better? What! is sitting alone, pensive under God's hand, reading the Scriptures, and hearing of sermons, etc., the way to be undone? The Lord open thine eyes, and make thee to see thine error.—*Bunyan's Come and Welcome.*

[5] To be *saved!* What is like being saved? To be saved from sin, from hell, from the wrath of God, from eternal damnation, what is like it? To be made an heir of God,—of his grace, his kingdom and eternal glory,—what is like it? And yet all this is included in this word, "saved." But this word is but of little use in the world, save to them that are heartily afraid of damning. This word lies in the Bible, as excellent salve lies in some men's houses, thrust into a hole, and not thought on for many months, because the household have no wounds nor sores: but in time of sickness, what so set by as the doctor's glasses and gally-pots full of his excellent things. . . . Oh! when men are

Christian no sooner leaves the world, but meets
Evangelist, who lovingly him greets
With tidings of another ; and doth show
Him how to mount to that from this below

I saw also that he looked this way, and that way, as if he would run; yet he stood still, because (as I perceived) he could not tell which way to go. I looked then and saw a man named Evangelist coming to him, and he asked, "Wherefore dost thou cry?"

He answered, "Sir, I perceive, by the book in my hand, that I am condemned to die, and after that to come to judgment, (Heb. ix, 27,) and I find that I am not willing to do the first, nor able to do the second."

Then said Evangelist, "Why not willing to die, since this life is attended with so many evils?" The man answered, "Because I fear that this burden that is upon my back will sink me lower than the grave, and I shall fall into Tophet. Isa. xxx, 33. And, sir, if I be not fit to go to prison, I am not fit to go to judgment, and from thence to execution; and the thoughts of these things make me cry."

Then said Evangelist, "If this be thy condition, why standest thou still?" He answered, "Because I know not whither to go." Then he gave him a parchment roll, and there was written within, "Fly from the wrath to come." Matt. iii, 7.

The man therefore read it, and, looking upon Evangelist very carefully, said, "Whither must I fly?" Then said Evangelist, (pointing with his finger over a very wide field,) "Do you see yonder wicket-gate?" The man said, "No." Then said the other, "Do you

sick of sin, and afraid of damning, what a text is that where this word *saved* is found? Yea, what a word of worth, and goodness, and blessedness, is it to him that lies continually upon the wrath of a guilty conscience. . . . He, and he only, knows what *saved* means that knows what hell, and death, and damnation mean. "What shall I do to be *saved?*" is the language of the trembling sinner. "Lord, *save* me," is the language of the sinking sinner.—*Bunyan's Strait Gate.*

see yonder shining light?"[6] He said, "I think I do." Then said Evangelist, "Keep that light in your eye, and go up directly thereto, so shalt thou see the gate; at which, when thou knockest, it shalt be told thee what thou shalt do."

So I saw in my dream that the man began to run. Now he had not run far from his own door when his wife and children, perceiving it, began to cry after him to return; but the man put his fingers in his ears, and ran on,[7] crying, "Life! life! eternal life!" So he looked not behind him, but fled toward the middle of the plain. Gen. xix, 17.

The neighbours also came out to see him run, and as he ran some mocked, others threatened, and some cried after him to return; and among those that did so, there were two that resolved to fetch him back by force. The name of the one was Obstinate, and the name of the other Pliable. Now by this time the man

[6]"THY word," says the Psalmist, (cxix, 105,) "is a lamp unto my feet, and a light unto my path." As the "shining light" was to guide Christian to the "wicket-gate," so the word of God directs the burdened sinner to Christ, who is represented by that gate: "I am the *door*," said our Lord; "by me if any man enter in he shall be saved:" and again, "Come unto me, all ye that labour and are heavy laden, and I will give you rest."

[7]Jesus says, "If any man come to me, and hate not his father, and mother, and wife, and children, and brethren, and sisters, yea, and his own life also, he cannot be my disciple." Luke xiv, 26. By this is meant, not that we are literally to "hate" our nearest relatives—for this is contrary to the spirit and teachings of Christianity—but only that we must not suffer our regard for them to stand in opposition to our duty to God: if things come to that point, that we must either give up our friends or our religion, we must not hesitate to choose the Lord for our portion. If our friends will not go to heaven with us, we must not hold back to keep them company. See the parallel passage in Matthew x, 37.

was got a good distance from them; but however they were resolved to pursue him, which they did, and in a little time they overtook him. Then said the man, "Neighbours, wherefore are ye come?" They said, "To persuade you to go back with us." But he said, "That can by no means be: you dwell," said he, "in the city of Destruction, the place also where I was born: I see it to be so; and dying there, sooner or later you will sink lower than the grave, into a place that burns with fire and brimstone: be content, good neighbours, and go along with me."

"What!" said Obstinate, "and leave our friends and our comforts behind us!"[8]

"Yes," said Christian, (for that was his name,) "because that all which you forsake is not worthy to be compared with a little of that I am seeking to enjoy,[9]

[8] *Objector.* But if I should run as you would have me, then I must run from all my friends; for none of them are running that way.

Ans. And if thou dost thou wilt run into the bosom of Christ and of God, and then what harm will that do thee?

Obj. But then if I run this way, I must run from all my sins.

Ans. That is true, indeed; yet if thou dost not thou wilt run into hell fire.

Obj. But if I run this way I shall lose the love of my friends and relations, and be mocked of all my relations.

Ans. And if thou dost not, thou art sure to lose the love and favour of God and Christ, the benefits of heaven and glory, and be mocked of God for thy folly.

Obj. But surely I may begin this time enough a year or two hence, may I not?

Ans. Hast thou a lease of thy life? Nay; it may be thou mayest not live so long. Then art thou a wise man to let thy immortal soul hang over hell by a thread of uncertain time, which may soon be cut asunder by death? Arise, man; set foot, and heart, and all, into the way of God, and run; the crown is at the end of the race.—***Bunyan' Heavenly Footman.***

[9] For the things that are seen are temporal, but the things that are not seen are eternal. 2 Cor. iv, 18

and if you will go along with me, and hold it, you shall fare as I myself; for there, where I go, is enough and to spare. Come away, and prove my words."

Obst. What are the things you seek, since you leave all the world to find them?

Chr. I seek an inheritance incorruptible, undefiled, and that fadeth not away, and it is laid up in heaven, (1 Pet. i, 4,) and safe there, to be bestowed, at the time appointed, on them that diligently seek it. Read it so, if you will, in my book.

"Tush," said Obstinate, "away with your book; will you go back with us or no?"

"No, not I," said the other, "because I have laid my hand to the plough."

Obst. Come, then, neighbour Pliable, let us turn again, and go home without him: there is a company of these crazy-headed coxcombs, that when they take a fancy by the end, are wiser in their own eyes than seven men that can render a reason.

Then said Pliable, "Don't revile; if what the good Christian says is true, the things he looks after are better than ours: my heart inclines to go with my neighbour."

Obst. What! more fools still! Be ruled by me, and go back; who knows whither such a brain-sick fellow will lead you? Go back, go back, and be wise.

Chr. Come with me, neighbour Pliable; there are such things to be had which I spoke of, and many more glories besides. If you believe not me, read here in this book; and for the truth of what is expressed therein, behold, all is confirmed by the blood of Him that made it. Heb. ix, 13–17.

"Well, neighbour Obstinate," said Pliable, "I begin

to come to a point; I intend to go along with this good man, and to cast in my lot with him: but, my good companion, do you know the way to this desired place?"

Chr. I am directed by a man, whose name is Evangelist, to speed me to a little gate that is before us, where we shall receive instruction about the way.

Pli. Come, then, good neighbour, let us be going.

Then they went both together.

"And I will go back to my place," said Obstinate: "I will be no companion of such misled fantastical fellows."

Now I saw in my dream, that when Obstinate was gone back, Christian and Pliable went talking over the plain; and thus they began their discourse.

Chr. Come, neighbour Pliable, how do you do? I am glad you are persuaded to go along with me. Had even Obstinate himself but felt what I have felt of the powers and terrors of what is yet unseen, he would not thus lightly have given us the back.

Pli. Come, neighbour Christian, since there are none but us two here, tell me now further, what the things are, and how to be enjoyed, whither we are going.

Chr. I can better conceive of them with my mind, than speak of them with my tongue; but yet, since you are desirous to know, I will read of them in my book.

Pli. And do you think that the words of your book are certainly true?

Chr. Yes, verily; for it was made by Him that cannot lie. Titus i, 2.

Pli. Well said; what things are they?

Chr. There is an endless kingdom to be inhabited,

and everlasting life to be given us, that we may inhabit that kingdom for ever.

Pli. Well said; and what else?

Chr. There are crowns of glory to be given us;[10] and garments that will make us shine like the sun in the firmament of heaven. Matt. xiii, 43.

Pli. This is excellent; and what else?

Chr. There shall be no more crying, nor sorrow, for he that is owner of the place will wipe all tears from our eyes. Isa. xxv, 8; Rev. vii, 16, 17; xxi, 4.

Pli. And what company shall we have there?

Chr. There we shall be with seraphims and cherubims; (Rev. v, 11;) creatures that will dazzle your eyes to look on them. There also you shall meet with thousands and ten thousands that have gone before us to that place; none of them are hurtful, but loving and holy; every one walking in the sight of God, and standing in his presence with acceptance for ever. In a word, there we shall see the elders with their golden crowns; (Rev. iv, 4;) there we shall see the holy virgins with their golden harps; (Rev. xiv, 1, 5;) there we shall see men, that by the world were cut in pieces, burnt in flames, eaten of beasts, drowned in the seas, for the love they bare to the Lord of the place, all well, and clothed with immortality as with a garment.

Pli. The hearing of this is enough to ravish one's heart. But are these things to be enjoyed? How shall we get to be sharers thereof?

Chr. The Lord, the governor of the country, hath recorded that in this book; (Isa. lv, 1, 2; John vi, 37;

10 Henceforth there is laid up for me a crown of righteousness, which the Lord, the righteous Judge, shall give me at that day; and not to me only, but unto all, also, that love his appearing 2 Tim. iv, 8.

viii, 37; Rev. xxii, 6; xxii, 17;) the substance of which is, if we be truly willing to have it, he will bestow it on us freely.

Pli. Well, my good companion, glad am I to hear of these things: come on, let us mend our pace.[11]

Chr. I cannot go so fast as I would, by reason of this burden that is on my back.

Now I saw in my dream, that just as they had ended this talk, they drew nigh to a very miry slough that was in the midst of the plain: and they being heedless, did both fall suddenly into the bog. The name of the slough was Despond. Here, therefore, they wallowed for a time, being grievously bedaubed with dirt; and Christian, because of the burden that was on his back. began to sink in the mire.[12]

Then said Pliable, "Ah, neighbour Christian, where are you now?"

"Truly," said Christian, "I do not know."

At this Pliable began to be offended, and angrily said to his fellow, "Is this the happiness you have told me all this while of? If we have such ill speed at our first setting out, what may we expect between this and our journey's end? May I get out again with my life, you shall possess the brave country alone for me." And with that he gave a desperate struggle or two, and got

11 Pliable is eager to push forward; but too *light*—having never felt the burden of sin—to travel far. Our Lord describes such as the "stony ground" hearers: they receive the word with joy, but it hath no root in their hearts; they believe awhile, but in time of temptation fall away.—*Mason's Notes.*

12 The Slough of Despond is intended to represent the state of distress and despondency into which, through temptation, ignorance, or unbelief, many fall when under convictions for sin. Bunyan makes use of the same figure in relating his own experience: "I found myself in a *miry bog*, that shook if I did but stir."

out of the mire on that side of the slough which was next to his own house; so away he went, and Christian saw him no more.

Wherefore Christian was left to tumble in the Slough of Despond alone; but still he endeavoured to struggle to that side of the slough that was furthest from his own house, and next to the wicket-gate; the which he did, but could not get out because of the burden that was upon his back: but I beheld in my dream, that a man came to him, whose name was Help, and asked him "what he did there?"

"Sir," said Christian, "I was bid to go this way by a man called Evangelist, who directed me also to yonder gate, that I might escape the wrath to come. And as I was going thither I fell in here."

Help. But why did not you look for the steps?[13]

Chr. Fear followed me so hard, that I fled the next way, and fell in.

"Then," said he, "give me thine hand:" so he gave him his hand, and he drew him out, and he set him upon sound ground, and bid him go on his way. Psa. xl, 2.

Then I stepped to him that plucked him out, and said, "Sir, wherefore, since over this place is the way from the city of Destruction to yonder gate, is it, that this plat is not mended, that poor travellers might go thither with more security?" And he said unto me, "This miry slough is such a place as cannot be mended: it is the descent whither the scum and filth that attend conviction for sin doth continually run, and therefore it is called the Slough of Despond; for still

[13] By the "steps" are meant the many precious promises of pardon and acceptance to penitent and believing souls, which are found in the word of God.

as the sinner is awakened about his lost condition, there arise in his soul many fears and doubts, and discouraging apprehensions, which all of them get together, and settle in this place: and this is the reason of the badness of the ground.

"It is not the pleasure of the King that this place should remain so bad. His labourers also have, by the direction of his Majesty's surveyors, been for above these sixteen hundred years employed about this patch of ground, if perhaps it might have been mended: yea, and to my knowledge," said he, "here have been swallowed up at least twenty thousand cart-loads, yea, millions of wholesome instructions, that have at all seasons been brought from all places of the King's dominions, (and they that can tell, say they are the best materials to make good ground of the place,) if so be it might have been mended; but it is the Slough of Despond still, and so will be when they have done what they can.

"True, there are, by the direction of the Lawgiver, certain good and substantial steps, placed even through the very midst of this slough; but at such time as this place doth much spew out its filth, as it doth against change of weather, these steps are hardly seen; or if they be, men, through the dizziness of their heads, step beside, and then they are bemired to purpose, notwithstanding the steps be there; but the ground is good when they are once got in at the gate."

Now, I saw in my dream, that by this time Pliable was got home to his house. So his neighbours came to visit him; and some of them called him wise man for coming back, and some called him fool for hazarding himself with Christian: others again did mock at his cowardliness; saying, "Surely, since you began to venture, I would not have been so base to have given out for a few difficulties;" so Pliable sat sneaking among them.[14] But at last he got more confidence, and then they all turned their tales, and began to deride poor Christian behind his back.[15] And thus much concerning Pliable.

[14] Though the men of the world often labour to turn aside from the way of life those who have set out for heaven, yet they will most commonly despise those who, through their endeavours, have been induced to give up their religious profession. The resolute, persevering Christian is more respected, even by the ungodly, than is the faint-hearted backslider.

[15] Sinners, did you but know what a blessed thing it is to come to Christ, you would hang and burn in hell a thousand years before you would turn your spirits as you do against him that God is drawing to Jesus Christ, and against the God that draws him. But, faithless sinner, let us a little expostulate the matter. What hath this man that is coming to Christ done against thee? Why dost thou make him the object of thy scorn? Doth his coming to Christ offend thee? Doth his pursuing of his own salvation offend thee? Doth his forsaking of his sins and pleasures offend thee? Is he ever the worse for coming to Jesus Christ? or is he ever the worse a fool for seeking eternal life, and flying from that which will drown thee in hell? Thou that wilt not come to Christ thyself, and hinderest him that would, what sayest thou? Wilt thou stand by thy doings? Wilt thou continue to reproach and contemn the living God? Thinkest thou that thou shalt weather it out well enough at the day of judgment? "Can thy heart endure, or thy hands be strong, in the day that I shall deal with thee, saith the Lord?"—*Bunyan's Come and Welcome*

CHAPTER II.

Christian is met by Mr. Worldly Wiseman, who condemns Evangelist's counsel, and prefers morality to the strait gate—Christian is snared by his words, and turned out of the way—He comes to Mt. Sinai, and fears it will fall on his head—Evangelist again meets him, and puts him in the right way—Christian arrives at the Wicket-gate—Conversation between Christian and Goodwill.

Now as Christian was walking solitary by himself, he espied one afar off, come crossing over the field to meet him; and their hap was to meet just as they were crossing the way of each other. The gentleman's name that met him was Mr. Worldly Wiseman: he dwelt in the town of Carnal Policy, a very great town, and also hard-by from whence Christian came. This man then, meeting with Christian, and having some inkling[1] of him, (for Christian's setting forth from the city of Destruction was much noised abroad, not only in the town where he dwelt, but also it began to be the town talk in some other places,) Mr. Worldly Wiseman, therefore, having some guess of him, by beholding his laborious going, by observing his sighs and groans, and the like, began thus to enter into some talk with Christian:—

World. How now, good fellow, whither away after this burdened manner?

Chr. A burdened manner, indeed, as ever I think poor creature had! And whereas you ask me, "Whither away?" I tell you, sir, I am going to yonder wicket-gate before me; for there, as I am informed, I shall be put into a way to be rid of my heavy burden.

[1] *Inkling*—a hint, intimation, or slight knowledge

World. Hast thou a wife and children?

Chr. Yes; but I am so laden with this burden that I cannot take that pleasure in them as formerly; methinks I am as if I had none.

World. Wilt thou hearken to me if I give thee counsel?

Chr. If it be good, I will; for I stand in need of good counsel.

World. I would advise thee then, that thou with all speed get thyself rid of thy burden; for thou wilt never be settled in thy mind till then: nor canst thou enjoy the benefits of the blessings which God hath bestowed upon thee, till then.

Chr. That is that which I seek for, even to be rid of this heavy burden: but get it off myself I cannot, nor is there any man in our country that can take it off my shoulders; therefore am I going this way, as I told you, that I may be rid of my burden.

World. Who bid thee go this way to be rid of thy burden?

Chr. A man that appeared to me to be a very great and honourable person: his name, as I remember, is Evangelist.

World. Beshrew him for his counsel! there is not a more dangerous and troublesome way in the world than is that into which he hath directed thee; and that thou shalt find, if thou wilt be ruled by his counsel. Thou hast met with something, as I perceive, already; for I see the dirt of the Slough of Despond is upon thee; but that slough is the beginning of the sorrows that do attend those that go on in that way. Hear me; I am older than thou: thou art like to meet with, in the way which thou goest, wearisomeness, painfulness, hunger, perils, nakedness, sword, lions, dragons, darkness, and, in a word, death, and what not. These things are certainly true, having been confirmed by many testimonies. And should a man so carelessly cast away himself by giving heed to a stranger?

Chr. Why, sir, this burden upon my back is more terrible to me than are all these things which you have mentioned; nay, methinks I care not what I meet with in the way, if so be I can also meet with deliverance from my burden.[2]

World. How camest thou by thy burden at first?

Chr. By reading this book in my hand.

World. I thought so; and it has happened unto thee as to other weak men, who, meddling with things too high for them, do suddenly fall into thy distractions; which distractions do not only unman men, as thine I perceive have done thee, but they run them upon desperate ventures, to obtain they know not what.

Chr. I know what I would obtain; it is ease from my heavy burden.

World. But why wilt thou seek for ease this way, seeing so many dangers attend it? especially since (hadst thou but patience to hear me) I could direct thee to the obtaining of what thou desirest, without the dangers that thou in this way wilt run thyself into. Yea, and the remedy is at hand. Besides, I will add, that instead of those dangers, thou shalt meet with much safety, friendship, and content.

Chr. Sir, I pray, open this secret to me.

[2] Such is the feeling of one that is truly convinced of his guilt as a sinner, and sensible of the condemnation to which he is thereby exposed: he *desires* nothing but deliverance from his burden of sin, he *fears* nothing but the wrath to come.

World. Why, in yonder village (the village is named Morality) there dwells a gentleman whose name is Legality, a very judicious man, and a man of a very good name, that has skill to help men off with such burdens as thine is from their shoulders; yea, to my knowledge, he hath done a great deal of good this way; ay, and besides he hath skill to cure those that are somewhat crazed in their wits with their burdens. To him, as I said, thou mayst go, and be helped presently. His house is not quite a mile from this place; and if he should not be at home himself, he hath a pretty young man to his son, whose name is Civility, that can do it (to speak on) as well as the old gentleman himself: there, I say, thou mayst be eased of thy burden; and if thou art not minded to go back to thy former habitation, (as indeed I would not wish thee,) thou mayest send for thy wife and children to thee to this village, where there are houses now standing empty, one of which thou mayst have at a reasonable rate: provision is there also cheap and good; and that which will make thy life the more happy is to be sure there thou shalt live by honest neighbours, in credit and good fashion.[3]

[3] The "village of Morality" is the residence of that class of professors who, having no just sense either of their own depravity or of the holiness of God, think to merit heaven by abstaining from open and scandalous vices, and by an outward conformity to some of the requirements of the law. Being "worldly-wisemen," they are of course not so puritanically strict as to allow their religion to interfere with their carnal pleasures or prosperity. "They feared the Lord, but served their own gods." 2 Kings xvii, 33. They pride themselves greatly on the idea that they are better than their neighbours: "Lord, I thank thee that I am not as other men are, extortioners, unjust, adulterers," &c. Luke xviii, 11. They think it proper to show some respect to public worship, and hence are often seen at church; but are moved thereto not so much by reverence to God, as by a de-

Now was Christian somewhat at a stand; but presently he concluded, If this be true which this gentleman hath said, my wisest course is to take his advice: and with that he thus further spake:—"Sir, which is my way to this honest man's house?"

World. Do you see yonder high hill?

Chr. Yes, very well.

World. By that hill you must go, and the first house you come at is his.

So Christian turned out of his way to go to Mr. Legality's house for help: but, behold, when he was got now hard by the hill, it seemed so high, and also that side of it that was next the way-side did hang so much over, that Christian was afraid to venture further, lest the hill should fall on his head; wherefore there he stood still, and wotted not what to do. Also his burden now seemed heavier to him than while he was in his way. There came also flashes of fire out of the hill, that made Christian afraid that he should be burnt: here, therefore, he did sweat, and quake for fear.[4]

sire to keep up their reputation for sanctity: "This people draw near me with their mouth, and with their lips do honour me, but have removed their heart far from me, and their fear toward me is taught by the precept of men." Isa. xxix, 14. True morality is in itself worthy of all commendation, but wo to that man who rests thereon his hopes of eternal salvation: "For I say unto you, that except your righteousness shall exceed the righteousness of the scribes and Pharisees, ye shall in no case enter into the kingdom of heaven." Matt. v, 20. "Not by works of righteousness which we have done, but according to his mercy he saved us, by the washing of regeneration, and renewing of the Holy Ghost; which he shed on us abundantly through Jesus Christ our Saviour." Titus iii, 5, 6.

[4] The convicted sinner, especially if he be not well instructed in the doctrine of Christ, is often tempted to take up his residence in "the village of Morality," or, in other words, to rest in a mere outward reformation; but if his conviction be deep and sincere, and his

And now he began to be sorry that he had taken Mr. Worldly Wiseman's counsel; and with that he saw Evangelist coming to meet him, at the sight also of whom he began to blush for shame. So Evangelist drew nearer and nearer; and coming up to him, he looked upon him with a severe and dreadful countenance, and thus began to reason with Christian :—

"What dost thou here, Christian?" said he: at which words Christian knew not what to answer; wherefore at present he stood speechless before him. Then said Evangelist further, "Art not thou the man that I found crying without the walls of the city of Destruction?"

Chr. Yes, dear sir, I am the man.

Evan. Did not I direct thee the way to the little wicket-gate?

"Yes, dear sir," said Christian.

Evan. How is it then that thou art so quickly turned aside? For thou art now out of the way

Chr. I met with a gentleman so soon as I had got over the Slough of Despond, who persuaded me that I might, in the village before me, find a man that could take off my burden.

distress be occasioned by a *sense of guilt*, as well as a fear of punishment, the vain attempts of his unrenewed heart to conform to "the righteousness of the law" will only serve to increase his distress, and give him to see and feel more deeply his inward corruption and wickedness. The thunderings and lightnings of Sinai—the terrors and threatenings of a broken law—will make him afraid. His experience in this matter will be like that of the pilgrim; or like that of Bunyan himself, who says, "I saw I had a heart that *would* sin, and that lay under a law that would condemn. . . Sin and corruption would as naturally bubble out of my heart as water would bubble out of a fountain. I thought now, that every one had a better heart than I had; I could have changed heart with anybody; I thought none but the devil himself could equalize me for inward wickedness and pollution I fell, therefore, at the sight of my own vileness, deeply in despair"

Evan. What was he?

Chr. He looked like a gentleman, and talked much to me, and got me at last to yield: so I came hither; but when I beheld this hill, and how it hangs over the way, I suddenly made a stand; lest it should fall on my head.

Evan. What said that gentleman to you?

Chr. Why, he asked me whither I was going; and I told him.

Evan. And what said he then?

Chr. He asked me if I had a family: and I told him. But, said I, I am so loaden with the burden that is on my back that I cannot take pleasure in them as formerly.

Evan. And what said he then?

Chr. He bid me with speed get rid of my burden, and I told him it was ease that I sought: and said I, I am therefore going to yonder gate, to receive further direction how I may get to the place of deliverance. So he said that he would show me a better way, and short, not so attended with difficulties as the way, sir, that you set me in; which way, said he, will direct you to a gentleman's house that hath skill to take off these burdens: so I believed him, and turned out of that way into this, if haply I might be soon eased of my burden. But when I came to this place, and beheld things as they are, I stopped, for fear (as I said) of danger: but I now know not what to do.

Then said Evangelist, "Stand still a little, that I may show thee the words of God." So he stood trembling. Then said Evangelist, "See that ye refuse not Him that speaketh: for if they escaped not who refused him that spake on earth, much more shall not we escape, if we turn away from Him that speaketh from heaven." Heb. xii, 25. He said, moreover, "Now the just shall live by faith ; but if any man draw back, my soul shall have no pleasure in him." Heb. x, 38. He also did thus apply them : Thou art the man that art running into misery ; thou hast begun to reject the counsel of the Most High, and to draw back thy foot from the way of peace, even almost to the hazarding of thy perdition.

Then Christian fell down at his feet as dead, crying "Wo is me, for I am undone !" At the sight of which Evangelist caught him by the right hand, saying, "All manner of sin and blasphemies shall be forgiven unto men." Matt. xii, 31. "Be not faithless, but believing." John xx, 27. Then did Christian again a little revive, and stood up trembling, as at first, before Evangelist.

Then Evangelist proceeded, saying, "Give more earnest heed to the things that I shall tell thee of. I will now show thee who it was that deluded thee, and who it was also to whom he sent thee. That man that met thee is one Worldly Wiseman ; and rightly is he so called ; partly because he savoureth only of the doctrine of this world ; (therefore he always goes to the town of Morality to church ;) and partly because he loveth that doctrine best, for it saveth him best from the cross ; and because he is of this carnal temper, therefore he seeketh to pervert my ways, though right. Now there are three things in this man's counsel that thou must utterly abhor :—

"1. His turning thee out of the way.

"2. His labouring to render the cross odious to thee.

"3. And his setting thy feet in that way that leadeth to the administration of death.

"First, Thou must abhor his turning thee out of the way; yea, and thine own consenting thereto; because this is to reject the counsel of God for the sake of the counsel of a Worldly Wiseman. The Lord says, 'Strive to enter in at the strait gate,' the gate to which I send thee; 'for strait is the gate that leadeth unto life, and few there be that find it.'[5] From this little wicket-gate, and from the way thereto, hath this wicked man turned thee, to the bringing of thee almost to destruction: hate, therefore, his turning thee out of the way, and abhor thyself for hearkening to him.

"Secondly, Thou must abhor his labouring to render the cross odious unto thee; for thou art to prefer it before the treasures of Egypt. Besides, the King of glory hath told thee, that he that will save his life shall lose it. And he that comes after him, and hates not his father, and mother, and wife, and children, and brethren, and sisters, yea, and his own life also, he cannot be my disciple. I say, therefore, for man to labour to persuade thee that that shall be thy death, without which, the truth hath said, thou canst not have eternal life; this doctrine thou must abhor.

"Thirdly, Thou must hate his setting of thy feet in the way that leadeth to the ministration of death. And for this thou must consider to whom he sent thee, and

[5] The straitness of this gate is not to be understood carnally, but mystically. You are not to understand it as if the entrance into heaven was some little pinching wicket; no, the straitness of this gate is quite another thing; this gate is wide enough for all them that are truly gracious and sincere lovers of Jesus Christ, but so strait, as that not one of the other can by any means enter in. . . The gates of the temple were six cubits wide; yet they were so strait that none that were unclean in anything might enter in thereat. 2 Chron. xxiii, 19.—*Bunyan's Strait Gate.*

also how unable that person was to deliver thee from thy burden.

"He to whom thou wast sent for ease, being by name Legality, is the son of the bond-woman which now is, and is in bondage with her children, (Gal. iv, 21, 27,) and is, in a mystery, this Mount Sinai, which thou hast feared will fall on thy head. Now if she with her children are in bondage, how canst thou expect by them to be made free? This Legality, therefore, is not able to set thee free from thy burden. No man was as yet ever rid of his burden by him; no, nor ever is like to be: ye cannot be justified by the works of the law; for by the deeds of the law no man living can be rid of his burden.[6] Therefore Mr. Worldly Wiseman is an alien, and Mr. Legality is a cheat; and for his son Civility, notwithstanding his simpering looks, he is but a hypocrite, and cannot help thee. Believe me, there is nothing in all this noise that thou hast heard of these sottish men, but a design to beguile thee of thy salvation, by turning thee from the way in which I had set thee." After this, Evangelist called aloud to the heavens for confirmation of what he had said; and with that there came words and fire out of the mountain under which poor Christian stood, which made the hair of his flesh stand up. The words were thus pronounced: "As many as are of the works of the law are under the curse; for it is written, Cursed is every one that continueth not in all things which are written in the book of the law to do them." Gal. iii, 10.

[6] "Knowing that a man is not justified by the works of the law, but by the faith of Jesus Christ, even we have believed in Jesus Christ, that we might be justified by the faith of Christ, and not by the works of the law: for by the works of the law shall no flesh be justified." Galatians ii, 16.

Now Christian looked for nothing but death, and began to cry out lamentably; even cursing the time in which he met with Mr. Worldly Wiseman; still calling himself a thousand fools for hearking to his counsel. He also was greatly ashamed to think that this gentleman's arguments, flowing only from the flesh, should have the prevalency with him so far as to cause him to forsake the right way. This done, he applied himself again to Evangelist in words and sense as follows:—

Chr. Sir, what think you? Is there any hope? May I now go back, and go up to the wicket-gate? Shall I not be abandoned for this, and sent back from thence ashamed? I am sorry I have hearkened to this man's counsel; but may my sin be forgiven?

Then said Evangelist to him, "Thy sin is very great, for by it thou hast committed two evils; thou hast forsaken the way that is good, to tread in forbidden paths. Yet will the man at the gate receive thee, for he has good will for men; only," said he, "take heed that thou turn not aside again, lest thou 'perish from the way, when his wrath is kindled but a little.'" Psa. ii, 12.

Then did Christian address himself to go back; and Evangelist, after he had kissed him, gave him one smile, and bid him God speed; so he went on with haste, neither spake he to any man by the way; nor if any asked him, would he vouchsafe them an answer. He went like one that was all the while treading on forbidden ground, and could by no means think himself safe, till again he was got into the way which he had left to follow Mr. Worldly Wiseman's counsel. So, in process of time, Christian got up to the gate. Now, over the gate there was written, "Knock, and it shall be opened unto you." Matt. vii, 7.

He that would enter in, must first without
Stand knocking at the Gate, nor need he doubt,
That is a knocker, but to enter in,
For God can love him, and forgive his sin.

He knocked, therefore, more than once or twice, saying,

> "May I now enter here? Will he within
> Open to sorry me, though I have been
> An undeserving rebel? Then shall I
> Not fail to sing his lasting praise on high."

At last there came a grave person to the gate, named Goodwill, who asked who was there, and whence he came, and what he would have.

Chr. Here is a poor burdened sinner. I come from the city of Destruction, but am going to Mount Zion, that I may be delivered from the wrath to come: I would therefore, sir, since I am informed that by this gate is the way thither, know if you are willing to let me in.

"I am willing with all my heart," said he; and with that he opened the gate. So when Christian was stepping in, the other gave him a pull. Then said Christian, "What means that?" The other told him, "A little distance from this gate there is erected a strong castle, of which Beelzebub is the captain: from thence both he and them that are with him shoot arrows at those that come up to this gate, if haply they may die before they enter in." Then said Christian, "I rejoice and tremble."

So when he was got in, the man of the gate asked him who directed him thither.

Chr. Evangelist bid me come hither and knock, as I did: and he said, that you, sir, would tell me what I must do.

Good. An open door is set before thee, and no man can shut it.

Chr. Now I begin to reap the benefits of my hazards.

Good. But how is it that you came alone?

Chr. Because none of my neighbours saw their danger, as I saw mine.

Good. Did any of them know of your coming?

Chr. Yes, my wife and children saw me at the first, and called after me to turn again: also, some of my neighbours stood crying and calling after me to return; but I put my fingers in my ears, and so came on my way.

Good. But did none of them follow you, to persuade you to go back?

Chr. Yes, both Obstinate and Pliable: but when they saw that they could not prevail, Obstinate went railing back, but Pliable came with me a little way.

Good. But why did he not come through?

Chr. We indeed came both together until we came to the Slough of Despond, into the which we also suddenly fell. And then was my neighbour Pliable discouraged, and would not venture further. Wherefore, getting out again on the side next to his own house, he told me I should possess the brave country alone for him: so he went his way, and I came mine: he after Obstinate, and I to this gate.

Then said Goodwill, "Alas, poor man! is the celestial glory of so little esteem with him, that he counteth it not worth running the hazard of a few difficulties to obtain it?"

"Truly," said Christian, "I have said the truth of Pliable; and if I should also say the truth of myself, it will appear there is no betterment betwixt him and myself. 'Tis true, he went back to his own house, but I also turned aside to go into the way of death, being persuaded thereto by the carnal argument of one Mr. Worldly Wiseman."

Good. O! did he light upon you? What! he would

have had you seek for ease at the hands of Mr. Legality! They are both of them a very cheat. But did you take his counsel?

Chr. Yes, as far as I durst. I went to find out Mr. Legality, until I thought that the mountain that stands by his house would have fallen upon my head; wherefore there I was forced to stop.

Good. That mountain has been the death of many, and will be the death of many more; it is well you escaped being by it dashed in pieces.

Chr. Why truly I do not know what had become of me there, had not Evangelist happily met me again as I was musing in the midst of my dumps; but it was God's mercy that he came to me again, for else I had never come hither. But now I am come, such a one as I am, more fit, indeed, for death by that mountain, than thus to stand talking with my Lord. But, O! what a favour is this to me, that yet I am admitted entrance here.

Good. We make no objections against any, notwithstanding all that they have done before they come hither: they are in no wise cast out. John vi, 37. And, therefore, good Christian, come a little way with me, and I will teach thee about the way thou must go. Look before thee; dost thou see this narrow way? That is the way thou must go. It was cast up by the patriarchs, prophets, Christ, and his apostles, and it is as straight as a rule can make it; this is the way thou must go.

"But," said Christian, "are there no turnings nor windings, by which a stranger may lose his way?"

Good. Yes, there are many ways butt down upon this; and they are crooked and wide; but thus thou mayst distinguish the right from the wrong, the right only being straight and narrow.[7]

Then I saw in my dream, that Christian asked him further, if he could not help him off with his burden that was upon his back. For as yet he had not got rid thereof, nor could he by any means get it off without help.

He told him, "As to thy burden, be content to bear it until thou comest to the place of deliverance; for there it will fall from thy back of itself."

Then Christian began to gird up his loins, and to address himself to his journey. So the other told him, that by that he was gone some distance from the gate, he would come to the house of the Interpreter, at whose door he should knock, and he would show him excellent things. Then Christian took his leave of his friend, and he again bid him God speed.

[7] Beware of by-paths; take heed thou dost not run into those lanes which lead out of the way. There are crooked paths—paths in which men go astray—paths that lead to death and damnation; but take heed of all these. Some of them are dangerous because of practice, some because of opinion, but mind them not; mind the path before thee; look right before thee; turn neither to the right nor to the left, but let thine eyes look right on, even right before thee: "Ponder the path of thy feet, and let all thy ways be established." Turn not to the right hand nor to the left: "Remove thy foot far from evil." This counsel being not so seriously taken as given, is the reason of that starting from opinion to opinion, reeling this way and that way, out of this lane into that lane, and so missing the way to the kingdom. Though the way to heaven be but one, yet there are many crooked lanes and by-paths shoot down upon it, as I may say.—*Bunyan's Heavenly Footman*

CHAPTER III.

Christian arrives at the Interpreter's house—The Interpreter shows and explains to him various representations and emblems of spiritual things, as the picture of the pilgrims' guide, the dusty parlour, Passion and Patience, the fire, the man in the iron cage, etc.

THEN he went on till he came at the house of the Interpreter, where he knocked over and over. At last one came to the door, and asked who was there.

Chr. Sir, here is a traveller, who was bid by an acquaintance of the good man of this house to call here for my profit; I would therefore speak with the master of the house.

So he called for the master of the house, who, after a little time, came to Christian, and asked him what he would have.

"Sir," said Christian, "I am a man that am come from the city of Destruction, and am going to Mount Zion; and I was told by the man that stands at the gate at the head of this way, that if I called here you would show me excellent things, such as would be helpful to me on my journey."

Then said the Interpreter, "Come in; I will show thee that which will be profitable to thee."[1] So he commanded his man to light the candle, and bid Christian follow him. So he had him into a private room, and bid his man open a door; the which when he had done, Christian saw the picture of a very grave person

[1] The Interpreter is intended to represent the Holy Spirit, whose office it is to enlighten and instruct the believer. John xvi, 13, 14; 1 Cor. ii, 10, 11. As the Interpreter led Christian from room to room "through his chambers of spiritual imagery," so the Spirit leads the humble, inquiring soul, step by step into all the truths of the gospel.

hang up against the wall; and this was the fashion of it: it had eyes lifted up to heaven, the best of books in its hand, the law of truth was written upon its lips, the world was behind its back; it stood as if it pleaded with men, and a crown of gold did hang over its head.

Then said Christian, "What meaneth this?"

Inter. The man whose picture this is, is one of a thousand; he can beget children,[2] travail in birth with children,[3] and nurse them himself when they are born. Whereas thou seest him with his eyes lift up to heaven, the best of books in his hand, and the law of truth writ on his lips, it is to show thee, that his work is to know, and unfold dark things to sinners; even as also thou seest him stand as if he pleaded with men. And whereas thou seest the world as cast behind him, and that a crown hangs over his head; that is to show thee, that slighting and despising the things that are present, for the love that he has to his Master's service, he is sure in the world that comes next to have glory for his reward.

"Now," said the Interpreter, "I have showed thee this picture first, because the man whose picture this is, is the only man whom the Lord of the place whither thou art going hath authorized to be thy guide in all difficult places thou mayst meet with in the way: wherefore take good heed to what I have showed thee, and bear well in thy mind what thou hast seen, lest in thy journey thou meet with some that pretend to lead thee right, but their way goes down to death."[4]

[2] 1 Corinthians iv, 15. [3] Galatians iv, 19.

[4] This "picture" is a portraiture of a true and faithful Christian minister; one who has been called and qualified by the Holy Spirit for the important and responsible work of preaching the everlasting gospel; an ambassador for Christ, praying sinners in Christ's stead to be reconciled to God, and guiding and instructing them in the way that

Then he took him by the hand, and led him into a very large parlour that was full of dust because never swept; the which after he had reviewed it a little while, the Interpreter called for a man to sweep. Now, when he began to sweep, the dust began so abundantly to fly about, that Christian had almost therewith been choked. Then said the Interpreter to a damsel that stood by, "Bring hither water, and sprinkle the room;" the which when she had done, it was swept and cleansed with pleasure.

Then said Christian, "What means this?"

The Interpreter answered, "This parlour is the heart of a man that was never sanctified by the sweet grace of the gospel. The dust is his original sin, and inward

leads to life eternal. Our Lord and his apostles warned the people that there were and would be *false* prophets—wolves in sheep's clothing—having a form of religion, but denying its power—teachers of false doctrines, who should involve in their own destruction those who trusted them as spiritual guides. "If the blind lead the blind, both shall fall into the ditch." The Interpreter, aware that Christian would in his journey meet with some of these pretenders who might lead him astray to his ruin, gives him the marks by which he may distinguish the man whose counsel and direction he may safely follow *His eyes are lifted up to heaven*—he trusts not in his own ability, but looks to God for grace and wisdom to discharge his duty aright, and give him success therein; *the law of truth is on his lips*—he preaches faithfully the doctrines of that "best of books," described as being "in his hand;" he *pleads* with men—shows his concern for their salvation by the earnestness with which he entreats them to turn to God; *the world is behind his back*—he seeks not, desires not, the honours or pleasures of the present life, "having respect unto the recompense of reward," the "crown" which God has promised to his faithful servants; and *he begets children*—that is, souls are converted through his instrumentality. Similar to these are the evidences which Mr. Wesley required of his "helpers" as proof of their ministry, GRACE, GIFTS, and FRUIT: "As long," he says, "as these marks concur in any one, we believe he is called of God to preach: these we receive as sufficient proof that he is moved thereto by the Holy Ghost."

corruptions, that have defiled the whole man. He that began to sweep at first, is the Law; but she that brought water, and did sprinkle it, is the Gospel. Now whereas thou sawest, that as soon as the first began to sweep, the dust did so fly about that the room could not by him be cleansed, but that thou wast almost choked therewith: this is to show thee, that the law, (by its working,) instead of cleansing the heart from sin, doth revive, put strength into, and increase [the sense of] it in the soul, even as it doth discover and forbid it, for it doth not give power to subdue.[5] Again, as thou sawest the damsel sprinkle the room with water, upon which it was cleansed with pleasure; this is to show thee, that when the gospel comes in the sweet and precious influences thereof to the heart, then, I say, even as thou sawest the damsel lay the dust by sprinkling the floor with water, so is sin vanquished and subdued, and the soul made clean, through the faith of it, and consequently fit for the King of glory to inhabit."[6]

I saw moreover in my dream, that the Interpreter took him by the hand, and had him into a little room, where sat two little children, each one in his chair. The name of the eldest was Passion, and the name of the other Patience. Passion seemed to be much discontented, but Patience was very quiet. Then Christian asked, "What is the reason of the discontent of Passion?" The Interpreter answered, "The governor of them would have him stay for his best things till the beginning of the next year; but he will have all now; but Patience is willing to wait."

Then I saw that one came to Passion, and brought him a bag of treasure, and poured it down at his feet: the

[5] Rom v,20; vii,7-9; 1 Cor. xv,56. [6] John. xv,3; Eph.v,26; Acts xv,9

which he took up and rejoiced therein, and withal laughed Patience to scorn. But I beheld but a while, and he had lavished all away, and had nothing left him but rags.

Then said Christian to the Interpreter, "Expound this matter more fully to me."

So he said, "These two lads are figures; Passion of the men of this world, and Patience of the men of that which is to come; for as here thou seest, Passion will have all now, this year, that is to say, in this world; so are the men of this world; they must have all their good things now; they cannot stay till the next year, that is, until the next world, for their portion of good. That proverb, 'A bird in the hand is worth two in the bush,' is of more authority with them than are all the divine testimonies of the good of the world to come. But as thou sawest that he had quickly lavished all away, and had presently left him nothing but rags, so will it be with all such men at the end of this world."

Then said Christian, "Now I see that Patience has the best wisdom, and that upon many accounts. 1. Because he stays for the best things. 2. And also because he will have the glory of his, when the other has nothing but rags."

Inter. Nay, you may add another, to wit, the glory of the next world will never wear out; but these are suddenly gone. Therefore Passion had not so much reason to laugh at Patience, because he had his good things first, as Patience will have to laugh at Passion, because he had his best things last; for first must give place to last, because last must have his time to come; but last gives place to nothing, for there is not another to succeed; he therefore that hath his portion first, must needs have a time to spend it; but he that hath his portion last, must have it lastingly: therefore it is said of Dives, "In thy lifetime thou receivedst thy good things, and likewise Lazarus evil things; but now he is comforted and thou art tormented." Luke xvi, 25.

Chr. Then I perceive it is not best to covet things that are now, but to wait for things to come.

Inter. You say truth: for "the things that are seen are temporal, but the things that are not seen are eternal." 2 Cor. iv, 18. But though this be so, yet since things present, and our fleshly appetite, are such near neighbours one to another; and again, because things to come and carnal sense are such strangers one to another; therefore it is, that the first of these so suddenly fall into amity, and that distance is so continued between the second.

Then I saw in my dream, that the Interpreter took Christian by the hand, and led him into a place where was a fire burning against a wall, and one standing by it, always casting much water upon it, to quench it yet did the fire burn higher and hotter.

Then said Christian, "What means this?"

The Interpreter answered, "This fire is the work of grace that is wrought in the heart; he that casts water upon it, to extinguish and put it out, is the devil: but in that thou seest the fire notwithstanding burn higher and hotter, thou shalt also see the reason of that. So he had him about to the back side of the wall, where he saw a man with a vessel of oil in his hand, of the which he did also continually cast (but secretly) into the fire.

Then said Christian, "What means this?"

The Interpreter answered, "This is Christ, who continually, with the oil of his grace, maintains the work already begun in the heart;[7] by the means of which, notwithstanding what the devil can do, the souls of his people prove gracious still.[8] And in that thou sawest, that the man stood behind the wall to maintain the fire; this is to teach thee, that it is hard for the tempted to see how this work of grace is maintained in the soul."

I saw also that the Interpreter took him again by the hand, and led him into a pleasant place, where was built a stately palace, beautiful to behold; at the sight of which Christian was greatly delighted. He saw also upon the top thereof certain persons walking, who were clothed all in gold.

Then said Christian, "May we go in thither?"

[7] The Lord will perfect that which concerneth me. Psa. cxxxviii, 8. My sheep hear my voice, and I know them, and they follow me: and I will give unto them eternal life; and they shall never perish, neither shall any man pluck them out of my hand. John x, 27, 28. Being confident of this very thing, that he which hath begun a good work in you will perform it unto the day of Jesus Christ. Phil. i, 6. Faithful is he that calleth you, who also will do it. 1 Thess. v, 24.

[8] The precious promises of persevering grace are sufficient to sustain the believing soul under the most severe trials, temptations, and discipline to which he can be exposed: under all these he will find that word of our Saviour to be true,—"My grace is sufficient for thee." But we should ever remember that with these promises there is always a condition on our part—continued faithfulness—either expressed or implied: "He that *endureth to the end*, the same shall be saved," Matt. x, 14; "Thou standest *by faith*," Rom. xi, 20; "Who are kept by the power of God, *through faith*, unto salvation," 1 Pet. i, 5; "Give diligence to make your calling and election sure: for *if ye do these things* ye shall never fall," 2 Pet. i, 10; "Be thou *faithful unto death*, and I will give thee a crown of life," Rev. ii, 10. It is only so long as the sheep continue to *follow* the good Shepherd that they cannot be plucked out of his hand. While therefore we rejoice in the promise, let us rejoice with trembling, assured that if we fail of the condition, it will avail us nothing. May "He who is able to keep us from falling," preserve us, and at the last "present us faultless before the presence of his glory with exceeding joy" Jude 24.

Then the Interpreter took him and led him up toward the door of the palace; and behold, at the door stood a great company of men, as desirous to go in, but durst not. There also sat a man at a little distance from the door, at a table-side, with a book and his ink-horn before him, to take the names of them that should enter therein; he saw also that in the doorway stood many men in armour to keep it, being resolved to do to the men that would enter, what hurt and mischief they could. Now was Christian somewhat in a maze. At last, when every man started back for fear of the armed men, Christian saw a man of a very stout countenance come up to the man that sat there to write, saying, "Set down my name, sir;" the which when he had done, he saw the man draw his sword, and put a helmet upon his head, and rush toward the door upon the armed men, who laid upon him with deadly force; but the man, not at all discouraged, fell to cutting and hacking most fiercely. So after he had received and given many wounds to those that attempted to keep him out, he cut his way through them all and pressed forward into the palace; at which there was a pleasant voice heard from those that were within, even of those that walked upon the top of the palace, saying,—

Come in, come in, Eternal glory shalt thou win

So he went in and was clothed with such garments as they. Then Christian smiled, and said, "I think verily I know the meaning of this."[9]

[9] He that would gain heaven must strive, yea, fight for it, for he will find that he hath many and subtle adversaries who will oppose themselves to his entering therein. "The kingdom of heaven suffereth violence, and the violent take it by force." Matt. xi, 12. "Put on the whole armour of God, that ye may be able to stand against

"Now," said Christian, "let me go hence."

"Nay, stay," said the Interpreter, "until I have showed thee a little more, and after that thou shalt go on thy way." So he took him by the hand again, and led him into a very dark room, where there sat a man in an iron cage.

Now the man, to look on, seemed very sad; he sat with his eyes looking down to the ground, his hands folded together, and he sighed as if he would break his heart. Then said Christian, "What means this?" At which the Interpreter bid him talk with the man.

Then said Christian to the man, "What art thou?"

The man answered, "I am what I was not once."

Chr. What wast thou once?

The man said, "I was once a fair and flourishing professor, both in mine own eyes, and also in the eyes of others: I was once, as I thought, fair for the celestial city, and had even joy at the thoughts that I should get thither."

Chr. Well, but what art thou now?

Man. I am now a man of despair, and am shut up in it, as in this iron cage. I cannot get out. O *now* I cannot!

Chr. But how camest thou into this condition?

Man. I left off to watch and be sober: I laid the reins upon the neck of my lusts; I sinned against the light of

the wiles of the devil. For we wrestle not against flesh and blood, but against principalities, against powers, against the rulers of the darkness of this world, against spiritual wickedness in high places. Wherefore take unto you the whole armour of God, that ye may be able to withstand in the evil day, and having done all, to stand." Eph. vi, 11–13. Bunyan wrote this book in a time of great religious intolerance, and he and many others of his day found that if they "would live godly in Christ Jesus," and "lay hold on eternal life," they must not only "fight the good fight of faith," but also "suffer persecution," and pass "through much tribulation." 1 Tim. vi, 12; Acts xiv, 22.

the word, and the goodness of God; I have grieved the Spirit, and he is gone; I tempted the devil, and he is come to me; I have provoked God to anger, and he has left me; I have so hardened my heart that I cannot repent.

Then said Christian to the Interpreter, "But are there no hopes for such a man as this?"

"Ask him," said the Interpreter.

Then said Christian, "Is there no hope, but you must be kept in the iron cage of despair?"

Man. No, none at all.

Chr. Why, the Son of the Blessed is very pitiful.

Man. I have crucified him to myself afresh. I have despised his person; I have despised his righteousness; I have counted his blood an unholy thing; I have done despite to the Spirit of grace; therefore I shut myelf out of all the promises, and there now remains to me nothing but threatenings, dreadful threatenings, fearful threatenings of certain judgment and fiery indignation, which shall devour me as an adversary.

Chr. For what did you bring yourself into this condition?

Man. For the lusts, pleasures, and profits of this world, in the enjoyment of which I did then promise myself much delight; but now every one of those things also bite me, and gnaw me, like a burning worm.

Chr. But canst thou not now repent and turn?

Man. God hath denied me repentance. His word gives me no encouragement to believe; yea, himself hath shut me up in this iron cage; nor can all the men in the world let me out. O eternity! eternity! how shall I grapple with the misery that I must meet with in eternity.[10]

[10] Because a man is in despair it does not necessarily follow that his case is really hopeless. There may be "a way of escape," though as

Then said the Interpreter to Christian, "Let this man's misery be remembered by thee, and be an everlasting caution to thee."

"Well," said Christian, "this is fearful! God help me to watch and be sober, and to pray that I may shun the cause of this man's misery. Sir, is it not time for me to go on my way now?"

Inter. Tarry till I shall show thee one thing more, and then thou shalt go on thy way.

So he took Christian by the hand again, and led him into a chamber where there was one rising out of bed; and as he put on his raiment, he shook and trembled. Then said Christian, "Why doth this man thus tremble?"

The Interpreter then bid him tell to Christian the reason of his so doing. So he began, and said, "This night, as I was in my sleep, I dreamed, and behold the

yet he cannot see it. The Scriptures do indeed speak of cases of aggravated apostacy respecting the subjects of which it is said that "it is impossible to renew them again to *repentance*," and that there remaineth for them nothing but a "fearful looking-for of judgment, and fiery indignation which shall devour the adversaries." Heb. vi, 4–6; x, 26–29. But these, it must be remembered, are not cases of simple backsliding, but of final and utter apostacy, after having received the grace of God, accompanied with a denial and rejection of Christ and his atonement. Now, as there is no other name given under heaven by which we can be saved, but the name of Jesus only, it is plain that for those who reject his offering, "there remaineth no more sacrifice for sin." But a reference to the passages quoted, will show that no true *penitent* can be in this desperate case: he, therefore, that hath a heart broken for sin, and is willing to be "saved by grace," may, however foully he hath fallen, draw near to the mercy seat with hope—yea, with full assurance of hope, for He "who is able to save to the uttermost" hath said, "Him that cometh unto me I will in no wise cast out." Penitence itself, being an "operation of the Holy Ghost," is an evidence that God hath *not* withdrawn his Spirit from those that are exercised thereby.

heavens grew exceeding black; also it thundered and lightened in most fearful wise, that it put me into an agony. So I looked up in my dream, and saw the clouds rack, at an unusual rate; upon which I heard a great sound of a trumpet, and saw also a man sitting upon a cloud, attended with the thousands of heaven; they were all in flaming fire; also the heavens were on a burning flame. I heard then a great voice, saying, 'Arise, ye dead, and come to judgment.' And with that the rocks rent, the graves opened, and the dead that were therein came forth: some of them were exceeding glad, and looked upward; and some sought to hide themselves under the mountains. Then I saw the man that sat upon the cloud, open the book and bid the world draw near. Yet there was, by reason of a fierce flame which issued out and came before him, a convenient distance betwixt him and them, as betwixt the judge and the prisoners at the bar. I heard it also proclaimed to them that attended on the man that sat on the cloud, 'Gather together the tares, the chaff, and stubble, and cast them into the burning lake.' And with that the bottomless pit opened, just whereabout I stood; out of the mouth of which there came, in an abundant manner, smoke, and coals of fire, with hideous noises. It was also said to the same persons, 'Gather my wheat into the garner.' And with that I saw many catched up and carried away into the clouds; but I was left behind. I also sought to hide myself, but I could not; for the man that sat upon the cloud still kept his eye upon me; my sins also came into my mind; and my conscience did accuse me on every side. Upon this I awakened from my sleep."

Chr. But what was it that made you so afraid of this sight?

Man. Why I thought that the day of judgment was come, and that I was not ready for it; but this frighted me most, that the angels gathered up several, and left me behind: also the pit of hell opened her mouth just where I stood. My conscience too afflicted me; and, as I thought, the Judge had always his eye upon me, showing indignation in his countenance.[11]

Then said the Interpreter to Christian, "Hast thou considered all these things?"

Chr. Yes, and they put me in hope and fear.

Inter. Well, keep all things so in thy mind, that they may be as a goad in thy sides, to prick thee forward in the way thou must go.

Then Christian began to gird up his loins, and to address himself to his journey. Then said the Interpreter, "The Comforter be always with thee, good Christian, to guide thee in the way that leads to the city." So Christian went on his way, saying,—

Here have I seen things rare and profitable,
Things pleasant, dreadful things to make me stable
In what I have begun to take in hand:
Then let me think on them, and understand
Wherefore they showed me were, and let me be
Thankful, O good Interpreter, to thee.

[11] There can be little doubt that Bunyan is here relating one of the fearful visions with which his own slumbers were disturbed, and his conscience alarmed, in the years of his youthful wickedness. Some of those dreams are recorded in the Life of Bunyan, pp. 13, 14, and will be found to bear a striking resemblance to this of the man in the Interpreter's house.

Must here the burden fall from off my back?
Must here the strings that bound it to me crack?
Blest cross! blest sepulchre! blest rather be
The Man that there was put to shame for me!

CHAPTER IV.

Christian loses his burden at the cross—Is saluted by three Shining Ones, who give him a change of raiment, etc.—Going on his way he finds Simple, Sloth, and Presumption, asleep—Meets Formalist and Hypocrisy—Climbs the hill Difficulty—Falls asleep in the Arbour, and loses his roll—Meets Timorous and Mistrust fleeing back—He misses his roll and returns to find it.

Now I saw in my dream, that the highway which Christian was to go was fenced on either side with a wall, and that wall was called Salvation. Up this way therefore did burdened Christian run, but not without great difficulty, because of the load on his back.

He ran thus till he came at a place somewhat ascending; and upon that place stood a cross, and a little below, in the bottom, a sepulchre. So I saw in my dream, that just as Christian came up with the cross his burden loosed from off his shoulders, and fell from off his back, and began to tumble, and so continued to do till it came to the mouth of the sepulchre, where it fell in, and I saw it no more.[1]

Then was Christian glad and lightsome, and said with a merry heart, "He hath given me rest by his sorrow, and life by his death."[2] Then he stood still

[1] There is no way to heaven but by the cross, nor any other means by which the sinner can be rid of his "burden" but by faith in Him who on that cross made atonement for his offences. When we truly repent of our sins, and, casting aside every other confidence, believe on the Lord Jesus Christ, with the heart unto righteousness, then, and then only, do we feel that the Father's wrath is passed away, and that we are accepted in the Beloved. "Other ground can no man lay; Jesus takes our sins away."

[2] I remember one day, as I was travelling in the country, and musing on the wickedness and blasphemy of my heart, and considering

a while to look and wonder; for it was very surprising to him that the sight of the cross should thus ease him of his burden. He looked, therefore, and looked again, even till the springs that were in his head sent the waters down his cheeks. Now as he stood looking and weeping, behold three Shining Ones came to him,[3] and saluted him with "Peace be to thee." So the first said to him, "Thy sins be forgiven thee," the second stripped him of his rags, and clothed him with change of raiment,[4] the third also set a mark on his forehead, and gave him a roll with a seal upon it,[5] which he bid

the enmity there was in me to God, this scripture came into my mind, "He hath made peace by the blood of his cross," Col. i, 20; by which I was made to see, both again and again, that day, that God and my soul were friends by his blood. This was a good day to me: I hope I shall never forget it.—*Bunyan's Grace Abounding.*

[3] The appearance of the "three Shining Ones" is thought by some to have reference to the "ministry of angels;" we think it more probable, however, that by it the author designed to point out the agency of the three persons in the Trinity in accomplishing the work of a sinner's salvation.

[4] And He answered and spake unto them that stood before him, saying, "Take away the filthy garments from him." And unto him he said, "Behold, I have caused thine iniquity to pass from thee, and I will clothe thee with change of raiment." Zech. iii, 4. I will greatly rejoice in the Lord; my soul shall be joyful in my God; for he hath clothed me with the garments of salvation, he hath covered me with the robe of righteousness. Isa. lxi, 10.

[5] In whom also, after that ye believed, ye were sealed with that Holy Spirit of promise, which is the earnest of our inheritance. Eph i, 13, 14. The "roll with a seal upon it," which was now given to Christian, denotes that assurance of divine acceptance which the believer receives at the time of his conversion, when "the Spirit witnesseth with his spirit that he is a child of God," Rom. viii, 16, and so long as he remains faithful to the grace given to him, it is his privilege to enjoy this "witness of the Spirit" as an abiding testimony of his adoption and sonship; "for hereby we know that God abideth in us, by the Spirit which he hath given us." 1 John iii, 24. We will here quote another passage from "Grace Abounding," de

him look on as he ran, and that he should give it in at the celestial gate: so they went their way. Then Christian gave three leaps for joy, and went on singing,—

Thus far did I come laden with my sin;
Nor could aught ease the grief that I was in,
Till I came hither: what a place is this!
Must here be the beginning of my bliss?
Must here the burden fall from off my back?
Must here the strings that bound it to me crack?
Blest cross! blest sepulchre! blest rather be
The Man that there was put to shame for me!

I saw then in my dream, that he went on thus, even until he came at a bottom, where he saw, a little out of the way, three men fast asleep, with fetters upon their heels. The name of the one was Simple, another Sloth, and the third Presumption.

Christian then seeing them lie in this case, went to them, if peradventure he might awake them, and cried, "You are like them that sleep on the top of a mast, for the dead sea is under you, a gulf that hath no bottom: awake, therefore, and come away; be willing, also, and I will help you off with your irons." He also told them, "If he that goeth about like a roaring lion (1 Pet. 5, 8)

scriptive of Bunyan's feelings at this stage of his own experience: "Now I had an evidence, as I thought, of my salvation, from heaven, with many golden seals thereon, all hanging in my sight; now I could remember this manifestation, and the other discovery of grace, with comfort; and should often long and desire that the last day were come, that I might be for ever inflamed with the sight and joy, and communion with Him whose head was crowned with thorns, whose face was spit upon, and body broken, and soul made an offering for my sins. For whereas, before I lay continually trembling at the mouth of hell; now methought I was got so far therefrom that I could not, when I looked back, scarce discern it; and O! thought I, that I were fourscore years old now, that I might die quickly, that my soul might be gone to rest" comes by, you will certainly become a prey to his teeth." With that they looked upon him, and began to answer him in this sort: Simple said, "I see no danger;" Sloth said, "Yet a little more sleep;" and Presumption said, "Every tub must stand upon its own bottom." And so they lay down to sleep again, and Christian went on his way.

Yet was he troubled to think, that men in that danger should so little esteem the kindness of him that so freely offered to help them, both by awakening of them, counselling of them, and proffering to help them off with their irons. And as he was troubled thereabout, he espied two men come tumbling over the wall on the left hand of the narrow way: and they made up apace to him. The name of the one was Formalist,[6] and the name of the other Hypocrisy.[7] So, as I said, they

[6] The Formalist is a man that hath lost all but [or never had more than] the *shell* of religion: he is hot, indeed, for his form; and no marvel, for that is his all to contend for: but his form being without the power and spirit of godliness, (2 Tim. iii, 5,) it will leave him in his sins; nay, he standeth now in them in the sight of God, and is one of the "many" that "will seek to enter in, and shall not be able."—*Bunyan's Strait Gate.* Bunyan himself, at one period of his life, furnished no inapt illustration of the character of the Formalist. See Life of Bunyan, pp. 22–25.

[7] Hypocrites, with rotten hearts, are not afraid to come before God in Zion. This conduct of theirs suggests unto us a prodigious kind of boldness and hardened fearlessness; for what presumption higher, and what attempt more desperate, than for a man that wanteth grace, and a true knowledge of God, to crowd himself in that condition into the house or church of God? or to make profession of, and desire that the name of God shall be called upon him? Men merely natural, I mean men that have not got the devilish art of hypocrisy, are afraid to think of doing thus. . . They have, therefore, learned this boldness of none in the visible world; they only took it of the devil, for he, and he only, with these his disciples, attempt thus to present themselves in the church before God. "The

drew up unto him, who thus entered with them into discourse.

Chr. Gentlemen, whence came you, and whither go you?

Form. and *Hyp.* We were born in the land of Vain-glory, and are going for praise to Mount Sion. Matt. xxiii, 5.

Chr. Why came ye not in at the gate which standeth at the beginning of the way? Know ye not that it is written, that "he that cometh not in by the door, but climbeth up some other way, the same is a thief and a robber?" John x, 1.

They said, that to go to the gate for entrance was by all their countrymen counted too far about; and that therefore their usual way was to make a short cut of it, and to climb over the wall, as they had done.

Chr. But will it not be counted a trespass against the Lord of the city whither we are bound, thus to violate his revealed will?

They told him that as for that, he needed not to trouble his head thereabout: for what they did they had custom for, and could produce, if need were, testimony that would witness it, for more than a thousand years.

"But," said Christian, "will it stand a trial at law?"

They told him, that custom, it being of so long standing as above a thousand years, would doubtless now be admitted as a thing legal by an impartial judge: and besides, said they, if we get into the way, what matters which way we get in? If we are in, we are in; thou

ares are the children of the wicked one." Matt. xiii, 38. The "tares," that is, the hypocrites, that are Satan's brood; the generation of vipers, that cannot escape the damnation of hell.—*Bunyan's Discourse on the Barren Fig-tree.*

art but in the way, who, as we perceive, came in at the gate; and we also are in the way, that came tumbling over the wall; wherein now is thy condition better than ours?

Chr. I walk by the rule of my Master: you walk by the rude working of your fancies. You are counted thieves already by the Lord of the way: therefore I doubt you will not be found true men at the end of the way. You come in by yourselves without his direction, and shall go out by yourselves without his mercy.

To this they made him but little answer; only they bid him look to himself. Then I saw that they went on every man in his way, without much conference one with another; save that these two men told Christian, that as to laws and ordinances, they doubted not but that they should as conscientiously do them as he. Therefore, said they, we see not wherein thou differest from us, but by the coat that is on thy back, which was, as we trow, given thee by some of thy neighbours, to hide the shame of thy nakedness.

Chr. By laws and ordinances you will not be saved; since you came not in by the door. Gal. ii, 16. And as for this coat that is on my back, it was given me by the Lord of the place whither I go; and that, as you say, to cover my nakedness with. And I take it as a token of his kindness to me; for I had nothing but rags before. And besides thus I comfort myself as I go. Surely think I, when I come to the gate of the city, the Lord thereof will know me for good, since I have his coat on my back; a coat that he gave me freely in the day that he stript me of my rags. I have, moreover, a mark in my forehead, of which perhaps you have taken no notice, which one of my Lord's most intimate associates fixed there in the day that my burden fell off my shoulders. I will tell you, moreover, that I had then given me a roll sealed, to comfort me by reading as I go in the way: I was also bid to give it in at the celestial gate, in token of my certain going in after it; all which things I doubt you want, and want them because you came not in at the gate.

To these things they gave him no answer; only they looked upon each other, and laughed. Then I saw that they all went on, save that Christian kept before, who had no more talk but with himself, and that sometimes sighingly, and sometimes comfortably; also he would be often reading in the roll that one of the Shining Ones gave him, by which he was refreshed.[8]

I beheld then, that they all went on till they came at the foot of the hill Difficulty, at the bottom of which was a spring. There were also in the same place two other ways besides that which came straight from the gate: one turned to the left hand, and the other to the right, at the bottom of the hill; but the narrow way lay right up the hill, and the name of the going [road] up the side of the hill is called Difficulty. Christian now went to the spring,[9] and drank thereof to refresh

[8] If thou wouldst be faithful to do that work that God hath allotted thee to do in this world for his name, labour to live in the savour and sense of thy freedom and liberty by Jesus Christ. This is of absolute use in this matter; yea, so absolute, that it is impossible for any Christian to do his work Christianly without some enjoyment of it.—*Bunyan on Paul's Departure and Crown.*

[9] "He that hath mercy on them shall lead them; even by the springs of water shall he guide them." Isa. xlix, 10. Unusual manifestations of grace frequently precede great trials. The Pilgrim had now a difficult task before him, and he is refreshed by the Spirit of grace to enable him to accomplish it; according to the promise, "As thy days, so shall thy strength be." Deut. xxxiii, 25.

himself, and then began to go up the hill, saying,—

> The hill, though high, I covet to ascend;
> The difficulty will not me offend;
> For I perceive the way to life lies here:
> Come, pluck up heart, let's neither faint nor fear
> Better, though *difficult*, the right way to go,
> Than wrong, though *easy*, where the end is wo[10]

The other two also came to the foot of the hill. But when they saw that the hill was steep and high, and that there were two other ways to go; and supposing

[10] If thou wouldst be faithful to do that work that God hath appointed thee, then beware thou do not stop and stick when hard work comes before thee. It is with Christians as it is with other scholars, they sometimes meet with hard lessons; but these thou must also learn, or thou canst not do thy work. The word and Spirit of God comes sometimes like chain-shot to us, as if it would cut down all; as when Abraham was to offer up Isaac, and the Levites to slay their brethren. Paul also must go from place to place to preach, though he knew beforehand he was to be afflicted there. These are hard things, but have not been rejected when God hath called to do them. O how willingly would our flesh and blood escape the cross for Christ! The comforts of the gospel, the sweetness of the promise, how pleasing is it to us! like Ephraim here, we love to tread out the corn, (Hos x, 11,) and to hear those pleasant songs and music that gospel sermons make, when only grace is preached, and nothing of our duty as to works of self-denial; but as for such, God will tread upon their fair neck, and yoke them with Christ's yoke; for there they have a work to do, even a work of self-denial. Now this work sometimes lieth in acts that seem to be desperate; as when a man must both leave and hate his life, and all he hath, for Christ, or else he cannot serve him, nor be counted his disciple Sometimes in acts that seem to be foolish; as when men deny them selves of those comforts, and pleasures, and friendships, and honours of the world, that formerly they used to have, and choose rather to associate themselves with the very abjects of this world—I mean such as carnal men count so. I might add many things of this nature, to show you what hard chapters God sometimes sets his best people: but thy work is, if thou wouldst be faithful, not to stop nor stick at anything.—*Bunyan on Paul's Departure and Crown*

also that these two ways might meet again with that up which Christian went, on the other side of the hill; therefore they were resolved to go in those ways. Now the name of one of those ways was Danger, and the name of the other Destruction. So the one took the way which is called Danger, which led him into a great wood; and the other took directly up the way to Destruction, which led him into a wide field, full of dark mountains, where he stumbled and fell, and rose no more.[11]

I looked then after Christian, to see him go up the hill, where I perceived he fell from running to going, and from going to clambering upon his hands and his knees, because of the steepness of the place. Now about the midway to the top of the hill was a pleasant Arbour, made by the Lord of the hill for the refreshment of weary travellers. Thither, therefore, Christian got, where also he sat down to rest him: then he pulled his roll out of his bosom, and read therein to his comfort; he also now began afresh to take a review of the coat or garment that was given to him as he stood by the cross. Thus pleasing himself awhile, he at last fell into a slumber, and thence into a fast sleep, which detained him in that place until it was almost night; and in his sleep his roll fell out of his hand. Now as he was sleeping, there came one to him, and awaked him, saying, "Go to the ant, thou sluggard;

[11] Some when they come at the cross, they will either there make a stop and go no further, or else, if they can, step over it; if not, they will go round about—turn aside to the left hand, or to the right hand, and so think to get to heaven another way; but they will be deceived. Do not thou do this; but take up the cross and kiss it, and bear it after Jesus.—*Bunyan's Paul's Departure* and *Heavenly Footman.*

consider her ways and be wise." Prov. vi, 6. And with that Christian suddenly started up, and sped him on his way, and went apace till he came to the top of the hill.

Now when he was got up to the top of the hill, there came two men running to meet him amain; the name of the one was Timorous, and of the other Mistrust: to whom Christian said, "Sirs, what's the matter? you run the wrong way." Timorous answered, that they were going to the city of Zion, and had got up that difficult place: "but," said he, "the further we go the more danger we meet with; wherefore we turned, and are going back again."[12]

[12] It is no great matter to begin to look for heaven, to begin to seek the Lord, to begin to shun sin; O, but it is a very great matter to continue with God's approbation! It is an easy matter for a man to run hard for a spurt, for a furlong, for a mile or two: O, but to hold out for a hundred, for a thousand, for ten thousand miles; that man that doth this, he must look to meet with cross, pain, and wearisomeness to the flesh, especially if as he goeth he meeteth with briers and quagmires, and other incumbrances, that make his journey so much the more painful. I could point out many, that, after they had followed the ways of God about a twelvemonth, others it may be two, three, or four (some more, some less) years, they have been beat out of wind, have taken up their lodging and rest before they have got half way to heaven, some in this, some in that sin; and have secretly, nay, sometimes openly, said, "The way is too strait, the race too long, the religion too holy, and I cannot hold out, I can go no further."

But what will become of them that are thus grown weary before they are got half way to heaven? Do you think those will ever come thither? Why, man, it is he that holdeth out to the end that must be saved; it is he that overcometh that shall inherit all things; it is not every one that begins. Agrippa gave a fair step for a sudden; he steps "almost" into the bosom of Christ in less than half an hour; he stept fair, indeed, but yet he stopped short. O this but *almost!* I tell you, this but almost, it lost his soul. Methinks I have seen sometimes how these poor wretches that get but almost to

"Yes," said Mistrust, "for just before us lie a couple of lions in the way, whether sleeping or waking we know not, and we could not think, if we came within reach, but they would presently pull us in pieces."

Then said Christian, "You make me afraid; but whither shall I flee to be safe? If I go back to my own country, that is prepared for fire and brimstone, and I shall certainly perish there; if I can get to the celestial city, I am sure to be in safety there: I must venture. To go back is nothing but death; to go forward is fear of death, and life everlasting beyond it. I will yet go forward." So Mistrust and Timorous ran down the hill, and Christian went on his way. But thinking again of what he heard from the men, he felt in his bosom for his roll, that he might read therein, and be comforted; but he felt and found it not. Then was Christian in great distress, and knew not what to do; for he wanted that which used to relieve him, and that which should have been his pass into the celestial city. Here therefore he began to be much perplexed, and knew not what to do. At last he bethought himself that he had slept in the arbour that is on the side of the hill; and falling down upon his knees, he asked God forgiveness for that his foolish act, and then went back to look for his roll. But all the way he

heaven, how fearfully their almost, and their but almost, will torment them in hell, when they cry out in the bitterness of their soul, saying, "Almost a Christian! I was almost got into the kingdom, almost got out of the hands of the devil, almost out of my sins, almost from under the curse of God, almost, and that was all; almost, but not altogether. O that I should be almost at heaven, and should not go quite through!" Friend, it is a sad thing to sit down before we are in heaven, and to grow weary before we come to the place of rest; and if this be thy case, I am sure thou dost not so run as to obtain.—*Bunyan's Heavenly Footman.*

went back, who can sufficiently set forth the sorrow of Christian's heart? Sometimes he sighed, sometimes he wept, and oftentimes he chid himself for being so foolish to fall asleep in that place, which was erected only for a little refreshment for his weariness. Thus, therefore, he went back, carefully looking on this side and on that, all the way as he went, if happily he might find his roll that had been his comfort so many times in his journey. He went thus till he came again within sight of the arbour where he sat and slept; but that sight renewed his sorrow the more, by bringing again, even afresh, his evil of sleeping into his mind. Thus, therefore, he now went on, bewailing his sinful sleep, saying, "O wretched man that I am, that I should sleep in the day-time! that I should sleep in the midst of difficulty! that I should so indulge the flesh as to use that rest for ease to my flesh which the Lord of the hill hath erected only for the relief of the spirits of pilgrims! How many steps have I taken in vain! Thus it happened to Israel; for their sin they were sent back again by the way of the Red Sea; and I am made to tread those steps with sorrow, which I might have trod with delight had it not been for this sinful sleep. How far might I have been on my way by this time! I am made to tread those steps thrice over, which I needed not to have trod but once: yea, now also I am like to be benighted, for the day is almost spent. O that I had not slept!"[13]

[13] In the "arbour," which was designed only as a temporary resting-place, where he might refresh himself for future toils, the Pilgrim fell asleep, and lost his roll. So it is often with the young Christian; favoured, it may be, with some intermission of his trials, or with a more than usual degree of spiritual consolation, he is too apt to re-

Now by this time he was come to the arbour again, where for a while he sat down and wept; but at last (as Providence would have it) looking sorrowfully down under the settle, there he espied his roll, the which he with trembling and haste catched up, and put into his bosom. But who can tell how joyful this man was when he had gotten his roll again? For this roll was the assurance of his life, and acceptance at the desired haven. Therefore he laid it up in his bosom, gave thanks to God for directing his eye to the place where it lay, and with joy and tears betook himself again to his journey. But O how nimbly now did he go up the rest of the hill! Yet, before he got up, the sun went

lax his diligence, and fondly imagining that his danger is past, and his warfare accomplished, he gives way to self-indulgence, lulling his soul to sleep with the song of the Psalmist. "My mountain stands strong, I shall never be moved." Nor does he awake from this dream of false security until some new danger, some severe trial, some arduous duty, or perhaps a fresh assault of the adversary, calls him to action, when he finds himself, like Samson after sleeping in the lap of Delilah, "shorn of his strength, and become weak as another man." We have always cause, and never more than in a time of apparent spiritual prosperity, to attend to the injunction given by our Lord to his drowsy disciples, "Watch and pray that ye enter not into temptation." Matt. xxvi, 41.

Reader, how is it with thee? Hast thou, through unwatchfulness, lost the evidence of thy adoption? Hast thou grieved the Spirit till he hath gone from thee? and art thou bemoaning thy sad condition, saying, "O that it were with me as in months past, as in the days when God preserved me; when his candle shined upon my head, and by his light I walked through darkness?" Job xxix, 3. If this be the case, examine thyself, wherein thou hast departed from the living God; "return to the Almighty, and thou shalt be built up: thou shalt make thy prayer unto him, and he shall heal thee." Job xxii, 23, 27. His word concerning thee is a word of mercy; hear it: "Return, thou backsliding Israel, and I will not cause mine anger to fall upon you: for I am merciful, saith the Lord, and I will heal your backslidings." Isa. iii, 12, 22.

down upon Christian; and this made him again recall the vanity of his sleeping to his remembrance; and thus he again began to condole with himself: "O thou sinful sleep! how for thy sake am I like to be benighted in my journey! I must walk without the sun, darkness must cover the path of my feet, and I must hear the noise of the doleful creatures, because of my sinful sleep!" Now also he remembered the story that Mistrust and Timorous told him, of how they were frighted with the sight of the lions. Then said Christian to himself again, "These beasts range in the night for their prey, and if they should meet with me in the dark, how should I shift them? How should I escape being by them torn in pieces?" Thus he went on his way. But while he was thus bewailing his unhappy miscarriage, he lift up his eyes, and behold there was a very stately palace before him, the name of which was Beautiful, and it stood just by the highway side.

CHAPTER V.

Christian arrives at the palace called Beautiful—His converse with the Porter—Admission into the palace—Discourse with Piety, Prudence, and Charity—The supper—The records of the house—Visit to the armoury—View of the Delectable Mountains—Christian is furnished with armour, and prepares to proceed on his journey.

So I saw in my dream that he made haste, and went forward, that if possible he might get lodging there. Now before he had gone far he entered into a very narrow passage, which was about a furlong off of the Porter's lodge; and looking very narrowly before him as he went he espied two lions in the way. Now, thought he, I see the danger that Mistrust and Timorous were driven back by. (The lions were chained, but he saw not the chains.) Then he was afraid, and thought also himself to go back after them; for he thought nothing but death was before him.[1] But the Porter at the lodge, whose name is Watchful, perceiving that Christian made a halt, as if he would go back, cried unto him, saying, "Is thy strength so small? Fear not the lions, for they are chained, and are placed

[1] If thou meet with the cross in thy journey, in what manner soever it be, be not daunted, and say, "Alas! what shall I do now?" But rather take courage, knowing that by the cross is the way to the kingdom. Can a man believe in Christ, and not be hated by the devil? Can he make profession of this Christ, and that sweetly and convincingly, and the children of Satan hold their tongue? Can darkness agree with light; or the devil endure that Christ Jesus should be honoured both by faith and a heavenly conversation, and let that soul alone at quiet? Did you never read, that "the dragon persecuted the woman?" Rev. xii, 13; and that Christ saith, "In the world ye shall have tribulation?" John xvi, 33.—*Bunyan's Heavenly Footman.*

there for trial of faith where it is, and for discovery of those that have none: keep in the midst of the path, and no hurt shall come unto thee."

Then I saw that he went on trembling for fear of the lions; but taking good heed to the directions of the Porter, he heard them roar, but they did him no harm. Then he clapped his hands, and went on till he came and stood before the gate where the Porter was. Then said Christian to the Porter, "Sir, what house is this? and may I lodge here to-night?" The Porter answered, "This house was built by the Lord of the hill, and he built it for the relief and security of pilgrims." The Porter also asked whence he was, and whither he was going.

Chr. I am come from the city of Destruction, and am going to Mount Zion; but because the sun is now set, I desire, if I may, to lodge here to-night.

Port. What is your name?

Chr. My name is now Christian, but my name at the first was Graceless: I came of the race of Japheth, whom God will persuade to dwell in the tents of Shem. Gen. ix, 27.

Port. But how doth it happen that you come so late? The sun is set.

Chr. I had been here sooner, but that (wretched man that I am!) I slept in the arbour that stands on the hill side. Nay, I had, notwithstanding that, been here much sooner, but that in my sleep I lost my evidence and came without it to the brow of the hill: and then feeling for it, and not finding it, I was forced with sorrow of heart to go back to the place where I slept my sleep, where I found it; and now I am come.

Port. Well, I will call out one of the virgins of this

place, who will, if she likes your talk, bring you in to the rest of the family, according to the rules of the house So Watchful, the Porter, rang a bell, at the sound of which came out of the door of the house a grave and beautiful damsel, named Discretion, and asked why she was called.

The Porter answered, "This man is on a journey from the city of Destruction to Mount Zion; but being weary and benighted, he asked me if he might lodge here to-night: so I told him I would call for thee, who, after discourse had with him, mayest do as seemeth thee good, even according to the law of the house."

Then she asked him whence he was, and whither he was going; and he told her. She asked him also how he got into the way; and he told her. Then she asked him what he had seen and met with in the way; and he told her. And at last she asked his name. So he said, "It is Christian; and I have so much the more a desire to lodge here to-night, because, by what I perceive, this place was built by the Lord of the hill for the relief and security of pilgrims." So she smiled, but the water stood in her eyes; and after a little pause she said, I will call forth two or three more of the family. So she ran to the door, and called out Prudence, Piety, and Charity, who after a little more discourse with him, had him in to the family; and many of them meeting him at the threshold of the house, said, Come in, thou blessed of the Lord; this house was built by the Lord of the hill on purpose to entertain such pilgrims in. Then he bowed his head, and followed them into the house. So when he was come in and sat down, they gave him something to drink, and consented together that, until supper was ready, some of them should have some particular discourse with Christian, for the best improvement of time, and they appointed Piety, Prudence, and Charity to discourse with him; and thus they began.[2]

Piety. Come, good Christian, since we have been so loving to you to receive you into our house this night, let us, if perhaps we may better ourselves thereby, talk with you of all things that have happened to you in your pilgrimage.[3]

Chr. With a very good will; and I am glad that you are so well disposed.

Piety. What moved you at first to betake yourself to a pilgrim's life?

Chr. I was driven out of my native country by a dreadful sound that was in mine ears: to wit, that unavoidable destruction did attend me, if I abode in that place where I was.

Piety. But how did it happen that you came out of your country this way?

Chr. It was as God would have it; for when I was under the fears of destruction I did not know whither

[2] The palace called Beautiful, into which Christian is now received, is intended to represent a visible church of Christ, of which Watchful, the Porter, is the pastor. The previous questioning of the Pilgrim by Watchful and the others denotes the carefulness with which churches should examine into the character and religious experience of those who apply to them for admission. The "supper" denotes the sacrament of the holy communion; and the Pilgrim's discourse with the inmates of the house after his reception, is designed to point out the nature and advantages of the "communion of saints."

[3] Then they that feared the Lord spake often one to another: and the Lord hearkened and heard it: and a book of remembrance was written before him for them that feared the Lord and that thought upon his name. And they shall be mine, saith the Lord of hosts, in that day when I make up my jewels. Malachi iii. 16, 17.

to go; but by chance there came a man, even to me, as I was trembling and weeping, whose name is Evangelist, and he directed me to the Wicket-Gate, which else I should never have found, and so set me into the way that hath led me directly to this house.

Piety. But did you not come by the house of the Interpreter?

Chr. Yes, and did see such things there, the remembrance of which will stick by me as long as I live, especially three things; to wit, how Christ, in despite of Satan, maintains his work of grace in the heart; how the man had sinned himself quite out of hopes of God's mercy, and also the dream of him that thought in his sleep the day of judgment was come.

Piety. Why, did you hear him tell his dream?

Chr. Yes, and a dreadful one it was, I thought; it made my heart ache as he was telling of it; but yet I am glad I heard it.

Piety. Was this all you saw at the house of the Interpreter?

Chr. No: he took me, and had me where he showed me a stately palace, and how the people were clad in gold that were in it; and how there came a venturous man, and cut his way through the armed men that stood in the door to keep him out; and how he was bid to come in, and win eternal glory. Methought those things did ravish my heart. I would have stayed at that good man's house a twelvemonth, but that I knew I had further to go.

Piety. And what saw you else in the way?

Chr. Saw? Why I went but a little further, and I saw one, as I thought in my mind, hang bleeding upon a tree; and the very sight of him made my burden fall off my back; for I groaned under a very heavy burden but then it fell down from off me. 'Twas a strange thing to me, for I never saw such a thing before: yea, and while I stood looking up, (for then I could not forbear looking,) three Shining Ones came to me. One of them testified that my sins were forgiven me, another stripped me of my rags, and gave me this broidered coat which you see; and the third set the mark which you see in my forehead, and gave me this sealed roll (and with that he plucked it out of his bosom.)

Piety. But you saw more than this, did you not?

Chr. The things that I have told you were the best; yet some other matters I saw, as namely, I saw three men, Simple, Sloth, and Presumption, lie asleep, a little out of the way, as I came, with irons upon their heels; but do you think I could awake them? I also saw Formality and Hypocrisy come tumbling over the wall, to go, as they pretended, to Zion; but they were quickly lost, even as I myself did tell them, but they would not believe. But, above all, I found it hard work to get up this hill, and as hard to come by the lions' mouths; and truly, if it had not been for the good man, the Porter, that stands at the gate, I do not know but that, after all, I might have gone back again; but I thank God I am here, and thank you for receiving me.

Then Prudence thought good to ask him a few questions, and desired his answer to them.

Pr. Do you not think sometimes of the country from whence you came?

Chr. Yea; but with much shame and detestation. Truly, if I had been mindful of that country from whence I came out, I might have had opportunity to have returned, but now I desire a better country, that is, a heavenly one. Heb. xi, 15, 16.

Pr. Do you not yet bear away with you some of the things that then you were conversant withal?

Chr. Yes; but greatly against my will; especially my inward and carnal cogitations, with which all my countrymen, as well as myself, were delighted. But now all those things are my grief; and might I but choose mine own things, I would choose never to think of those things more; but when I would be a-doing of that which is best, that which is worst is with me.[4]

Pr. Do you not find sometimes as if those things were vanquished, which at other times are your perplexity?

Chr. Yes; but that is but seldom; but they are to me golden hours in which such things happen to me.

[4] The Christian, even after justification, finds in his heart the remains of the carnal mind,—the seeds of pride, anger, evil desire, and the like,—a proneness often to that which is evil, and a backwardness to that which is good. He hath, as it were, two natures; the one contrary to the other; for "the flesh lusteth against the Spirit, and the Spirit against the flesh." Gal. v, 17. Hence he is called to watch and pray against "the enemy within," and to contend against the "flesh," as well as the world and the devil. But whereas in his unrenewed state he followed after the lusts of the flesh, now, though they trouble him, they have not dominion over him; and if he be faithful to the grace given to him, it is his privilege to be "sanctified, body, soul, and spirit," 1 Thess. v, 23, and delivered from the inbeing as well as the dominion of the carnal mind. "If we walk in the light, as He is in the light, we have fellowship one with another, and the blood of Jesus Christ his Son cleanseth us from all sin." 1 John i, 7. "Then will I sprinkle clean water upon you, and ye shall be clean: from all your filthiness, and from all your idols, will I cleanse you. A new heart also will I give you, and a new spirit will I put within you." Ezek. xxxvi, 25, 26. "Having therefore these promises, dearly beloved, let us cleanse ourselves from all filthiness of the flesh and spirit, perfecting holiness in the fear of God." 2 Cor. vii, 1.

Pr. Can you remember by what means you find your annoyances at times as if they were vanquished?

Chr. Yes; when I think of what I saw at the cross, that will do it; and when I look upon my broidered coat, that will do it; and when I look into the roll that I carry in my bosom, that will do it; and when my thoughts wax warm about whither I am going, that will do it.

Pr. And what is it that makes you so desirous to go to Mount Zion?

Chr. Why, there I hope to see Him alive that did hang on the cross; and there I hope to be rid of all those things that to this day are in me an annoyance to me: there they say there is no death, (Isa. xxv, 8; Rev. xxi, 4;) and there I shall dwell with such company as I like best. For, to tell you truth, I love him because I was by him eased of my burden; and I am weary of my inward sickness. I would fain be where I shall die no more, and with the company that shall continually cry, "Holy, holy, holy."

Then said Charity to Christian, "Have you a family? are you a married man?"

Chr. I have a wife and four small children.

Char. And why did you not bring them along with you?

Then Christian wept, and said, "O, how willingly would I have done it! but they were all of them utterly averse to my going on pilgrimage."

Char. But you should have talked with them, and endeavoured to have shown them the danger of staying behind.

Chr. So I did; and told them also what God had shown to me of the destruction of our city; but I seemed to them as one that mocked, and they believed me not. Gen. xix, 14.

Char. And did you pray to God that he would bless your counsel to them?

Chr. Yes, and that with much affection; for you must think that my wife and poor children were very dear to me.

Char. But did you tell them of your own sorrow, and fear of destruction? for I suppose that destruction was visible enough to you.

Chr. Yes, over, and over, and over. They might also see my fears in my countenance, in my tears, and also in my trembling under the apprehension of the judgment that did hang over our heads; but all this was not sufficient to prevail with them to come with me.

Char. But what could they say for themselves why they came not?

Chr. Why, my wife was afraid of losing this world, and my children were given to the foolish delights of youth; so, what by one thing, and what by another, they left me to wander in this manner alone.

Char. But did you not with your vain life damp all that you, by words, used by way of persuasion to bring them away with you?

[5] Dost thou love thy friends? dost thou love thine enemies? dost thou love thy family, or relations, or the church of God? then cry for strength from heaven, and for wisdom, to walk wisely before them. For if a man be remiss, negligent, and careless in his conversation, not much mattering whom he offends, displeases, or discourages, by doing this or that, so he may save himself, please his foolish heart and get this world, or the like, this man hath lost a good report of them that are without: he is fallen into reproach, and is slighted, and disdained, both he and his profession, and all he says, either by way of reproof, rebuke, or exhortation. "Physician, cure thyself," say all to such a one: "This man is a sayer but not a doer,"

Chr. Indeed I cannot commend my life, for I am conscious to myself of many failings therein. I know also, that a man, by his conversation, may soon overthrow what by argument or persuasion he doth labour to fasten upon others for their good. Yet this I can say, I was very wary of giving them occasion, by any unseemly action, to make them averse to going on pilgrimage. Yea, for this very thing, they would tell me I was too precise, and that I denied myself of things (for their sakes) in which they saw no evil. Nay, I think I may say, that if what they saw in me did hinder them, it was my great tenderness in sinning against God, or of doing any wrong to my neighbour.

Char. Indeed, Cain hated his brother, (1 John iii, 12,) because his own works were evil, and his brother's righteous; and if thy wife and children have been offended with thee for this, they thereby show themselves to be implacable to good; thou hast delivered thy soul from their blood. Ezek. iii, 19.

Now I saw in my dream, that thus they sat talking together until supper was ready. So when they had made ready they sat down to meat. Now the table was furnished with fat things, and wine that was well refined; (Isa. xxv, 6;) and all their talk at the table was about the Lord of the hill; as namely, about what

say they; "he believeth not what he says:" yea, religion itself is made to stink by this man's ungodly life. This is he that hardens his children, that stumbleth the world, that grieveth the tender and godly Christian; but I say he that walketh uprightly, that tenders the name of God, the credit of the gospel, and the welfare of others, seeking with Paul, not his own profit, but the profit of others, that they may be saved,—this man holds forth the word of life; this man is a good savour of Christ among them that are saved; yea, may prove, by so doing, the instrument in God's hand of saving many souls.—*Bunyan on Paul's Departure and Crown.*

he had done, and wherefore he did what he did, and why he had builded that house; and by what they said, I perceived that he had been a great warrior, and had fought with and slain him that had the power of death; (Heb. ii, 14, 15;) but not without great danger to himself, which made me love him the more.

For, as they said, and as I believe said Christian, he did it with the loss of much blood. But that which put the glory of grace into all he did, was, that he did it out of pure love to this country. And besides, there were some of them of the household that said they had been and spoke with him since he did die on the cross; and they have attested, that they had it from his own lips, that he is such a lover of poor pilgrims, that the like is not to be found from the east to the west. They, moreover, gave an instance of what they affirmed; and that was, he had stripped himself of his glory that he might do this for the poor; and that they had heard him say and affirm, that he would not dwell in the mountain of Zion alone. They said, moreover, that he had made many pilgrims princes, though by nature they were beggars born, and their original had been the dunghill.

Thus they discoursed together till late at night; and after they had committed themselves to their Lord for protection, they betook themselves to rest. The pilgrim they laid in a large upper chamber, whose window opened toward the sun-rising. The name of the chamber was Peace, where he slept till break of day, and then he awoke and sung,—

> Where am I now? Is this the love and care
> Of Jesus, for the men that pilgrims are,
> Thus to provide! that I should be forgiven
> And dwell already the next door to heaven!

So in the morning they all got up; and after some more discourse, they told him that he should not depart till they had showed him the rarities of that place. And first they had him into the study, where they showed him Records of the greatest antiquity; in which, as I remember my dream, they showed him the pedigree of the Lord of the hill, that he was the Son of the Ancient of days, and came by that eternal generation. Here also was more fully recorded the acts that he had done, and the names of many hundreds that he had taken into his service; and how he had placed them in such habitations, that could neither by length of days, nor decays of nature, be dissolved.

Then they read to him some of the worthy acts that some of his servants had done; as how they had subdued kingdoms, wrought righteousness, obtained promises, stopped the mouths of lions, quenched the violence of fire, escaped the edge of the sword, out of weakness were made strong, waxed valiant in fight, and turned to flight the armies of the aliens. Heb. xi, 33, 34.

Then they read again another part of the records of the house, where it was shown how willing their Lord was to receive into his favour any, even any, though they in time past had offered great affronts to his person and proceedings. Here also were several other histories of many other famous things, of al which Christian had a view; as of things both ancient and modern, together with prophecies and predictions of things that have their certain accomplishment, both to the dread and amazement of enemies, and the comfort and solace of pilgrims.

The next day they took him, and had him into the armoury, where they showed him all manner of furniture which their Lord had provided for pilgrims, as sword, shield, helmet, breastplate, all-prayer, and shoes that would not wear out. Eph. vi, 13–18. And there was here enough of this to harness out as many men for the service of their Lord as there be stars in the heaven for multitude.

They also showed him some of the engines with which some of his servants had done wonderful things. They showed him Moses' rod; the hammer and nail with which Jael slew Sisera; the pitchers, trumpets, and lamps too, with which Gideon put to flight the armies of Midian. Then they showed him the ox's goad wherewith Shamgar slew six hundred men. They showed him also the jaw-bone with which Samson did such mighty feats. They showed him moreover the sling and stone with which David slew Goliath of Gath, and the sword also with which their Lord will kill the man of sin in the day that he shall rise up to the prey. They showed him besides many excellent things, with which Christian was much delighted. This done, they went to their rest again.

Then I saw in my dream, that on the morrow he got up to go forward, but they desired him to stay till the next day also; and then, said they, we will, if the day be clear, show you the Delectable Mountains; which, they said, would yet further add to his comfort, because they were nearer the desired haven than the place where at present he was; so he consented and stayed. When the morning was up, they had him to the top of the house, and bid him look south. So he did, and behold, at a great distance, he saw a most pleasant, mountainous country, beautified with woods, vineyards, fruits of all sorts, flowers also, with springs and fountains, very delectable to behold. Then he asked the name of the country. They said it was Immanuel's land; "and it is as common," said they, "as this hill is, to and for all the pilgrims. And when thou comest there, from thence thou mayest see to the gate of the Celestial City, as the shepherds that live there will make appear."[6]

Now he bethought himself of setting forward, and they were willing he should. But first, said they, let us go again into the armoury. So they did, and when they came there they harnessed him from head to foot with what was of proof, lest perhaps he should meet with assaults in the way. He being therefore thus accoutred, walked out with his friends to the gate; and there he asked the Porter if he saw any pilgrim pass by. Then the Porter answered, "Yes."

"Pray did you know him?" said he.

Port. I asked his name, and he told me it was Faithful.

"O," said Christian, "I know him; he is my townsman, my near neighbour; he comes from the place where I was born. How far do you think he may be before?"

Port. He has got by this time below the hill.

"Well," said Christian, "good Porter, the Lord be with thee, and add to all thy blessings much increase for the kindness thou hast showed me."

[6] The Delectable Mountains lay in the Pilgrim's way to the Celestial City; this previous sight of them, with which he was now favoured, must therefore be understood to point out "those distinct views of the privileges and consolations attainable in this life, with which believers are sometimes favoured while attending on the means of grace, or making a subsequent improvement of them," and by which they are animated to press forward through dangers and hardships "toward the mark for the prize of the high calling of God in Christ Jesus."

CHAPTER VI.

Christian, accompanied by Piety, Prudence, and Discretion, leaves the Beautiful Palace—Goes down the hill, into the Valley of Humiliation—His terrible conflict with Apollyon—His perilous passage through the Valley of the Shadow of Death—He passes without danger the cave of giants Pope and Pagan.

THEN he began to go forward; but Discretion, Piety, Charity, and Prudence would accompany him down to the foot of the hill. So they went on together, reiterating their former discourses, till they came to go down the hill. Then said Christian, "As it was difficult coming up, so, so far as I can see, it is dangerous going down."

"Yes," said Prudence, "so it is; for it is a hard matter for a man to go down into the Valley of Humiliation, as thou art now, and to catch no slip by the way; therefore," said they, "are we come out to accompany thee down the hill." So he began to go down, but very warily; yet he caught a slip or two.[1]

[1] By the Valley of Humiliation we are to understand those circumstances of humiliation and affliction into which God often sees fit to bring his people; such as loss of property, reputation, and friends, the reproach of the world, severe bodily affliction, or other painful dispensations of providence. In these circumstances they are sometimes tempted to murmur and despond. Like the Pilgrim, they often find it "a hard matter to go down into this valley," and unless they "watch unto prayer," they will be very apt, like him, to "catch a slip or two," to fall into temptation, question the dealings of God with them, and thus expose themselves to the assaults of the adversary. This, however, need not be the case; for these "chasten ings" of our heavenly Father are designed "for our profit, that we might be partakers of his holiness," Heb. xii, 10; for "tribulation," if it be rightly endured, "worketh patience; and patience, expe rience; and experience, hope; and hope maketh not ashamed: be-

Then I saw in my dream, that these good companions, when Christian was got down to the bottom of the hill, gave him a loaf of bread, a bottle of wine, and a cluster of raisins; and then he went on his way.

> When Christian is among his godly friends,
> These golden months make him sufficient mends
> For all his griefs; and when they let him go
> He's clad with northern steel from top to toe.

But now, in the Valley of Humiliation, poor Christian was hard put to it; for he had gone but a little way before he espied a foul fiend coming over the field to meet him: his name is Apollyon. Then did Christian begin to be afraid, and to cast in his mind whether to go back or to stand his ground. But he considered again that he had no armour for his back, and therefore thought that to turn the back to him might give him greater advantage with ease to pierce him with his darts; therefore he resolved to venture, and stand his ground; for, thought he, had I no more in mine eye than the saving of my life, 'twould be the best way to stand.

So he went on, and Apollyon met him. Now the monster was hideous to behold; he was clothed with scales like a fish, and they are his pride; he had wings like a dragon, feet like a bear, and out of his belly came fire and smoke; and his mouth was as the mouth of a lion. When he came up to Christian he beheld

cause the love of God is shed abroad in our hearts by the Holy Ghost which is given to us." Rom. v, 3-5. So Bunyan, in another place, tells us that "this Valley of Humiliation is of itself as fruitful a place as any the crow flies over;" that our Lord himself, in former days, loved to walk there; and that it is a spot where pilgrims should love to dwell. (See the Second Part, pp. 370.)

him with a disdainful countenance, and thus began to question him.

Apollyon. Whence come you, and whither are you bound?

Chr. I am come from the city of Destruction, which is the place of all evil, and I am going to the city of Zion.

Apol. By this I perceive that thou art one of my subjects; for all that country is mine, and I am the prince and god of it. How is it, then, that thou hast run away from thy king? Were it not that I hope thou mayest do me more service, I would strike thee now at one blow to the ground.

Chr. I was, indeed, born in your dominions, but your service was hard, and your wages such as a man could not live on; for the wages of sin is death; (Rom. vi, 23;) therefore when I was come to years, I did, as other considerate persons do, look out, if perhaps I might mend myself.

Apol. There is no prince that will thus lightly lose his subjects, neither will I as yet lose thee; but since thou complainest of thy service and wages, be content to go back; what the country will afford, I do here promise to give thee.

Chr. But I have let myself to another, even to the King of princes; and how can I with fairness go back with thee?

Apol. Thou hast done in this according to the proverb, "Changed a bad for a worse;" but it is ordinary for those that have professed themselves his servants, after a while to give him the slip, and return again to me. Do thou so too, and all shall be well.

Chr. I have given him my faith, and sworn my allegiance to him; how then can I go back from this, and not be hanged as a traitor?

Apol. Thou didst the same to me, and yet am I willing to pass by all, if now thou wilt yet turn and go back.

Chr. What I promised thee was in my nonage: and besides, I count that the Prince, under whose banner now I stand, is able to absolve me, yea, and to pardon also what I did as to my compliance with thee. And besides, O thou destroying Apollyon, to speak truth, I like his service, his wages, his servants, his government, his company, and country, better than thine; therefore leave off to persuade me further: I am his servant, and I will follow him.

Apol. Consider again, when thou art in cool blood, what thou art to meet with in the way that thou goest. Thou knowest that for the most part his servants come to an ill end, because they are transgressors against me and my ways. How many of them have been put to shameful deaths! And besides, thou countest his service better than mine; whereas he never yet came from the place where he is, to deliver any that served him out of my hands; but as for me, how many times, as all the world very well knows, have I delivered, either by power or fraud, those that have faithfully served me, from him and his, though taken by them: and so I will deliver thee.

Chr. His forbearing at present to deliver them, is on purpose to try their love, whether they will cleave to him to the end; and as for the ill end thou sayest they come to, that is most glorious in their account. For, for present deliverance, they do not much expect it; for they *stay* for their glory; and then they shall have it, when their Prince comes in his, and the glory of the angels.

Apol. Thou hast already been unfaithful in thy service to him; and how dost thou think to receive wages of him?

Chr. Wherein, O Apollyon, have I been unfaithful tc him?

Apol. Thou didst faint at first setting out, when thou wast almost choked in the Gulf of Despond. Thou didst attempt wrong ways to be rid of thy burden, whereas thou shouldst have stayed till thy Prince had taken it off. Thou didst sinfully sleep, and lose thy choice things. Thou wast also almost persuaded to go back at the sight of the lions. And when thou talkest of thy journey, and of what thou hast heard and seen, thou art inwardly desirous of vain glory in all that thou sayest or doest.

Chr. All this is true, and much more which thou hast left out; but the Prince whom I serve and honour is merciful and ready to forgive. But besides, these infirmities possessed me in thy country; for there I sucked them in, and I have groaned under them, been sorry for them, and have obtained pardon of my Prince.

Then Apollyon broke out into a grievous rage, saying, "I am an enemy to this Prince; I hate his person, his laws, and people: I am come out on purpose to withstand thee."

Chr. Apollyon, beware what you do, for I am in the king's highway, the way of holiness; therefore ake heed to yourself.

Then Apollyon straddled quite over the whole breadth of the way, and said, "I am void of fear in this matter. Prepare thyself to die; for I swear by my infernal den, thou shalt go no further; here will I spill thy soul." And with that he threw a flaming dart at his breast; but Christian had a shield in his hand, with which he caught it, and so prevented the danger of that.[2]

Then did Christian draw, for he saw it was time to bestir him; and Apollyon as fast made at him, throwing darts as thick as hail; by the which, notwithstanding all that Christian could do to avoid it, Apollyon wounded him in his head, his hand, and foot.[3] This made Christian give a little back: Apollyon, therefore, followed his work amain, and Christian again took courage, and resisted as manfully as he could. This sore combat lasted for above half a day, even till Christian was almost quite spent. For you must know, that Christian, by reason of his wounds, must needs grow weaker and weaker.

Then Apollyon, espying his opportunity, began to gather up close to Christian, and, wrestling with him, gave him a dreadful fall; and with that Christian's sword flew out of his hand. Then said Apollyon, I am sure of you now. And with that he had almost pressed him to death: so that Christian began to despair of life. But, as God would have it, while Apollyon was fetching his last blow, thereby to make a full end of this good man, Christian nimbly reached out his hand for his sword, and caught it, saying, "Rejoice not against me, O mine enemy: when I fall, I shall arise,"

[2] The shield of faith, wherewith ye shall be able to quench all the fiery darts of the wicked. Eph. vi, 16.

[3] In a marginal note to the above, the author thus explains his meaning: "Christian is wounded in his understanding, his faith, and his conversation." The word *conversation* is used by Bunyan in the same sense as by the translators of our Bible; to signify our whole conduct and deportment in our intercourse with our fellow men.

Micah vii, 8; and with that gave him a deadly thrust, which made him give back, as one that had received his mortal wound. Christian perceiving that, made at him again, saying, "Nay, in all these things we are more than conquerors through Him that loved us." Rom. viii, 37. And with that, Apollyon spread forth his dragon wings, and sped him away, that Christian saw him no more.[4]

In this combat no man can imagine, unless he had seen and heard as I did, what yelling and hideous roaring Apollyon made all the time of the fight; he spake like a dragon; and on the other side, what sighs and groans burst from Christian's heart. I never saw him all the while give so much as one pleasant look, till he perceived he had wounded Apollyon with his two-edged sword; then, indeed, he did smile, and look upward! But 'twas the dreadfullest fight that ever I saw.[5]

So when the battle was over, Christian said, "I will here give thanks to Him that hath delivered me out of the mouth of the lion; to him that did help me against Apollyon." And so he did, saying,—

> "Great Beelzebub, the captain of this fiend,
> Design'd my ruin; therefore to this end

[4] Your adversary the devil, as a roaring lion, walketh about, seeking whom he may devour; whom resist steadfast in the faith. 1 Pet. v, 8, 9. Resist the devil, and he will flee from you. James iv, 7.

[5] In the Second Part, the author treats more at length on the Valley of Humiliation, and Christian's terrible combat there. He also gives the reasons why the Pilgrim was there so "hard put to it:" these were, first, the "slips," already spoken of, which he made in going down the hill; and second, his forgetfulness of past mercies and his own ill-deservings. The scene of the combat he calls "Forgetful Green," and says, "It is the most dangerous place in all these parts, for if at any time pilgrims meet with any brunt, it is when they forget what favours they have received, and how unworthy they are of them."

He sent him harness'd out; and he, with rage
That hellish was, did fiercely me engage:
But blessed Michael helped me, and I,
By dint of sword, did quickly make him fly:
Therefore to Him let me give lasting praise,
And thank and bless his holy name always."

Then there came to him a hand with some of the leaves of the tree of life, the which Christian took, and applied to the wounds that he had received in the battle, and was healed immediately.[6] He also sat down in that place to eat bread, and to drink of the bottle that was given him a little before; so being refreshed, he addressed himself to his journey, with his sword drawn in his hand; for, he said, I know not but some other enemy may be at hand. But he met with no other affront from Apollyon quite through this valley.

Now at the end of this valley was another, called the Valley of the Shadow of Death; and Christian must needs go through it, because the way to the Celestial City lay through the midst of it. Now this valley is a very solitary place. The prophet Jeremiah thus describes it: "A wilderness, a land of deserts and of pits; a land of drought, and of the Shadow of Death; a land that no man (but a Christian) passeth through, and where no man dwelt." Jer. ii, 6.

6 "The leaves of the tree were for the healing of the nations." Rev. xxii, 2. By "leaves" here, we may understand the blessed and precious promises, consolations, and encouragements, that by virtue of Christ's undertaking for us, we have everywhere growing upon the new covenant; which promises and encouragements, they are and will be most freely handed to the wounded conscience that is tossed upon the restless waves of doubt and unbelief. As a leaf for medicine, when applied to a sore in the body, doth supple, mollify, and heal the wound; so the word of promise, when rightly applied to the soul, it doth supple, mollify, and heal the wounded conscience: "He sent his word and healed them."—*Bunyan's Holy City*

Now here Christian was worse put to it than in his fight with Apollyon, as by the sequel you shall see.

I saw then in my dream, that when Christian was got to the borders of the Shadow of Death, there met him two men, children of them that brought up an evil report of the good land, (Num. xiii,) making haste to go back; to whom Christian spake as follows:—

Chr. Whither are you going?

They said, "Back! back! and we would have you do so too, if either life or peace is prized by you."

"Why, what's the matter?" said Christian.

"Matter," said they; "we were going that way, as you are going, and went as far as we durst: and, indeed, we were almost *past* coming back; for had we gone a little further, we had not been here to bring the news to thee."

"But what have you met with?" said Christian.

Men. Why, we were almost in the Valley of the Shadow of Death, but that by good hap we looked before us, and saw the danger before we came to it.

"But what have you seen?" said Christian.

Men. Seen! why the valley itself, which is as dark as pitch: we also saw there the hobgoblins, satyrs, and dragons of the pit: we heard also in that valley a continual howling and yelling, as of a people under unutterable misery, who there sat bound in affliction and irons: and over that valley hang the discouraging clouds of confusion: Death also doth always spread his wings over it. In a word, it is every whit dreadful, being utterly without order.[7]

[7] A place of dragons, and covered with the shadow of death. Psa. xliv, 19. A land of darkness, as darkness itself; and of the shadow of death, without any order, and where the light is as darkness. Job x, 22

Poor man! where art thou now? thy day is night
Good man, be not cast down; thou yet art right:
The way to heaven lies by the gates of hell;
Cheer up, hold out, with thee it shall go well

"Then," said Christian, "I perceive not yet, by what you have said, but that this is my way to the desired haven."

Men. Be it thy way; we will not choose it for ours.

So they parted, and Christian went on his way; but still with his sword drawn in his hand, for fear lest he should be assaulted.

I saw then in my dream, so far as this valley reached, there was on the right hand a very deep ditch; that ditch is it, into which the blind have led the blind in all ages, and have both there miserably perished. Again, behold on the left hand there was a very dangerous quag, into which, if even a good man falls, he finds no bottom for his foot to stand on: into that quag King David once did fall, and had, no doubt, therein been smothered, had not He that is able plucked him out. Psa. lxix, 14.

The pathway was here also exceeding narrow, and therefore good Christian was the more put to it; for when he sought in the dark to shun the ditch on the one hand, he was ready to tip over into the mire on the other: also, when he sought to escape the mire, without great carefulness he would be ready to fall into the ditch. Thus he went on, and I heard him here sigh bitterly; for besides the danger mentioned above, the pathway was here so dark, that ofttimes when he lifted up his foot to set forward, he knew not where, or upon what, he should set it next.

About the midst of this valley I perceived the mouth of hell to be, and it stood also hard by the wayside. Now, thought Christian, what shall I do? And ever and anon the flame and smoke would come out in such abundance, with sparks and hideous noises, (things that cared not for Christian's sword, as did Apollyon before,) that he was forced to put up his sword, and betake himself to another weapon, called All-prayer, (Eph. vi, 18;) so he cried in my hearing, "O Lord, I beseech thee, deliver my soul." Psa. cxvi, 4.[8]

Thus he went on a great while, yet still the flames would be reaching toward him; also he heard doleful voices, and rushings to and fro, so that sometimes he thought he should be torn in pieces, or trodden down like mire in the streets. This frightful sight was seen, and these dreadful noises were heard by him for several miles together; and coming to a place where he thought he heard a company of fiends coming forward to meet him, he stopped, and began to muse what he had best to do. Sometimes he had half a thought to go back; then again he thought he might be half way through the valley: he remembered also, how he had

[8] There are particular times more eminently dangerous and hazardous to saints. There are their young days, the days of their childhood in grace. This day is usually attended with much evil to him that is asking the way to Zion with his face thitherward. Now the devil has lost a sinner; there is a captive has broke prison, and one run away from his master. Now hell seems awakened from sleep, the devils are come out, they roar, and roaring they seek to recover their runaway: now tempt him, theaten him, flatter him, stigmatize him, throw dust in his eyes, poison him with errors; anything to keep him from coming to Jesus Christ. And is not this a needy time? doth not such an one want abundance of grace; is it not of absolute necessity that thou, if thou art the man thus beset, should ply it at the throne of grace, for mercy and grace to help thee at such a time as this? To want a spirit of prayer now, is as much as thy life is worth. O! therefore, you that know what I say, you that are broke loose from hell, that are fled for refuge to lay hold on the hope set before you, and that do hear the lion roar after you, and that are kept awake with the continual voice of his chinking chain, cry as you fly; yea, the promise is that they that come to God with weeping, with supplication, he will lead them.—*Bunyan's Saint's Privilege.*

already vanquished many a danger ; and that the danger of going back might be much more than for to go forward. So he resolved to go on : yet the fiends seemed to come nearer and nearer ; but when they were come even almost at him, he cried out with a most vehement voice, "I will walk in the strength of the Lord God." So they gave back, and came no further.

One thing I would not let slip : I took notice that now poor Christian was so confounded that he did not know his own voice ; and thus I perceived it : just when he was come over against the mouth of the burning pit, one of the wicked ones got behind him, and stepped up softly to him, and, whisperingly, suggested many grievous blasphemies to him, which he verily thought had proceeded from his own mind. This put Christian more to it than anything that he met with before ; even to think that he should now blaspheme Him that he loved so much before : yet if he could have helped it, he would not have done it ; but he had not the discretion either to stop his ears, or to know from whence those blasphemies came.[9]

When Christian had travelled in this disconsolate condition some considerable time, he thought he heard the voice of a man, as going before him, saying, "Though I walk through the Valley of the Shadow of Death, I will fear no ill ; for Thou art with me." Psa. xxiii, 4.

[9] In this passage the author evidently has reference to a period in his own experience, when "*whole floods of blasphemies*," he tells us, '*were poured upon his spirit*, to his great confusion and astonishment ; and did so overweigh his heart, both with their number, continuance, and fiery force, that he felt as if God had, in very wrath to his soul, given him up to them, to be carried away with them, as with a mighty whirlwind."

Then was he glad, and that for these reasons :—

First. Because he gathered from thence, that some who feared God were in this valley as well as himself.

Secondly. For that he perceived God was with them, though in that dark and dismal state : and why not, thought he, with me; though by reason of the im pediment, that attends this place, I cannot perceive it Job ix, 11.

Thirdly. For that he hoped (could he overtake them to have company by and by.

So he went on, and called to him that was before; but he knew not what to answer, for that he also thought himself to be alone. And by and by the day broke: then said Christian, "He hath turned the shadow of death into the morning." Amos v, 8.

Now morning being come, he looked back; not out of desire to return, but to see, by the light of the day, what hazards he had gone through in the dark : so he saw more perfectly the ditch that was on the one hand, and the quag that was on the other; also, how narrow the way was which led betwixt them both: also now he saw the hobgoblins, and satyrs, and dragons of the pit, but all afar off; for after break of day they came not nigh; yet they were discovered to him, according to that which is written, "He discovereth deep things out of darkness, and bringeth out to light the shadow of death." Job xii, 22.

Now was Christian much affected with this deliverance from all the dangers of his solitary way; which dangers, though he feared them much before, yet he saw them more clearly now, because the light of the day made them conspicuous to him. And about this time the sun was rising, and this was another mercy to

Christian; for you must note, that though the first part of the Valley of the Shadow of Death was dangerous, yet this second part, which he was yet to go, was, if possible, far more dangerous; for from the place where he now stood, even to the end of the valley, the way was all along set so full of snares, traps, gins, and nets here, and so full of pits, pitfalls, deep holes, and shelvings-down there, that had it now been dark, as it was when he came the first part of the way, had he had a thousand souls, they had in reason been cast away; but, as I said, just now the sun was rising. Then said he, "His candle shineth on my head, and by his light I go through darkness." Job xxix, 3.[10]

In this light, therefore, he came to the end of the valley. Now I saw in my dream, that at the end of the valley lay blood, bones, ashes, and mangled bodies of men, even of pilgrims that had gone this way formerly; and while I was musing what should be the reason, I espied a little before me a cave, where two giants, Pope and Pagan, dwelt in old time; by whose power and tyranny the men whose bones, blood, ashes, &c., lay there, were cruelly put to death. But by this place Christian went without much danger, whereat I somewhat wondered; but I have learned since, that Pagan has been dead many a day; and as for the other,

[10] Perhaps few Christians are assailed with such fiery trials and fierce temptations as are indicated by Christian's terrible combat with Apollyon, and his perilous passage through the Valley of the Shadow of Death. These terribly-expressive scenes were doubtless suggested to the author by his own extraordinary temptations and spiritual conflicts in the early part of his religious experience, and a perusal of his account of these would probably furnish the best exposition of this part of the Pilgrim's adventures. See the Life of Bunyan, pages 68-116.

though he be yet alive, he is, by reason of age, and also of the many shrewd brushes that he met with in his younger days, grown so crazy and stiff in his joints, that he can now do little more than sit in his cave's mouth, grinning at pilgrims as they go by, and biting his nails because he cannot come at them.

So I saw that Christian went on his way; yet, at the sight of the old man that sat at the mouth of the cave, he could not tell what to think, especially because he spoke to him, though he could not go after him, saying, "You will never mend till more of you be burned." But he held his peace, and set a good face on it, and so went by and catched no hurt. Then sang Christian:

"O world of wonders! (I can say no less,)
That I should be preserved in that distress
That I have met with here! O blessed be
That hand that from it hath delivered me!
Dangers in darkness, devils, hell, and sin,
Did compass me while I this vale was in:
Yea, snares, and pits, and traps, and nets, did lie
My path about, that worthless, silly I
Might have been catch'd, entangled, and cast down:
But since I live, let Jesus wear the crown."

CHAPTER VII.

Christian overtakes Faithful—Their talk about the country whence they came—How Pliable was accounted of when he got home—How Faithful was assaulted by Wanton, and by Adam the first—Also, in the Valley of Humiliation, by Discontent and Shame.

Now as Christian went on his way, he came to a little ascent, which was cast up on purpose that pilgrims might see before them: up there, therefore, Christian went; and looking forward, he saw Faithful before him upon his journey. Then said Christian aloud, "Ho, ho! so-ho! stay, and I will be your companion." At that Faithful looked behind him; to whom Christian cried again, "Stay, stay, till I come up to you." But Faithful answered, "No, I am upon my life, and the avenger of blood is behind me."[1]

At this Christian was somewhat moved, and putting to all his strength, he quickly got up with Faithful, and did also overrun him; so the last was first. Then did Christian vaingloriously smile, because he had gotten the start of his brother; but not taking good heed to his feet, he suddenly stumbled and fell, and could not rise again until Faithful came up to help him.[2]

[1] Men that run, you know, if any do call after them, saying, "I would speak with you;" or, "Go not too fast, and you shall have my company with you;" if they run for some great matter, they use to say, "Alas, I cannot stay for you; I am in haste; I am running for a wager: if I win I am made; if I lose I am undone; therefore hinder me not." Thus wise are men when they run for corruptible things, and thus shouldst thou do; and thou hast more cause to do so than they, forasmuch as they run but for things that last not, but thou for an incorruptible glory.—*Bunyan's Heavenly Footman.*

[2] How soon doth spiritual pride show its cursed head, in thinking we have outstripped another! Then danger is near—a fall is at

Then I saw in my dream, they went very lovingly on together, and had sweet discourse of all things that had happened to them in their pilgrimage; and thus Christian began:—"My honoured and well-beloved brother Faithful, I am glad that I have overtaken you, and that God has so tempered our spirits, that we can walk as companions in this so pleasant a path."

Faith. I had thought, dear friend, to have had your company quite from our town, but you did get the start of me; wherefore I was forced to come thus much of the way alone.

Chr. How long did you stay in the City of Destruction, before you set out after me on your pilgrimage?

Faith. Till I could stay no longer; for there was great talk presently after you were gone out, that our city would, in a short time, with fire from heaven be burnt down to the ground.

Chr. What! did your neighbours talk so?

Faith. Yes, it was for a while in everybody's mouth.

Chr. What! and did no more of them but you come out to escape the danger?

Faith. Though there was, as I said, a great talk thereabout, yet I do not think they did firmly believe it.[3] For in the heat of the discourse, I heard some of

hand, if we humble not ourselves before the Lord. That very person's hand we need to help us, whom before we had undervalued and thought we had excelled.—*Mason's Notes.*

[3] Let me tell thee, soul, whoever thou art, that if thou didst but verily *believe* that thou must die and come to judgment, it would make thee turn over a new leaf. But this is the misery; the devil doth labour by all means, to keep out of the heart, as much as in him lies, the thoughts of passing from this life into another world; for he knows, if he can but keep them from the serious thoughts of death, he shall the more easily keep them in their sins, and so from closing with Christ. Because there is no fear of death and a judgment to

them deridingly speak of you, and of your desperate journey; for so they called this your pilgrimage. But I did believe, and do still, that the end of our city will be with fire and brimstone from above; and therefore I have made my escape.

Chr. Did you hear no talk of neighbour Pliable?

Faith. Yes, Christian, I heard that he followed you till he came to the Slough of Despond, where, as some said, he fell in; but he would not be known to have so done; but I am sure he was soundly bedabbled with that kind of dirt.

Chr. And what said the neighbours to him?

Faith. He hath, since his going back, been had greatly in derision, and that among all sorts of people: some do mock and despise him, and scarce will any set him on work. He is now seven times worse than if he had never gone out of the city.

Chr. But why should they be so set against him, since they also despise the way that he forsook?

Faith. O, they say, "Hang him; he is a turncoat; he was not true to his profession!" I think God has stirred up even His enemies to hiss at him, and make him a proverb, because he hath forsaken the way.

Chr. Had you no talk with him before you came out?

Faith. I met him once in the streets, but he leered away on the other side, as one ashamed of what he had done; so I spake not to him.

Chr. Well, at my first setting out I had hopes of that man; but now I fear he will perish in the overthrow of the city. For it has happened to him accord-

come, therefore they do put off God and his ways, and spend their days in their sins, and in a moment, that is, before they are aware, go down to the grave.—*Bunyan's Sighs from Hell.*

ing to the true proverb, "The dog is turned to his vomit again, and the sow that was washed to her wallowing in the mire." 2 Peter ii, 22.

Faith. These are my fears of him too; but who can hinder that which will be?[4]

"Well, neighbour Faithful," said Christian, "let us leave him, and talk of things that more immediately concern ourselves. Tell me now what you have met with in the way as you came; for I know you have met with some things, or else it may be writ for a wonder."

Faith. I escaped the slough that I perceived you fell into, and got up to the gate without that danger; only I met with one whose name was Wanton, that had like to have done me mischief.

Chr. It is well you escaped her net; Joseph was hard put to it by her, and he escaped her as you did; but it had liked to have cost him his life. Gen. xxxix, 11–13. But what did she do to you?

Faith. You cannot think (but that you know something) what a flattering tongue she had; she lay at me hard to turn aside with her, promising me all manner of content.[5]

Chr. Nay, she did not promise you the content of a good conscience.

[4] When a man who has set out for heaven, turns again to his evil ways, and exhibits, as did Pliable, so little shame for his fall as to despise and deride the profession that once he made, he becomes more hardened in sin than before, and there seems to human apprehension no hope of his restoration; and our Lord himself declares, that "the last state of that man is worse than the first." Matt. xii, 45. But however desperate the case of such a one may seem, it is yet, while his day of probation lasts, not utterly hopeless; and therefore it is our duty still to labour and pray for his recovery, knowing that though "with men this is impossible, yet with God all things are possible"

[5] Abstain from fleshly lusts, which war against the soul. 1 Pet. ii, 11

Faith. You know that I mean all carnal and fleshly content.

Chr. Thank God you have escaped her; the abhorred of the Lord[6] shall fall into her ditch. Prov. xxii, 14.

Faith. Nay, I know not whether I did wholly escape her or no.

Chr. Why, I trow, you did not consent to her desires?

Faith. No, not to defile myself; for I remembered an old writing that I had seen, which said, "Her steps take hold on hell." Prov. v, 5. So I shut mine eyes, because I would not be bewitched with her looks. Then she railed on me, and I went my way.

Chr. Did you meet with no other assault as you came?

Faith. When I came to the foot of the hill called Difficulty, I met with a very aged man, who asked me what I was, and whither bound. I told him that I was a pilgrim, going to the Celestial City. Then said the old man, "Thou lookest like an honest fellow; wilt thou be content to dwell with me, for the wages that I shall give thee?" Then I asked him his name, and where he dwelt. He said his name was Adam the first, and that he dwelt in the town of Deceit.[7] I asked him then, what was his work, and what the wages that he would give. He told me that his work was *many delights;* and his wages, that I should be his *heir* at last. I further asked him what house he kept, and what other servants he had. So he told me, that his

[6] They committed all these things, and therefore I abhorred them Lev. xx, 23. If ye walk in my statutes and keep my commandments, my soul shall not abhor you. Lev. xxvi, 3, 11.

[7] "Adam the first," represents man's original carnal and corrupt nature, described by the apostle as "the old man which is corrupt according to the deceitful lusts." Eph. iv, 22.

house was maintained with all the dainties of the world, and that his servants were those of his own begetting. Then I asked him how many children he had. He said that he had but three daughters, the Lust of the Flesh, the Lust of the Eyes, and the Pride of Life, (1 John ii, 16;) and that I should marry them if I would. Then I asked how long time he would have me live with him; and he told me, as long as he lived himself.

Chr. Well, and what conclusion came the old man and you to at last?

Faith. Why, at first I found myself somewhat inclinable to go with the man, for I thought he spake very fair; but looking in his forehead, as I talked with him, I saw there written, "Put off the old man with his deeds." Col. iii, 9.

Chr. And how then?

Faith. Then it came burning hot into my mind, whatever he said, and however he flattered, when he got me home to his house he would sell me for a slave. So I bid him forbear to talk, for I would not come near the door of his house. Then he reviled me, and told me he would send such a one after me that should make my way bitter to my soul. So I turned to go away from him; but just as I turned myself to go thence I felt him take hold of my flesh, and give me such a deadly twitch back, that I thought he had pulled part of me after himself: this made me cry, "O wretched man!" Rom. vii, 24. So I went on my way up the hill.

Now when I had got about half way up, I looked behind me, and saw one coming after me, swift as the wind; so he overtook me just about the place where the settle stands.

"Just there," said Christian, "did I sit down to rest

me; but being overcome with sleep, I there lost this roll out of my bosom."

Faith. But, good brother, hear me out. So soon as the man overtook me, he was but a word and a blow, for down he knocked me, and laid me for dead. But when I was a little come to myself again, I asked him wherefore he served me so. He said, because of my secret inclining to Adam the first. And with that he struck me another deadly blow on the breast, and beat me down backward; so I lay at his foot as dead, as before. So when I came to myself again, I cried him mercy: but he said, "I know not how to show mercy;" and with that he knocked me down again. He had doubtless made an end of me, but that one came by, and bid him forbear.

Chr. Who was that that bid him forbear?

Faith. I did not know him at first; but as he went by, I perceived the holes in his hands and his side: then I concluded that he was our Lord. So I went up the hill.

Chr. That man that overtook you was Moses. He spareth none; neither knoweth he how to show mercy to those that transgress his law.[8]

Faith. I know it very well; it was not the first time

[8] The law is itself so perfectly holy and good, as not to admit of the least failure, either in the matter or manner of obedience. All the promises annexed to the law are by the first sin null and void. It neither giveth nor worketh repentance unto life, if thou break it. "Do this and live; break it and die;" this is the voice of the law. "Sin and die," is for ever its language. There is no middle way in the law. It stays no man from the due reward of his deeds: it hath no ears to hear, nor heart to pity its penitent ones. Alas! he who boasteth himself in the works of the law, doth not hear the law. When *that* speaks it shakes Mount Sinai, and writeth death upon all faces; and makes the church itself cry out, "A Mediator! else we die."—*Bunyan on Justification.*

that he has met with me. 'Twas he that came to me when I dwelt securely at home, and that told me he would burn my house over my head if I stayed there.

Chr. But did not you see the house that stood there, on the top of the hill on the side of which Moses met you?

Faith. Yes, and the lions too, before I came at it. But for the lions, I think they were asleep, for it was about noon; and because I had so much of the day before me, I passed by the Porter, and came down the hill.

Chr. He told me, indeed, that he saw you go by; but I wish that you had called at the house, for they would have showed you so many rarities, that you would scarce have forgot them to the day of your death.[9] But pray tell me, did you meet nobody in the Valley of Humility?

Faith. Yes, I met with one Discontent, who would willingly have persuaded me to go back again with him: his reason was, for that the valley was altogether without honour. He told me, moreover, that there to go was the way to disoblige all my friends, as Pride, Arrogancy, Self-Conceit, Worldly Glory, with others, who he knew, as he said, would be very much offended if I made such a fool of myself as to wade through this valley.

Chr. Well, and how did you answer him?

Faith. I told him, that although all these that he named might claim a kindred of me, and that rightly,

[9] Though Faithful passes the house called Beautiful without entering, we may not infer that our author considered it a matter of indifference whether Christians united themselves with the visible church. It was essential to his narrative that Christian and Faithful should first meet, as they did, immediately beyond the Valley of the Shadow of Death, and to this end he makes the latter pass the house while the former was within. Christian's expression of his wish that his fellow-pilgrim had called at the house, and his opinion of the advantage he would have derived thereby, sufficiently explain Bunyan's views on the subject, and should prevent any improper inference

(for indeed they were my relations according to the flesh,) yet since I became a pilgrim they have disowned me, and I also have rejected them; and therefore they were to me now no more than if they had never been of my lineage. I told him, moreover, that as to this valley, he had quite misrepresented the thing; for "before honour is humility," and "a haughty spirit before a fall." Therefore, said I, I had rather go through this valley to the honour that was so accounted by the wisest, than choose that which he esteemed most worthy of our affections.

Chr. Met you with nothing else in that valley?

Faith. Yes, I met with Shame; but of all the men that I met with on my pilgrimage, he, I think, bears the wrong name. The other would be said nay, after a little argumentation, and somewhat else; but this bold-faced Shame would never have done.

Chr. Why, what did he say to you?

Faith. What! why he objected against religion itself. He said it was a pitiful, low, sneaking business for a man to mind religion. He said that a tender conscience was an unmanly thing; and that for a man to watch over his words and ways, so as to tie up himself from that hectoring liberty that the brave spirits of the times accustom themselves unto, would make him the ridicule of the times.[10] He objected also, that but few

[10] He that cometh unto God by Christ is no little-spirited fellow. There are a generation of men in this world that count themselves men of the largest capacities, when yet the greatness of their desires lift themselves no higher than to things below. If they can, with their net of craft and policy, encompass a bulky lump of earth, O, what a treasure they have engrossed to themselves! Meanwhile, the man that comes to Christ, has laid siege to heaven, has found out the way to get into the city, and is resolved, in and by God's help, to

of the mighty, rich, or wise, were ever of my opinion; nor any of them neither, before they were persuaded to be fools, and to be of a voluntary fondness to venture the loss of all, for nobody else knows what. He moreover objected the base and low estate and condition of those that were chiefly the pilgrims of the times in which they lived; also their ignorance and want of understanding in all natural science. Yea, he did hold me to it at that rate also about a great many more things than here I relate; as, that it was a shame to sit whining and mourning under a sermon, and a shame to come sighing and groaning home; that it was a shame to ask my neighbour forgiveness for my petty faults, or to make restitution where I have taken from any. He said also, that religion made a man grow strange to the great, because of a few vices, (which he called by finer names,) and made him own and respect the base, because of the same religious fraternity: and is not this, said he, a shame?

Chr. And what did you say to him?

Faith. Say! I could not tell what to say at first. Yea, he put me so to it, that my blood came up in my face; even this Shame fetched it up, and had almost beat me quite off. But at last I began to consider, that that which is highly esteemed among men, is had in abomination with God. And I thought again, This Shame tells me what men are; but he tells me nothing what God, or the word of God, is. And I thought, moreover, that at the day of doom we shall not be

make that his own. Earth is a drossy thing in this man's account; earthly greatness and splendours are but like vanishing bubbles in this man's esteem: none but God, as the end of his desires, none but Christ, as the means to accomplish this end, are things counted great by this man.—*Bunyan's Christ a Complete Saviour.*

doomed to death or life, according to the hectoring spirits of the world, but according to the wisdom and law of the Highest. Therefore, thought I, what God says is best, indeed, is best, though all the men in the world are against it. Seeing, then, that God prefers his religion; seeing God prefers a tender conscience; seeing they that make themselves fools for the kingdom of heaven are wisest, and that the poor man that loveth Christ is richer than the greatest man in the world that hates him; Shame, depart! thou art an enemy to my salvation. Shall I entertain thee against my sovereign Lord? how then shall I look him in the face at his coming? Should I now be ashamed of his ways and servants, how can I expect the blessing? Mark viii, 38. But indeed this Shame was a bold villain; I could scarcely shake him out of my company; yea, he would be haunting of me, and continually whispering me in the ear with some one or other of the infirmities that attend religion. But at last I told him that it was but in vain to attempt further in this business; for those things that he disdained, in those did I see most glory: and so at last I got past this importunate one. And when I had shaken him off, then I began to sing:—

The trials that those men do meet withal,
That are obedient to the heavenly call,
Are manifold, and suited to the flesh,
And come, and come, and come again afresh;
That now, or some time else, we by them may
Be taken, overcome, and cast away.
O let the pilgrims, let the pilgrims then,
Be vigilant, and quit themselves like men.

Chr. I am glad, my brother, that thou didst withstand this villain so bravely; for of all, as thou sayest, I think he has the wrong name; for he is so bold as to follow us into the streets, and to attempt to put us to shame before all men; that is, to make us ashamed of that which is good. But if he was not himself audacious, he would never attempt to do as he does. But let us still resist him; for notwithstanding all his bravadoes, he promoteth the fool and none else. "The wise shall inherit glory," said Solomon; "but shame shall be the promotion of fools." Prov. iii, 35.

Faith. I think we must cry to Him for help against Shame, that would have us to be valiant for truth upon the earth.

Chr. You say true; but did you meet nobody else in that valley?

Faith. No, not I; for I had sunshine all the rest of the way through that, and also through the Valley of the Shadow of Death.

Chr. 'Twas well for you; I am sure it fared far otherwise with me. I had for a long season, as soon almost as I entered into that valley, a dreadful combat with that foul fiend Apollyon; yea, I thought verily he would have killed me, especially when he got me down, and crushed me under him, as if he would have crushed me to pieces; for as he threw me, my sword flew out of my hand; nay, he told me he was sure of me; but I cried to God, and he heard me, and delivered me out of all my troubles. Then I entered into the Valley of the Shadow of Death, and had no light for almost half the way through it. I thought I should have been killed there over and over; but at last day brake, and the sun rose, and I went through that which was behind with far more ease and quiet.

CHAPTER VIII.

The pilgrims fall in with one Talkative of Prating-Row—Faithful enters into conversation with him, and is at first deceived by his fine discourse—Christian discovers to Faithful the real character of his new companion—Faithful begins to discourse with him about heart-religion, with which he is not pleased, and they soon part.

Moreover I saw in my dream, that as they went on, Faithful, as he chanced to look on one side, saw a man whose name is Talkative, walking at a distance beside them; for in this place there was room enough for them all to walk. He was a tall man and something more comely at a distance than at hand. To this man Faithful addressed himself in this manner:—

Faith. Friend, whither away? Are you going to the heavenly country?

Talk. I am going to the same place.

Faith. That is well; then I hope we may have your good company?

Talk. With a very good will, will I be your companion.

Faith. Come on, then, and let us go together, and let us spend our time in discoursing of things that are profitable.

Talk. To talk of things that are good, to me is very acceptable, with you or with any other; and I am glad that I have met with those that incline to so good a work; for, to speak the truth, there are but few who care thus to spend their time as they are in their travels, but choose much rather to be speaking of things to no profit; and this hath been a trouble to me.

Faith. That is, indeed, a thing to be lamented; for

what thing so worthy of the use of the tongue and mouth of men on earth, as are the things of the God of heaven?

Talk. I like you wonderful well, for your sayings are full of conviction; and I will add, What thing is so pleasant, and what so profitable as to talk of the things of God? What things so pleasant? that is, if a man hath any delight in things that are wonderful. For instance: if a man doth delight to talk of the history or the mystery of things; or if a man doth love to talk of miracles, wonders, or signs, where shall he find things recorded so delightful, and so sweetly penned, as in the Holy Scripture.

Faith. That's true; but to be profited by such things in our talk, should be our chief design.

Talk. That is it that I said; for to talk of such things is most profitable; for by so doing, a man may get knowledge of many things; as of the vanity of earthly things, and the benefit of things above. Thus in general: but more particularly, by this a man may learn the necessity of the new birth, the insufficiency of our works, the need of Christ's righteousness, &c. Besides, by this a man may learn what it is to repent, to believe, to pray, to suffer, or the like; by this, also, a man may learn what are the great promises and consolations of the gospel, to his own comfort. Further, by this a man may learn to refute false opinions, to vindicate the truth, and also to instruct the ignorant.

Faith. All this is true; and glad am I to hear these things from you.

Talk. Alas! the want of this is the cause that so few understand the need of faith, and the necessity of a work of grace in their soul, in order to eternal life, but ignorantly live in the works of the law, by which a man can by no means obtain the kingdom of heaven.

Faith. But, by your leave, heavenly knowledge of these is the gift of God; no man attaineth to them by human industry, or only by the talk of them.

Talk. All that I know very well: for a man can receive nothing, except it be given him from heaven; all is of grace, not of works. I could give you a hundred scriptures for the confirmation of this.

"Well, then," said Faithful, "what is that one thing that we shall at this time found our discourse upon?"

Talk. What you will. I will talk of things heavenly, or things earthly; things moral, or things evangelical; things sacred, or things profane; things past, or things to come; things foreign, or things at home; things more essential, or things circumstantial; provided that all be done to our profit.[1]

Now did Faithful begin to wonder; and stepping to Christian, (for he walked all this while by himself,) he said to him, but softly, "What a brave companion have we got! Surely this man will make a very excellent pilgrim."

At this Christian modestly smiled, and said, "This man, with whom you are so taken, will beguile with this tongue of his twenty of them that know him not."

Faith. Do you know him, then?

Chr. Know him! Yes, better than he knows himself.

Faith. Pray what is he?

Chr. His name is Talkative: he dwelleth in our town. I wonder that you should be a stranger to him; only I consider that our town is large.

[1] O brave Talkative!—*Bunyan's Marginal Note.*

Faith. Whose son is he? And whereabout doth he dwell?

Chr. He is the son of one Say-well. He dwelt in Prating-Row; and he is known to all that are acquainted with him by the name of Talkative, of Prating-Row; and, notwithstanding his fine tongue, he is but a sorry fellow.

Faith. Well, he seems to be a very pretty man.

Chr. That is, to them that have not a thorough acquaintance with him, for he is best abroad: near home he is ugly enough. Your saying that he is a pretty man, brings to my mind what I have observed in the work of the painter, whose pictures show best at a distance, but very near more unpleasing.

Faith. But I am ready to think you do but jest, because you smiled.

Chr. God forbid that I should jest (though I smiled) in this matter, or that I should accuse any falsely. I will give you a further discovery of him. This man is for any company and for any talk; as he talketh now with you, so will he talk when he is on the ale-bench, and the more drink he hath in his crown, the more of these things he hath in his mouth. Religion hath no place in his heart, or house, or conversation; all he hath lieth in his tongue, and his religion is to make a noise therewith.

Faith. Say you so? Then am I in this man greatly deceived.

Chr. Deceived! you may be sure of it. Remember the proverb, "They say and do not," Matt. xxiii, 3; but the kingdom of God is not in word, but in power. 1 Cor. iv, 20. He talketh of prayer, of repentance, of faith, and of the new birth; but he knows but only to talk of them. I have been in his family, and have observed him both at home and abroad; and I know what I say of him is the truth. His house is as empty of religion as the white of an egg is of savour. There is there neither prayer, nor sign of repentance for sin; yea, the brute, in his kind, serves God far better than he. He is the very stain, reproach, and shame of religion to all that know him; it can hardly have a good word in all that end of the town where he dwells, through him. Thus say the common people that know him, "A saint abroad, and a devil at home." His poor family finds it so; he is such a churl, such a railer at, and so unreasonable with, his servants, that they neither know how to do for or speak to him. Men that have any dealings with him say, It is better to deal with a Turk than with him, for fairer dealings they shall have at their hands. This Talkative (if it be possible) will go beyond them, defraud, beguile, and overreach them. Besides, he brings up his sons to follow his steps; and if he finds in any of them a foolish timorousness, (for so he calls the first appearance of a tender conscience,) he calls them fools and blockheads, and by no means will employ them in much, or speak to their commendation before others.[2] For my part, I am of opinion that he has, by his wicked life,

[2] A professor! and practise such villanies as these! such an one is not worthy to bear that name any longer. We may say to such, as the prophet spake to their like, to wit, to the rebellious that were in the house of Israel, *Go ye, serve every man his idols*—if you will not hearken to the law and testament of God, to lead your lives hereafter; *but pollute God's holy name no more with your gift, and with your idols.* Go, professors, go; leave off profession, unless you will lead your lives according to your profession. Better never profess, than make profession as talking horse to sin, deceit, to the devil and hell.—*Bunyan's Life and Death of Mr. Badman.*

caused many to stumble and fall; and will be, if God prevents not, the ruin of many more.

Faith. Well, my brother, I am bound to believe you, not only because you say you know him, but also because, like a Christian you make your reports of men. For I cannot think that you speak these things of ill will, but because it is even so as you say.

Chr. Had I known him no more than you, I might, perhaps, have thought of him as at the first you did; yea, had I received this report at their hands only that are enemies to religion, I should have thought it had been a slander, a lot that oft falls from bad men's mouths upon good men's names and professions. But all these things, yea, and a great many more as bad, of my own knowledge, I can prove him guilty of. Besides, good men are ashamed of him; they can neither call him brother nor friend; the very naming of him among them makes them blush, if they know him.

Faith. Well, I see that saying and doing are two things, and hereafter I shall better observe this distinction.

Chr. They are two things indeed, and are as diverse as are the soul and the body; for as the body without the soul is but a dead carcass, so *saying*, if it be alone, is but a dead carcass also. The soul of religion is the practical part. "Pure religion and undefiled before God and the Father, is this, to visit the fatherless and widows in their affliction, and to keep himself unspotted from the world." James i, 27. This Talkative is not aware of; he thinks that hearing and saying will make a good Christian; and thus he deceiveth his own soul. Hearing is but as the sowing of the seed; talking is not sufficient to prove that fruit is indeed in the heart and life. And let us assure ourselves, that at the day of doom men shall be judged according to their fruits. It will not be said then, Did you believe? but, Were you doers, or talkers only? and accordingly shall they be judged. The end of the world is compared to our harvest, (Matt. xiii, 30,) and you know men at harvest regard nothing but fruit. Not that anything can be accepted that is not of faith; but I speak this to show you how insignificant the profession of Talkative will be at that day.

Faith. This brings to my mind that of Moses, by which he describeth the beast that is clean. Lev. xi; Deut. xiv. He is such an one that parteth the hoof, and cheweth the cud; not that parteth the hoof only, or that cheweth the cud only. The hare cheweth the cud, but yet is unclean, because he parteth not the hoof. And this truly resembleth Talkative: he cheweth the cud, he seeketh knowledge; he cheweth upon the word, but he divideth not the hoof. He parteth not with the way of sinners; but as the hare, retaineth the foot of a dog or bear, and therefore he is unclean.

Chr. You have spoken, for aught I know, the true gospel sense of these texts. And I will add another thing: Paul calleth some men, yea, and those great talkers too, sounding brass, and tinkling cymbals, 1 Cor. xiii, 1, 3; that is, as he expounds them in another place, things without life giving sound. 1 Cor. xiv, 7. Things without life; that is, without the true faith and grace of the gospel; and, consequently, things that shall never be placed in the kingdom of heaven among those that are the children of life; though their sound, by their talk, be as if it were the tongue or voice of an angel.

Faith. Well, I was not so fond of his company at

first, but I am as sick of it now. What shall we do to be rid of him?

Chr. Take my advice, and do as I bid you, and you shall find that he will soon be sick of your company too, except God shall touch his heart and turn it.

Faith. What would you have me to do?

Chr. Why, go to him and enter into some serious discourse about the power of religion, and ask him plainly, (when he has approved of it, for that he will,) whether this thing be set up in his heart, house, or conversation.

Then Faithful stepped forward again, and said to Talkative, "Come, what cheer? How is it now?"

Talk. Thank you, well: I thought we should have had a great deal of talk by this time.

Faith. Well, if you will, we will fall to it now; and since you left it with me to state the question, let it be this: How doth the saving grace of God discover itself when it is in the heart of man?

Talk. I perceive, then, that our talk must be about the power of things. Well, it is a very good question, and I shall be willing to answer you. And take my answer in brief, thus: First, when the grace of God is in the heart, it causeth there a great outcry against sin. Secondly—

Faith. Nay, hold, let us consider of one at once. I think you should rather say, It shows itself by inclining the soul to abhor its sin.

Talk. Why, what difference is there between crying out against, and abhorring of sin?

Faith. O! a great deal. A man may cry out against sin of policy; but he cannot abhor it but by virtue of a godly antipathy against it. I have heard many cry out against sin in the pulpit, who yet can abide it well enough in the heart, house, and conversation. Joseph's mistress cried out with a loud voice, as if she had been very chaste; but she would willingly, notwithstanding that, have committed uncleanness with him. Gen. xxxix, 15. Some cry out against sin, even as the mother cries out against her child in her lap, when she calleth it slut and naughty girl, and then falls to hugging and kissing it.

Talk. You lie at the *catch*, I perceive.

Faith. No, not I; I am only for setting things right. But what is the second thing whereby you would prove a discovery of a work of grace in the heart?

Talk. Great knowledge of gospel mysteries.

Faith. This sign should have been first: but first or last, it is also false; for knowledge, great knowledge, may be obtained in the mysteries of the gospel, and yet no work of grace in the soul. Yea, if a man have "all knowledge," he may yet be nothing, and so, consequently, be no child of God. 1 Cor. xiii, 2. When Christ said, "Do you know all these things?" and the disciples had answered, Yes, he addeth, "Blessed are ye if ye do them." He doth not lay the blessing in the knowing of them, but in the doing of them. For there is a knowledge that is not attended with doing: "He that knoweth his Master's will, and doth it not." A man may know like an angel, and yet be no Christian; therefore your sign of it is not true. Indeed, to *know*, is a thing that pleaseth talkers and boasters; but to *do*, is that which pleaseth God. Not that the heart can be good without knowledge, for without that the heart is naught. There are, therefore, two sorts of knowledge, knowledge that resteth in the bare speculation of things, and knowledge that is accompanied with the grace of faith and love, which puts a man upon doing even the will of God from the heart: the first of these will serve the talker; but without the other the true Christian is not content. "Give me understanding, and I shall keep thy law; yea, I shall observe it with my whole heart." Psa. cxix, 34.

Talk. You lie at the catch again: this is not for edification.

Faith. Well, if you please, propound another sign how this work of grace discovereth itself where it is.

Talk. Not I, for I see we shall not agree.

Faith. Well, if you will not, will you give me leave to do it?

Talk. You may use your liberty.

Faith. A work of grace in the soul discovereth itself, either to him that hath it, or to standers by. To him that hath it, thus: It gives him conviction of sin, especially the defilement of his nature, and the sin of unbelief, for the sake of which he is sure to be damned, if he findeth not mercy at God's hand by faith in Jesus Christ. This sight and sense of things worketh in him sorrow and shame for sin. He findeth, moreover, revealed in him the Saviour of the world, and the absolute necessity of closing with him for life; at the which he findeth hungerings and thirstings after him; to which hungerings, &c., the promise is made. Matt. v, 6; Rev. xxi, 6. Now, according to the strength or weakness of his faith in his Saviour, so is his joy and peace, so is his love to holiness, so are his desires to know him more, and also to serve him in this world. But though, I say, it discovereth itself thus unto him, yet it is but seldom that he is able to conclude that this is a work of grace; because his corruptions now, and his abused reason, make his mind to misjudge in this matter; therefore in him that hath this work there is required a very sound judgment before he can with steadiness conclude that this is a work of grace.

To others it is thus discovered: 1. By an experimental confession of faith in Christ. 2. By a life answerable to that confession; to wit, a life of holiness; heart-holiness, family-holiness, (if he hath a family,) and by conversation-holiness in the world; which in the general teacheth him inwardly to abhor his sin, and himself for that, in secret; to suppress it in his family, and to promote holiness in the world; not by talk only, as a hypocrite or talkative person may do, but by a practical subjection in faith and love to the power of the word. John xiv, 15; Phil. i, 27. And now, sir, as to this brief description of the work of grace, and also the discovery of it, if you have aught to object, object; if not, then give me leave to propound to you a second question.

Talk. Nay, my part is not now to object, but to hear; let me, therefore, have your second question.

Faith. It is this: Do you experience this first part of the description of it? And doth your life and conversation testify the same? or standeth your religion in word or tongue, and not in deed and truth? Pray, if you incline to answer me in this, say no more than you know the God above will say Amen to; and also nothing but what your conscience can justify you in; "for not he that commendeth himself is approved, but whom the Lord commendeth." Besides, to say I am thus and thus, when my conversation, and all my neighbours tell me I lie, is great wickedness.

Then Talkative at first began to blush; but, recovering himself, thus he replied: "You come now to experience, to conscience, and God; and to appeal to him for justification of what is spoken. This kind of discourse I did not expect; nor am I disposed to give an answer to such questions, because I count not myself bound thereto, unless you take upon you to be a catechiser; and though you should so do, yet I may refuse to make you my judge. But I pray, will you tell me why you ask me such questions?

Faith. Because I saw you forward to talk, and because I knew not that you had aught else but notion. Besides, to tell you the truth, I have heard of you that you are a man whose religion lies in talk, and that your conversation gives this your mouth-profession the lie. They say you are a spot among Christians, and that religion fareth the worse for your ungodly conversation; that some already have stumbled at your wicked ways, and that more are in danger of being destroyed thereby; your religion, and an ale-house, and covetousness, and uncleanness, and swearing, and lying, and vain company-keeping, &c., will stand together. The proverb is true of you which is said of a whore, to wit, "That she is a shame to all women;" so are you a shame to all professors.

Talk. Since you are so ready to take up reports, and to judge so rashly as you do, I cannot but conclude you are some peevish or melancholy man, not fit to be discoursed with; and so, adieu.[3]

[3] Let me a little expostulate the matter with you, O ye professors whose religion lieth only in your tongues; I mean you who are little or nothing known from the rest of the rabble of the world, only you can *talk* better than they. Hear me a word or two: "If I speak with the tongues of men and angels, and have not charity"—that is, love

Then came up Christian, and said to his brother "I told you how it would happen; your words and his lusts could not agree. He had rather leave your company than reform his life. But he is gone, as I said; let him go; the loss is no man's but his own; he has saved us the trouble of going from him; for he continuing (as I suppose he will do) as he is, he would have been but a blot in our company. Besides, the apostle says, 'From such withdraw thyself.'"[4]

Faith. But I am glad we had this little discourse with him; it may happen that he will think of it again: however, I have dealt plainly with him, and so am clear of his blood, if he perisheth.

Chr. You did well to talk so plainly to him as you did. There is but little of this faithful dealing with men now-a-days, and that makes religion to stink in

to God, and Christ, and saints, and holiness—"I am nothing"—no child of God, and so have nothing to do with heaven. 1 Cor. xiii. A prating tongue will not unlock the gates of heaven, nor blind the eyes of thy Judge: look to it; "The wise in heart will receive commandments; but a prating fool shall fall." Prov. x, 8.—*Bunyan's Discourse on the Strait Gate.*

[4] There is nothing more seemly in this world, than to see a Christian walk as becomes the gospel, nor anything more unbecoming a reasonable creature, than to hear a man say, "I believe in Christ," and yet see in his life debauchery and profaneness. Might I, such men should be counted the basest of men; such men should be counted by all, unworthy of the name of Christian, and should be shunned by every good man, as such who are the very plague of profession. For so it is written we should carry it toward them. Whoso have a form of godliness, and deny the power thereof, from such we must turn away.—*Bunyan's Jerusalem Sinner.*

"Receive us," says the apostle, "we have wronged no man, we have corrupted no man, we have defrauded no man;" intimating, that those that are guilty of wronging, corrupting, or defrauding of any, should not be admitted to the fellowship of saints, no, nor into the common catalogue of brethren with them.—*Bunyan's Life and Death of Mr. Badman.*

the nostrils of so many as it doth; for they are these talkative fools, whose religion is only in word, and who are debauched and vain in their conversation, that (being so much admitted into the fellowship of the godly) do puzzle the world, blemish Christianity, and grieve the sincere. I wish that all men would deal with such as you have done; then should they either be made more conformable to religion, or the company of saints would be too hot for them.

Then did Faithful say:—

> "How Talkative at first lifts up his plumes!
> How bravely doth he speak! How he presumes
> To drive down all before him! But so soon
> As Faithful talks of heart-work, like the moon
> That's past the full, into the wane he goes;
> And so will all but he that heart-work knows."

Thus they went on, talking of what they had seen by the way, and so made that way easy, which would otherwise no doubt have been tedious to them, for now they went through a wilderness.

CHAPTER IX.

Evangelist overtakes the Pilgrims—He predicts the troubles they will meet with in Vanity-Fair, and encourages them to steadfastness—Account of Vanity-Fair—The Pilgrims enter the Fair—The Fair is in a hubbub about them—They are taken prisoners and put in the cage—The trial—Faithful is put to death.

Now when they were got almost quite out of this wilderness, Faithful chanced to cast his eye back, and espied one coming after them, and he knew him. "O," said Faithful to his brother, "who comes yonder?" Then Christian looked, and said, "It is my good friend Evangelist." "Ay, and my good friend too," said Faithful, "for 'twas he that set me on the way to the gate."

Now was Evangelist come up to them, and thus saluted them, "Peace be to you, dearly beloved, and peace be to your helpers."

Chr. Welcome, welcome, my good Evangelist, the sight of thy countenance brings to my remembrance thy ancient kindness and unwearied labours for my eternal good.

"And a thousand times welcome," said good Faithful, "thy company, O sweet Evangelist; how desirable is it to us poor pilgrims!"

Then said Evangelist, "How hath it fared with you, my friends, since the time of our last parting? What have you met with, and how have you behaved yourselves?"

Then Christian and Faithful told him of all things that had happened to them in the way; and how, and with what difficulty, they had arrived to that place.

"Right glad am I," said Evangelist, "not that you have met with trials, but that you have been victors; and for that you have, notwithstanding many weaknesses, continued in the way to this very day. I say, right glad am I of this thing, and that for mine own sake and yours; I have sowed, and you have reaped; and the day is coming, when both he that sowed, and they that reaped, shall rejoice together, John iv, 36; that is, if you hold out: for in due time ye shall reap, if ye faint not. Gal. vi, 9. The crown is before you, and it is an incorruptible one; so run that you may obtain it. 1 Cor. ix, 24–27. Some there be that set out for this crown, and after they have gone far for it, another comes in and takes it from them: 'hold fast, therefore, that you have; let no man take your crown.' Rev. iii, 11. You are not yet out of the gun-shot of the devil; 'you have not yet resisted unto blood, striving against sin.' Let the kingdom be always before you, and believe steadfastly concerning things that are invisible. Let nothing that is on this side the other world get within you. And, above all, look well to your own hearts and to the lusts thereof, for they are 'deceitful above all things, and desperately wicked.' Set your faces like a flint; you have all power in heaven and earth on your side."

Then Christian thanked him for his exhortation; but told him withal, that they would have him speak further to them for their help the rest of the way; and the rather, for that they well knew that he was a prophet, and could tell them of things that might happen unto them, and also how they might resist and overcome them. To which request Faithful also consented. So Evangelist began as followeth:

"My sons, you have heard in the words of the truth of the gospel, that you must 'through many tribulations enter into the kingdom of heaven;' and again, that 'in every city, bonds and afflictions abide you;' and therefore you cannot expect that you should go long on your pilgrimage without them, in some sort or other. You have found something of the truth of these testimonies upon you already, and more will immediately follow; for now, as you see, you are almost out of this wilderness, and therefore you will soon come into a town that you will by and by see before you; and in that town you will be hardly beset with enemies, who will strain hard but they will kill you; and be you sure that one or both of you must seal the testimony which you hold with blood; but be you faithful unto death, and the King will give you a crown of life. Rev. ii, 10. He that shall die there, although his death will be unnatural, and his pain, perhaps, great, he will yet have the better of his fellow; not only because he will be arrived at the celestial city soonest, but because he will escape many miseries that the other will meet with in the rest of his journey. But when you are come to the town, and shall find fulfilled what I have here related, then remember your friend, and quit yourselves like men, and 'commit the keeping of your souls to God in well-doing, as unto a faithful Creator.'"

Then I saw in my dream, that when they were got out of the wilderness, they presently saw a town before them, and the name of that town is Vanity; and at the town there is a fair kept, called Vanity Fair. It is kept all the year long. It beareth the name of Vanity Fair, because the town where it is kept is lighter than vanity; and also, because all that is there sold, or that cometh thither, is vanity; as is the saying of the wise, "All that cometh is vanity." Eccl. i, 2–14; xi, 8.[1]

This fair is no new-erected business, but a thing of ancient standing. I will show you the original of it. Almost five thousand years ago there were pilgrims walking to the celestial city, as these two honest persons are; and Beelzebub, Apollyon, and Legion, with their companions, perceiving by the path that the pilgrims made, that their way to the city lay through this town of Vanity, they contrived here to set up a fair; a fair wherein should be sold all sorts of vanity, and that it should last all the year long. Therefore at this fair are all such merchandise sold as houses, lands, trades, places, honours, preferments, titles, countries, kingdoms, lusts, pleasures; and delights of all sorts, as whores, bawds, wives, husbands, children, masters, servants, lives, blood, bodies, souls, silver, gold, pearls, precious stones, and what not. And moreover, at this fair there is at all times to be seen jugglings, cheats, games, plays, fools, apes, knaves, and rogues, and that of every kind. Here are to be seen, too, and that for nothing, thefts, murders, adulteries, false swearers, and that of a blood-red colour. And as in other fairs of less moment there are the several rows and streets under their proper names, where such and such wares are vended; so here likewise you have the proper places, rows, streets, (namely, countries and kingdoms,) where the wares of this fair are soonest to be found. Here is the Britain Row, the French Row,

[1] Vanity Fair is described by one, as being "the City of Destruction in its gala dress." Both are intended to represent our fallen world, which by nature "lieth in wickedness," under bondage to Satan, who is called in Scripture, "the god of this world," 2 Corinthians, iv, 4

the Italian Row, the Spanish Row, the German Row, where several sorts of vanities are to be sold. But as in other fairs some one commodity is the chief of all the fair, so the ware of Rome and her merchandise is greatly promoted in this fair; only our English nation, with some others, have taken a dislike thereat.

Now, as I said, the way to the Celestial City lies just through this town where this lusty fair is kept; and he that would go to the city, and yet not go through this town, "must needs go out of the world." 1 Cor. v, 10. The Prince of princes himself, when here, went through this town to his own country, and that upon a fair-day too; yea, and, as I think, it was Beelzebub, the chief lord of this fair, that invited him to buy of his vanities, yea, would have made him lord of the fair, would he but have done him reverence as he went through the town. Yea, because he was such a person of honour, Beelzebub had him from street to street, and showed him all the kingdoms of the world in a little time, that he might, if possible, allure that blessed One to cheapen and buy some of his vanities; but he had no mind to the merchandise, and, therefore, left the town without laying out so much as one farthing upon these vanities.[2] Matt. iv, 8–10. This fair, therefore, is an ancient thing of long standing, and a very great fair.

[2] Much of this world and its glory is permitted of God to be disposed of by the devil, and he is called both the prince (John xii, 31) and god (2 Cor. iv, 4) thereof; yea, when Satan told Christ he could give it to whom he would, Christ did not say, Thou liest; but answered by the word, "It is written, Thou shalt worship the Lord thy God, and him only shalt thou serve." Implying, also, that commonly when men get much of the honours and glory of this world, it is by bending the knee too low to the prince and god thereof.—*Bunyan on Paul's Departure and Crown.*

Now these pilgrims, as I said, must needs go through this fair. Well, so they did; but, behold, even as they entered into the fair, all the people in the fair were moved, and the town itself, as it were, in a hubbub about them, and that for several reasons: for,

First. The pilgrims were clothed with such kind of raiment as was diverse from the raiment of any that traded in that fair. The people, therefore, of the fair, made a great gazing upon them; some said they were fools; some they were bedlams; and some they were outlandish men.[3]

Secondly. And as they wondered at their apparel, so they did likewise at their speech; for few could understand what they said. They naturally spoke the language of Canaan; but they that kept the fair were the men of this world. So that from one end of the fair to the other, they seemed barbarians each to the other.

[3] He is no fool that cometh to God by Christ. The world, indeed, will count him one, for the things that be of the Spirit of God are foolishness to them; but indeed, and in the verdict of true judgment, he is not so. It is not a sign of foolishness, timely to prevent ruin, is it? They are the prudent men that foresee an evil, and hide themselves; and the fools that go and are punished. Why, this man foresees an evil, the greatest evil—sin, and the punishment of the soul for sin in hell—and flies to Christ, who is the refuge that God has provided for penitent sinners; and is this the sign of a fool? God make me such a fool, and thee that readest these lines such a fool, and then we shall be wiser than all men that are counted wise by the wisdom of this world. Is he a fool that chooseth for himself long lasters, or he whose best things will rot in a day? Sinners, before your pots can feel the thorns, before you can see where you are, God shall take you away as with a whirlwind, both living and in his wrath. Psa. lviii, 9. But *this* man hath provided for things; like the tortoise, he has got a shell on his back so strong and sound that he fears not to suffer a loaden cart to go over him. The Lord is his rock, his defence, his refuge, his high tower, unto which he doth continually resort. Ps. xviii, 2; lxxi, 3; cxliv, 2.—*Bunyan's Christ a Complete Saviour*

Thirdly. But that which did not a little amuse the merchandisers was, that these pilgrims set very light by all their wares. They cared not so much as to look upon them; and if they called upon them to buy, they would put their fingers in their ears, and cry, "Turn away mine eyes from beholding vanity," Psa. cxix, 37; and look upward, signifying that their trade and traffic was in heaven. Phil. iii, 20, 21.[4]

One chanced mockingly, beholding the carriage of

[4] If thou wouldst be faithful, labour always to possess thy heart with a right understanding, both of the things that this world yieldeth, and of the things that shall be hereafter. I am confident that most if not all the miscarriages of the saints and people of God have their rise from deceivable thoughts here. The things of this world appear to us more, and those that are to come less, than they are; and hence it is that many are so hot and eager for things that be in the world, and so cold and heartless for those that be in heaven. Satan is here a mighty artist, and can show us all earthly things in a multiplying glass; but when we look up to things above, we see them as through sackcloth of hair: but take thou heed; be not ruled by thy sensual appetite that can only savour fleshly things, neither be thou ruled by carnal reason, which always darkeneth the things of heaven. But go to the Word, and as that says, so judge thou. That tells thee all things under the sun are "vanity," nay, worse, "vexation of spirit;" that tells thee the world is not, even then when it doth most appear to be: wilt thou set thine heart upon that which is not? for riches certainly make themselves wings and fly away. The same may be said of honours, pleasures, and the like; they are poor, low, base things to be entertained by a Christian's heart; the man that hath most of them may in the fulness of his sufficiency be in straits; yea, when he is about to fill his belly with them, God may cast the fury of his wrath upon him: "so is every one that layeth up treasure for himself upon earth, and is not rich toward God." A horse that is loaden with gold and pearls all day, may have a foul stable and a galled back at night: and "wo be to him that increaseth that which is not his, and that ladeth himself with thick clay." Hab. ii, 6. O man of God, throw this bone to the dogs; suck not at it, there is no marrow there. "Set thine affections on things that are above, where Christ sitteth on the right hand of God." Col. iii, 1, 2.—*Bunyan on Paul's Departure and Crown.*

the men, to say unto them, "What will ye buy?" But they, looking gravely upon him, said, "We buy the truth." Prov. xxiii, 23. At that, there was an occasion taken to despise the men the more, some mocking, some taunting, some speaking reproachfully, and some calling upon others to smite them. At last things came to a hubbub and great stir in the fair, insomuch that all order was confounded. Now was word presently brought to the great one of the fair, who quickly came down and deputed some of his most trusty friends to take those men into examination about whom the fair was almost overturned. So the men were brought to examination; and they that sat upon them asked whence they came, whither they went, and what they did there in such an unusual garb. The men told them that they were pilgrims and strangers in the world, and that they were going to their own country, which was the heavenly Jerusalem, Heb. xi, 13–16 : and that they had given no occasion to the men of the town, nor yet to the merchandisers, thus to abuse them, and to let them in their journey, except it was for that, when one asked them what they would buy, they said they would buy the truth. But they that were appointed to examine them did not believe them to be any other than bedlams and mad, or else such as came to put all things into a confusion in the fair. Therefore they took them and beat them, and besmeared them with dirt, and then put them into the cage, that they might be made a spectacle to all the men of the fair. There, therefore, they lay for some time, and were made the objects of any man's sport, or malice, or revenge; the great one of the fair laughing still at all that befell them. But the men being patient, and "not rendering railing for railing, but contrariwise blessing," and giving good words for bad, and kindness for injuries done, some men in the fair, that were more observing and less prejudiced than the rest, began to check and blame the baser sort for their continual abuses done by them to the men.[5] They, therefore, in angry manner let fly at *them* again, counting them as bad as the men in the cage, and telling them that they seemed confederates, and should be made partakers of their misfortunes. The others replied, that, for aught they could see, the men were quiet and sober, and intended nobody any harm; and that there were many that traded in their fair that were more worthy to be put into the cage, yea, and pillory too, than were the men that they had

[5] Love your enemies, bless them that curse you, do good to them that hate you, and pray for them which despitefully use you, and persecute you; that ye may be the children of your Father which is in heaven: for he maketh his sun to rise on the evil and on the good. Matt. v, 44, 45.

O, it is hard work to pocket up the reproaches of all the foolish people, as if we had found great spoil, and to suffer all their revilings, lies, and slanders, without cursing them, as Elisha did the children; to answer them with prayers and blessings for their curses. It is far more easy to give them taunt for taunt, and reviling for reviling; to give them blow for blow; yea, to call for fire from heaven against them. But to "bless them that curse us, and to pray for them that despitefully use and persecute us," even of malice, and on purpose to vex and afflict our mind, and to make us break out into a rage, this is work above us; now our patience should look up to unseen things, now remember Christ and his carriage to them that spilt his blood; or all is in danger of bursting, and thou of miscarrying in these things. Now, for thy better performing this piece of service for our Lord and Saviour Jesus Christ: 1. Remember often that thou art not the first that hath met with these things in the world: "It hated me," saith Christ, "before it hated you." 2. Arm thyself with a patient and quiet mind, to bear and suffer for His sake. 3. Pray that thou mayst hear the voice of the rod, and have an heart to answer the end of God therein. 4. Remember the promise, "all things shall work together for good to them that love God."—*Bunyan on Paul's Departure and Crown.*

abused. Thus, after divers words had passed on both sides, (the men behaving themselves all the while very wisely and soberly before them,) they fell to some blows among themselves, and did harm one to another. Then were these two poor men brought before their examiners again, and were charged as being guilty of the late hubbub that had been in the fair. So they beat them pitifully, and hanged irons upon them, and led them in chains up and down the fair, for an example and terror to others, lest any should speak in their behalf, or join themselves unto them. But Christian and Faithful behaved themselves yet more wisely, and received the ignominy and shame that was cast upon them with so much meekness and patience, that it won to their side (though but few in comparison of the rest) several of the men in the fair. This put the other party yet into a greater rage, insomuch that they concluded the death of these two men. Wherefore they threatened, that neither cage nor irons should serve their turn, but that they should die for the abuse they had done, and for deluding the men of the fair.

Then were they remanded to the cage again, until further order should be taken with them. So they put them in, and made their feet fast in the stocks.

Here, therefore, they called again to mind what they had heard from their faithful friend Evangelist, and were the more confirmed in their way and sufferings, by what he told them would happen to them. They also now comforted each other, that whose lot it was to suffer, even he should have the best on't; therefore each man secretly wished that he might have that preferment: but committing themselves to the all-wise disposal of Him that ruleth all things, with much content they abode in the condition in which they were, until they should be otherwise disposed of.[6]

Then a convenient time being appointed, they brought them forth to their trial, in order to their condemnation. When the time was come, they were brought before their enemies, and arraigned. The judge's name was Lord Hategood: their indictment was one and the same in substance, though somewhat varying in form; the contents whereof were these:—"That they were enemies to, and disturbers of, the trade; that they had made commotions and divisions in the town, and had

[6] As the afflictions of saints abound for Christ, so do their consolations by him: so, did I say? they abound much more. . . . They drink of the cup that is exceeding bitter, and of that which is exceeding sweet; and they complain not of the bitter, because the sweet overcomes it. "I am filled with comfort," saith the apostle, "I am exceeding joyful in all our tribulations."—*Bunyan's House of the Forest of Lebanon.*

Bunyan himself knew something of this from his own experience, as he testifies in the following homely rhymes, which we extract from his Prison Meditations:—

"This prison very sweet to me
Hath been since I came here;
And so would hanging also be,
If God would there appear.

When they do talk of banishment,
Of death or such like things,
Then God to me sends heart's content,
That like a fountain springs.

If they do give me gall to drink,
Then God doth sweetening cast
So much thereto, that they can't think
How bravely it doth taste.

Alas, they little think what peace
They help me to, for by
Their rage my comforts do increase;
Bless God, therefore do I."

won a party to their own most dangerous opinions, in contempt of the law of their prince."

Then Faithful began to answer, that he had only set himself against that which had set itself against Him that is higher than the highest. "And," said he, "as for disturbance, I make none, being myself a man of peace: the parties that were won to us, were won by beholding our truth and innocence, and they are only turned from the worse to the better. And as to the king you talk of, since he is Beelzebub, the enemy of our Lord, I defy him and all his angels."

Then proclamation was made, that they that had aught to say for their lord the king against the prisoner at the bar should forthwith appear, and give in their evidence. So there came in three witnesses, to wit, Envy, Superstition, and Pickthank. They were then asked, if they knew the prisoner at the bar; and what they had to say for their lord the king against him.

Then stood forth Envy, and said to this effect: "My lord, I have known this man a long time, and will attest upon oath before this honourable bench, that he is"—

Judge. Hold! give him his oath.

So they sware him. Then he said, "My lord, this man, notwithstanding his plausible name, is one of the vilest men in our country; he neither regardeth prince nor people, law nor custom, but doeth all that he can to possess all men with certain of his disloyal notions, which he in the general calls principles of faith and holiness. And in particular, I heard him once myself affirm, that Christianity and the customs of our town of Vanity were diametrically opposite, and could not be reconciled. By which saying, my lord, he doth at once not only condemn all our laudable doings, but us in the doing of them."

Then did the judge say to him, "Hast thou any more to say?"

Envy. My lord, I could say much more, only I would not be tedious to the court. Yet if need be, when the other gentlemen have given in their evidence, rather than anything shall be wanting that will despatch him, I will enlarge my testimony against him.

So he was bid to stand by.

Then they called Superstition, and bid him look upon the prisoner at the bar. They also asked what he could say for their lord the king against him. Then they sware him; so he began:—"My lord, I have no great acquaintance with this man, nor do I desire to have further knowledge of him. However, this I know, that he is a very pestilent fellow, from some discourse that the other day I had with him, in this town; for then, talking with him, I heard him say, that our religion was naught, and such by which a man could by no means please God. Which saying of his, my lord, your lordship very well knows what necessarily thence will follow, to wit, that we still do worship in vain, are yet in our sins, and finally shall be damned. And this is that which I have to say."

Then was Pickthank sworn, and bid say what he knew in the behalf of their lord the king, against the prisoner at the bar.

Pick. My lord, and you gentlemen all, this fellow I have known of a long time, and have heard him speak things that ought not to be spoken; for he hath railed on our noble prince Beelzebub, and hath spoken contemptibly of his honourable friends, whose names are, the Lord Old Man, the Lord Carnal Delight, the Lord Luxurious, the Lord Desire of Vain Glory, my old Lord Lechery, Sir Having Greedy, with all the rest of our nobility: and he hath said, moreover, that if all men were of his mind, if possible, there is not one of these noblemen should have any longer a being in this town. Besides, he hath not been afraid to rail on you, my lord, who are now appointed to be his judge, calling you an ungodly villain, with many other such like vilifying terms, with which he hath bespattered most of the gentry of our town.

When this Pickthank had told his tale, the judge directed his speech to the prisoner at the bar, saying, "Thou runagate, heretic, and traitor, hast thou heard what these honest gentlemen have witnessed against thee?"

Faith. May I speak a few words in my own defence?

Judge. Sirrah, sirrah, thou deservest to live no longer, but to be slain immediately upon the place; yet that all men may see our gentleness toward thee, let us hear what thou, vile runagate, hast to say.

Faith. 1. I say, then, in answer to what Mr. Envy hath spoken, I never said aught but this, that what rule, or laws, or custom, or people, were flat against the word of God, are diametrically opposite to Christianity. If I have said amiss in this, convince me of my error, and I am ready here before you to make my recantation.

2. As to the second, to wit, Mr. Superstition, and his charge against me, I said only this, That in the worship of God there is required a divine faith; but there can be no divine faith without a divine revelation of the will of God. Therefore, whatever is thrust into the worship of God, that is not agreeable to divine revela-

tion, cannot be done but by a human faith; which faith will not be profitable to eternal life.

3. As to what Mr. Pickthank hath said, I say, (avoiding terms, as that I am said to rail, and the like,) that the prince of this town, with all the rabblement, his attendants, by this gentleman named, are more fit for a being in hell than in this town and country. And so the Lord have mercy upon me.

Then the judge called to the jury, (who all this while stood by to hear and observe,) "Gentlemen of the jury, you see this man about whom so great an uproar hath been made in this town; you have also heard what these worthy gentlemen have witnessed against him; also you have heard his reply and confession: it lieth now in your breasts to hang him, or save his life; but yet I think meet to instruct you in our law.

"There was an act made in the days of Pharaoh the great, servant to our prince, that, lest those of a contrary religion should multiply, and grow too strong for him, their males should be thrown into the river. Exod. i. There was also an act made in the days of Nebuchadnezzar the great, another of his servants, that whoever would not fall down and worship his golden image, should be thrown into a fiery furnace. Dan. iii. There was also an act made in the days of Darius, that whoso for some time called upon any God but him, should be cast into the lion's den. Dan. vi. Now the substance of these laws this rebel has broken, not only in thought, (which is not to be borne,) but also in word and deed; which must, therefore, needs be intolerable.

"For that of Pharaoh, his law was made upon a supposition, to prevent mischief, no crime being yet apparent; but here is a crime apparent. For the second and third, you see he disputeth against our religion; and for the treason that he hath confessed, he deserveth to die the death."

Then went the jury out, whose names were Mr. Blindman, Mr. Nogood, Mr. Malice, Mr. Lovelust, Mr. Liveloose, Mr. Heady, Mr. Highmind, Mr. Enmity, Mr. Liar, Mr. Cruelty, Mr. Hatelight, and Mr. Implacable; who every one gave in his private verdict against him among themselves, and afterward unanimously concluded to bring him in guilty before the judge. And first among themselves, Mr. Blindman, the foreman, said, "I see clearly that this man is a heretic." Then said Mr. Nogood, "Away with such a fellow from the earth." "Ay," said Mr. Malice, "for I hate the very looks of him." Then said Mr. Lovelust, "I could never endure him." "Nor I," said Mr. Liveloose, "for he would always be condemning my way." "Hang him! hang him!" said Mr. Heady. 'A sorry scrub," said Mr. Highmind. "My heart riseth against him," said Mr. Enmity. "He is a rogue," said Mr. Liar. "Hanging is too good for him," said Mr. Cruelty. "Let us despatch him out of the way," said Mr. Hatelight. Then said Mr. Implacable, "Might I have all the world given me, I could not be reconciled to him; therefore let us forthwith bring him in guilty of death."

And so they did; therefore he was presently condemned to be had from the place where he was, to the place from whence he came, and there to be put to the most cruel death that could be invented.

They, therefore, brought him out to do with him according to their law; and first they scourged him, then they buffeted him, then they lanced his flesh with knives; after that they stoned him with stones; then pricked him with their swords; and last of all, they burned him to ashes at the stake. Thus came Faithful to his end.[7]

Now I saw, that there stood behind the multitude a chariot and a couple of horses waiting for Faithful, who (so soon as his adversaries had despatched him) was taken up into it, and straightway was carried up through the clouds with sound of trumpet, the nearest way to the celestial gate. But as for Christian, he had some respite, and was remanded back to prison; so he there remained for a space. But He who overrules all things, having the power of their rage in his own

[7] The description of Faithful's trial is a picture drawn to the life if not *from* the life, of some of the proceedings against those who were persecuted for religion's sake, by a professedly Protestant church and government, in Bunyan's own day. The character of "Lord Hategood" finds more than a counterpart in that of the infamous Judge Jeffreys, whose cruelty, hatred of religion, and perversions of justice, were as great as are attributed to Hategood by our author; and his language to those who were so unfortunate as to be brought before him, was even more intemperate and abusive. On the trial of Richard Baxter (in 1684) "old blockhead; unthankful villain; conceited, stubborn, fanatical dog," were the epithets which he applied to that holy man. "Hang him," said he, "this one old fellow hath cast more reproach upon the constitution and discipline of our church than will be wiped off this hundred years; but I'll handle him for it: he deserves to be whipped through the city." . . . "I know thou hast a mighty party, but by the grace of Almighty God, I'll crush you all. Come, what do you say for yourself, you old knave; come, speak up I am not afraid of you, for all the snivelling calves you have got about you," alluding to some persons who were in tears about Mr. Baxter. The burning scene, which followed Faithful's trial, belongs to an earlier period, when Mary, and Bonner, and Gardner, kindled the fires of Smithfield, for those who would not bow the knee to the Baal of Popery.

hand, so wrought it about, that Christian for that time escaped them, and went on his way.

And as he went he sang, saying,—

> "Well, Faithful, thou hast faithfully profest
> Unto thy Lord, with whom thou shalt be blest,
> When faithless ones, with all their vain delights,
> Are crying out under their hellish plights:
> Sing, Faithful, sing, and let thy name survive;
> For though they killed thee, thou art yet alive."[8]

[8] Was not this man, think you, a giant? Had he not also hold of the shield of faith? And did he not behave himself valiantly? Was not his mind elevated a thousand degrees beyond sense, carnal reason, fleshly love, self-concerns, and the desires of embracing temporal things? This man had got that by the end that pleased him, neither could threats nor reproaches make him once listen to, or desire to inquire after, what the world or the glory of it could afford. His mind was captivated with delights invisible; he coveted to show his love to his Lord, by laying down his life for his sake; he longed to be there where there shall be no more pain, nor sorrow, nor sighing, nor fears, nor troubles. He was a man of a thousand.—*Bunyan's House of the Forest of Lebanon.*

CHAPTER X.

Christian finds another companion in Hopeful, who accompanies him from Vanity Fair—They overtake By-ends, with whom Christian enters into discourse—By-ends leaves the Pilgrims and falls in with company more to his mind—Demas invites the Pilgrims to turn aside to see a silver mine—By-ends and his companions go to the mine and are seen no more—A strange monument.

Now I saw in my dream, that Christian went not forth alone; for there was one whose name was Hopeful, (being so made by the beholding of Christian and Faithful in their words and behaviour, in their sufferings at the fair,) who joined himself unto him, and entering into a brotherly covenant, told him that he would be his companion. Thus one died to bear testimony to the truth, and another rises out of his ashes to be a companion with Christian in his pilgrimage. This Hopeful also told Christian that there were many more of the men in the fair that would take their time and follow after.[1]

So I saw, that quickly after they were got out of the fair they overtook one that was going before them, whose name was By-ends; so they said to him, "What

[1] The faithful Christian, in his patient sufferings, knows not what work he may do for God. Thy blood will have a voice before men, and that possibly for their good. Who knows but thy blood may be so remembered by thy children, neighbours, and enemies, as to convince them thou wert for the truth? Yea, who knows but their thoughts of thy resolution for Christ, in thy resisting unto blood, may have so good an effect upon some, as to persuade them to close with his ways? The three children in the fiery furnace made Nebuchadnezzar cry out, There was no God like theirs. Indeed this is hard la bour; but be content; the dearer thou payest for it to win the souls of others, the greater will be thy crown when the Lord the righteous judge shall appear.—*Bunyan on Paul's Departure and Crown.*

countryman, sir? and how far go you this way?" He told them that he came from the town of Fairspeech, and he was going to the celestial city; but told them not his name.

"From Fairspeech," said Christian; "is there any good that lives there?" Prov. xxvi, 25.

"Yes," said By-ends, "I hope."

Chr. Pray, sir, what may I call you?

By-ends. I am a stranger to you, and you to me: if you be going this way, I shall be glad of your company; if not, I must be content.

Chr. This town of Fairspeech: I have heard of it; and, as I remember, they say it's a wealthy place.

By-ends. Yes, I will assure you that it is; and I have very many rich kindred there.

Chr. Pray who are your kindred there, if a man may be so bold?

By-ends. Almost the whole town; but in particular my Lord Turnabout, my Lord Timeserver, my Lord Fairspeech, from whose ancestors that town took its name; also Mr. Smoothman, Mr. Facing-both-ways, Mr. Anything; and the parson of our parish, Mr. Two-tongues, was my mother's own brother, by father's side; and, to tell you the truth, I am become a gentleman of good quality; yet my great grand-father was but a waterman, looking one way and rowing another, and I got most of my estate by the same occupation.

Chr. Are you a married man?

By-ends. Yes, and my wife is a very virtuous woman, the daughter of a virtuous woman; she was my Lady Feigning's daughter; therefore she came of a very honourable family, and is arrived to such a pitch of breeding, that she knows how to carry it to all, even to prince and peasant. 'Tis true, we somewhat differ in religion from those of the stricter sort, yet but in two small points; First, we never strive against wind and tide. Secondly, we are always most zealous when Religion goes in his silver slippers; we love much to walk with him in the street if the sun shines and the people applaud him.

Then Christian stepped a little aside to his fellow Hopeful, saying, "It runs in my mind that this is one By-ends, of Fairspeech; and if it be he, we have as very a knave in our company as dwelleth in all these parts." Then said Hopeful, "Ask him; methinks he should not be ashamed of his name." So Christian came up with him again, and said, "Sir, you talk as if you knew something more than all the world doth; and, if I take not my mark amiss, I deem I have half a guess of you. Is not your name Mr. By-ends, of Fairspeech?"

By-ends. This is not my name; but indeed, it is a nick name that is given me by some that cannot abide me, and I must be content to bear it as a reproach, as other good men have borne theirs before me.

Chr. But did you never give an occasion to men to call upon you by this name?

By-ends. Never, never! The worst that ever I did to give them occasion to give me this name was, that I had always the luck to jump in my judgment with the present way of the times, whatever it was, and my chance was to *get* thereby; but if things are thus cast upon me, let me count them a blessing; but let not the malicious load me, therefore, with reproach.

Chr. I thought, indeed, that you were the man that I heard of; and to tell you what I think, I fear this name belongs to you more properly than you are willing we should think it doth.

By-ends. Well, if you will thus imagine, I cannot help it. You shall find me a fair company-keeper, if you will still admit me your associate.

Chr. If you will go with us, you must go against wind and tide; the which, I perceive, is against your opinion. You must also own Religion in his rags, as well as when in his silver slippers; and stand by him, too, when bound in irons, as well as when he walketh the streets with applause.

By-ends. You must not impose nor lord it over my faith; leave me to my liberty, and let me go with you.

Chr. Not a step further, unless you will do, in what I propound, as we.

Then said By-ends, "I shall never desert my old principles, since they are harmless and profitable. If I may not go with you, I must do as I did before you overtook me, even go by myself, until some overtake me that will be glad of my company."

Now I saw in my dream, that Christian and Hopeful forsook him, and kept their distance before him; but one of them, looking back, saw three men following Mr. By-ends; and, behold, as they came up with him, he made them a very low congée; and they also gave him a compliment. The men's names were, Mr. Hold-the-world, Mr. Money-love, and Mr. Save-all, men that Mr. By-ends had formerly been acquainted with, for in their minority they were school-fellows, and were taught by one Mr. Gripeman, a schoolmaster in Love-gain, which is a market-town in the county of Coveting, in the North. This schoolmaster taught them the art of getting, either by violence, cozenage, flattery, lying.

or by putting on a guise of religion; and these four gentlemen had attained much of the art of their master, so that they could each of them have kept such a school themselves.

Well, when they had, as I said, thus saluted each other, Mr. Money-love said to Mr. By-ends, "Who are they upon the road before us?" for Christian and Hopeful were yet within view.

By-ends. They are a couple of far countymen, that, after their mode, are going on pilgrimage.

Money-love. Alas! why did not they stay, that we might have had their good company? for they, and we, and you, sir, I hope, are all going on pilgrimage.

By-ends. We are so, indeed; but the men before us are so rigid, and love so much their own notions, and do also so lightly esteem the opinions of others, that let a man be never so godly, yet if he jumps not with them in all things, they thrust him quite out of their company.

Save-all. That's bad; but we read of some that are righteous overmuch; and such men's rigidness prevails with them to judge and condemn all but themselves. But I pray, what, and how many, were the things wherein you differed?

By-ends. Why they, after their headstrong manner, conclude that it is their duty to rush on their journey all weathers; and I am for waiting for wind and tide. They are for hazarding all for God at a clap; and I am for taking all advantages to secure my life and estate. They are for holding their notions, though all other men be against them; but I am for religion in what, and so far as, the times and my safety will bear it. They are for Religion when in rags and contempt; but

I am for him when he walks in his silver slippers, in the sunshine, and with applause.

Hold-the-world. Ay, and hold you there still, good Mr. By-ends; for, for my part, I can count him but a fool, that having the liberty to keep what he has, shall be so unwise as to lose it. Let us be wise as serpents. It is best to make hay while the sun shines. You see how the bee lieth still all winter, and bestirs her only when she can have profit with pleasure. God sends sometimes rain, and sometimes sunshine; if they be such fools to go through the first, yet let us be content to take fair weather along with us. For my part, I like that religion best that will stand with the security of God's good blessings unto us;[2] for who can imagine, that is ruled by his reason, since God has bestowed upon us the good things of this life, but that he would have us keep them for his sake? Abraham and Solomon grew rich in religion; and Job says, that "a good man shall lay up gold as dust;" but he must not be

[2] They that look upon their outward enjoyments to be [of themselves] tokens of God's special grace unto them, are deceived: for, as it is in the parable, (of the rich man and Lazarus,) a man of wealth and a child of the devil may make but one person; or a man may have abundance of outward enjoyments, and yet be carried by devils into eternal burning. But this is a trap in which the devil hath caught many thousands of poor souls, namely, by getting them to judge according to outward appearance, or according to God's outward blessings. Do but ask a poor, carnal, covetous wretch, how he should know a man to be in a happy state; and he will answer, "Those that God blesseth, and giveth abundance of this world unto." They are so ignorant as to think that because a man is increased in outward things, therefore God doth love that man with a special love, or else he would never so prosper the work of his hands. Ah, poor soul! take heed that it be not said to you hereafter, when you would very willingly have heaven, "Remember, in your lifetime you had your good things, in your lifetime you had your portion."—*Bunyan's Sighs from Hell.*

such as the men before us, if they be as you have described them.

Save-all. I think that we are all agreed in this matter; and therefore there needs no more words about it.

Money-love. No, there needs no more words about this matter indeed; for he that believes neither Scripture nor reason, (and you see we have both on our side,) neither knows his own liberty nor seeks his own safety.

By-ends. My brethren, we are, as you see, going all on pilgrimage; and for our better diversion from things that are bad, give me leave to propound unto you this question:—

Suppose a man, a minister, or a tradesman, &c., should have an advantage lie before him to get the good blessings of this life, yet so as that he can by no means come by them, except, in appearance at least, he becomes extraordinary zealous in some points of religion that he meddled not with before; may he not use this means to attain his end, and yet be a right honest man?

Money-love. I see the bottom of your question; and with these gentlemen's good leave, I will endeavour to shape you an answer. And first, to speak to your question as it concerneth a minister himself: suppose a minister, a worthy man, possessed but of a very small benefice, and has in his eye a greater, more fat and plump by far; he has also now an opportunity of getting it, yet so as by being more studious, by preaching more frequently and zealously, and, because the temper of the people requires it, by altering of some of his principles: for my part, I see no reason why a man may not do this, (provided he has a call,) ay, and more a great deal besides, and yet be an honest man. For why?

1. His desire of a greater benefice is lawful, (this cannot be contradicted,) since it is set before him by Providence; so then he may get it if he can, making no question for conscience' sake.

2. Besides, his desire after that benefice makes him more studious, a more zealous preacher, &c., and so makes him a better man; yea, makes him better improve his parts, which is according to the mind of God.

3. Now, as for his complying with the temper of his people, by deserting, to serve them, some of his principles, this argueth, (1) that he is of a self-denying temper; (2) of a sweet and winning deportment; and (3) so more fit for the ministerial function.

4. I conclude, then, that a minister that changes a small for a great, should not, for so doing, be judged as covetous; but rather, since he is improved in his parts and industry thereby, be counted as one that pursues his call, and the opportunity put into his hand to do good.

And now to the second part of the question, which concerns the tradesman you mentioned. Suppose such an one to have but a poor employ in the world, but by becoming religious, he may mend his market, perhaps get a rich wife, or more and far better customers to his shop; for my part, I see no reason but this may be lawfully done. For why?

1. To become religious is a virtue, by what means soever man becomes so.

2. Nor is it unlawful to get a rich wife, or more custom to my shop.

3. Besides, the man that gets these by becoming re-

ligious, gets that which is good of them that are good, by becoming good himself; so then here is a good wife, and good customers, and good gain, and all these by becoming religious, which is good: therefore, to become religious to get all these is a good and profitable design.[3]

This answer, thus made by Mr. Money-love to Mr. By-ends' question, was highly applauded by them all; wherefore they concluded upon the whole, that it was most wholesome and advantageous. And because, as they thought, no man was able to contradict it, and because Christian and Hopeful were yet within call, they jointly agreed to assault them with the question as soon as they overtook them; and the rather because they had opposed Mr. By-ends before. So they called after them, and they stopped and stood still till they came up to them; but they concluded as they went, that not Mr. By-ends, but old Mr. Hold-the-world, should propound the question to them, because, as they supposed, their answer to him would be without the remainder of that heat that was kindled betwixt Mr. By-ends and them at their parting a little before.

[3] No man that either feareth God, regardeth the credit of religion, or the salvation of his own soul, will do thus. Professors perhaps there may be, who make profession a stalking-horse to beguile their neighbours out of their estates, as Mr. Badman himself did, when he beguiled her that is now with sorrow his wife; and who can help it? How can we help it if men ascribe to themselves the title of godly ones, and while they thus call themselves, should be the veriest rogues imaginable? True they are a scandal to religion, a grief to the honest-hearted, an offence to the world, and a stumbling-block to the weak; and these offences have come, and will come, do what all the world can; *but wo be to them through whom they come.* Let such professors, therefore, be disowned by all true Christians, and reckoned among those base men of the world whom by such actions they most resemble. They are Mr. Badman's kindred. They are a shame to religion, and religious men should be ashamed of them.—*Bunyan's Life and Death of Mr. Badman*

So they came up to each other, and after a short salutation, Mr. Hold-the-world propounded the question to Christian and his fellow, and bid them to answer it, if they could.

Then said Christian, "Even a babe in religion may answer ten thousand such questions. For if it be unlawful to follow Christ for loaves, as it is, (John vi, 26,) how much more abominable is it to make of him and religion a stalking-horse to get and enjoy the world! Nor do we find any other than heathens, hypocrites, devils, and witches, that are of this opinion:

"1. Heathens: for when Hamor and Shechem had a mind to the daughter and cattle of Jacob, and saw that there was no way for them to come at them but by becoming circumcised, they said to their companions, 'If every male of us be circumcised, as they are circumcised, shall not their cattle, and their substance, and every beast of theirs be ours?' Their daughters and their cattle were that which they sought to obtain, and their religion the stalking-horse they made use of to come at them. Read the whole story. Gen. xxxiv.

"2. The hypocritical Pharisees were also of this religion: long prayers were their pretence; but to get widows' houses was their intent, and greater damnation was from God their judgment. Luke xx, 46, 47.

"3. Judas the devil was also of this religion; he was religious for the bag, that he might be possessed of what was put therein; but he was lost, cast away, and the very son of Perdition.

"4. Simon the wizard was of this religion too: for he would have had the Holy Ghost, that he might have got money therewith; and his sentence from Peter's mouth was according. Acts viii, 19–22.

"5. Neither will it out of my mind, but that that man that takes up religion for the world, will throw away religion for the world; for so surely as Judas designed the world in becoming religious, so surely did he also sell religion and his Master for the same. To answer the question, therefore, affirmatively, as I perceive you have done, and to accept of, as authentic, such answer, is both heathenish, hypocritical, and devilish; and your reward will be according to your works."

Then they stood staring one upon another, but had not wherewith to answer Christian. Hopeful also approved of the soundness of Christian's answer; so there was a great silence among them. Mr. By-ends and his company also staggered, and kept behind, that Christian and Hopeful might outgo them. Then said Christian to his fellow, "If these men cannot stand before the sentence of men, what will they do with the sentence of God? And if they are mute when dealt with by vessels of clay, what will they do when they shall be rebuked by the flames of a devouring fire?"

Then Christian and Hopeful outwent them again, and went till they came at a delicate plain, called Ease, where they went with much content; but that plain was but narrow, so they were quickly got over it. Now at the further side of that plain was a little hill, called Lucre, and in that hill a silver mine, which some of them that had formerly gone that way, because of the rarity of it, had turned aside to see; but going too near the brim of the pit, the ground being deceitful under them, broke, and they were slain: some also had been maimed there, and could not, to their dying day, be their own men again.

Then I saw in my dream, that a little off the road

over against the silver mine, stood Demas (gentleman-like) to call to passengers to come and see; who said to Christian and his fellow, "Ho! turn aside hither, and I will show you a thing."

Chr. What thing so deserving as to turn us out of the way to see it?

Demas. Here is a silver mine, and some digging in it for treasure; if you will come, with a little pains you may richly provide for yourselves.

Then said Hopeful, "Let us go see."

"Not I," said Christian; "I have heard of this place before now, and how many have there been slain; and besides, that treasure is a snare to those that seek it, for it hindereth them in their pilgrimage."

Then Christian called to Demas, saying, "Is not the place dangerous? Hath it not hindered many in their pilgrimage?" Mark x, 23; 1 Tim. vi, 9.

Demas. Not very dangerous, except to those that are careless.—But withal, he blushed as he spake.

Then said Christian to Hopeful, "Let us not stir a step, but still keep on our way."

Hope. I will warrant you, when By-ends comes up, if he hath the same invitation as we, he will turn in thither to see.

Chr. No doubt thereof, for his principles lead him that way; and a hundred to one but he dies there.

Then Demas called again, saying, "But will you not come over and see?"

Then Christian roundly answered, saying, "Demas, thou art an enemy to the right ways of the Lord of this way, and hast been already condemned for thine own turning aside, by one of his Majesty's judges, (2 Tim. iv, 10;) and why seekest thou to bring us into the like condemnation? Besides, if we at all turn aside, our Lord the King will certainly hear thereof, and will there put us to shame, where we would stand with boldness before him."

Demas cried again, that he also was one of their fraernity; and that if they would tarry a little he also himself would walk with them.

Then said Christian, "What is thy name? Is it not the same by the which I have called thee?"

Demas. Yes, my name is Demas; I am the son of Abraham.

Chr. I know you; Gehazi was your great grandfather, and Judas your father, and you have trod in their steps; it is but a devilish prank that thou usest; thy father was hanged for a traitor, and thou deservest no better reward. Assure thyself, that when we come to the King, we will tell him of this thy behaviour.—Thus they went their way.

By this time By-ends and his companions were come again within sight, and they at the first beck went over to Demas. Now, whether they fell into the pit by looking over the brink thereof, or whether they went down to dig, or whether they were smothered in the bottom by the damps that commonly arise, of these things I am not certain; but this I observed, that they were never seen again in the way. Then sang Christian:—

"By-ends and silver Demas both agree;
One calls, the other runs, that he may be
A sharer in his lucre: so these do
Take up in this world, and no further go."

Now I saw that, just on the other side of this plain, the pilgrims came to a place where stood an old monument hard by the highway-side, at the sight of which they were both concerned, because of the strangeness of the form thereof; for it seemed to them as if it had been a woman transformed into the shape of a pillar. Here, therefore, they stood looking and looking upon it, but could not for a time tell what they should make thereof. At last Hopeful espied, written above upon the head thereof, a writing in an unusual hand; but he, being no scholar, called to Christian (for he was learned) to see if he could pick out the meaning: so he came, and after a little laying of letters together, he found the same to be this, "Remember Lot's wife." So he read it to his fellow; after which they both concluded that that was the pillar of salt into which Lot's wife was turned, for her looking back with a covetous heart when she was going from Sodom for safety, (Gen. xix, 26;) which sudden and amazing sight gave them occasion of this discourse.

Chr. Ah, my brother! this is a seasonable sight; it came opportunely to us after the invitation which Demas gave us to come over to view the hill Lucre; and had we gone over as he desired us, and as thou wast inclined to do, my brother, we had, for aught I know, been made ourselves a spectacle for those that shall come after, to behold.

Hope. I am sorry that I was so foolish, and made to wonder that I am not now as Lot's wife; for wherein was the difference betwixt her sin and mine? She only looked back, and I had a desire to go see. Let grace be adored; and let me be ashamed that ever such a thing should be in mine heart.

Chr. Let us take notice of what we see here, for our help for time to come. This woman escaped one judgment, for she fell not by the destruction of Sodom: yet she was destroyed by another; as we see she is turned into a pillar of salt.

Hope. True; and she may be to us both caution and example: caution, that we should shun her sin, or a sign of what judgment will overtake such as shall not be prevented by this caution; so Korah, Dathan, and Abiram, with the two hundred and fifty men that perished in their sin, did also become a sign or example to others to beware. Num. xvi, 31, 32; xxvi, 9, 10. But above all, I muse at one thing, to wit, how Demas and his fellows can stand so confidently yonder to look for that treasure, which this woman but for looking behind her after (for we read not that she stepped one foot out of the way) was turned into a pillar of salt; especially since the judgment which overtook her did but make her an example within sight of where they are; for they cannot choose but see her, did they but lift up their eyes.

Chr. It is a thing to be wondered at, and it argueth that their hearts are grown desperate in the case; and I cannot tell who to compare them to so fitly, as to them that pick pockets in the presence of the judge, or that will cut purses under the gallows. It is said of the men of Sodom, that "they were sinners exceedingly," because they were sinners "before the Lord," that is, in his eye-sight and notwithstanding the kind nesses that he had showed them; for the land of Sodom was now like the garden of Eden heretofore. Gen. xiii, 10–13. This, therefore, provoked him the more to jealousy, and made their plague as hot as the fire of the Lord out of heaven could make it. And it is most rationally to be concluded, that such, even such as these are that shall sin in the sight, yea, and that too in despite of such examples that are set continually before them to caution them to the contrary, must be partakers of severest judgments.

Hope. Doubtless thou hast said the truth; but what a mercy is it that neither thou, but especially I, am not made myself this example! This ministereth occasion to us to thank God, to fear before him, and always to remember Lot's wife.

CHAPTER XI.

The pilgrims come to a pleasant river, and travel awhile by its side—Finding the way difficult after they leave the river, they turn aside into By-path Meadow—They are caught by Giant Despair trespassing on his grounds, and are thrust into Doubting Castle—Their sad condition there—Deliverance comes at last.

I SAW then that they went on their way to a pleasant river, which David the king called "the river of God," Psalm lxv, 9; but John, "the river of the water of life." Rev. xxii, 1. Now their way lay just upon the bank of this river: here, therefore, Christian and his companion walked with great delight; they drank also of the water of the river, which was pleasant and enlivening to their weary spirits.[1] Besides, on the banks of this river, on either side, were green trees with all manner of fruit; and the leaves they ate to prevent surfeits, and other diseases that are incident to those that heat their blood by travel. On either side of the river was also a meadow, curiously beautified with lilies; and it was green all the year long. In this meadow they lay down and slept, for here they might lie down safely.

[1] This water of life is nothing else but the manifold grace of God in Christ, for both the words, *water* and *life*, are but metaphorical sayings, under which is held forth some better and more excellent thing. And indeed it is frequent with God in Scripture to speak of his grace and mercy under the notion of waters. It is called water, because it quencheth the spiritual thirst of them that by faith do drink thereof: "I will give," saith Christ, "to him that is a-thirst, of the water of life freely;" and again, "He that drinketh of the water that I shall give him shall never thirst." From this water of life come all those heavenly and spiritual quickenings and revivings that do fetch again and cheer up the sinking soul. "There is a river, the streams whereof make glad the city of God."—*Bunyan's Holy City.*

Psa. xxiii, 2. When they awoke, they gathered again of the fruit of the trees, and drank again of the water of the river, and then lay down again to sleep. Thus they did several days and nights. Then they sang:—

"Behold ye how these crystal streams do glide,
To comfort pilgrims by the highway-side!
The meadows green, besides their fragrant smell,
Yield dainties for them; and he who can tell
What pleasant fruit, yea, leaves, these trees do yield,
Will soon sell all, that he may buy this field."

So when they were disposed to go on, (for they were not as yet at their journey's end,) they ate, and drank, and departed.

Now I beheld in my dream, that they had not journeyed far, but the river and the way for a time parted, at which they were not a little sorry; yet they durst not go out of the way. Now the way from the river was rough, and their feet tender by reason of their travel; so the souls of the pilgrims were much discouraged because of the way. Wherefore still as they went on, they wished for a better way. Now a little before them, there was on the left hand of the road a meadow, and a stile to go over into it, and that meadow is called By-path Meadow. Then said Christian to his fellow, "If this meadow lieth along by our way-side, let's go over into it." Then he went to the stile to see, and behold a path lay along by the way on the other side of the fence. "It is according to my wish," said Christian; "here is the easiest going; come, good Hopeful, and let us go over."

Hope. But how if this path should lead us out of the way?

"That is not likely," said the other. "Look, doth

it not go along by the way-side?" So Hopeful, being persuaded by his fellow, went after him over the stile. When they were gone over, and were got into the path, they found it very easy for their feet; and withal, they, looking before them, espied a man walking as they did, and his name was Vain Confidence: so they called after him, and asked him whither that way led. He said, "To the celestial gate." "Look," said Christian, "did not I tell you so? by this you may see we are right." So they followed, and he went before them. But behold the night came on, and it grew very dark; so that they that were behind lost the sight of him that went before.

He therefore that went before, (Vain Confidence by name,) not seeing the way before him, fell into a deep pit, which was on purpose there made, by the prince of those grounds, to catch vain-glorious fools withal, and was dashed in pieces with his fall.

Now Christian and his fellow heard him fall. So they called to know the matter, but there was none to answer, only they heard a groaning. Then said Hopeful, "Where are we now?" Then was his fellow silent, as mistrusting that he had led him out of the way. And now it began to rain, and thunder and lighten in a most dreadful manner, and the water rose amain.[2]

[2] Though the path of duty may sometimes be difficult, thou must not therefore turn aside from it, but cry for help to Him who hath promised that his grace shall be sufficient for thee; and he will,

"Though rough and thorny be the way,
Thy strength proportion to thy day."

Other ways may offer themselves that seem to be "easier going," and also appear at first to lead to the Celestial City; but if thou valuest thy soul, if thou wouldst escape hell and gain heaven, beware of these "by-paths;" set not thy foot in them, though they seem ever so

Then Hopeful groaned in himself, saying, "O that I had kept on my way!"

Chr. Who could have thought that this path should have led us out of the way?

Hope. I was afraid on't at the very first, and therefore gave you that gentle caution. I would have spoke plainer, but that you are older than I.

Chr. Good brother, be not offended; I am sorry I have brought thee out of the way, and that I have put thee into such imminent danger. Pray, my brother, forgive me; I did not do it of an evil intent.

Hope. Be comforted, my brother, for I forgive thee; and believe, too, that this shall be for our good.

Chr. I am glad I have with me a merciful brother; but we must not stand here; let us try to go back again.

Hope. But, good brother, let me go before.

Chr. No, if you please let me go first, that if there be any danger, I may be first therein, because by my means we are both gone out of the way.

"No," said Hopeful, "you shall not go first, for your mind being troubled may lead you out of the way again." Then for their encouragement they heard the voice of one saying, "Let thine heart be toward the highway, even the way that thou wentest; turn again." Jer. xxxi, 21. But by this time the waters were greatly risen, by reason of which the way of going back

smooth and tempting. Remember what the wise man hath said: "There is a way that seemeth right unto a man, but the end thereof are the ways of death." Prov. iv, 12. Therefore, "Let thine eyes look right on, and let thine eyelids look straight before thee. Ponder the path of thy feet, and let all thy ways be established. Turn not to the right hand nor to the left: remove thy foot from evil." Prov. iv, 25–27.

was very dangerous. (Then I thought that it is easier going out of the way when we are in, than going in when we are out.) Yet they adventured to go back; but it was so dark, and the flood was so high, that in their going back they had like to have been drowned nine or ten times.[3]

Neither could they, with all the skill they had, get again to the stile that night. Wherefore at last, lighting under a little shelter, they sat down there till the day brake; but, being weary, they fell asleep. Now there was, not far from the place they lay, a castle, called Doubting Castle, the owner whereof was Giant Despair, and it was in his grounds they now were sleeping: wherefore he, getting up in the morning early, and walking up and down in his fields, caught Christian and Hopeful asleep in his grounds. Then with a grim and surly voice he bid them awake, and asked them whence they were, and what they did in his grounds.

[3] It is easier, not only to go out of the way, but also to *keep in it*, than it is to get back when once out, however sincere the backsliding soul may be in its desires, and earnest in its efforts to return. A feeling of shame and self-abhorrence at his unfaithfulness will often so overwhelm the poor wanderer as to cause him to sink into despondency, and a "horror of great darkness" to fall upon him. So deep is the sense of his unworthiness, that he really doubts the willingness of Christ to receive him again; and hence he has but little heart or confidence to pray, but, like Peter when he essayed to walk on the sea, he fears he is sinking even while he is coming to the Saviour. "Indeed I have found it," says Bunyan in his Grace Abounding, "as difficult to come to God by prayer, after backsliding from him, as to do any other thing. O, the shame that did now attend me! especially when I thought I am now a-going to pray to Him for mercy that I had so lightly esteemed but awhile before. It was hard for me now to have the face to pray to this Christ for mercy, against whom I had so vilely sinned. I was ashamed; yea, even confounded. O, who knows how hard a thing I found it to come to God in prayer!" These things are for our admonition

The pilgrims now, to gratify the flesh,
Will seek its ease; but O, how they afresh
Do plunge themselves new griefs into!
Who seek to please the flesh themselves undo.

They told him they were pilgrims, and that they had lost their way. Then said the giant, "You have this night trespassed on me by trampling in and lying on my grounds, and therefore you must go along with me." So they were forced to go, because he was stronger than they. They also had but little to say, for they knew themselves in a fault. The giant, therefore, drove them before him, and put them into his castle, into a very dark dungeon, nasty, and stinking to the spirits of these two men. Here, then, they lay from Wednesday morning till Saturday night, without one bit of bread or drop of drink, or light, or any to ask how they did: they were, therefore, here in evil case, and were far from friends and acquaintance. Now in this place Christian had double sorrow, because it was through his unadvised counsel that they were brought into this distress.

Now Giant Despair had a wife, and her name was Diffidence: so when he was gone to bed he told his wife what he had done, to wit, that he had taken a couple of prisoners, and cast them into his dungeon for trespassing on his grounds. Then he asked her also what he had best to do further with them. So she asked him what they were, whence they came, and whither they were bound, and he told her. Then she counselled him, that when he arose in the morning he should beat them without mercy. So when he arose, he getteth him a grievous crabtree cudgel, and goes down into the dungeon to them, and there first falls to rating of them as if they were dogs, although they never gave him a word of distaste. Then he falls upon them, and beats them fearfully, in such sort that they were not able to help themselves, or to turn them upon the floor. This done, he withdraws and leaves them there to condole their misery, and to mourn under their distress: so all that day they spent their time in nothing but sighs and bitter lamentations. The next night she, talking with her husband further about them, and understanding that they were yet alive, did advise him to counsel them to make away with themselves. So when morning was come, he goes to them in a surly manner, as before, and perceiving them to be very sore with the stripes that he had given them the day before, he told them, that since they were never like to come out of that place, their only way would be forthwith to make an end of themselves, either with knife, halter, or poison: "for why," said he, "should you choose to live, seeing it is attended with so much bitterness?" But they desired him to let them go. With that he looked ugly upon them, and rushing to them, had doubtless made an end of them himself, but that he fell into one of his fits, (for he sometimes in sunshiny weather fell into fits,) and lost for a time the use of his hands; wherefore he withdrew, and left them as before to consider what to do.[4] Then did the prisoners consult between themselves, whether it was best to take his counsel or no; and thus they began to discourse:—

[4] The "sunshiny weather," in which the giant was subject to "fits," represents those transient glimmerings of hope which the desponding soul is sometimes enabled to obtain, and which for the time paralyze the power of despair. Such as these our author was sometimes favoured with when he was shut up in "Doubting Castle." He says, "I had some supports in this temptation; but they were but hints, touches, and short visits, though very sweet when present; only they lasted not, but, like to Peter's sheet, of a sudden were caught up from me to heaven again." He caught a glimpse of the promises, but his faith was as yet too weak to lay hold upon them.

"Brother," said Christian, "what shall we do? The life that we now live is miserable. For my part, I know not whether is best to live thus, or to die out of hand. My soul chooseth strangling rather than life, and the grave is more easy for me than this dungeon. Job vii, 15. Shall we be ruled by the giant?"

Hope. Indeed our present condition is dreadful, and death would be far more welcome to me than thus for ever to abide; but yet let us consider, the Lord of the country to which we are going hath said, "Thou shalt do no murder," no, not to another man's person; much more then are we forbidden to take his counsel to kill ourselves. Besides, he that kills another, can but commit murder upon his body; but for one to kill himself, is to kill body and soul at once. And, moreover, my brother, thou talkest of ease in the grave, but hast thou forgotten the hell whither for certain the murderers go? for "no murderer hath eternal life," &c. And let us consider again, that all the law is not in the hand of Giant Despair; others, so far as I can understand, have been taken by him as well as we, and yet have escaped out of his hands. Who knows but that God, who made the world, may cause that Giant Despair may die; or that at some time or other he may forget to lock us in; or but he may, in a short time, have another of his fits before us, and he may lose the use of his limbs? And if ever that should come to pass again, for my part, I am resolved to pluck up the heart of a man, and to try my utmost to get from under his hand. I was a fool that I did not try to do it before. But, however, my brother, let us be patient, and endure awhile; the time may come that may give us a happy release; but let us not be our own murderers. With these words Hopeful at present did moderate the mind of his brother; so they continued together in the dark that day, in their sad and doleful condition.

Well, toward evening the giant goes down into the dungeon again, to see if his prisoners had taken his counsel. But when he came there he found them alive; and truly, alive was all; for now, what for want of bread and water, and by reason of the wounds they received when he beat them, they could do little but breathe. But I say he found them alive; at which he fell into a grievous rage, and told them that seeing they had disobeyed his counsel, it should be worse with them than if they had never been born.

At this they trembled greatly, and I think that Christian fell into a swoon; but coming a little to himself again, they renewed their discourse about the giant's counsel, and whether yet they had best take it or no. Now Christian again seemed for doing it; but Hopeful made his second reply as followeth:—

"My brother," said he, "rememberest thou not how valiant thou hast been heretofore? Apollyon could not crush thee, nor could all that thou didst hear, or see, or feel, in the Valley of the Shadow of Death. What hardship, terror, and amazement hast thou already gone through! and art thou now nothing but fears! Thou seest that I am in the dungeon with thee, a far weaker man by nature than thou art. Also this giant hath wounded me as well as thee, and also cut off the bread and water from my mouth, and with thee I mourn without the light. But let us exercise a little more patience. Remember how thou playedst the man at Vanity Fair, and wast neither afraid of the chain nor cage, nor yet of bloody death: wherefore let us (at least to avoid the shame that it becomes not a Christian to be found in) bear up with patience as well as we can."[5]

Now night being come again, and the giant and his wife being in bed, she asked him concerning the prisoners, and if they had taken his counsel: to which he replied, "They are sturdy rogues; they choose rather to bear all hardships than to make away with themselves." "Then," said she, "take them into the castle-yard to-morrow, and show them the bones and skulls of those that thou hast already despatched, and make them believe, ere a week comes to an end, thou wilt tear them in pieces, as thou hast done their fellows before them."

So when the morning was come, the giant goes to them again, and takes them into the castle-yard, and shows them as his wife had bidden him. "These," said he, "were pilgrims, as you are, once, and they trespassed on my grounds as you have done; and when I thought fit I tore them in pieces, and so within ten days I will do you.[6] Go get you down to your den

[5] The remembrance of former deliverances should excite confidence in, as well as gratitude to, the great Author of them. While we "praise Him for that which is past," we should remember that it is not less our duty to "trust him for what is to come." "The salvation of the righteous is of the Lord; he is their strength in the time of trouble. And the Lord shall help them, and deliver them, because they trust in him." Psa. xxxvii, 39, 40. Cheer up, then, desponding pilgrim, who art ready to say, "I shall now assuredly fall by the hand of the enemy:" why art thou cast down, and why is thy soul disquieted within thee; hope thou in God, and thou shalt yet praise him for the help of his countenance. Be faithful, and "He who delivered thee out of the paw of the lion, and out of the paw of the bear, will also deliver thee out of the hand of this Philistine." 1 Sam. xvii, 37.

[6] This is no uncommon device of the adversary. Bunyan himself, in relating one of his fearful conflicts with Satan, when he was almost shut up in despair, says, "Then hath the tempter come upon me with

again." And with that he beat them all the way thither. They lay, therefore, all day on Saturday in lamentable case, as before. Now when night was come, and when Mrs. Diffidence and her husband, the giant, were got to bed, they began to renew their discourse of their prisoners; and withal the old giant wondered, that he could neither by his blows nor counsel bring them to an end. And with that his wife replied, "I fear," said she, "that they live in hopes that some will come to relieve them; or that they have picklocks about them, by the means of which they hope to escape." "And sayest thou so, my dear?" said the giant; "I will therefore search them in the morning."

Well, on Saturday, about midnight, they began to pray, and continued in prayer till almost break of day.[7]

such discouragements as these: 'You are very hot after mercy, but I will cool you; this frame shall not last always; many have been as hot as you for a spirt, but I have quenced their zeal:' and with this, *such and such who were fallen off would be set before mine eyes.* Then I would be *afraid that I should do so too!*" Thus do these miserable backsliders not only make shipwreck of their own souls, but also prove a stumbling-block and a snare to the souls of others.

[7] The time of guilt contracted, and of the hiding of God's face, is a time of need—a dangerous time. If thou now shalt forbear to pray, thou art undone; for the natural tendency of guilt is to drive a man from God. So it served our first father; and ofttimes when God hides his face, men run into desperation, and so throw up all duties, and say as he of old, "Why should I wait upon the Lord any longer?" Now thy great help against this is prayer—continuing in prayer. Prayer wrestleth with the devil, and will overthrow him; prayer wrestleth with God, and will overcome him; prayer wrestleth with all temptations, and makes them fly. Great things have been done by prayer, even by the prayer of those that have contracted guilt, and by their sins lost the smiles and sense of the favour of God. Therefore when this needy, this evil time has overtaken thee, *pray!* ply it hard; "come boldly to the throne of grace, to obtain mercy, and find grace to help in time of need."—*Bunyan's Saint's Privilege*

Now, a little before it was day, good Christian, as one half amazed, brake out into this passionate speech: "What a fool," quoth he, "am I to lie in a stinking dungeon, when I may as well walk at liberty! I have a key in my bosom, called Promise, that will, I am persuaded, open any lock in Doubting Castle." Then said Hopeful, "That's good news; good brother, pluck it out of thy bosom, and try."

Then Christian pulled it out of his bosom, and began to try at the dungeon door, whose bolt, as he turned the key, gave back, and the door flew open with ease, and Christian and Hopeful both came out. Then he went to the outward door that leads into the castle-yard, and with his key opened that door also. After that he went to the iron gate, for that must be opened too, but that lock went desperate hard, yet the key did open it. Then they thrust open the gate to make their escape with speed; but that gate, as it opened, made such a creaking that it waked Giant Despair, who, hastily rising to pursue his prisoners, felt his limbs to fail; for his fits took him again, so that he could by no means go after them. Then they went on, and came to the King's highway again, and so were safe, because they were out of his jurisdiction.

Now when they were gone over the stile, they began to contrive with themselves what they should do at that stile, to prevent those that shall come after from falling into the hands of Giant Despair. So they consented to erect there a pillar, and to engrave upon the side thereof this sentence:—"Over this stile is the way to Doubting Castle, which is kept by Giant Despair, who despiseth the King of the celestial country, and seeks to destroy his holy pilgrims." Many, therefore, that followed after, read what was written, and es caped the danger. This done, they sang as follows :—

> "Out of the way we went, and then we found
> What 'twas to tread upon forbidden ground:
> And let them that come after have a care
> Lest they, for trespassing, his pris'ners are,
> Whose castle's Doubting, and whose name's Despair."

The following lines, from one of Charles Wesley's hymns "for backsliders recovered," are exceedingly appropriate to the cases of all those who, like the pilgrims, have been a second time delivered from the "snare of the fowler:"—

> "Son of God, if thy free grace
> Again hath raised me up;
> Call'd me still to seek thy face,
> And given me back my hope:
> Still thy timely help afford,
> And all thy loving kindness show,
> Keep me, keep me, gracious Lord,
> And never let me go.
>
> "By me, O my Saviour, stand,
> In sore temptation's hour;
> Save me with thine outstretch'd hand,
> And show forth all thy power;
> O be mindful of thy word!
> Thy all-sufficient grace bestow;
> Keep me, keep me, gracious Lord,
> And never let me go.
>
> "Give me, Lord, a holy fear,
> And fix it in my heart;
> That I may from evil near,
> With timely care depart;
> Let thy love my heart constrain,
> And all my restless passions sway:
> Keep me lest I turn again
> Out of the narrow way."

CHAPTER XII.

The Pilgrims come to the Delectable Mountains—Their talk with the Shepherds—The Shepherds welcome them—The names of the Shepherds—The Mountain of Error—Mount Caution—A by-way to Hell—The Shepherds' perspective glass—A two-fold caution.

THEY then went till they came to the Delectable Mountains, which mountains belong to the Lord of that hill of which we have spoken before. So they went up to the mountains, to behold the gardens and orchards, the vineyards and fountains of water; where also they drank and washed themselves, and did freely eat of the vineyards. Now there were on the tops of these mountains shepherds feeding their flocks, and they stood by the highway-side. The pilgrims therefore went to them, and leaning upon their staffs, (as is common with weary pilgrims when they stand to talk with any by the way,) they asked, "Whose delectable mountains are these, and whose be the sheep that feed upon them?"

Shep. These mountains are Immanuel's land, and they are within sight of his city; and the sheep also are his, and he laid down his life for them.

Chr. Is this the way to the Celestial City?

Shep. You are just in your way.

Chr. How far is it thither?

Shep. Too far for any but those that shall get thither indeed.

Chr. Is the way safe or dangerous?

Shep. Safe for those for whom it is to be safe;[1] but transgressors shall fall therein. Hos. xiv, 9.

[1] Keep sound wisdom and discretion: then shalt thou walk in thy way safely, and thy foot shall not stumble. Prov. iii, 21, 23

Chr. Is there in this place any relief for pilgrims that are weary and faint in the way?

Shep. The Lord of these mountains hath given us a charge not to be forgetful to entertain strangers, Heb. xiii, 2; therefore the good of the place is before you.[2]

I saw also in my dream, that when the shepherds perceived that they were wayfaring men, they also put questions to them, (to which they made answer as in other places,) as, "Whence came you?" and, "How got you into the way?" and, "By what means have you so persevered therein? for but few of them that begin to come hither, do show their face on these mountains." But when the shepherds heard their answers, being pleased therewith, they looked very lovingly upon them, and said, "Welcome to the Delectable Mountains."[3]

The shepherds, I say, whose names were Knowledge, Experience, Watchful, and Sincere,[4] took them

[2] If ye be willing and obedient, ye shall eat the good of the land. Isaiah i, 19. How excellent is thy loving-kindness, O God! therefore the children of men shall put their trust under the shadow of thy wings. They shall be abundantly satisfied with the fatness of thine house; and thou shalt make them drink of the river of thy pleasures. For with thee is the fountain of life; in thy light shall we see light. Psalm xxxvi, 7–9.

[3] "Weeping may endure for a night, but joy cometh in the morning." The pilgrims who but a while since were bemoaning their sad condition in the gloomy dungeon of Doubting Castle, are now walking in the light of God's countenance, among the fountains and gardens of the Delectable Mountains. "It is," says Bunyan, "as ordinary as for the light to shine, for God to make black and dismal dispensations to usher in bright and pleasing; yea, and the more frightful that is which goes before, the more comfortable is that which follows after."—*Bunyan's Antichrist and its Ruin.*

[4] The "Shepherds" represent those who are called by the Spirit of God to feed the flock of Christ; while the names by which they are distinguished, indicate those gifts and graces which are essential to the proper discharge of the duties of a spiritual pastor.

by the hand, and had them to their tents, and made them partake of what was ready at present. They said, moreover, "We would that you should stay here a while, to be acquainted with us, and yet more to solace yourselves with the good of these Delectable Mountains." They then told them that they were content to stay. So they went to rest that night, because it was very late.

Then I saw in my dream, that in the morning the shepherds called up Christian and Hopeful to walk with them upon the mountains. So they went forth with them, and walked a while, having a pleasant prospect on every side. Then said the shepherds one to another, "Shall we show these pilgrims some wonders?" So when they had concluded to do it, they had them first to the top of a hill, called Error, which was very steep on the farthest side, and bid them look down to the bottom. So Christian and Hopeful looked down, and saw at the bottom several men dashed all to pieces by a fall that they had from the top. Then said Christian, "What meaneth this?" The shepherds answered, "Have you not heard of them that were made to err, by hearkening to Hymenæus and Philetus, as concerning the faith of the resurrection of the body?" 2 Tim. ii, 17, 18. They answered, "Yes." Then said the shepherds, "Those that you see dashed in pieces at the bottom of this mountain are they; and they have continued to this day unburied, as you see, for an example to others to take heed how they clamber too high, or how they come too near the brink of this mountain."

Then I saw that they had them to the top of another mountain, and the name of that is Caution, and bid them look afar off; which, when they did, they perceived, as they thought, several men walking up and down among the tombs that were there; and they perceived that the men were blind, because they stumbled sometimes upon the tombs, and because they could not get out from among them. Then said Christian, "What means this?"

The shepherds then answered, "Did you not see a little below these mountains a stile that led into a meadow, on the left hand of this way?" They answered, "Yes." Then said the shepherds, "From that stile there goes a path that leads directly to Doubting Castle, which is kept by Giant Despair; and these men (pointing to them among the tombs) came once on pilgrimage, as you do now, even until they came to that same stile. And because the right way was rough in that place, they chose to go out of it into that meadow, and there were taken by Giant Despair, and cast into Doubting Castle, where, after they had awhile been kept in the dungeon, he at last did put out their eyes, and led them among those tombs, where he has left them to wander to this very day, that the saying of the wise man might be fulfilled, 'He that wandereth out of the way of understanding shall remain in the congregation of the dead.'" Prov. xxi, 16. Then Christian and Hopeful looked one upon another, with tears gushing out, but yet said nothing to the shepherds.

Then I saw in my dream, that the shepherds had them to another place, in a bottom, where was a door in the side of a hill; and they opened the door, and bid them look in. They looked in, therefore, and saw that within it was very dark and smoky; they also thought that they heard there a rumbling noise, as of fire, and a cry of some tormented, and that they smelt the scent of brimstone. Then said Christian, "What means this?" The shepherds told them, "This is a by-way to hell, a way that hypocrites go in at; namely, such as sell their birthright, with Esau; such as sell their Master, with Judas; such as blaspheme the gospel, with Alexander; and that lie and dissemble, with Ananias and Sapphira his wife."

Then said Hopeful to the shepherds, "I perceive that these had on them, even every one, a show of pilgrimage, as we have now; had they not?"

Shep. Yes, and held it a long time, too.

Hope. How far might they go on in pilgrimage in their day, since they, notwithstanding, were thus miserably cast away?

Shep. Some further, and some not as far as these mountains.

Then said the pilgrims one to another, "We have need to cry to the Strong for strength."

Shep. Ay, and you will have need to use it, when you have it, too.[5]

By this time the pilgrims had a desire to go forward, and the shepherds a desire they should; so they walked together toward the end of the mountains. Then said the shepherds one to another, "Let us here show the pilgrims the gates of the Celestial City, if they have skill to look through our perspective glass." The pilgrims then lovingly accepted the motion: so they had them to the top of a high hill, called Clear, and gave them the glass to look.

[5] The falling away of others should be a warning to us, and excite us to more constant prayer, and greater watchfulness and diligence, "lest we also fall after the same example of unbelief."

Then they tried to look; but the remembrance of that last thing that the shepherds had shown them made their hands shake, by means of which impediment they could not look steadily through the glass; yet they thought they saw something like the gate, and also some of the glory of the place.[6] Thus they went away and sang:—

"Thus by the shepherds secrets are reveal'd,
Which from all other men are kept conceal'd:
Come to the shepherds, then, if you would see
Things deep, things hid, and that mysterious be."

When they were about to depart, one of the shep herds gave them a note of the way. Another of them bid them beware of the Flatterer. The third bid them take heed that they slept not upon the Enchanted Ground. And the fourth bid them God speed. So I awoke from my dream.

[6] Looking through the glass of God's word, with the eye of faith, the advanced Christian, especially as he approaches the termination of his pilgrimage, is often privileged to "behold the land that is very far off," and enjoy a lively anticipation of the promised inheritance.

By faith we already behold
That lovely Jerusalem here;
Her walls are of jasper and gold,
As crystal her buildings are clear.
Immoveably founded in grace,
She stands as she ever hath stood,
And brightly her Builder displays,
And flames with the glory of God.—*Wesley.*

CHAPTER XIII.

The Pilgrims meet with Ignorance—Christian has some talk with him—The destruction of one Turnaway—Christian tells his companion a story of Little Faith—The Flatterer seduces the Pilgrims —They are taken in a net—A Shining One lets them out—They are whipped and sent on their way—Atheist meets the Pilgrims.

AND I slept, and dreamed again, and saw the same two pilgrims going down the mountains along the highway toward the city. Now a little below these mountains, on the left hand, lieth the country of Conceit; from which country there comes into the way in which the pilgrims walked a little crooked lane. Here, therefore, they met with a very brisk lad that came out of that country, and his name was Ignorance. So Christian asked him from what parts he came, and whither he was going.

Ignor. Sir, I was born in the country that lieth off there, a little on the left hand, and I am going to the Celestial City.

Chr. But how do you think to get in at the gate, for you may find some difficulty there?

"As other good people do," said he.

Chr. But what have you to show at that gate, that he gate should be opened to you?

Ignor. I know my Lord's will, and have been a good liver: I pay every man his own; I pray, fast, pay tithes, and give alms, and have left my country for whither I am going.

Chr. But thou camest not in at the wicket-gate that is at the head of this way; thou camest in hither through that same crooked lane; and therefore I fear however thou mayest think of thyself, when the reckoning day shall come, thou wilt have laid to thy charge, that thou art a thief and a robber, instead of getting admittance into the city.

Ignor. Gentlemen, ye be utter strangers to me; I know you not: be content to follow the religion of your country, and I will follow the religion of mine.[1] I hope all will be well. And as for the gate that you talk of, all the world knows that that is a great way off of our country. I cannot think that any man in all our parts doth so much as know the way to it; nor need they matter whether they do or no, since we have, as you see, a fine, pleasant, green lane, that comes down from our country, the next way into the way.[2]

When Christian saw that the man was wise in his own conceit, he said to Hopeful, whisperingly, "'There is more hope of a fool than of him.'" Prov. xxvi, 12. And said, moreover, "'When he that is a fool walketh by the way, his wisdom faileth him, and he saith to every one, that he is a fool.' Eccles. x, 3. What, shall we talk further with him, or outgo him at present, and so leave him to think of what he hath heard already,

[1] There is the wilfully ignorant professor, or him who is afraid to know more, for fear of the cross. He is for picking and choosing of truth, and loveth not to hazard his all for that worthy name by which he would be called. When he is at any time overtaken by arguments, or awakenings of conscience, he uses to heal all by, "I was not brought up in this faith:" as if it were unlawful for Christians to know more than hath been taught them at first. There are many scriptures that lie against this man, as the mouths of great guns, and he is one of the many that "will seek to enter in and shall not be able." Luke xii, 24.—*Bunyan's Strait Gate.*

[2] The way of peace they know not; and there is no judgment in their goings; they have made them crooked paths: whosoever goeth therein shall not know peace. Isa. lix, 8. The way of a fool is right in his own eyes; but he that hearkeneth unto counsel is wise. Prov. xii, 15

and then stop again for him afterward, and see if by degrees we can do any good by him?"[3] Then said Hopeful,—

"Let Ignorance a little while now muse
On what is said, and let him not refuse
Good counsel to embrace, lest he remain
Still ignorant of what's the chiefest gain.
God saith, those that no understanding have,
(Although he made them,) them he will not save."

He farther added, "It is not good, I think, to say to him all at once; let us pass him by, if you will, and talk to him anon, even as he is able to bear it." So they both went on, and Ignorance he came after.

Now when they had passed him a little way, they entered into a very dark lane, where they met a man whom seven devils had bound with seven strong cords, and were a-carrying back to the door that they saw on the side of the hill.[4] Now good Christian began to tremble, and so did Hopeful, his companion; yet, as the devils led away the man, Christian looked to see if he knew him; and he thought it might be one Turn-away, that dwelt in the town of Apostacy. But he did not perfectly see his face, for he did hang his head like a thief that is found. But being gone past, Hopeful looked after him, and espied on his back a paper,

[3] Prudence will often dictate the propriety of this course. When a person is obstinately bent on pursuing his own way, and unwilling to listen to reason, especially if it be one with whom we have frequent opportunities of speaking, it will be best after a brief admonition to leave him awhile to his own reflections, carefully watching for an occasion when he may be in a better frame to receive good counsel.

[4] Then goeth he, and taketh with himself seven other spirits more wicked than himself, and they enter in and dwell there: and the last state of that man is worse than the first. Matthew xii, 45. His own iniquities shall take the wicked himself, and he shall be holden with the cords of his sins. Proverbs v, 22.

with this inscription, "Wanton professor, and damnable apostate."[5]

Then said Christian to his fellow, "Now I call to my remembrance that which was told me of a thing that happened to a good man hereabout. The name of that man was Little-Faith; but a good man, and he dwelt in the town of Sincere. The thing was this: At the entering in at this passage, there comes down from Broadway-gate a lane, called Deadman's-lane; so called, because of the murders that are commonly done there; and this Little-Faith, going on pilgrimage, as we do now, chanced to sit down there and sleep.

[5] Fearful is the crime and fearful will be the doom of final apostacy. By their going back from Christ, these *turn-away* professors proclaim to the world, that in their estimation, the pleasures of sin are more to be desired than the hopes and consolations of religion, and that heaven is a prize not worth the pursuing. These are false witnesses for Christ; spies who after having seen the "good land and the fruit of it," turn back again to the wilderness, sigh for the flesh-pots of Egypt, and by their evil report discourage others from entering into the promised inheritance. Such are far more guilty in the sight of God, than those who never "named the name of Christ," and will, if they repent not, "receive the greater condemnation." Read 2 Peter ii, 20, 21. If they shall not escape that "neglect," then how shall they escape that *reject* and *turn their back* upon so great salvation? "O," says our author, "if Judas the traitor, or Francis Spira the backslider, were but now alive in this world, to whisper these men in the ear a little, and tell them what it hath cost *their* souls for backsliding, surely it would stick by them, and make them afraid of running back again, so long as they had one day to live in this world."

Ah! Lord, with trembling I confess,
A gracious soul may fall from grace;
The salt may lose its seasoning power,
And never, never find it more!

Lest that my fearful case should be,
Each moment knit my soul to thee:
And lead me to the mount above,
Through the low vale of humble love.—*Wesley.*

Now there happened at that time to come down the lane from Broadway-gate three sturdy rogues, and their names were Faint-Heart, Mistrust, and Guilt, three brothers; and they espying Little-Faith, where he was, came galloping up with speed. Now the good man was just awakened from his sleep, and was getting up to go on his journey. So they came up all to him, and with threatening language bid him stand. At this, Little-Faith looked as white as a clout, and had neither power to fight nor fly. Then said Faint-Heart, "Deliver thy purse;" but he making no haste to do it, (for he was loth to lose his money,) Mistrust ran up to him, and thrusting his hand into his pocket, pulled out thence a bag of silver. Then he cried out, "Thieves, thieves!" With that Guilt, with a great club that was in his hand, struck Little-Faith on the head, and with that blow felled him flat to the ground, where he lay bleeding as one that would bleed to death. All this while the thieves stood by. But at last, they hearing that some were upon the road, and fearing lest it should be one Great-Grace that dwells in the town of Good-Confidence, they betook themselves to their heels, and left this good man to shift for himself. Now, after a while, Little-Faith came to himself, and getting up, made shift to scramble on his way. This was the story.

Hope. But did they take from him all that ever he had?

Chr. No; the place where his jewels were they never ransacked; so those he kept still. But, as I was told, the good man was much afflicted for his loss; for the thieves got most of his spending-money. That which they got not, as I said, were jewels; also he had a little odd money left, but scarce enough to bring him to his journey's end. Nay, (if I was not misinformed,) he was forced to beg as he went, to keep himself alive, for his jewels he might not sell; but beg and do what he could, he went, as we say, with many a hungry belly the most part of the rest of the way.[6]

Hope. But is it not a wonder they got not from him his certificate, by which he was to receive his admittance at the Celestial Gate?

Chr. It is a wonder: but they got not that, though they missed it not through any good cunning of his; for he, being dismayed by their coming upon him, had neither power nor skill to hide anything: so it was more by good providence than by his endeavour that they missed of that good thing.

Hope. But it must needs be a comfort to him, that they got not this jewel from him.

Chr. It might have been great comfort to him, had he used it as he should; but they that told me the story

[6] This Little-Faith, who was attacked by thieves in his sleep and robbed of his "spending money," is a type of those feeble and sickly, yet sincere professors, who, giving way to spiritual sloth and remissness in Christian duties, become weary and *faint* in their minds, give way to *mistrust*, and thus contract *guilt*, and deprive themselves of all present comfort and enjoyment in religion. Such poor souls, if they do not finally make shipwreck of the little faith they have, yet drag heavily along, and go mourning all their days, continually hovering, as it were, between life and death: "whereas," says Bunyan, "if they had but the grace to add to their faith, virtue, &c., they might have more peace, live better lives, and not have their heads so often in a bag as they have. 'To him that ordereth his conversation aright will I show the salvation of God.' Psa. l, 23. To him that disposeth his way aright; now this cannot be done without a constant supplicating at the throne of grace for more grace. This then is the reason why every new temptation so foils, so overcomes them: they are not upon their watch, and have not been before with God to be inlaid with grace proportionable to what may come upon them."

said, that he made but little use of it all the rest of the way; and that because of the dismay that he had in their taking away his money. Indeed, he forgot it a great part of the rest of his journey; and besides, when at any time it came into his mind, and he began to be comforted therewith, then would fresh thoughts of his loss come again upon him, and these thoughts would swallow up all.

Hope. Alas, poor man, this could not but be a great grief unto him.

Chr. Grief! Ay, a grief indeed. Would it not have been so to any of us, had we been used as he, to be robbed and wounded too, and that in a strange place, as he was? It is a wonder he did not die with grief, poor heart! I was told that he scattered almost all the rest of the way with nothing but doleful and bitter complaints; telling also to all that overtook him, or that he overtook in the way as he went, where he was robbed, and how; who they were that did it, and what he had lost; how he was wounded, and that he hardly escaped with life.

Hope. But it is a wonder that his necessity did not put him upon selling or pawning some of his jewels, that he might have wherewith to relieve himself in his journey.

Chr. Thou talkest like one upon whose head is the shell to this very day. For what should he pawn them? or to whom should he sell them? In all that country where he was robbed, his jewels were not accounted of; nor did he want that relief which could from thence be administered to him. Besides, had his jewels been missing at the gate of the Celestial City, he had (and that he knew well enough) been excluded from an inheritance there, and that would have been worse to him than the appearance and villany of ten thousand thieves.

Hope. Why art thou so tart, my brother? Esau sold his birthright, and that for a mess of pottage, (Heb. xii, 16;) and that birthright was his greatest jewel: and if he, why might not Little-Faith do so too?

Chr. Esau did sell his birthright indeed, and so do many besides, and by so doing exclude themselves from the chief blessing, as also that caitiff did; but you must put a difference betwixt Esau and Little-Faith, and also betwixt their estates. Esau's birthright was typical; but Little-Faith's jewels were not so. Esau's belly was his god; but Little-Faith's belly was not so. Esau's want lay in his fleshly appetite; Little-Faith's did not so. Besides, Esau could see no further than to the fulfilling of his lusts; "For I am at the point to die," said he; "and what good will this birthright do me?" Genesis xxv, 32. But Little-Faith, though it was his lot to have but a little faith, was by his little faith kept from such extravagances, and made to see and prize his jewels more than to sell them, as Esau did his birthright. You read not anywhere that Esau had faith, no, not so much as a little; therefore no marvel, where the flesh only bears sway, (as it will in that man where no faith is to resist,) if he sells his birthright, and his soul and all, and that to the devil of hell; for it is with such as it is with the ass, who in her occasion cannot be turned away, Jer. ii, 24. When their minds are set upon their lusts, they will have them whatever they cost. But Little-Faith was of another temper; his mind was on things divine; his livelihood was upon things that were spiritual, and from above; therefore to what end should he that is of such a temper sell his jewels, (had there been any that would have bought them,) to fill his mind with empty things? Will a man give a penny to fill his belly with hay? or can you persuade the turtle dove to live upon carrion, like the crow? Though faithless ones can, for carnal lusts, pawn or mortgage, or sell what they have, and themselves outright to boot; yet they that have faith, saving faith, though but a little of it, cannot do so. Here, therefore, my brother, is thy mistake.

Hope. I acknowledge it; but yet your severe reflection had almost made me angry.

Chr. Why, I did but compare thee to some of the birds that are of the brisker sort, who will run to and fro in untrodden paths with the shell upon their heads. But pass by that, and consider the matter under debate, and all shall be well betwixt thee and me.

Hope. But, Christian, these three fellows, I am persuaded in my heart, are but a company of cowards: would they have run else, think you, as they did at the noise of one that was coming on the road? Why did not Little-Faith pluck up a greater heart? He might, methinks, have stood one brush with them, and have yielded when there had been no remedy.

Chr. That they are cowards, many have said, but few have found it so in the time of trial. As for a great heart, Little-Faith had none; and I perceive by thee, my brother, hadst thou been the man concerned, thou art but for a brush, and then to yield. And, verily, since this is the height of thy stomach now they are at a distance from us, should they appear to thee, as they did to him, they might put thee to second thoughts.

But consider again, they are but journeymen thieves, they serve under the king of the bottomless pit, who, if need be, will come in to their aid himself, and his voice is as the roaring of a lion. 1 Pet. v, 8. I myself have been engaged as this Little-Faith was, and I found it a terrible thing. These three villans set upon me, and I beginning like a Christian to resist, they gave but a call, and in came their master. I would, as the saying is, have given my life for a penny, but that, as God would have it, I was clothed with armour of proof. Ay, and yet, though I was so harnessed, I found it hard work to quit myself like a man; no man can tell what in that combat attends us, but he that hath been in the battle himself.

Hope. Well, but they ran, you see, when they did but suppose that one Great-Grace was in the way.

Chr. True, they often have fled, both they and their master, when Great-Grace hath but appeared: and no marvel, for he is the King's champion. But I trow, you will put some difference betwixt Little-Faith and the King's champion. All the King's subjects are not his champions; nor can they, when tried, do such feats of war as he. Is it meet to think that a little child should handle Goliath as David did? or that there should be the strength of an ox in a wren? Some are strong, some are weak; some have great faith, some have little: this man was one of the weak, and therefore he went to the wall.

Hope. I would it had been Great-Grace for their sakes.

Chr. If it had been he, he might have had his hands full; for I must tell you, that though Great-Grace is excellent good at his weapons, and has, and can, so long as he keeps them at sword's point, do well enough with them; yet if they get within him, even Faint-Heart, Mistrust, or the other, it shall go hard but they will throw up his heels. And when a man is down, you know, what can he do?

Whoso looks well upon Great-Grace's face, will see those scars and cuts there, that shall easily give demonstration of what I say. Yea, once I heard that he should say, (and that when he was in the combat,) "We despaired even of life." How did these sturdy rogues and their fellows make David groan, mourn, and roar! Psalm lxxxviii. Yea, Heman, and Hezekiah too, though champions in their days, were forced to bestir them, when by these assaulted; and yet, notwithstanding, they had their coats soundly brushed by them. Peter, upon a time, would go try what he could do; but though some do say of him that he is the prince of the apostles, they handled him so that they made him at last afraid of a sorry girl.

Besides, their king is at their whistle; he is never out of hearing; and if at any time they be put to the worst, he, if possible, comes in to help them; and of him it is said, "The sword of him that layeth at him cannot hold; the spear, the dart, nor the habergeon. He esteemed iron as straw, and brass as rotten wood. The arrow cannot make him fly; sling-stones are turned with him into stubble. Darts are counted as stubble; he laugheth at the shaking of a spear." What can a man do in this case? It is true, if a man could at every turn have Job's horse, and had skill and courage to ride him, he might do notable things. "For his neck is clothed with thunder. He will not be afraid as the grasshopper; the glory of his nostrils is terrible. He paweth in the valley, rejoiceth in his strength, and goeth out to meet the armed men. He mocketh at fear, and is not affrighted, neither turneth back from the sword. The quiver rattleth against him, the glittering spear and the shield. He swalloweth the ground with fierceness and rage; neither believeth he that it is the sound of the trumpet. He saith among the trumpets, Ha, ha; and he smelleth the battle afar off, the thundering of the captains, and the shoutings." Job xxxix, 19–25.

But for such footmen as thee and I are, let us never desire to meet with an enemy, nor vaunt as if we could do better when we hear of others that have been foiled; nor be tickled at the thoughts of our own manhood; for such commonly come by the worst when tried. Witness Peter, of whom I made mention before; he would swagger, ay, he would; he would, as his vain mind prompted him to say, do better, and stand more for his Master than all men; but, who so foiled and run down by these villans as he?

When, therefore, we hear that such robberies are done on the King's highway, two things become us to do.

1. To go out harnessed, and to be sure to take a shield with us; for it was for the want of that, that he that laid so lustily at Leviathan could not make him yield; for, indeed, if that be wanting, he fears us not at all. Therefore, he that hath skill hath said, "Above all, take the shield of faith, wherewith ye shall be able to quench all the fiery darts of the wicked." Eph. vi, 16.

2. It is good, also, that we desire of the King a convoy, yea, that he will go with us himself. This made David rejoice when in the Valley of the Shadow of Death; and Moses was rather for dying where he

stood, than to go one step without his God. Exod. xxxiii, 15. O my brother, if He will but go along with us, what need we be afraid of ten thousands that shall set themselves against us? But without him, the proud helpers fall under the slain. Psalm iii, 5–8; xxvi, 1–3; Isaiah x, 4.

I, for my part, have been in the fray before now; and though, through the goodness of Him that is best, I am, as you see, alive, yet I cannot boast of my manhood. Glad shall I be if I meet with no more such brunts; though I fear we are not got beyond all danger. However, since the lion and the bear have not as yet devoured me, I hope God will also deliver us from the next uncircumcised Philistine.

> Poor Little-Faith! hast been among the thieves?
> Wast robb'd? Remember this, whoso believes,
> And get more faith; then shall you victors be
> Over ten thousand, else scarce over three.

So they went on, and Ignorance followed. They went then till they came at a place where they saw a way put itself into their way, and seemed withal to lie as straight as the way which they should go; and here they knew not which of the two to take, for both seemed straight before them; therefore here they stood still to consider. And as they were thinking about the way, behold, a man black of flesh, but covered with a very light robe, came to them, and asked them why they stood there. They answered, they were going to the Celestial City, but knew not which of these ways to take. "Follow me," said the man; "it is thither that I am going." So they followed him in the way that but now came into the road, which by degrees turned, and turned them so from the city that they desired to go to, that in a little time their faces were turned away from it: yet they followed him. But by and by, before they were aware, he led them both within the compass of a net, in which they were both so entangled that they knew not what to do; and with that the white robe fell off the black man's back. Then they saw where they were. Wherefore there they lay crying for some time, for they could not get themselves out.[7]

Then said Christian to his fellow, "Now do I see myself in an error. Did not the shepherds bid us beware of the Flatterer? As is the saying of the wise man, so we have found it this day: 'A man that flattereth his neighbour, spreadeth a net for his feet.'" Prov. xxix, 5.[8]

Hope. They also gave us a note of directions about the way, for our more sure finding thereof; but therein

7 "They lay crying,"—bewailing their misfortune and crying to God for deliverance. "Mine eyes are ever toward the Lord; for he shall pluck my feet out of the net. Turn thee unto me, and have mercy upon me; for I am desolate and afflicted. The troubles of my heart are enlarged: O bring thou me out of my distress. Look upon mine affliction and my pain; and forgive all my sins." Psa. xxv, 15-18.

8 The Flatterer is a teacher of some false doctrine pleasing to the flesh, and made plausible by specious arguments, by means of which the pilgrims, forgetting the caution of the shepherds, are led astray, entangled in the mazes of error, and fallen into condemnation, almost before they are aware. The way into which they wandered seemed to them at first "as straight as the way they should go," and afterward it turned from it so gradually, that they knew not of their danger, until, "as the fishes that are taken in an evil net, and as the birds that are caught in the snare, so were they snared in an evil time, when it fell suddenly upon them." Eccles. ix, 12. How important then is it that we attend to the admonition of our Lord, "Take heed what ye hear;" and also to that of the apostle, "Beloved, believe not every spirit, but try the spirits whether they are of God: because many false prophets are gone out into the world." 1 John iv, 1.

we have also forgotten to read, and not kept ourselves from the paths of the destroyer. Here David was wiser than we, for, saith he, "Concerning the works of men, by the word of thy lips I have kept me from the paths of the destroyer." Psa. xvii, 4.[9]

Thus they lay bewailing themselves in the net. At last they espied a Shining One coming toward them with a whip of small cords in his hand. When he was come to the place where they were, he asked them whence they came, and what they did there. They told him that they were poor pilgrims going to Zion, but were led out of their way by a black man clothed in white, who bid us, said they, follow him, for he was going thither too. Then said he with a whip, "It is Flatterer, a false apostle, that hath transformed himself into an angel of light." 2 Cor. xi, 13, 14. So he rent the net, and let the men out.[10] Then said he to them, "Follow me, that I may set you in your way again." So he led them back to the way which they had left to follow the Flatterer. Then he asked them, saying, "Where did you lie the last night?" They said, "With the shepherds upon the Delectable Mountains." He asked them then if they had not a note of directions for the way. They answered, "Yes." "But did you not," said he, "when you were at a stand, pluck

[9] In all cases of doubt and perplexity as to his course, the Christian should seek for counsel in "the word of God, and prayer." Show me thy ways, O Lord; teach me thy paths. Lead me in thy truth, and teach me; for thou art the God of my salvation. Psa. xxv, 4, 5. Wherewithal shall a young man cleanse his way? By taking heed thereto, according to thy word. Thy word is a lamp unto my feet, and a light unto my path. Psa. cxix, 9, 105.

[10] Our soul is escaped as a bird out of the snare of the fowler: the snare is broken, and we are escaped. Psalm cxxiv, 6, 7.

out and read your note?" They answered, "No." He asked them, "Why?" They said they forgot. He asked, moreover, if the shepherds did not bid them beware of the Flatterer. They answered, "Yes; but we did not imagine," said they, "this fine-spoken man had been he."[11]

Then I saw in my dream that he commanded them to lie down; which when they did, he chastised them sore, to teach them the good way wherein they should walk; and as he chastised them, he said, "As many as I love I rebuke and chasten; be zealous, therefore, and repent." Rev. iii, 19. This done, he bids them go on their way, and take good heed to the other directions of the shepherds. So they thanked him for all their kindness, and went softly along the right way, singing:—

"Come hither, you that walk along the way,
See how the pilgrims fare that go astray:
They catched are in an entangled net,
'Cause they good counsel lightly did forget:
'Tis true they rescued were; but yet you see,
They're scourged to boot: let this your caution be."

Now, after a while, they perceived, afar off, one coming softly, and alone, all along the highway to meet them. Then said Christian to his fellow, "Yonder is a man with his back toward Zion, and he is coming to meet us."

Hope. I see him: let us take heed to ourselves now lest he should prove a Flatterer also.

[11] Now I beseech you, brethren, mark them which cause divisions and offences, contrary to the doctrine which ye have learned; and avoid them. For they that are such serve not our Lord Jesus Christ, but their own belly; and by good words and fair speeches, deceive the hearts of the simple. Romans xvi, 16, 17.

So he drew nearer and nearer, and at last came up to them. His name was Atheist, and he asked them whither they were going.

Chr. We are going to the Mount Zion.

Then Atheist fell into a very great laughter.

Chr. What's the meaning of your laughter?

Atheist. I laugh to see what ignorant persons you are, to take upon you so tedious a journey, and yet are like to have nothing but your travel for your pains.

Chr. Why, man, do you think we shall not be received?

Atheist. Received! There is not such a place as you dream of in all this world.

Chr. But there is in the world to come.

Atheist. When I was at home in mine own country, I heard as you now affirm; and from that hearing went out to see, and have been seeking this city these twenty years, but find no more of it than I did the first day I set out.

Chr. We have both heard, and believe, that there is such a place to be found.

Atheist. Had not I, when at home, believed, I had not come thus far to seek; but finding none, (and yet I should, had there been such a place to be found, for I have gone to seek it further than you,) I am going back again, and will seek to refresh myself with the things that I then cast away for hopes of that which I now see is not.

Then said Christian to Hopeful, his companion, "Is it true which this man hath said?"

Hope. Take heed, he is one of the Flatterers. Remember what it hath cost us once already for hearkening to such kind of fellows. What! no Mount Zion!

Did we not see from the Delectable Mountains the gate of the City? Also, are we not now to walk by faith? 2 Cor. v, 7. Let us go on, lest the man with the whip overtake us again. You should have taught me that lesson, which I will round you in the ears withal: "Cease, my son, to hear the instruction that causeth to err from the words of knowledge." Prov. xix, 27. I say, my brother, cease to hear him, and let us believe to the saving of the soul.[12]

Chr. My brother, I did not put the question to thee for that I doubted of the truth of our belief myself, but to prove thee, and to fetch from thee a fruit of the honesty of thy heart. As for this man, I know that he is blinded by the god of this world. Let thee and me go on, knowing that we have belief of the truth; and "no lie is of the truth." 1 John ii, 21.

Hope. Now do I rejoice in hope of the glory of God.

So they turned away from the man; and he, laughing at them, went his way.

[12] If any man draw back, my soul shall have no pleasure in him. But we are not of them who draw back unto perdition; but of them that believe to the saving of the soul. Heb. x, 38, 39

CHAPTER XIV.

The pilgrims come to the Enchanted Ground—To prevent drowsiness they fall into good discourse—Hopeful relates his experience—His life before conversion—He falls under conviction—Endeavours to mend his life—Finding no relief, he breaks his mind to Faithful, who tells him the way to be saved—He doubts of acceptation—Is better instructed, and bid to pray—Christ is revealed to him.

I THEN saw in my dream, that they went on until they came into a certain country, whose air naturally tended to make one drowsy, if he came a stranger into it. And here Hopeful began to be very dull, and heavy to sleep; wherefore he said unto Christian, "I do now begin to grow so drowsy, that I can scarcely hold open mine eyes; let us lie down here and take one nap."

"By no means," said the other, "lest sleeping we never awake more."

Hope. Why, my brother? sleep is sweet to the labouring man; we may be refreshed if we take a nap.

Chr. Do you not remember that one of the shepherds bid us beware of the Enchanted Ground? He meant by that, that we should beware of sleeping: "wherefore let us not sleep as others do, but let us watch and be sober." 1 Thess. v, 6.[1]

[1] The Enchanted Ground seems to represent a state of spiritual quiet, accompanied with temporal prosperity, which, strange as it may at first appear, often proves most dangerous to the Christian pilgrim. Although, when things go well with us, and God makes our way to prosper, we ought to be most mindful of his mercies and most active in his service, yet, alas! (such is the deceitfulness of man's heart) this is the time when we are most prone to forget him. When "Ephraim waxed fat," then it was that he "kicked;" and of how many who were once zealous and devoted Christians, may it be said that their "prosperity hath destroyed them." When Israel "dwells

Hope. I acknowledge myself in a fault; and had I been here alone, I had by sleeping run the danger of death. I see it is true that the wise man saith, "Two are better than one." Eccles. iv, 9. Hitherto hath thy company been my mercy; and thou shalt have a good reward for thy labour.[2]

"Now, then," said Christian, "to prevent drowsiness in this place, let us fall into good discourse."

"With all my heart," said the other.

Chr. Where shall we begin?

in a quiet habitation"—when he enjoys a fulness of temporal blessings and a cessation of spiritual conflicts—when heaven and earth seem to smile upon, and hell, as it were, to withdraw from him,—he is too apt to indulge an overweening confidence, and a dangerous sense of security, and, like the Psalmist, to say in his prosperity, "I shall never be moved." O thou prosperous professor, thou hast need to be doubly jealous of thyself, and to watch and pray continually, that thou fall not into temptation. O let not thy blessings be made a snare to thee. Do not become slothful in spiritual things, careless and self-indulgent. Say not in thine heart, "Soul, take thine ease; thou hast endured long, hast laboured hard, hast passed through many dangers, and now God hath given thee rest; thou hast much goods laid up, therefore sit down and enjoy the fruit of thy labours." Thou art now upon the Enchanted Ground; stand not still, lie not down, give no place to drowsiness, or inactivity; for if thou fall asleep here, there is fearful danger, unless God arouse thee by his judgments, that thou "sleep the sleep of death." Therefore remember the admonition of the shepherds, and "take heed that thou sleep not upon the Enchanted Ground."

[2] See here one of the advantages of Christian fellowship. "Two are better than one: for if they fall the one will lift up his fellow; but wo to him that is alone when he falleth." Eccles. iv, 9. Had it not been for Christian's admonition, Hopeful had doubtless now fallen asleep on the Enchanted Ground; and had not Hopeful encouraged his brother, the latter had most likely made an end of himself in Doubting Castle. Thus, and in many other ways, may Christians prove a mutual benefit; bearing one another's burdens, helpers of each other's joy. Calvin says, "There is none, however weak, in the Church of Christ, who cannot be of some use for our advance in grace."

Hope. Where God began with us.[3] But do you begin, if you please.

Chr. I will sing you first this song:—

When saints do sleepy grow, let them come hither,
And hear how these two pilgrims talk together;
Yea, let them learn of them in any wise,
Thus to keep ope their drowsy, slumb'ring eyes.
Saints' fellowship, if it be managed well,
Keeps them awake, and that in spite of hell.

Then Christian began and said, "I will ask you a question: How came you to think at first of doing as you do now?"

Hope. Do you mean, how I came at first to look after the good of my soul?

Chr. Yes, that is my meaning.

Hope. I continued a great while in the delight of those things which were seen and sold at our Fair; things which I believe now would have, had I continued in them still, drowned me in perdition and destruction.

Chr. What things were they?

Hope. All the treasures and riches of the world. Also I delighted much in rioting, revelling, drinking swearing, lying, uncleanness, sabbath-breaking, and what not, that tended to destroy the soul. But I found at last, by hearing and considering of things that are divine, which, indeed, I heard of you, as also of beloved Faithful that was put to death for his faith and good living in Vanity Fair, that "the end of these things is death," and that for these things' sake "the wrath of God cometh upon the children of disobedience." Eph. v, 6.

[3] It is profitable for Christians to be often calling to mind the very beginnings of grace within their souls.—*Bunyan's Grace Abounding.*

Chr. And did you presently fall under the power of this conviction?

Hope. No; I was not willing presently to know the evil of sin, nor the damnation that follows upon the commission of it; but endeavoured, when my mind at first began to be shaken with the word, to shut mine eyes against the light thereof.

Chr. But what was the cause of your carrying of it thus to the first workings of God's blessed Spirit upon you?

Hope. The causes were, 1. I was ignorant that this was the work of God upon me. I never thought that by awakenings for sin, God at first begins the conversion of a sinner. 2. Sin was very sweet to my flesh, and I was very loth to leave it. 3. I could not tell how to part with mine old companions, their presence and actions were so desirable unto me. 4. The hours in which convictions were upon me, were such troublesome and such heart-affrighting hours, that I could not bear, no, not so much as the remembrance of them upon my heart.

Chr. Then, as it seems, sometimes you got rid of your trouble?

Hope. Yes, verily; but it would come into my mind again, and then I should be as bad, nay, worse than I was before.

Chr. Why, what was it that brought your sins to mind again?

Hope. Many things; as, 1. If I did but meet a good man in the streets;[4] or, 2. If I have heard any read in

[4] Bunyan says, when under conviction, "I trembled at the sight of the saints of God, especially those that greatly loved him; for they did, both in their words, their carriage, and all their expressions of tenderness and fear to sin against their precious Saviour, condemn, and also add continual affliction to my soul.—*Grace Abounding.*

the Bible; or, 3. If my head did begin to ache; or, 4. If I were told that some of my neighbours were sick; or, 5. If I heard the bell toll for some that were dead; or, 6. If I thought of dying myself; or, 7. If I heard that sudden death happened to others; 8. But especially when I thought of myself, that I must quickly come to judgment.

Chr. And could you at any time, with ease, get off the guilt of sin, when by any of these ways it came upon you?

Hope. No, not I; for then they got faster hold of my conscience; and then, if I did but think of going back to sin, (though my mind was turned against it,) it would be double torment to me.

Chr. And how did you then?

Hope. I thought I must endeavour to mend my life; or else, thought I, I am sure to be damned.

Chr. And did you endeavour to mend?

Hope. Yes; and fled from, not only my sins, but sinful company too; and betook me to religious duties, as praying, reading, weeping for sin, speaking truth to my neighbours, &c. These things did I, with many others, too much here to relate.

Chr. And did you think yourself well then?

Hope. Yes, for a while; but at the last my trouble came tumbling upon me again, and that over the neck of all my reformations.[5]

[5] Whosoever thou art, who desirest to be forgiven and reconciled to the favour of God, do not say in thy heart, "I must *first do this*; I must *first* conquer every sin; break off every evil word and work, and do good to all men; or, I must *first* go to church, receive the Lord's supper, hear more sermons, and say more prayers." Alas, my brother! thou art clean gone out of the way. Thou art still "ignorant of the righteousness of God," and art "seeking to establish thy

Chr. How came that about, since you were now reformed?

Hope. There were several things brought it upon me, especially such sayings as these: "All our righteousnesses are as filthy rags," Isa. lxiv, 6; "By the works of the law shall no flesh be justified," Gal. ii, 16; "When ye have done all these things, say, We are unprofitable," Luke xvii, 10; with many more such like. From whence I began to reason with myself thus: If all my righteousnesses are as filthy rags, if by the deeds of the law no man can be justified, and if, when we have done all, we are yet unprofitable, then 'tis but a folly to think of heaven by the law. I further thought thus: If a man runs a hundred pounds into the shop-keeper's debt, and after that shall pay for all that he shall fetch; yet if his old debt stands still upon the book uncrossed, the shop-keeper may sue him for it, and cast him into prison till he shall pay the debt.

Chr. Well, and how did you apply this to yourself?

Hope. Why, I thougnt tnus with myself: I have by my sins run a great way into God's book, and that my now reforming will not pay off that score; therefore I should think still, under all my present amendments, But how shall I be freed from that damnation that I brought myself in danger of by my former transgressions?

Chr. A very good application: but pray go on.

own righteousness," as the ground of thy reconciliation. (Rom. x, 3.) Knowest thou not that thou canst do nothing but sin, till thou art reconciled to God? Wherefore, then, dost thou say, "I must do this or this *first*, and then I shall believe?" Nay, but *first believe!* Believe in the Lord Jesus Christ, the propitiation for thy sins. Let this good foundation first be laid, and then thou shalt do all things well.—*Wesley' Sermon on the Righteousness of Faith.*

Hope. Another thing that hath troubled me ever since my late amendments is, that if I look narrowly into the best of what I do now, I still see sin, new sin, mixing itself with the best of that I do; so that now I am forced to conclude, that notwithstanding my former fond conceits of myself and duties, I have committed sin enough in one day to send me to hell, though my former life had heen faultless.

Chr. And what did you then?

Hope. Do! I could not tell what to do, until I broke my mind to Faithful; for he and I were well acquainted: and he told me, that unless I could obtain the righteousness of a man that never had sinned, neither mine own, nor all the righteousness of the world could save me.

Chr. And did you think he spake true?

Hope. Had he told me so when I was pleased and satisfied with mine own amendments, I had called him fool for his pains; but now, since I see mine own infirmity, and the sin which cleaves to my best performance, I have been forced to be of his opinion.

Chr. But did you think, when at first he suggested it to you, that there was such a man to be found, of whom it might justly be said that he never committed sin?

Hope. I must confess the words at first sounded strangely; but after a little more talk and company with him, I had full conviction about it.

Chr. And did you ask him what man this was, and how you must be justified by him?

Hope. Yes, and he told me it was the Lord Jesus, that dwelleth on the right hand of the Most High. And thus, said he, you must be justified by him, even by trusting to what he hath done by himself in the days of his flesh, and suffered when he did hang on the tree. I asked him further, how that man's righteousness could be of that efficacy, to justify another before God. And he told me, he was the mighty God, and did what he did, and died the death also, not for himself, but for me; to whom his doings, and the worthiness of them, should be imputed, if I believed on him.[6]

Chr. And what did you do then?

Hope. I made my objections against my believing, for that I thought he was not willing to save me.[7]

[6] By the "righteousness" of Christ is meant all that he did and suffered to redeem us from the curse of the law; and by virtue of which, "all that believe in him are justified from all things, from which they could not be justified by the law of Moses." Acts xiii, 39. We must not, however, understand that Christ's righteousness is accounted ours, or imputed to us as though we had performed it, as some have erroneously supposed. It is not the righteousness of Christ, but our "*faith*" in it, which is "imputed unto us for righteousness," Rom. iv, 20–25; and hence our righteousness—or justification—is termed in some places "the righteousness of *faith*," Rom. ix, 30; x, 6; Gal v, 5; Heb. xi, 7; and in others, "the righteousness of God which is by faith of Jesus Christ," &c. Rom. iii, 22; Phil. iii, 9. The doctrine which our author would inculcate, is, that the penitent soul is not forgiven and accepted for the sake of anything that he himself has done or can do, but solely on the ground of his faith in the atonement of Christ who hath undertaken for him. Eph. ii, 8, 9.

"As soon as in him we believe,
By faith of his Spirit we take;
And freely accepted, receive
Forgiveness for Jesus's sake."

[7] The awakened sinner doth not so easily question the power of Christ, as his willingness to save him: "Lord, if thou *wilt*, thou canst," said one. He did not put the "if" upon his power, but upon his *will*: he concluded he could, but he was not so fully of persuasion that he would. But we have the same ground to believe he will, as we have to believe he can. If he was not willing, why did he promise? Why did he say he would receive the coming sinner? "Him that cometh to me I will in no wise cast out." John vi, 37. Here is

Chr. And what said Faithful to you then?

Hope. He bid me go to him and see. Then I said it was presumption. He said, No; for I was invited to come. Matt. xi, 28. Then he gave me a book of Jesus's inditing, to encourage me the more freely to come; and he said concerning that book, that every jot and tittle thereof stood firmer than heaven and earth. Matt. xxiv, 35. Then I asked him what I must do when I came; and he told me I must entreat upon my knees, with all my heart and soul, the Father to reveal him to me. Then I asked him further, how I must make my supplications to him; and he said, Go, and thou shalt find him upon a mercy-seat, where he sits all the year long to give pardon and forgiveness to them that come.[8] I told him that I knew not what to say when I came; and he bid me say to this effect: "God be merciful to me a sinner, and make me to know and believe in Jesus Christ; for I see, if his righteousness had not been, or I have not faith in that righteousness, I am utterly cast away. Lord, I have heard that thou

his willingness asserted, as well as his power suggested. These words, therefore, are sufficient ground to encourage any coming sinner, that Christ is willing to receive him; and, since he hath power also to do what he will, there is no ground at all left to the coming sinner any more to doubt; but to come in full hope of acceptance, and to be received unto grace and mercy.—*Bunyan's Come and Welcome.*

"Ah, wherefore did I ever doubt?
Thou wilt in no wise cast me out,
A helpless soul that comes to thee,
With only sin and misery."

[8] And thou shalt put the mercy-seat above upon the ark. And there I will meet with thee, and I will commune with thee from above the mercy-seat. Exodus xxv, 21, 22. Let us therefore come boldly unto the throne of grace, that we may obtain mercy, and find grace to help in time of need. Hebrews iv, 16.

art a merciful God, and hast ordained that thy Son Jesus Christ should be the Saviour of the world; and moreover, that thou art willing to bestow him upon such a poor sinner as I am, and I am a sinner indeed. Lord, take therefore this opportunity, and magnify thy grace in the salvation of my soul, through thy Son Jesus Christ. Amen."

Chr. And did you do as you were bidden?

Hope. Yes, over, and over, and over.

Chr. And did the Father reveal the Son to you?

Hope. No, not at first, nor second, nor third, nor fourth, nor fifth; no, nor at the sixth time neither.

Chr. What did you do then?

Hope. What! why I could not tell what to do.

Chr. Had you no thoughts of leaving off praying?

Hope. Yes; and a hundred times twice told.

Chr. And what was the reason you did not?

Hope. I believed that it was true which hath been told me, to wit, that without the righteousness of this Christ, all the world could not save me; and, therefore, thought I with myself, if I leave off, I die, and I can but die at the throne of grace. And withal this came into my mind, "If it tarry, wait for it; because it will surely come, and will not tarry." Hab. ii, 3.[9] So I continued praying until the Father showed me his Son.

Chr. And how was he revealed unto you?

Hope. I did not see him with my bodily eyes, but with the eyes of my understanding, (Eph. i, 18,) and

[9] Do not conclude thy cause is lost, because at present thou dost not hear from court. Cry, if thou wilt, "O when wilt thou come unto me?" Psalm ci, 2; but never let such a wicked thought pass through thy heart, saying, "Why should I wait upon the Lord any longer?" 2 Kings vi, 33.—*Bunyan's Advocateship of Jesus Christ*

thus it was: One day I was very sad, I think sadder than at any one time in my life: and this sadness was through a fresh sight of the greatness and vileness of my sins. And as I was then looking for nothing but hell, and the everlasting damnation of my soul, suddenly, as I thought, I saw the Lord Jesus look down from heaven upon me, and saying, "Believe on the Lord Jesus Christ, and thou shalt be saved." Acts xvi, 31.

But I replied, Lord, I am a great, a very great sinner: and he answered, "My grace is sufficient for thee." 2 Cor. xii, 9. Then I said, But, Lord, what is believing? And then I saw from that saying, "He that cometh to me shall never hunger, and he that believeth on me shall never thirst," (John vi, 35,) that believing and coming was all one; and that he that came, that is, that ran out in his heart and affections after salvation by Christ, he indeed believed in Christ. Then the water stood in mine eyes, and I asked further, But, Lord, may such a great sinner as I am be indeed accepted of thee, and be saved by thee? And I heard him say, "And him that cometh to me I will in no wise cast out." John vi, 37. Then I said, But how, Lord, must I consider of thee in my coming to thee, that my faith may be placed aright upon thee? Then he said, "Christ Jesus came into the world to save sinners." 1 Tim. i, 15. "He is the end of the law for righteousness to every one that believes." Rom. x, 4, and chapter iv. "He died for our sins, and rose again for our justification." Rom. iv, 25. "He loved us and washed us from our sins in his own blood." Rev. i, 5. "He is Mediator betwixt God and us." 1 Tim. ii, 5. "He ever liveth to make intercession for us." Heb. vii, 25. From all which I gathered, that I must look for righteousness in his person, and for satisfaction for my sins by his blood; that what he did in obedience to his Father's law, and in submitting to the penalty thereof, was not for himself, but for him that will accept it for his salvation, and be thankful. And now was my heart full of joy, mine eyes full of tears, and mine affections running over with love to the name, people, and ways of Jesus Christ.

Chr. This was a revelation of Christ to your soul indeed. But tell me particularly what effect this had upon your spirit.

Hope. It made me see that all the world, notwithstanding all the righteousness thereof, is in a state of condemnation. It made me see that God the Father, though he be just, can justly justify the coming sinner. It made me greatly ashamed of the vileness of my former life, and confounded me with the sense of mine own ignorance; for there never came thought into my heart before now that showed me so the beauty of Jesus Christ. It made me love a holy life, and long to do something for the honour and glory of the name of the Lord Jesus. Yea, I thought that had I now a thousand gallons of blood in my body, I could spill it all for the sake of the Lord Jesus

CHAPTER XV.

The Pilgrims have another conference with Ignorance, who will not be convinced of his error—The good use of right fear—Why ignorant persons stifle conviction—Talk about one Temporary—The reasons why such as he turn back—How the apostate goes back.

I SAW then in my dream, that Hopeful looked back, and saw Ignorance, whom they had left behind, coming after. "Look," said he to Christian, "how far yonder youngster loitereth behind."

Chr. Ay, ay, I see him; he careth not for our company.

Hope. But I trow it would not have hurt him had he kept pace with us hitherto.

Chr. That is true, but I warrant you he thinketh otherwise.

Hope. That I think he doth; but, however, let us tarry for him. (So they did.)

Then Christian said to him, "Come away, man; why did you stay so behind?"

Ignor. I take my pleasure in walking alone, even more a great deal than in company, unless I like it the better.

Then said Christian to Hopeful, (but softly,) "Did I not tell you he cared not for our company? But however," said he, "come up, and let us talk away the time in this solitary place." Then directing his speech to Ignorance, he said, "Come, how do you do? How stands it between God and your soul now?"

Ignor. I hope, well; for I am always full of good motions that come into my mind to comfort me as I walk.

Chr. What good motions? pray tell us.

Ignor. Why, I think of God and heaven.

Chr. So do the devils and damned souls.

Ignor. But I think of them and desire them.

Chr. So do many that are never likely to come there. "The soul of the sluggard desires, and hath nothing." Prov. xiii, 4.

Ignor. But I think of them, and leave all for them.

Chr. That I doubt, for to leave all is a very hard matter; yea, a harder matter than any are aware of. But why, or for what, art thou persuaded that thou hast left all for God and heaven?

Ignor. My heart tells me so.

Chr. The wise man says, "He that trusteth in his own heart is a fool." Prov. xxviii, 26.

Ignor. That is spoken of an evil heart; but mine is a good one.

Chr. But how dost thou prove that?

Ignor. It comforts me in hopes of heaven.

Chr. That may be through its deceitfulness; for a man's heart may minister comfort to him in the hopes of that thing for which he has yet no ground to hope.

Ignor. But my heart and life agree together; and therefore my hope is well grounded.

Chr. Who told thee that thy heart and life agree together?

Ignor. My heart tells me so.

Chr. "Ask my fellow if I be a thief." Thy heart tells thee so! Except the word of God beareth witness in this matter, other testimony is of no value.

Ignor. But is it not a good heart that hath good thoughts? and is not that a good life that is according to God's commandments?

Chr. Yes, that is a good heart that hath good

thoughts, and that is a good life that is according to God's commandments; but it is one thing indeed to have these, and another thing only to think so.

Ignor. Pray, what count you good thoughts, and a life according to God's commandments?

Chr. There are good thoughts of divers kinds; some respecting ourselves, some God, some Christ, and some other things.

Ignor. What be good thoughts respecting ourselves?

Chr. Such as agree with the word of God.

Ignor. When do our thoughts of ourselves agree with the word of God?

Chr. When we pass the same judgment upon ourselves which the word passes. To explain myself, the word of God saith of persons in a natural condition, "There is none righteous, there is none that doeth good." Rom. iii, 10. It saith also, that "every imagination of the heart of man is only evil, and that continually." Gen. vi, 5. And again, "The imagination of man's heart is evil from his youth." Gen. viii, 21. Now, then, when we think thus of ourselves, having sense thereof, then are our thoughts good ones, because according to the word of God.

Ignor. I will never believe that my heart is thus bad.

Chr. Therefore thou never hadst one good thought concerning thyself in thy life. But let me go on. As the word passeth a judgment upon our hearts, so it passeth a judgment upon our ways; and when the thoughts of our hearts and ways agree with the judgment which the word giveth of both, then are both good, because agreeing thereto.

Ignor. Make out your meaning.

Chr. Why, the word of God saith, that man's ways are crooked ways, not good, but perverse: it saith, they are naturally out of the good way, that they have not known it.[1] Now when a man thus thinketh of his ways, I say when he doth sensibly, and with heart-humiliation, thus think, then hath he good thoughts of his own ways, because his thoughts now agree with the judgment of the word of God.

Ignor. What are good thoughts concerning God?

Chr. Even as I have said concerning ourselves, when our thoughts of God do agree with what the word saith of him; and that is, when we think of his being and attributes as the word hath taught; of which I cannot now discourse at large. But to speak of him with reference to us: then have we right thoughts of God when we think that he knows us better than we know ourselves, and can see sin in us when and where we can see none in ourselves: when we think he knows our inmost thoughts, and that our heart, with all its depths, is always open unto his eyes; also when we think that all our righteousness stinks in his nostrils, and that therefore he cannot abide to see us stand before him in any confidence, even of all our best performances.

Ignor. Do you think that I am such a fool as to think that God can see no further than I; or that I would come to God in the best of my performances?

Chr. Why, how dost thou think in this matter?

[1] As it is written, There is none righteous, no not one: there is none that understandeth, there is none that seeketh after God. They are all gone out of the way, they are together become unprofitable: there is none that doeth good, no, not one. Destruction and misery are in their ways: and the way of peace have they not known There is no fear of God before their eyes. Romans iii, 10–12, 16–18.

Ignor. Why, to be short, I think I must believe in Christ for justification.

Chr. How! think thou must believe in Christ, when thou seest not thy need of him! Thou neither seest thy original nor actual infirmities; but hast such an opinion of thyself, and of what thou doest, as plainly renders thee to be one that did never see a necessity of Christ's personal righteousness to justify thee before God. How, then, dost thou say, I believe in Christ?

Ignor. I believe well enough for that.

Chr. How dost thou believe?

Ignor. I believe that Christ died for sinners; and that I shall be justified before God from the curse, through his gracious acceptance of my obedience to his law. Or thus, Christ makes my duties, that are religious, acceptable to his Father by virtue of his merits, and so shall I be justified.

Chr. Let me give an answer to this confession of thy faith:—

1. Thou believest with a fantastical faith; for this faith is nowhere described in the word.

2. Thou believest with a false faith; because it taketh justification from the personal righteousness of Christ, and applies it to thy own.

3. This faith maketh not Christ a justifier of thy person, but of thy actions; and of thy person for thy actions' sake, which is false.

4. Therefore this faith is deceitful, even such as will leave thee under wrath in the day of God Almighty: for true justifying faith puts the soul, as sensible of its lost condition by the law, upon flying for refuge unto Christ's righteousness; (which righteousness of his is not an act of grace by which he maketh, for justifica-

tion, thy obedience accepted with God, but his personal obedience to the law, in doing and suffering for us what that required at our hands;) this righteousness, I say, true faith accepteth; under the skirt of which the soul being shrouded, and by it presented as spotless before God, it is accepted, and acquitted from condemnation.

Ignor. What! would you have us trust to what Christ in his own person has done without us? This conceit would loosen the reins of our lust, and tolerate us to live as we list: for what matter how we live, if we may be justified by Christ's personal righteousness from all, when we believe it?

Chr. Ignorance is thy name, and as thy name is, so art thou: even this thy answer demonstrateth what I say. Ignorant thou art of what justifying righteousness is, and as ignorant how to secure thy soul through the faith of it, from the heavy wrath of God. Yea, thou also art ignorant of the true effects of saving faith in this righteousness of Christ, which is to bow and win over the heart to God in Christ, to love his name, his word, ways, and people, and not as thou ignorantly imaginest.

Hope. Ask him if ever he had Christ revealed to him from heaven.

Ignor. What! you are a man for revelations! I believe, that what both you and all the rest of you say about that matter, is but the fruit of distracted brains.

Hope. Why man! Christ is so hid in God from the natural apprehensions of all flesh, that he cannot by any man be savingly known, unless God the Father reveals him to him.

Ignor. That is your faith, but not mine; yet mine,

I doubt not, is as good as yours, though I have not in my head so many whimsies as you.[2]

Chr. Give me leave to put in a word. You ought not so slightly to speak of this matter: for this I will boldly affirm, even as my good companion hath done, that no man can know Jesus Christ but by the revelation of the Father: yea, and faith too, by which the soul layeth hold upon Christ (if it be right) must be wrought by the exceeding greatness of his mighty power;[3] the working of which faith, I perceive, poor Ignorance, thou art ignorant of. Be awakened then, see thine own wretchedness, and fly to the Lord Jesus; and by his righteousness, which is the righteousness of God, (for he himself is God,) thou shalt be delivered from condemnation.

[2] There is no man more at ease in his mind (with such ease as it is) than the man that hath not closed with the Lord Jesus, but is shut up in unbelief. O! but this is the man that stands convict before God, and that is bound over to the *great assize!* This is the man whose sins are still his own, and upon whom the wrath of God abideth; for the ease and peace of such, though it keep them far from fear, is but like to that of the secure thief that is ignorant that the *constable standeth at the door;* the first sight of an officer makes his peace to give up the ghost. Ah! how many thousands there be that can now glory that they never were troubled for sin against God, whom God will trouble worse than he troubled cursed Achan; because their peace (though false and of the devil) was rather chosen by them than "peace by Jesus Christ," than "peace with God by the blood of his cross." Awake! careless sinners, awake! and arise from the dead. Content not yourselves either with sin or righteousness, if you be destitute of Christ.—*Bunyan on Justification.*

[3] That the God of our Lord Jesus Christ, the Father of glory, may give unto you the spirit of wisdom and revelation in the knowledge of him: the eyes of your understanding being enlightened; that ye may know what is the hope of his calling, and what the riches of the glory of his inheritance in the saints, and what is the exceeding greatness of his power to us-ward who believe, according to the working of his mighty power. Ephesians i. 17–19.

Ignor. You go so fast I cannot keep pace with you; do you go on before: I must stay awhile behind.

Then they said,—

"Well, Ignorance, wilt thou yet foolish be,
To slight good counsel, ten times given thee
And if thou yet refuse it, thou shalt know,
Ere long, the evil of thy doing so.
Remember, man, in time; stoop, do not fear;
Good counsel, taken well, saves; therefore hear.
But if thou yet shalt slight it, thou wilt be
The loser, Ignorance, I'll warrant thee"

Then Christian addressed himself thus to his fellow: "Well, come, my good Hopeful, I perceive that thou and I must walk by ourselves again."

So I saw in my dream that they went on apace before, and Ignorance he came hobbling after. Then said Christian to his companion, "It pities me much for this poor man: it will certainly go ill with him at last."

Hope. Alas! there are abundance in our town in his condition, whole families, yea, whole streets, and that of pilgrims too; and if there be so many in our parts, how many think you must there be in the place where he was born!

Chr. Indeed, the word saith, "He hath blinded their eyes, lest they should see," &c.[4]

But, now we are by ourselves, what do you think of such men? have they at no time, think you, convictions of sin, and so, consequently, fears that their state is dangerous?

[4] For the heart of this people is waxed gross, and their ears are dull of hearing, and their eyes have they closed; lest they should see with their eyes, and hear with their ears, and understand with their hearts, and should be converted, and I should heal them. Acts xxviii, 27.

Hope. Nay, do you answer that question for yourself, for you are the elder man.

Chr. Then I say, sometimes (as I think) they may; but they being naturally ignorant, understand not that such convictions tend to their good; and therefore they do desperately seek to stifle them, and presumptuously continue to flatter themselves in the way of their own hearts.

Hope. I do believe, as you say, that fear tends much to men's good, and to make them right at their beginning to go on pilgrimage.

Chr. Without all doubt it doth, if it be right: for so says the word, "The fear of the Lord is the beginning of wisdom." Psa. cxi, 10; Prov. ix, 10.

Hope. How will you describe right fear?

Chr. True or right fear is discovered by three things:

1. By its rise: it is caused by saving convictions for sin.

2. It driveth the soul to lay fast hold of Christ for salvation.

3. It begetteth and continueth in the soul a great reverence of God, his word, and ways; keeping it tender, and making it afraid to turn from them, to the right hand or to the left, to anything that may dishonour God, break its peace, grieve the Spirit, or cause the enemy to speak reproachfully.

Hope. Well said; I believe you have said the truth. Are we now almost got past the Enchanted Ground?

Chr. Why? are you weary of this discourse?

Hope. No, verily, but that I would know where we are.

Chr. We have not now above two miles further to go thereon. But let us return to our matter. Now the ignorant know not that such convictions as tend to put them in fear are for their good, and therefore they seek to stifle them.

Hope. How do they seek to stifle them?

Chr. 1. They think that those fears are wrought by the devil, (though indeed they are wrought of God,) and, thinking so, they resist them as things that directly tend to their overthrow. 2. They also think that these fears tend to the spoiling of their faith; (when, alas for them, poor men that they are, they have none at all;) and therefore they harden their hearts against them. 3. They presume they ought not to fear, and, therefore, in despite of them, wax presumptuously confident. 4. They see that these fears tend to take away from them their pitiful old self-holiness, and therefore they resist them with all ther might.

Hope. I know something of this myself; for before I knew myself it was so with me.

Chr. Well, we will leave, at this time, our neighbour Ignorance by himself, and fall upon another profitable question.

Hope. With all my heart; but you shall still begin.

Chr. Well, then, did you know, about ten years ago, one Temporary in your parts, who was a forward man in religion then?

Hope. Know him! yes; he dwelt in Graceless, a town about two miles off of Honesty, and he dwelt next door to one Turnback.

Chr. Right; he dwelt under the same roof with him. Well, that man was much awakened once: I believe that then he had some sight of his sins, and of the wages that were due thereto.

Hope. I am of your mind, for (my house not being above three miles from him) he would oftentimes come to me, and that with many tears. Truly I pitied the man, and was not altogether without hope of him; but one may see, it is not every one that cries, "Lord, Lord!"

Chr. He told me once that he was resolved to go on pilgrimage, as we go now; but all on a sudden he grew acquainted with one Save-self, and then he became a stranger to me.

Hope. Now, since we are talking about him, let us a little inquire into the reason of the sudden backsliding of him and such others.

Chr. It may be very profitable; but do you begin.

Hope. Well, then, there are, in my judgment, four reasons for it:—

1. Though the consciences of such men are awakened, yet their minds are not changed: therefore, when the power of guilt weareth away, that which provoked them to be religious ceaseth; wherefore they naturally turn to their old course again: even as we see the dog that is sick of what he hath eaten, so long as his sickness prevails, he vomits and casts up all; not that he doth this of a free mind, (if we may say a dog has a mind,) but because it troubleth his stomach: but now, when his sickness is over, and so his stomach eased, his desires being not all alienated from his vomit, he turns him about, and licks up all; and so it is true which is written, "The dog is turned to his own vomit again." 2 Pet. ii, 22. Thus, I say, being hot for heaven, by virtue only of the sense and fear of the torments of hell, as their sense of hell and fear of damnation chills and cools, so their desires for heaven and salvation cool also. So then it comes to pass, that when their guilt and fear is gone, their desires for heaven and happiness die, and they return to their course again.

2. Another reason is, they have slavish fears that do overmaster them: I speak now of the fears that they have of men; "for the fear of man bringeth a snare." Prov. xxix, 25. So then, though they seem to be hot for heaven so long as the flames of hell are about their ears, yet, when that terror is a little over, they betake themselves to second thoughts, namely, that it is good to be wise, and not to run (for they know not what) the hazard of losing all, or at least of bringing themselves into unavoidable and unnecessary troubles; and so they fall in with the world again.

3. The shame that attends religion lies also as a block in their way; they are proud and haughty, and religion in their eye is low and contemptible: therefore when they have lost their sense of hell and the wrath to come, they return again to their former course.

4. Guilt, and to meditate terror, are grievous to them; they like not to see their misery before they come into it; though perhaps the sight of it first, if they loved that sight, might make them fly whither the righteous fly, and are safe; but because they do, as I hinted before, even shun the thoughts of guilt and terror, therefore, when once they are rid of their awakenings about the terrors and wrath of God, they harden their hearts gladly, and choose such ways as will harden them more and more.

Chr. You are pretty near the business, for the bottom of all is for want of a change in their mind and will. And therefore they are but like the felon that standeth before the judge: he quakes and trembles, and seems to repent most heartily; but the bottom of all is the fear of the halter; not that he hath any detestation of the offence, as is evident; because, let but this man have his liberty, and he will be a thief, and so a rogue still; whereas, if his mind was changed, he would be otherwise.

Hope. Now I have showed you the reasons of their going back, do you show me the manner thereof.

Chr. So I will willingly:—

1. They draw off their thoughts, all that they may, from the remembrance of God, death, and judgment to come.

2. Then they cast off by degrees private duties, as closet prayer, curbing their lusts, watching, sorrow for sin, and the like.

3. Then they shun the company of lively and warm Christians.

4. After that, they grow cold to public duty, as hearing, reading, godly conference, and the like.

5. They then begin to pick holes, as we say, in the coats of some of the godly; and that devilishly, that they may have a seeming colour to throw religion (for the sake of some infirmities they have espied in them) behind their backs.

6. Then they begin to adhere to, and associate themselves with, carnal, loose, and wanton men.

7. They then give way to carnal and wanton discourses in secret; and glad are they if they can see such things in any that are counted honest, that they may the more boldly do it through their example.

8. After this they begin to play with little sins openly.

9. And then, being hardened, they show themselves as they are. Thus, being launched again into the gulf of misery, unless a miracle of grace prevent it, they everlastingly perish in their own deceivings.

No night is here for to eclipse
Its spangling rays so bright;
Nor doubt, nor fear to shut the lips
Of those within this light

CHAPTER XVI.

The Pilgrims, having got over the Enchanted Ground, enter the country of Beulah—They come to a river without a bridge, which they must pass—Christian's conflict at the hour of death—He is delivered from his fears—The angels wait for them as soon as they are passed out of this world—Their admission into the City—Ignorance comes up to the river—Vain-Hope ferries him over—What becomes of him.

Now I saw in my dream, that by this time the pilgrims were got over the Enchanted Ground, and entering into the country of Beulah, (Isa. lxii, 4–12,) whose air was very sweet and pleasant, the way lying directly through it, they solaced themselves there for a season. Yea, here they heard continually the singing of birds, and saw every day the flowers appear in the earth, and heard the voice of the turtle in the land. In this country the sun shineth night and day: wherefore this was beyond the Valley of the Shadow of Death, and also out of the reach of Giant Despair; neither could they from this place so much as see Doubting Castle. Here they were within sight of the City they were going to: also here met them some of the inhabitants thereof; for in this land the shining ones commonly walked, because it was upon the borders of heaven. In this land also the contract between the Bride and the Bridegroom was renewed; yea, here "as the bridegroom rejoiceth over the bride, so doth their God rejoice over them." Here they had no want of corn and wine; for in this place they met with abundance of what they had sought for in all their pilgrimages. Here they heard voices from out of the City, loud voices, saying, "Say ye to the daughter of Zion, Behold, thy salvation cometh! Behold, his reward is with him!" Here all the inhabitants of the country called them "the holy people, the redeemed of the Lord, sought out," &c.[1]

[1] The pleasant country of Beulah, where the pilgrims "solaced themselves for a season," before they passed the river of death, seems to shadow forth the highest state of spiritual enjoyment attainable in the present life,—the sweet peace and confidence, the joyful assurance, the blissful anticipations often vouchsafed to the tried believer before he quits the scene of mortality to enter into rest. The following extract from Coxe's Life of that holy man, J. Fletcher of Madeley, furnishes, we think, a good illustration of this portion of Bunyan's allegory: "His general attainments in divine things had long been of a very exalted kind. His uncommon power over sin, his habitual recollection, his uninterrupted communion with God, together with his extensive enjoyment of the graces and consolations of the Holy Spirit, had for many years marked him out as a Christian of no ordinary standard. But toward the close of his life he was in the habit of expecting a yet greater fulness of spiritual enjoyments. The following lines, expressive of his desires, were frequently uttered by him as the language of his ardent mind:—

'Stretch my faith's capacity
Wider and yet wider still;
Then with all that is in Thee
My soul for ever fill.' Eph. iii, 19.

And in answer to these his pious breathings, he seemed, for a short time previous to his death, to have lived within the very precincts of the celestial world. 'A few days before his dissolution,' says Mr. Gilpin, 'he appeared to have reached that desirable point, where the last rapturous discoveries are made to the souls of dying saints. Roused, as it were, with the shouts of angels, and kindled into rapture with visions of glory, he broke forth into a song of holy triumph, which began and ended with praises of God's unfathomable love. He laboured to declare the secret manifestations he enjoyed; but his sensations were too powerful for utterance; and, after *looking* unutterable things, he contented himself with calling upon all around him to celebrate that adorable love which can never be fully comprehended nor adequately expressed. This triumphant frame of mind was not a transient feeling, but a state that he continued to enjoy, with little or no discernible interruption, to the moment of his death. While he possessed the power of speech, he spake as one whose lips

Now, as they walked in this land, they had more rejoicing than in parts more remote from the kingdom to which they were bound; and drawing near to the City, they had yet a more perfect view thereof. It was builded of pearls and precious stones, also the streets thereof were paved with gold; so that, by reason of the natural glory of the City, and the reflection of the sunbeams upon it, Christian with desire fell sick. Hopeful also had a fit or two of the same disease; wherefore here they lay by it awhile, crying out because of their pangs, "If you see my Beloved, tell him that I am sick of love."[2]

But, being a little strengthened, and better able to bear their sickness, they walked on their way, and

had been touched with a *live coal from the altar;* and, when deprived of that power, his countenance discovered that he was secretly engaged in the contemplation of eternal things.'"

[2] The ravishing views of the heavenly world described in the preceding paragraph induce in the soul that enjoys them, a longing to be freed from the shackles that bind it to earth. Then its language is, "O that I had wings like a dove, then would I fly away and be at rest." "I have a desire to depart and be with Christ, which is far better" than to abide in this tabernacle of clay. "My heart and my flesh crieth out for the living God, When shall I come and appear before God?"

> "I long to behold Him array'd
> With glory and light from above
> The King in his beauty display'd,
> His beauty of holiest love:
> I languish and sigh to be there
> Where Jesus hath fix'd his abode:
> O when shall we meet in the air,
> And fly to the mountain of God!"

These feelings of "earnest expectation" and ardent desire are tempered in the believing soul by the most perfect resignation to the divine will: while, in the language of one inspired writer he prays that he may "go over and see the good land;" in the words of another he submissively adds, "all the days of my appointed time will I wait till my change come."

came yet nearer and nearer, where were orchards, vineyards, and gardens, and their gates opened into the highway. Now, as they came up to these places, behold the gardener stood in the way; to whom the pilgrims said, "Whose goodly vineyards and gardens are these?" He answered, "They are the King's, and are planted here for his own delights, and also for the solace of pilgrims." So the gardener had them into the vineyards, and bid them refresh themselves with the dainties; he also showed them there the King's walks and the arbours, where he delighteth to be: and here they tarried and slept.

Now I beheld in my dream that they talked more in their sleep at this time than ever they did in all their journey; and, being in a muse thereabout, the gardener said even to me, "Wherefore musest thou at the matter; it is the nature of the fruit of the grapes of these vineyards 'to go down so sweetly as to cause the lips of them that are asleep to speak.'" Cant. vii, 9.

So I saw that when they awoke they addressed themselves to go up to the City. But, as I said, the reflection of the sun upon the City (for the city was pure gold, Rev. xxi, 18) was so extremely glorious that they could not as yet with open face behold it, but through an instrument made for that purpose. 2 Cor. iii, 18. So I saw, that as they went on, there met them two men in raiment that shone like gold, also their faces shone as the light.

These men asked the pilgrims whence they came; and they told them. They also asked them where they had lodged, what difficulties and dangers, what comforts and pleasures, they had met in the way; and they told them. Then said the men that met them,

"You have but two difficulties more to meet with, and then you are in the City."

Christian then and his companion asked the men to go along with them: so they told them that they would; "But," said they, "you must obtain it by your own faith." So I saw in my dream that they went on together till they came in sight of the gate.

Now I further saw, that betwixt them and the gate was a river; but there was no bridge to go over, and the river was very deep. At the sight therefore of this river the pilgrims were much stunned; but the men that went with them said, "You must go through or you cannot come at the gate."[3]

The pilgrims then began to inquire if there was no other way to the gate. To which they answered, "Yes; but there hath not any, save two, to wit, Enoch and Elijah, been permitted to tread that path since the foundation of the world, nor shall until the last trumpet shall sound." The pilgrims then, especially Christian, began to despond in his mind, and looked this way and that, but no way could be found by them by which they

[3] The day of death, when I am to pack up all to be gone from hence, is a "time of need." Now the greatest trial is come, excepting that of the day of judgment. Now a man is to be stripped of all but "that which cannot be shaken." Now a man grows near the borders of eternity: now he begins to see into the skirts of the next world: now death is death, and the grave the grave indeed. Now the dark entry, and the thoughts of what is in the way from a death-bed to the gate of the holy heaven, comes nearer the heart than when health and prosperity do compass a man about. Wherefore this is like to be a trying time, a "time of need," indeed. A prudent man will make it one of the great concerns of his whole life to get and lay up a stock of grace for this day; for he knows all will be little enough to keep him warm in his soul while cold death strokes his hand over his face, and over his heart; while strong death is loosing his silver cord, and breaking his golden bowl.—*Bunyan's Saint's Priv*

Then said the other, "Be of good cheer, my brother; I feel the bottom, and it is good."

might escape tne river. Then they asked the men if the waters were all of a depth. They said, "No;" yet they could not help them in that case; "for," said they, "you shall find it deeper or shallower as you believe in the King of the place."

They then addressed themselves to the water, and entering, Christian began to sink, and, crying out to his good friend Hopeful, he said, "I sink in deep waters, the billows go over my head; all his waves go over me." Selah.

Then said the other, "Be of good cheer, my brother; I feel the bottom, and it is good." Then said Christian, "Ah! my friend, the sorrows of death have compassed me about, I shall not see the land that flows with milk and honey." And with that a great darkness and horror fell upon Christian, so that he could not see before him. Also here he in a great measure lost his senses, so that he could neither remember nor orderly talk of any of those sweet refreshments that he had met with in the way of his pilgrimage. But all the words that he spoke still tended to discover that he had horror of mind, and heart-fears that he should die in that river and never obtain entrance in at the gate. Here also, as they that stood by perceived, he was much in the troublesome thoughts of the sins that he had committed, both since and before he began to be a pilgrim. It was also observed, that he was troubled with apparitions of hobgoblins and evil spirits; for ever and anon he would intimate so much by words.

Hopeful therefore here had much ado to keep his brother's head above water; yea, sometimes he would be quite gone down, and then, ere awhile, he would rise up again half dead. Hopeful also would endeavour to comfort him, saying, "Brother, I see the gate, and men standing by to receive us;" but Christian would answer, "'Tis you, 'tis you they wait for; you have been hopeful ever since I knew you." "And so have you," said he to Christian. "Ah, brother, (said he,) surely if I was right he would now arise to help me; but for my sins he hath brought me into the snare, and hath left me." Then said Hopeful, "My brother, you have quite forgot the text where it is said of the wicked, 'There are no bands in their death, but their strength is firm; they are not troubled as other men, neither are they plagued like other men,' Psa. lxxiii, 4, 5. These troubles and distresses that you go through in these waters, are no sign that God hath forsaken you; but are sent to try you, whether you will call to mind that which heretofore you have received of his goodness, and live upon him in your distresses."[4]

Then I saw in my dream, that Christian was in a muse awhile. To whom also Hopeful added these words, "Be of good cheer, Jesus Christ maketh thee whole." And with that Christian brake out with a loud voice, "O, I see him again! and he tells me, 'When thou passest through the waters, I will be with thee; and through the rivers, they shall not overflow thee.'" Isa. xliii, 2. Then they both took courage, and the enemy was after that as still as a stone, until they were gone over. Christian, therefore, presently found ground to stand upon, and so it followed that the rest of the river was but shallow. Thus they got over.

[4] Sick-bed temptations are ofttimes the most violent, because then the devil is to play his last game with us; he is never to assault us more. But out of all these the LORD will deliver his people. He shall save Israel "out of all his troubles," out of sick-bed troubles as well as others. Psalm xxxiv, 6; xlviii, 14.—*Bunyan's Saved by Grace*

Now upon the bank of the river, on the other side, they saw the two shining men again, who there waited for them. Wherefore, being come out of the river, they saluted them, saying, "We are ministering spirits, sent forth to minister for those that shall be heirs of salvation." Thus they went along toward the gate.

Now you must note, that the City stood upon a mighty hill: but the pilgrims went up that hill with ease, because they had these two men to lead them up by the arms; they had likewise left their mortal garments behind them in the river; for though they went in with them, they came out without them. They therefore went up here with much agility and speed, though the foundation upon which the City was framed was higher than the clouds: they therefore went up through the regions of the air, sweetly talking as they went, being comforted because they safely got over the river, and had such glorious companions to attend them.

The talk that they had with the shining ones was about the glory of the place; who told them that the beauty and glory of it was inexpressible. "There," said they, "is the Mount Sion, the heavenly Jerusalem, the innumerable company of angels, and the spirits of just men made perfect." Heb. xii, 22-24. "You are going now," said they, "to the paradise of God, wherein you shall see the tree of life, and eat of the never-fading fruits thereof; and when you come there you shall have white robes given you, and your walk and talk shall be every day with the King, even all the days of eternity. There you shall not see again such things as you saw when you were in the lower region upon the earth; to wit, sorrow, sickness, affliction, and death; 'For the former things are passed away.' Rev. xxi, 4.

You are going now to Abraham, to Isaac, and Jacob, and to the prophets, men that God hath taken away from the evil to come, and that are now 'resting upon their beds, each one walking in his righteousness.'"

The men then asked, "What must we do in the holy place?" To whom it was answered, "You must there receive the comfort of all your toil, and have joy for all your sorrow; you must reap what you have sown, even the fruit of all your prayers, and tears, and sufferings for the King by the way. In that place you must wear crowns of gold, and enjoy the perpetual sight and vision of the Holy One; for 'there you shall see him as he is.' 1 John iii, 2. There also you shall serve Him continually with praise, with shouting and thanksgiving, whom you desired to serve in the world, though with much difficulty, because of the infirmity of your flesh. There your eyes shall be delighted with seeing, and your ears with hearing the pleasant voice of the Mighty One. There you shall enjoy your friends again that are gone thither before you; and there you shall with joy receive even every one that follows into the holy place after you. There also you shall be clothed with glory and majesty, and put into an equipage fit to ride out with the King of glory. When he shall come with sound of trumpet in the clouds, as upon the wings of the wind, you shall come with him; and when he shall sit upon the throne of judgment, you shall sit by him; yea, and when he shall pass sentence upon all the workers of iniquity, let them be angels or men, you also shall have a voice in that judgment, because they were his and your enemies. 1 Cor. vi, 2, 3. Also when he shall again return to the City, you shall go too, with sound of trumpet, and be ever with him. 1 Thes. iv, 13-18

Now while they were thus drawing toward the gate, behold a company of the heavenly host came out to meet them; to whom it was said by the other two shining ones, "These are the men that have loved our Lord, when they were in the world, and that have left all for his holy name; and he hath sent us to fetch them, and we have brought them thus far on their desired journey, that they may go in and look their Redeemer in the face with joy." Then the heavenly host gave a great shout, saying, "Blessed are they that are called to the marriage-supper of the Lamb." Rev. xix, 9. There came out also at this time to meet them several of the King's trumpeters, clothed in white and shining raiment, who, with melodious voices and loud, made even the heavens to echo with their sound. These trumpeters saluted Christian and his fellow with ten thousand welcomes from the world; and this they did with shouting and sound of trumpet.

This done, they compassed them round on every side; some went before, some behind, and some on the right hand, and some on the left, (as it were to guard them through the upper regions,) continually sounding as they went, with melodious noise, in notes on high: so that the very sight was to them that could behold it as if heaven itself was come down to meet them. Thus therefore they walked on together; and, as they walked, ever and anon these trumpeters, even with joyful sound, would, by mixing their music with looks and gestures, still signify to Christian and his brother how welcome they were into their company, and with what gladness they came to meet them. And now were these two men, as it were, in heaven, before they came at it, being swallowed up with the sight of angels, and with hearing their melodious notes. Here also they had the City itself in view; and they thought they heard all the bells therein to ring, to welcome them thereto. But, above all, the warm and joyful thoughts that they had about their own dwelling there with such company, and that for ever and ever, O, by what tongue or pen can their glorious joy be expressed! Thus they came up to the gate.

Now when they were come up to the gate, there was written over it in letters of gold, (Rev. xxii, 14,)

BLESSED ARE THEY THAT DO HIS COMMANDMENTS,

THAT THEY MAY HAVE RIGHT TO THE TREE OF LIFE,

AND MAY ENTER IN THROUGH THE GATES INTO THE CITY

Then I saw in my dream that the shining men bid them call at the gate: the which when they did, some from above looked over the gate, to wit, Enoch, Moses, and Elijah, &c., to whom it was said, "These pilgrims are come from the City of Destruction, for the love that they bear to the King of this place:" and then the pilgrims gave in unto them each man his certificate, which they had received in the beginning; those therefore were carried in unto the King, who, when he had read them, said, "Where are the men?" To whom it was answered, "They are standing without the gate." The King then commanded to open the gate, "That the righteous nation (said he) that keepeth the truth may enter in." Isaiah xxvi, 2.

Now I saw in my dream that these two men went in at the gate; and lo! as they entered, they were transfigured; and they had raiment put on that shone like gold. There were also that met them with harps and crowns, and gave them to them; the harps to praise withal, and the crowns in token of honour. Then I heard in my dream that all the bells in the City rang again for joy, and that it was said unto them,

ENTER YE INTO THE JOY OF OUR LORD.

I also heard the men themselves, that they sang with a loud voice, saying, "BLESSING, AND HONOUR, AND GLORY, AND POWER, BE UNTO HIM THAT SITTETH UPON THE THRONE, AND UNTO THE LAMB, FOR EVER AND EVER." Rev. v, 13.

Now, just as the gates were opened to let in the men, I looked in after them, and behold the City shone like the sun; the streets also were paved with gold; and in them walked many men, with crowns on their heads, palms in their hands, and golden harps, to sing praises withal.

They were also of them that had wings, and they answered one another without intermission, saying, "Holy, holy, holy is the Lord." And after that they shut up the gates: which, when I had seen, I wished myself among them.[5]

Now, while I was gazing upon all these things, I turned my head to look back, and saw Ignorance come up to the river side; but he soon got over, and that without half the difficulty which the other two men met with. For it happened that there was then in the place one Vain-Hope, a ferryman, that with his boat helped him over: so he, as the others I saw, did as-

5 "Here assuredly," says Mr. Montgomery, "the story ought to have ended, leaving the reader to shut the book, with the closing gates of heaven in his eye, and the author's pious wish in his heart. But the stern justice of John Bunyan to every part of his subject, compelled him to add what, indeed, is a very seasonable warning to those who go on pilgrimage—that though the right-minded Christian cannot fail at last, the presumptuous sinner cannot escape."

cend the hill, to come up to the gate; only he came alone; neither did any meet him with the least encouragement.[6] When he was come up to the gate, he looked up to the writing that was above, and then began to knock, supposing that entrance should have been quickly administered to him: but he was asked by the men that looked over the top of the gate, "Whence come you? and what would you have?" He answered, "I have eat and drank in the presence of the King, and he has taught in our streets." Then they asked him for his certificate, that they might go in and show it to the King: so he fumbled in his bosom for one, and found none. Then said they, "Have you none?" but the man answered never a word. So they told the King, but he would not come down to see him, but commanded the two shining ones, that conducted Christian and Hopeful to the City, to go out, and take Ignorance,

[6] Some there are that will speak as confidently of their eternal state, and the welfare of their souls, as if they had the most excellent experience of any man or woman in the world, saying, "I shall have peace," when they are as ignorant of the new birth, of the nature and operation of faith, of the witness of the Spirit, as if there was no new birth, no faith, no witness of the Spirit of Christ in any of the saints in the world. Nay, thus many of them are even an hour or less before their departure. They go away here like a lamb, as the world says. Now by this one thing doth the devil take great advantage on the hearts of the ignorant, suggesting to them, that because the deceased departed so quietly, without all doubt they are gone to rest and joy, when, alas! the reason why they went away so quietly, was because they were senseless and hardened in their consciences Had they but had some awakenings on their death-beds, they would have made all the town ring of their doleful condition: but because they are seared and ignorant, and so depart quietly, the world takes heart, and makes no great matter of living and dying they cannot tell how. But let them look to themselves, for if they have not an interest in the Lord Jesus, they will, whether they die raging or still, go to the same place, and lift up their eyes in hell.—*Bunyan's Sighs from Hell*

and bind him, hand and foot, and have him away. Then they took him up, and carried him through the air, to the door that I saw in the side of the hill, and put him in there. Then I saw that there was a way to hell, even from the gate of heaven, as well as from the City of Destruction.[7] So I awoke, and behold it was a dream.

[7] What a strange disappointment will many professors meet with at the day of judgment! Let us therefore fear, lest a promise being left us of entering into rest, any of us should seem to come short of it. O, to come short! nothing kills like it, nothing will burn like it. I intend not discouragements, but awakenings: the churches have need of awakening, and so have all professors. Do not despise me, therefore, but hear me over again: What a strange disappointment will many professors meet with at the day of God Almighty! 1. They will look to escape hell, and yet fall just into the mouth of hell: what a disappointment will here be! 2. They will look for heaven; but the gate of heaven will be shut against them: what a disappointment is here! 3. They will expect that Christ should have compassion for them: but will find that he hath shut up all bowels of compassion from them: what a disappointment is here! As this disappointment will be fearful, so certainly it will be very full of amazement. 1. Will it not amaze them to be unexpectedly excluded from life and salvation? 2. Will it not be amazing to them to see their own madness and folly, while they consider how they have dallied with their own souls, and took lightly for granted, that they had that grace that would save them? 3. Will they not also be amazed one at another, while they remember how in their lifetime they counted themselves fellow-heirs of bliss? 4. Will it not be amazing to some of the damned themselves to see some come to hell that then they shall see come thither? to see preachers of the word, professors of the word come thither? They that see thee shall narrowly look upon thee, and consider thee, saying, Is this the man? Is this he that professed, and disputed, and forsook us; but now he is come to us again? Is this he that separated from us, but now is he fallen with us into the same eternal damnation? .... O my friends, did you but know what a miserable condition they are in that go out of this world without an interest in the Son of God, it would make you smite upon your thigh, and in the bitterness of your souls cry out, "Men and brethren, what shall we do to be saved?" and not only so, but thou wouldst not be comforted until thou didst find a rest for thy soul in the Lord Jesus Christ.—*Bunyan's Sighs from Hell.*

CONCLUSION.

Now, Reader, I have told my dream to thee,
See if thou canst interpret it to me,
Or to thyself, or neighbour; but take heed
Of misinterpreting, for that, instead
Of doing good, will but thyself abuse:
By misinterpreting, evil ensues.

Take heed also that thou be not extreme
In playing with the outside of my dream:
Nor let my figure or similitude
Put thee into a laughter, or a feud;
Leave this for boys and fools; but as for thee
Do thou the substance of my matter see.

Put by the curtains, look within the veil,
Turn up my metaphors, and do not fail;
There, if thou seekest them, such things thou'lt find
As will be helpful to an honest mind.

What of my dross thou findest there, be bold
To throw away, but yet preserve the gold.
What if my gold be wrapped up in ore?
None throws away the apple for the core.
But if thou shalt cast all away as vain,
I know not but 'twill make me dream again.

THE

PILGRIM'S PROGRESS

FROM

THIS WORLD TO THAT WHICH IS TO COME.

DELIVERED UNDER THE SIMILITUDE OF A DREAM

PART II.

WHEREIN IS SET FORTH THE MANNER OF THE SETTING OUT OF CHRISTIAN'S WIFE AND CHILDREN; THEIR DANGEROUS JOURNEY; AND SAFE ARRIVAL AT THE DESIRED COUNTRY.

I have used similitudes. Hosea xii, 10.

THE AUTHOR'S WAY

OF SENDING FORTH HIS

SECOND PART OF THE PILGRIM.

Go now, my little Book, to every place
Where my *First Pilgrim* has but shown his face:
Call at their door: if any say, *Who's there?*
Then answer thou, CHRISTIANA *is here.*
If they bid thee, *Come in,* then enter thou,
With all thy boys; and then, as thou know'st how,
Tell who they are, also from whence they came:
Perhaps they'll know them by their looks or name:
But if they should not, ask them yet again,
If formerly they did not entertain
One CHRISTIAN, *a Pilgrim?* If they say
They did, and were delighted in his way;
Then let them know, that these related were
Unto him: yea, his Wife and Children are.
Tell them, that they have left their house and home,
Are turned Pilgrims; seek a world to come:
That they *have* met with hardships in the way;
That they *do* meet with troubles night and day;
That they have trod on serpents; fought with devils,
Have also overcome a many evils:
Yea tell them also of the next who have,
Of love to Pilgrimage, been stout and brave
Defenders of that Way; and how they still
Refuse this World, to do their Father's will.

Go tell them also of those dainty things
That Pilgrimage unto the Pilgrims brings.
Let them acquainted be too, how they are
Beloved of their King, under his care;
What goodly mansions he for them provides;
Though they meet with rough winds and swelling tides,
How brave a calm they will enjoy at last,
Who to their Lord and by his ways hold fast.
  Perhaps with heart and hand they will embrace
Thee as they did my firstling; and will grace
Thee and thy fellows with such cheer and fare
As show well, they of Pilgrims lovers are.

OBJECTION I.

But how, if they will not believe of me
That I am truly thine? 'cause some there be
That counterfeit the Pilgrim and his name,
Seek, by disguise, to seem the very same;
And by that means have brought themselves into
The hands and houses of I know not who.

ANSWER.

'Tis true some have of late, to counterfeit
My Pilgrim, to their own my title set;
Yea, others half my name, and title too,
Have stitched to their books to make them do;
But yet they, by their features, do declare
Themselves not mine to be, whose e'er they are.
  If such thou meet'st with, then thine only way,
Before them all, is to *say out thy say*
In thine own native language, which no man
Now useth, nor with ease dissemble can.
  If, after all, they still of you shall doubt,
Thinking that you like Gipsies go about,
In naughty wise the country to defile;
Or that you seek good people to beguile
With things unwarrantable; send for me,
And I will testify you Pilgrims be;

Yea, I will testify that only you
My Pilgrims are ; and that alone will do.

OBJECTION II.

But yet, perhaps, I may inquire for him
Of those who wish him damned life and limb :
What shall I do, when I at such a door
For Pilgrims ask, and they shall rage the more?

ANSWER.

Fright not thyself, my Book, for such bugbears
Are nothing else but ground for groundless fears
My Pilgrim's book has travell'd sea and land,
Yet could I never come to understand
That it was slighted, or turn'd out of door,
By any kingdom, were they rich or poor.
In France and Flanders, where men kill each other,
My Pilgrim is esteem'd a friend, a brother.
In Holland too, 'tis said, as I am told,
My Pilgrim is with some worth more than gold.
Highlanders and wild Irish can agree
My Pilgrim should familiar with them be.
'Tis in New-England under such advance,
Receives there so much loving countenance,
As to be trimm'd, new clothed, and deck'd with gems,
That it might show its features and its limbs,
Yet more, so comely doth my Pilgrim walk,
That of him thousands daily sing and talk.
If you draw nearer home, it will appear
My Pilgrim knows no ground of shame or fear.
City or country will him entertain
With, *Welcome, Pilgrim;* yea, they can't refrain
From smiling, if my Pilgrim be but by,
Or shows his head in any company.
Brave gallants do my Pilgrim hug and love,
Esteem it much, yea, value it above
Things of a greater bulk; yea, with delignt,
Say, my lark's leg is better than a kite.

Young ladies and young gentlewomen too
Do no small kindness to my Pilgrim show.
Their cabinets, their bosoms, and their hearts,
My Pilgrim has; 'cause he to them imparts
His pretty riddles in such wholesome strains
As yield them profit double to their pains
Of reading; yea, I think I may be bold
To say, some prize him far above their gold.
The very children that do walk the street,
If they do but my holy Pilgrim meet,
Salute him will; will wish him well, and say,
He is the only stripling of the day.
They that have never seen him, yet admire
What they have heard of him, and much desire
To have his company, and hear him tell
Those *pilgrim stories* which he knows so well.
Yea, some that did not love him at the first,
But call'd him *fool* and *noddy*, say they must,
Now they have seen and heard him, him commend·
And to those whom they love, they do him send.
Wherefore, my SECOND PART, thou need'st not be
Afraid to show thy head: none can hurt thee
That wish but well to him that went before;
Cause thou com'st after with a second store
Of things as good, as rich, as profitable,
For young, for old, for staggering, and for stable.

OBJECTION III.

But some there be that say, He laughs too loud.
And some do say, His head is in a cloud.
Some say, His words and stories are so dark
They know not how by them to find his mark.

ANSWER.

One may, I think, say, Both his laughs and cries
May well be guess'd at by his wat'ry eyes.
Some things are of that nature as to make
One's fancy chuckle, while his heart doth ache.

When Jacob saw his Rachel with the sheep,
He did, at the same time, both kiss and weep.
Whereas some say, *A cloud is in his head;*
That doth but show his wisdom's covered
With his own mantle, and to stir the mind
To search well after what it fain would find;
Things that seem to be hid in words obscure,
Do but the godly mind the more allure
To study what those sayings should contain,
That speak to us in such a cloudy strain.
I also know a dark similitude
Will on the curious fancy more intrude,
And will stick faster in the heart and head
Than things from similes not borrowed.
Wherefore, my Book, let no discouragement
Hinder thy travels. Behold! thou art sent
To friends, not foes; to friends that will give place
To thee, thy Pilgrims, and thy words embrace.
Besides, what my First Pilgrim left conceal'd,
Thou, my brave Second Pilgrim, hast reveal'd;
What Christian left lock'd up, and went his way,
Sweet Christiana opens with her key.

OBJECTION IV.

But some love not the method of your First:
Romance they count it; throw't away as dust.
If I should meet with such, what should I say?
Must I slight them as they slight me, or nay?

ANSWER.

My Christiana, if with such thou meet,
By all means, in all loving wise them greet·
Render them not reviling for revile:
But if they frown, I pr'ythee, on them smile:
Perhaps 'tis nature, or some ill report,
Has made them thus despise, or thus retort.
Some love no fish, some love no cheese, and some
Love not their friends, nor their own house or home·

Some start at pig, slight chicken, love not fowl,
More than they love a cuckoo or an owl.
Leave such, my Christiana, to their choice,
And seek those who to find thee will rejoice
By no means strive, but in most humble wise
Present thee to them in thy Pilgrim's guise.
Go then, my little Book, and show to all
That entertain and bid thee welcome shall,
What thou shalt keep close shut up from the rest;
And wish what thou shalt show them may be bless'd
To them for good, and make them choose to be
Pilgrims by better far than thee and me.
Go then, I say, tell all men who thou art:
Say, I am Christiana; and my part
Is now, with my four sons, to tell you what
It is for men to take a Pilgrim's lot.
Go also, tell them who and what they be
That now do go on pilgrimage with thee;
Say, Here's my neighbour Mercy; she is one
That has long time with me a pilgrim gone;
Come see her in her virgin face, and learn
'Twixt idle ones and pilgrims to discern.
Yea, let young damsels learn of her to prize
The world which is to come, in any wise.
When little tripping maidens follow God,
And leave old doating sinners to his rod,
'Tis like those days wherein the young ones cried
Hosanna! when the old ones did deride.
Next tell them of old Honest, whom you found
With his white hairs, treading the Pilgrim's ground;
Yea, tell them how plain-hearted this man was,
How after his good Lord he bare the cross.
Perhaps with some gray head this may prevail
With Christ to fall in love, and sin bewail.
Tell also them, how Master Fearing went
On pilgrimage, and how the time he spent
In solitariness, with fears and cries;
And how at last he won the joyful prize.

He *was* a good man, though much down in spirit,
He *is* a good man, and doth life inherit.
  Tell them of Master Feeble-Mind also,
Who not before, but still behind would go.
Show them also, how he had like been slain,
And how one Great-Heart did his life regain.
This man was true of heart, though weak in grace,
One might true godliness read in his face.
  Then tell them of Master Ready-to-Halt,
A man with crutches, but much without fault.
Tell them how Master Feeble-Mind and he
Did love, and in opinion much agree;
And let all know, though weakness was their chance,
Yet sometimes one could sing, the other dance.
  Forget not Master Valiant-for-the-Truth,
That man of courage, though a very youth.
Tell every one his spirit was so stout
No man could ever make him face about;
And how Great-Heart and he could not forbear,
But put down Doubting Castle, slay Despair!
  Overlook not Master Despondency,
Nor Much-afraid, his daughter, though they lie
Under such mantles, as may make them look
(With some) as if their God had them forsook.
They softly went, but sure; and at the end,
Found that the Lord of Pilgrims was their friend.
  When thou hast told the world of all these things,
Then turn about, my Book, and touch these strings.
Which, if but touch'd, will such music make,
They'll make a cripple dance, a giant quake.
  Those riddles that lie couch'd within thy breast
Freely propound, expound; and for the rest
Of thy mysterious lines, let them remain
For those whose nimble fancies shall them gain.
  Now may this little Book a blessing be
To those that love this little Book and me;
And may its buyer have no cause to say,
His money is but lost or thrown away.

Yea, may this Second Pilgrim yield that fruit
As may with each good Pilgrim's fancy suit;
And may it some persuade that go astray,
To turn their feet and heart to the right way

Is the hearty prayer of the author

JOHN BUNYAN.

THE

PILGRIM'S PROGRESS

CHAPTER I.

The author dreams again—Is accosted by Mr. Sagacity, who gives him tidings of Christian's wife and Children—Christiana's dream—She is visited by Secret—Prepares, with her four sons, to go on pilgrimage—Mrs. Timorous and Mercy call on her; the former attempts to dissuade, but the latter inclines to go with her—Mrs. Timorous acquaints her friends with what Christiana intends to do.

OURTEOUS COMPANIONS: Some time since, to tell you my dream that I had of Christian the pilgrim, and of his dangerous journey toward the Celestial Country, was pleasant to me, and profitable to you. I told you then also what I saw concerning his wife and children, and how unwilling they were to go with him on pilgrimage; insomuch that he was forced to go on his progress without them; for he durst not run the danger of that destruction which he feared would come by staying with them in the City of Destruction: wherefore, as I then showed you, he left them and departed.

Now it hath so happened, through the multiplicity of business, that I have been much hindered and kept back from my wonted travels into those parts whence he went, and so could not, till now, obtain an opportunity to make further inquiry after these whom he left behind, that I might give you an account of them. But having had some concerns that way of late, I went down again thitherward. Now having taken up my lodgings in a wood, about a mile off the place, as I slept, I dreamed again.

And, as I was in my dream, behold an aged gentleman came by where I lay; and because he was to go some part of the way that I was travelling, methought I got up and went with him. So as we walked, and as travellers usually do, I was as if we fell into a discourse; and our talk happened to be about Christian and his travels; for thus I began with the old man:

"Sir," said I, "what town is that there below, that lieth on the left hand of our way?"

Then said Mr. Sagacity, (for that was his name,) "It is the City of Destruction, a populous place, but possessed with a very ill-conditioned and idle sort of people."

"I thought that was that city," quoth I; "I went myself through that town; and therefore know that this report you give of it is true."

Sag. Too true! I wish I could speak truth in speaking better of them that dwell therein.

"Well, sir," quoth I, "then I perceive you to be a well-meaning man, and so one that takes pleasure to hear and tell of that which is good. Pray, did you never hear what happened to a man some time ago of this town, (whose name was Christian,) that went on a pilgrimage up toward the higher regions?"

Sag. Hear of him! Ay, and I also heard of the mo

astations, troubles, wars, captivities, cries, groans, frights, and fears, that he met with and had in his journey. Besides, I must tell you all our country rings of him; there are but few houses that have heard of him and his doings, but have sought after and got the records of his pilgrimage; yea, I think I may say, that his hazardous journey has got many well-wishers to his ways; for, though when he was here he was fool in every man's mouth, yet now he is gone he is highly commended of all. For 'tis said he lives bravely where he is: yea, many of them that are resolved never to run his hazards, yet have their mouths water at his gains.

"They may," quoth I, "well think, if they think anything that is true, that he liveth well where he is; for he now lives at, and in the Fountain of life, and has what he has without labour and sorrow, for there is no grief mixed therewith. But pray what talk have the people about him?"

Sag. Talk! the people talk strangely about him: some say that he now walks in white, Rev. iii, 4; that he has a chain of gold about his neck; that he has a crown of gold, beset with pearls, upon his head: others say, that the shining ones, who sometimes showed themselves to him in his journey, are become his companions, and that he is as familiar with them in the place where he is, as here one neighbour is with another. Besides, it is confidently affirmed concerning him, that the King of the place where he is has bestowed upon him already a very rich and pleasant dwelling at court, and that he every day eateth and drinketh, and walketh and talketh with him, and receiveth of the smiles and favours of him that is Judge of all there. Moreover, it is expected of some, that his Prince, the Lord of that country, will shortly come into these parts, and will know the reason, if they can give any, why his neighbours set so little by him, and had him so much in derision, when they perceived that he would be a pilgrim. For they say, that now he is so in the affections of his Prince, and that his Sovereign is so much concerned with the indignities that were cast upon Christian when he became a pilgrim, that he will look upon all as if done unto himself; and no marvel, for it was for the love that he had to his Prince that he ventured as he did. Luke x, 16.

"I dare say," quoth I, "I am glad on't; I am glad for the poor man's sake, for that he now has rest from his labour, and for that he reapeth the benefit of his tears with joy;[1] and for that he has got beyond the gunshot of his enemies, and is out of the reach of them that hate him. I also am glad for that a rumour of these things is noised abroad in this country; who can tell but that it may work some good effect on some that are left behind? But, pray sir, while it is fresh in my mind, do you hear anything of his wife and children? Poor hearts! I wonder in my mind what they do."

Sag. Who? Christiana and her sons? They are like to do as well as Christian did himself; for though they all played the fool at first, and would by no means be persuaded by either the tears or entreaties of Christian, yet second thoughts have wrought wonderfully with them: so they have packed up, and are also gone after him.

[1] I heard a voice from heaven, saying unto me, Write, blessed are the dead which die in the Lord from henceforth: Yea, saith the Spirit, that they may rest from their labours; and their works do follow them. Rev. xiv, 3. They that sow in tears shall reap in joy. Psa. cxxvi, 5

"Better and better," quoth I: "but, what! wife and children, and all?"

Sag. It is true: I can give you an account of the matter, for I was upon the spot at the instant, and was thoroughly acquainted with the whole affair.

Then said I, "A man, it seems, may report it for a truth."

Sag. You need not fear to affirm it: I mean that they are all gone on pilgrimage, both the good woman and her four boys. And being we are, as I perceive, going some considerable way together, I will give you an account of the whole matter.

This Christiana, (for that was her name from the day that she with her children betook herself to a pilgrim's life,) after her husband was gone over the river, and she could hear of him no more, her thoughts began to work in her mind. First, for that she had lost her husband, and for that the loving bond of that relation was utterly broken betwixt them. For you know, (said he to me,) nature can do no less but entertain the living with many a heavy cogitation, in the remembrance of the loss of loving relations. This, therefore, of her husband did cost her many a tear. But this was not all; for Christiana did also begin to consider with her self, whether her unbecoming behaviour toward her husband was not one cause that she saw him no more, and that in such sort he was taken away from her. And upon this came into her mind, by swarms, all her unkind, unnatural, and ungodly carriage to her dear friend; which also clogged her conscience, and did load her with guilt. She was, moreover, much broken with recalling to remembrance the restless groans, brinish tears, and self-bemoanings of her husband, and how she did harden her heart against all his entreaties and loving persuasions of her and her sons to go with him; yea, there was not anything that Christian either said to her, or did before her all the while that his burden did hang on his back, but it returned upon her like a flash of lightning, and rent the caul of her heart in sunder; especially that bitter outcry of his, "What shall I do to be saved?" did ring in her ears most dolefully.[2]

Then said she to her children, "Sons, we are all undone. I have sinned away your father, and he is gone: he would have had us with him, but I would not go myself: I also have hindered you of life." With that the boys fell all into tears, and cried out to go after their father. "O! (said Christiana) that it had been but our lot to go with him! then had it fared well with us, beyond what it is like to do now. For, though I formerly foolishly imagined, concerning the troubles of your father, that they proceeded of a foolish fancy that he had, or for that he was overrun with melancholy humours; yet now it will not out of my mind, but that they sprang from another cause; to wit, for that the light of life was given him, (John viii, 12;) by the help of which, as I perceive, he has escaped the snares of death." Prov. xiv, 27. Then they all wept again, and cried out, "O! wo worth the day!"

The next night Christiana had a dream; and, behold, she saw as if a broad parchment was opened before her, in which were recorded the sum of her ways; and the crimes, as she thought, looked very black upon her. Then she cried out aloud in her sleep, "Lord, have mercy upon me, a sinner," Luke xviii, 13; and the little children heard her.

[2] Mark this you that are churls to your godly relations.—*Bunyan.*

After this she thought she saw two very ill-favoured ones standing by her bed-side, and saying, "What shall we do with this woman? for she cries out for mercy, waking and sleeping; if she be suffered to go on as she begins, we shall lose her as we have lost her husband. Wherefore we must, by one way or other, seek to take her off from the thoughts of what shall be hereafter, else all the world cannot help, but she will become a pilgrim."

Now she awoke in a great sweat; also a trembling was upon her; but after a while she fell to sleeping again. And then she thought she saw Christian her husband in a place of bliss among many immortals, with a harp in his hand, standing and playing upon it before One that sat upon a throne with a rainbow about his head. She also saw, as if he bowed his head with his face to the paved work that was under his Prince's feet, saying, "I heartily thank my Lord and King for bringing me into this place." Then shouted a company of them that stood round about, and harped with their harps; but no man living could tell what they said but Christian and his companions.

Next morning, when she was up, had prayed to God, and talked with her children a while, one knocked hard at the door; to whom she spake out, saying, "If thou comest in God's name, come in." So he said, "Amen;" and opened the door and saluted her with, "Peace be to this house." The which when he had done, he said, "Christiana, knowest thou wherefore I am come?" Then she blushed and trembled; also her heart began to wax warm with desires to know from whence he came, and what was his errand to her. So he said unto her, "My name is Secret; I dwell with those that are on high. It is talked of where I dwell as if thou hadst a desire to go thither: also there is a report that thou art aware of the evil thou hast formerly done to thy husband, in hardening of thy heart against his way, and in keeping of these babes in their ignorance. Christiana, the Merciful One hath sent me to tell thee, that he is a God ready to forgive, and that he taketh delight to multiply the pardon of offences. He also would have thee to know, that he inviteth thee to come into his presence, to his table, and that he will feed thee with the fat of his house, and with the heritage of Jacob thy father.[3] There is Christian, thy husband that was, with legions more, his companions, ever beholding that face that doth minister life to beholders; and they will all be glad when they shall hear the sound of thy feet step over thy Father's threshold."

Christiana at this was greatly abashed in herself, and bowed her head to the ground. This visiter proceeded and said, "Christiana, here is also a letter for thee, which I have brought from thy husband's King;" so she took it, and opened it, but it smelt after the manner of the best perfume. Also it was written in letters of gold. The contents of the letter were these, That the King would have her to do as did Christian her husband; for that was the way to come to his City and to dwell in his presence with joy for ever. At this the good woman was quite overcome; so she cried out to her visiter, "Sir, will you carry me and my children with you, that we also may go and worship the King?"

Then said the visiter, "Christiana, the bitter is be-

[3] God had by his Spirit convinced Christiana of sin; and now that she is truly penitent, "Secret"—the Holy Spirit, the Comforter—is sent to second conviction with tidings of God's readiness to pardon

fore the sweet. Thou must through troubles, as did he that went before thee, enter this Celestial City. Wherefore I advise thee to do as did Christian thy husband: go to the wicket-gate yonder, over the plain, for that stands at the head of the way up which thou must go; and I wish thee all good speed. Also advise, that thou put this letter in thy bosom; that thou read therein to thyself, and to thy children, until you have got it by rote of heart; for it is one of the songs that thou must sing while thou art in this house of thy pilgrimage, (Ps. cxix, 54;) also this thou must deliver in at the further gate."

Now I saw in my dream, that this old gentleman, as he told me the story, did himself seem to be greatly affected therewith. He moreover proceeded, and said, So Christiana called her sons together, and began thus to address herself unto them: "My sons, I have, as you may perceive, been of late under much exercise in my soul about the death of your father: not for that I doubt at all of his happiness; for I am satisfied now that he is well. I have also been much affected with the thoughts of mine own estate and yours, which I verily believe is by nature miserable. My carriage also to your father in his distress is a great load to my conscience; for I hardened both mine own heart and yours against him, and refused to go with him on pilgrimage. The thoughts of these things would now kill me outright, but that for a dream which I had last night, and but that for the encouragement that this stranger has given me this morning. Come, my children, let us pack up, and begone to the gate that leads to the celestial country, that we may see your father, and be with him and his companions in peace, according to the laws of that land."

Then did her children burst out into tears, for joy that the heart of their mother was so inclined. So their visitor bid them farewell; and they began to prepare to set out for their journey.

But while they were thus about to be gone, two of the women that were Christian's neighbours came up to her house, and knocked at her door. To whom she said as before, "If you come in God's name, come in." At this the women were stunned; for this kind of language they used not to hear, or to perceive to drop from the lips of Christiana. Yet they came in: but behold, they found the good woman preparing to be gone from her house.

So they began, and said, "Neighbour, pray what is your meaning by this?"

Christiana answered, and said to the eldest of them, whose name was Mrs. Timorous, "I am preparing for a journey."

This Timorous was daughter to him that met Christian upon the Hill of Difficulty, and would have had him go back for fear of the lions.

Tim. For what journey, I pray you?

Chr. Even to go after my good husband. (And with that she fell a weeping.)

Tim. I hope not so, good neighbour; pray, for your poor children's sake, do not so unwomanly cast away yourself.

Chr. Nay, my children shall go with me; not one of them is willing to stay behind.

Tim. I wonder in my very heart what or who has brought you into this mind!

Chr. O, neighbour! knew you but as much as I do, I doubt not but that you would go along with me.

Tim. Prithee, what new knowledge hast thou got that so worketh off thy mind from thy friends, and that tempteth thee to go nobody knows where?

Then Chistiana replied, "I have been sorely afflicted since my husband's departure from me; but especially since he went over the river. But that which troubleth me most is, my churlish carriage to him when he was under his distress. Besides I am now as he was then; nothing will serve me but going on pilgrimage. I was a dreaming last night that I saw him. O, that my soul was with him! He dwelleth in the presence of the King of the country; he sits and eats with him at his table; he is become a companion of immortals, and has a house now given him to dwell in, to which the best palace on earth, if compared, seems to me but as a dunghill. 2 Cor. v, 1–4. The Prince of the palace has also sent for me, with promises of entertainment if I shall come to him; his messenger was here even now, and has brought me a letter, which invites me to come." And with that she plucked out her letter, and read it, and said to them, "What now will you say to this?"

Tim. O, the madness that has possessed thee and thy husband, to run yourselves upon such difficulties! You have heard, I am sure, what your husband did meet with, even in a manner at the first step that he took on his way, as our neighbour Obstinate can yet testify, for he went along with him; yea, and Pliable too, until they, like wise men, were afraid to go any further. We also heard, over and above, how he met with the lions, Apollyon, the Shadow of Death, and many other things. Nor is the danger he met with at Vanity Fair to be forgotten by thee. For if he, though a man, was so hard put to it, what canst thou, being but a poor woman, do? Consider also, that these four sweet babes are thy children, thy flesh and thy bones. Wherefore, though thou shouldest be so rash as to cast away thyself, yet for the sake of the fruit of thy body, keep thou at home.

But Christiana said unto her, "Tempt me not, my neighbour: I have now a price put into my hands to get gain, and I should be a fool of the greatest size if I should have no heart to strike in with the opportunity. And for that you tell me of all these troubles which I am like to meet with in the way, they are so far from being to me a discouragement, that they show I am in the right. The bitter must come before the sweet, and that also will make the sweet sweeter. Wherefore, since you came not to my house in God's name, as I said, I pray you to be gone, and not to disquiet me further."

Then Timorous reviled her, and said to her fellow, "Come, neighbour Mercy, let us leave her in her own hands, since she scorns our counsel and company." But Mercy was at a stand; and could not so readily comply with her neighbour; and that for a twofold reason. 1. Her bowels yearned over Christiana. So she said within herself, If my neighbour will needs be gone, I will go a little way with her, and help her. 2. Her bowels yearned over her own soul; for what Christiana had said had taken some hold upon her mind. Wherefore she said within herself again, I will yet have more talk with this Christiana; and if I find truth and life in what she shall say, myself with my heart shall also go with her. Wherefore Mercy began thus to reply to her neighbour Timorous:

Mer. Neighbour, I did indeed come with you to see Christiana this morning; and, since she is, as you see, taking her last farewell of her country, I think to walk this sunshiny morning a little with her, to help her on her way. (But she told her not of her second reason, but kept it to herself.)

Tim. Well, I see you have a mind to go a fooling too; but take heed in time, and be wise: while we are out of danger, we are out; but when we are in, we are in.

So Mrs. Timorous returned to her house, and Christiana betook herself to her journey. But when Timorous was got home to her house she sends for some of her neighbours, to wit, Mrs. Bat's-Eyes, Mrs. Inconsiderate, Mrs. Light-Mind, and Mrs. Know-Nothing. So when they were come to her house, she falls to telling of the story of Christiana, and of her intended journey. And thus she began her tale:

Tim. Neighbours, having had little to do this morning, I went to give Christiana a visit; and when I came at the door I knocked, as you know it is our custom: and she answered, "If you come in God's name, come in." So in I went, thinking all was well: but when I came in I found her preparing herself to depart the town, she, and also her children. So I asked her what was her meaning by that. And she told me in short, that she was now of a mind to go on pilgrimage, as did her husband. She told me also of a dream that she had, and how the King of the country where her husband was had sent her an inviting letter to come thither.

Then said Mrs. Know-Nothing, "And what! do you think she will go?"

Tim. Ay, go she will, whatever comes on't; and methinks I know it by this; for that which was my great argument to persuade her to stay at home, (to wit, the troubles she was like to meet with on the way, is one great argument with her to put her forward on her journey. For she told me in so many words, "The bitter goes before the sweet: yea, and forasmuch as it so doth, it makes the sweet the sweeter."

Mrs. Bat's-Eyes. O, this blind and foolish woman! and will she not take warning by her husband's afflictions? For my part, I see if he were here again he would rest himself content in a whole skin, and never run so many hazards for nothing.

Mrs. Inconsiderate also replied, saying, "Away with such fantastical fools from the town! a good riddance, for my part, I say, of her! should she stay where she dwells, and retain this her mind, who could live quietly by her? for she will either be dumpish, or unneighbourly, or talk of such matters as no wise body can abide. Wherefore, for my part, I shall never be sorry for her departure; let her go, and let better come in her room: it was never a good world since these whimsical fools dwelt in it."

Then Mrs. Light-Mind added as followeth: "Come, put this kind of talk away. I was yesterday at Madam Wanton's, where we were as merry as the maids. For who do you think should be there but I and Mrs. Love-the-Flesh, and three or four more, with Mrs. Lechery, Mrs. Filth, and some others: so there we had music and dancing, and what else was meet to fill up the pleasure. And I dare say, my lady herself is an admirable well-bred gentlewoman, and Mr. Lechery is as pretty a fellow.

CHAPTER II.

Christiana with her children and Mercy set out on their journey—Christiana's discourse with Mercy by the way—They reach the Slough of Despond, and get over without much difficulty—They arrive at the Wicket-Gate, where they are well received by the keeper—Their discourse at the gate—They proceed on their pilgrimage.

By this time Christiana was got on her way, and Mercy went along with her: so as they went, her children being there also, Christiana began to discourse. "And, Mercy," said Christiana, "I take this as an unexpected favour that thou shouldest set forth out of doors with me to accompany me a little in my way."

Then said young Mercy, (for she was but young,) "If I thought it would be to purpose to go with you, I would never go near the town any more."

"Well, Mercy," said Christiana, "cast in thy lot with me. I well know what will be the end of our pilgrimage: my husband is where he would not but be for all the gold in the Spanish mines. Nor shalt thou be rejected, though thou goest but upon my invitation.[1] The

[1] Think much of them that are gone before; how safe they are in the arms of Jesus. Would they be here again for a thousand worlds? Or if they were, would they be afraid that God would not make them welcome? Keep thine eye upon the prize—upon the profit thou art like to get. The reason why men are so apt to faint in their race for heaven, lieth chiefly in either of these two things: they do not seriously consider the worth of the prize; or else, if they do, they are afraid t is too good for them. But most lose heaven for want of considering the prize and the worth of it: and therefore that thou mayest not do the like, keep thine eye much upon the excellency, the sweetness, the beauty, the comfort, the peace, that is to be had there by those that win the prize. This was that which made the apostle run through anything—good report, evil report, persecution, affliction, hunger, nakedness, peril by sea, peril by land, bonds and imprison-

King, who hath sent for me and my children, is one that delighteth in mercy. Besides, if thou wilt, I will hire thee, and thou shalt go along with me as my servant. Yet we will have all things in common betwix thee and me: only go along with me.

Mer. But how shall I be ascertained that I also shall be entertained? Had I this hope but from one that can tell, I would make no stick at all, but would go, being helped by Him that can help, though the way was never so tedious.

Chr. Well, loving Mercy, I will tell thee what thou shalt do: go with me to the Wicket-Gate, and there I will further inquire for thee; and if there thou shalt not meet with encouragement, I will be content that thou return to thy place; I also will pay thee for the kindness which thou showest to me and my children in the accompanying of us in our way as thou dost.

Mer. Then will I go thither, and will take what shall follow; and the Lord grant that my lot may there fall, even as the King of heaven shall have his heart upon me.

Christiana then was glad at her heart: not only that

ments. Also it made others endure to be stoned, sawn asunder, to have their eyes bored with augers, their tongues cut out, to be thrown to the wild beasts, burned at the stake, and a thousand other fearful torments, "while they looked not at the things that are seen —as the things of this world—but at the things that are not seen; for the things that are seen are temporal, but the things that are not seen are eternal." O this word "eternal;" that was it that made them, when they might have had deliverance, not accept of it; for they knew, in the world to come, they should have a better resurrection.... And do not let the thoughts of the rareness of the place make thee say in thine heart, "This is too good for me;" for I tell thee, heaven is prepared for whoever will accept of it, and they shall be entertained with a hearty welcome. As bad as thou have got thither. Therefore, take heart, and run.—*Bunyan's Heavenly Footman.*

she had a companion; but also for that she had prevailed with this poor maid to fall in love with her own salvation. So they went on together, and Mercy began to weep. Then said Christiana, "Wherefore weepeth my sister so?"

"Alas," said she, "who can but lament, that shall but rightly consider what a state and condition my poor relations are in that yet remain in our sinful town? And that which makes my grief the more heavy is, because they have no instructor, nor any to tell them what is to come."[2]

Chr. Bowels become pilgrims; and thou dost weep for thy friends, as my good Christian did for me when he left me: he mourned for that I would not heed nor regard him; but his Lord and ours did gather up his tears, and put them into his bottle; (Psa. lvi, 8;) and now both I and thou, and these my sweet babes, are reaping the fruit and benefit of them.[3] I hope, Mercy, that these tears of thine will not be lost; for the truth hath said, that "they that sow in tears shall reap in joy;" and "he that goeth forth and weepeth, bearing precious

[2] Those who have experienced any measure of the drawings of divine love upon their souls, feel in their hearts a kindling toward others, and especially their own kindred, that they may with them be partakers of the "great salvation." So strong was this feeling in the apostle Paul toward the Jews, his "brethren after the flesh," that he had, as he tells us, "great heaviness and continual sorrow of heart" on their account: his "heart's desire and prayer to God" for them was, "that they might be saved." Romans ix, 2, 3; x, 1. He who feels nothing of this desire may pretty safely conclude that, whatever else may be in his heart, the love of God dwells not there: "for he that loveth not his brother whom he hath seen, how can he love God whom he hath not seen?" 1 John iv, 20.

[3] Thus Christiana's prayers were answered for his relations after he was dead.—*Bunyan's Marginal Note.*

seed, shall doubtless come again with rejoicing, bringing his sheaves with him." Psalm cxxvi, 5, 6

Then said Mercy,—

"Let the Most Blessed be my guide,
If it be his blessed will,
Unto his gate, into his fold,
Up to his holy hill.

"And let Him never suffer me
To swerve, or turn aside
From his free grace and holy ways,
Whate'er shall me betide.

"And let Him gather them of mine
That I have left behind;
Lord, make them pray they may be thine,
With all their heart and mind."

Now my old friend proceeded and said, "But when Christiana came to the Slough of Despond, she began to be at a stand; 'For,' said she, 'this is the place in which my dear husband had like to have been smothered with mud.' She perceived, also, that notwithstanding the command of the King to make this place for pilgrims good, yet it was rather worse than formerly." So I asked if that was true. "Yes," said the old gentleman, "too true; for many there be that pretend to be the King's labourers, and that say they are for mending the King's highways, that bring dirt and dung instead of stones, and so mar instead of mending.[4] Here Christiana, therefore, with her boys did make a stand. 'But,' said Mercy, 'come, let us venture, only let us be

[4] By those who "pretend to be the King's labourers," are meant the preachers of false doctrine. They bring "dirt instead of stones," that is, as Bunyan explains in the margin, "their own carnal conclusions instead of the word of life." They distress and discourage sincere seeking souls by proposing to them other terms than the simple, Scriptural way of salvation through faith in the atonement of Christ

wary.' Then they looked well to their steps, and made a shift to get staggering over. Yet Christiana had like to have been in, and that not once or twice.

"Now they had no sooner got over, but they thought they heard words that said unto them, 'Blessed is she that believeth, for there shall be a performance of those things which were told her from the Lord.' Luke i, 45.

"Then they went on again; and said Mercy to Christiana, 'Had I as good ground to hope for a loving reception at the Wicket-Gate as you, I think no Slough of Despond would discourage me.'

"'Well,' said the other, 'you know your sore, and I know mine; and, good friend, we shall all have enough evil before we come to our journey's end. For can it be imagined that the people who design to attain such excellent glories as we do, and that are so envied that happiness as we are, but that we shall meet with what fears and snares, with what troubles and afflictions they can possibly assault us with that hate us?'"

And now Mr. Sagacity left me to dream out my dream by myself. Wherefore, methought I saw Christiana, and Mercy, and the boys, go all of them up to the gate: to which when they were come, they betook themselves to a short debate, about how they must manage their calling at the gate, and what should be said unto him that did open to them:[5] so it was concluded, since Christiana was the eldest, that she should knock for entrance, and that she should speak to him that did open, for the rest. So Christiana began to knock, and as her poor husband did, she knocked and

[5] Prayer should be made with consideration and fear, as well as in faith and hope.—*Bunyan's Marginal Note.*

knocked again. But instead of any that answered, they all thought that they heard as if a dog came barking upon them; a dog, and a great one too: and this made the women and children afraid. Nor durst they for a while to knock any more, for fear the mastiff should fly upon them. Now therefore they were greatly tumbled up and down in their minds, and knew not what to do; knock they durst not, for fear of the dog; go back they durst not, for fear the keeper of that gate should espy them as they so went, and should be offended with them; at last they thought of knocking again, and knocked more vehemently than they did at first.[6] Then said the keeper of the gate, "Who is there?" So the dog left off to bark, and he opened unto them.

Then Christiana made low obeisance, and said, "Let not our Lord be offended with his hand-maidens, for that we have knocked at his princely gate." Then said the keeper, "Whence come ye? And what is it that you would have?"

Christiana answered, "We are come from whence Christian did come, and upon the same errand as he; to wit, to be, if it shall please you, graciously admitted by this gate into the way that leads unto the Celestial City. And I answer, my Lord, in the next place, that I am Christiana, once the wife of Christian, that now is gotten above."

With that the keeper of the gate did marvel, saying

[6] "The dog—the devil—is an enemy to prayer," and often sadly perplexes and harasses penitent souls when they engage in that exercise: but it is well when these assaults of the adversary only make them, (as they did Christiana and her companions,) to knock the louder, and be the more importunate at the throne of grace.

"What! is she now become a pilgrim, that but a while ago abhorred that life?" Then she bowed her head, and said, "Yea; and so are these my sweet babes also."

Then he took her by the hand and led her in, and said also, "Suffer little children to come unto me;" and with that he shut up the gate. This done, he called to a trumpeter that was above, over the gate, to entertain Christiana with shouting, and the sound of trumpet for joy. So he obeyed, and sounded, and filled the air with his melodious notes.

Now all this while poor Mercy did stand without, trembling and crying for fear that she was rejected. But when Christiana had got admittance for herself and her boys, then she began to make intercession for Mercy.

And she said, "My Lord, I have a companion of mine that stands yet without, that is come hither upon the same account as myself; one that is much dejected in her mind, for that she comes, as she thinks, without sending for: whereas I was sent for by my husband's King to come."

Now Mercy began to be very impatient, and each minute was as long to her as an hour; wherefore she prevented Christiana from a fuller interceding for her, by knocking at the gate herself. And she knocked then so loud that she made Christiana to start. Then said the keeper of the gate, "Who is there?" And Christiana said, "It is my friend."

So he opened the gate, and looked out, but Mercy was fallen down without in a swoon, for she fainted, and was afraid that no gate should be opened to her.

Then he took her by the hand, and said, "Damsel, I bid thee arise."

"O, sir," said she, "I am faint; there is scarce life left in me." But he answered, that "one once said, 'When my soul fainted within me I remembered the Lord: and my prayer came unto thee into thy holy temple.' Jonah ii, 7. Fear not, but stand upon thy feet, and tell me wherefore thou art come."

Mer. I am come for that unto which I was never invited, as my friend Christiana was. Hers was from the King, and mine was but from her. Wherefore I fear I presume.

Keep. Did she desire thee to come with her to this place?

Mer. Yes; and as my Lord sees, I am come. And if there is any grace and forgiveness of sins to spare, I beseech that thy poor handmaid may be a partaker thereof.

Then he took her again by the hand, and led her gently in, and said, "I pray for all them that believe on me, by what means soever they come unto me." Then said he to those that stood by, "Fetch something and give it Mercy to smell on, thereby to stay her faintings." So they fetched her a bundle of myrrh, and a while after she was revived.

And now were Christiana and her boys, and Mercy, received of the Lord at the head of the way, and spoken kindly unto by him. Then said they yet further unto him, "We are sorry for our sins, and beg of our Lord his pardon, and further information what we must do."

"I grant pardon," said he, "by word and deed: by word in the promise of forgiveness; by deed in the way I obtained it. Take the first from my lips with a kiss, and the other as it shall be revealed."

Now I saw in my dream, that he spake many good words unto them, whereby they were greatly gladded. He also had them up to the top of the gate, and showed them by what deed they were saved; and told them withal, that that sight they would have again as they went along the way, to their comfort.

So he left them a while in a summer parlour below, where they entered into talk by themselves; and thus Christiana began: "O Lord, how glad am I that we are got in hither!"

Mer. So you well may: but I, of all, have cause to leap for joy.

Chr. I thought one time, as I stood at the gate, (because I had knocked and none did answer,) that all our labour had been lost, especially when that ugly cur made such a heavy barking against us.

Mer. But my worst fear was, after I saw that you were taken into his favour, and that I was left behind. Now, thought I, it is fulfilled which is written, "Two women shall be grinding together; the one shall be taken, and the other left." Matt. xxiv, 41. I had much ado to forbear crying out, Undone! And afraid I was to knock any more; but when I looked up to what was written over the gate, I took courage.[6] I also thought

[6] The inscription over the gate was, (as we are told in the First Part, p. 69,) "KNOCK, AND IT SHALL BE OPENED TO YOU." What a precious promise to the coming sinner! What an encouragement to persevering prayer! No wonder that when Mercy looked up and saw this, she took courage and urged her suit with increased earnestness.

"Fainting soul, be bold, be strong, Wait the coming of thy Lord;
Though it seem to tarry long, True and faithful is his word!
On his word my soul I cast, (He cannot himself deny,)
Surely it shall speak at last; It shall speak and shall not lie.
Every one that seeks, shall find: Every one that asks shall have
Christ the Saviour of mankind, Willing, able, all to save."

that I must either knock again or die; so I knocked, but I cannot tell how; for my spirit now struggled between life and death.

Chr. Can you not tell how you knocked? I am sure your knocks were so earnest that the very sound of them made me start; I thought I never heard such knocking in all my life; I thought you would a-come in by a violent hand, or a-took the kingdom by storm. Matthew xi, 12.

Mer. Alas! to be in my case, who that so was could but have done so? You saw that the door was shut upon me, and that there was a most cruel dog thereabout. Who, I say, that was so faint-hearted as I, would not have knocked with all their might? But pray, what said my Lord to my rudeness? Was he not angry with me?

Chr. When he heard your lumbering noise, he gave a wonderful innocent smile: I believe what you did pleased him well, for he showed no sign to the contrary.[7] But I marvel in my heart why he keeps such a dog: had I known that afore, I should not have had heart enough to have ventured myself in this manner. But now we are in, we are in, and I am glad with all my heart.

Mer. I will ask, if you please, next time he comes down, why he keeps such a filthy cur in his yard: I hope he will not take it amiss.

"Do so," said the children, "and persuade him to hang him; for we are afraid he will bite us when we go hence."

So at last he came down to them again, and Mercy fell to the ground on her face before him, and worship-

[7] Christ is pleased with loud and restless prayer.—*Bunyan's Note*

ped, and said, "Let my Lord accept the sacrifice of praise which I now offer unto him with the calves of my lips." Hosea xiv, 2.

So he said unto her, "Peace be to thee; stand up." But she continued upon her face, and said, "'Righteous art thou, O Lord, when I plead with thee; yet let me talk with thee of thy judgments.' Jer. xii, 1. Wherefore dost thou keep so cruel a dog in thy yard, at the sight of which, such women and children as we are ready to fly from the gate with fear?"

He answered and said, "That dog has another owner: he also is kept close in another man's ground, only my pilgrims hear his barking: he belongs to the castle which you see there at a distance, but can come up to the walls of this place. He has frighted many an honest pilgrim from worse to better, by the great voice of his roaring. Indeed, he that owneth him doth not keep him out of any good will to me or mine, but with intent to keep the pilgrims from coming to me, and that they may be afraid to come and knock at this gate for entrance. Sometimes also he has broken out, and has worried some that I loved; but I take all at present patiently. I also give my pilgrims timely help, so that they are not delivered to his power, to do with them what his doggish nature would prompt him to. But what! my purchased one, I trow, hadst thou known never so much beforehand, thou wouldest not have been afraid of a dog. The beggars that go from door to door, will, rather than lose a supposed alms, run the hazard of the bawling, barking and biting too of a dog: and shall a dog, a dog in another man's yard, a dog whose barking I turn to the profit of pilgrims, keep any one from coming to me? I deliver them from the lions, and my darling from the power of the dog. Psa. xxii, 20, 21."

Then said Mercy, "I confess my ignorance: I spake what I understand not: I acknowledge that thou dost all things well."

Then Christiana began to talk of their journey, and to inquire after the way. So he fed them and washed their feet, and set them in the way of his steps, according as he had dealt with her husband before. So I saw in my dream that they walked on their way, and had the weather very comfortable to them.

Then Christiana began to sing, saying,—

"Bless'd be the day that I began
A pilgrim for to be;
And blessed also be the man
That thereto moved me.

"'Tis true, 'twas long ere I began
To seek to live for ever;
But now I run fast as I can:
'Tis better late than never.

"Our tears to joy, our fears to faith,
Are turned as we see;
Thus our beginning (as one saith)
Shows what our end will be."

CHAPTER III.

The Devil's Garden—Two ill-favoured ones assault Christiana and Mercy—The Reliever comes to their rescue—The pilgrims reach the Interpreter's house—Joy at their arrival—The Interpreter takes them into his Significant Rooms—The man with the muck-rake—The spider—Hen and chickens—Butcher and sheep—The garden—The field—Tree that is rotten at the heart—The supper—The pilgrims wash in the Bath of Sanctification—They are sealed and clothed—Greatheart is given them for a guide—Their departure.

Now there was on the other side of the wall that fenced in the way up which Christiana and her companions were to go, a garden, and that garden belonged to him whose was that barking dog, of whom mention was made before. And some of the fruit trees that grew in that garden shot their branches over the wall; and being mellow, they that found them did gather them up, and eat of them to their hurt. So Christiana's boys, (as boys are apt to do,) being pleased with the trees, and with the fruit that hung thereon, did pluck them, and began to eat. Their mother did also chide them for so doing, but still the boys went on.[1]

"Well," said she, "my sons, you transgress, for that fruit is none of ours:" but she did not know that it belonged to the enemy: I'll warrant you if she had she would have been ready to die for fear. But that passed, and they went on their way.

Now by that they were gone about two bow-shots from the place that led them into the way, they espied two very ill-favoured ones coming down apace to meet

[1] By the fruit of the devil's garden, of which the children ate, is meant those sinful pleasures and amusements which are so alluring to the young.

them. With that Christiana and Mercy her friend covered themselves with their veils, and so kept on their journey: the children also went on before; so at last they met together. Then they that came down to meet them, came just up to the women, as if they would embrace them; but Christiana said, "Stand back, or go peaceably as you should." Yet these two, as men that are deaf, regarded not Christiana's words, but began to lay hands upon them; at that Christiana, waxing very wroth, spurned at them with her feet. Mercy also, as well as she could, did what she could to shift them. Christiana again said to them, "Stand back, and be gone, for we have no money to lose, being pilgrims, as you see, and such too as live upon the charity of our friends."

Then said one of the two men, "We make no assault upon you for money, but are come out to tell you, that if you will but grant one small request which we shall ask, we will make women of you for ever."

Now Christiana, imagining what they should mean, made answer again, "We will neither hear, nor regard, nor yield to what you shall ask. We are in haste, and cannot stay, our business is a business of life and death." So again she and her companion made a fresh essay to go past them; but they letted them in their way.

And they said, "We intend no hurt to your lives; it is another thing we would have."

"Ay," quoth Christiana, "you would have us body and soul, for I know it is for that you are come; but we will die rather upon the spot, than to suffer ourselves to be brought into such snares as shall hazard our well-being hereafter." And with that they both shrieked out and cried, Murder! murder! and so put themselves under those laws that are provided for the protection of women. Deut. xxii, 25–27. But the men still made their approach upon them, with design to prevail against them. They therefore cried out again.[2]

Now, they being, as I said, not far from the gate in at which they came, their voice was heard from whence they were, thither: wherefore some of the house came out, and knowing that it was Christiana's tongue, they made haste to her relief.[3] But by that they were got within sight of them the women were in a very great scuffle; the children also stood crying by. Then did he that came in for their relief call out to the ruffians, saying, "What is that thing you do; would you make my Lord's people to transgress?" He also attempted to take them, but they did make their escape over the wall into the garden of the man to whom the great dog belonged; so the dog became their protector. This Reliever then came up to the women, and asked them how they did. So they answered, "We thank thy Prince, pretty well, only we have been somewhat affrighted: we thank thee also for that thou camest in to our help, otherwise we had been overcome."

So after a few more words this Reliever said as followeth: "I marvelled much when you were entertain-

[2] Carnal lusts will seek entertainment in the Christian's heart: but we must strive against them, as did these pilgrims, and cry mightily to God for power to overcome them; for they "war against the soul." 1 Pet. ii, 11. It is no sin to be tempted, unless we have put ourselves in the way of temptation: but if we yield to the temptation, then we grieve the Spirit of God, and sin against our own souls.

[3] Thou heardest the voice of my supplications when I cried unto thee. Psa. xxxi, 22. The Lord knoweth how to deliver the godly out of temptations. 2 Peter ii, 9.

ed at the gate above, being ye knew that ye were but weak women, that you petitioned not the Lord for a conductor; then might you have avoided these troubles and dangers; for he would have granted you one."

"Alas!" said Christiana, "we were so taken with our present blessing, that dangers to come were forgotten by us.[4] Besides, who could have thought, that so near the King's palace there could have lurked such naughty ones? Indeed, it had been well for us had we asked our Lord for one; but since our Lord knew it would be for our profit, I wonder he sent not one along with us."

Rel. It is not always necessary to grant things not asked for, lest by so doing they become of little esteem; but when the want of a thing is felt, it then comes under, in the eyes of him that feels it, that estimate that properly is its due, and so consequently it will be thereafter used. Had my Lord granted you a conductor, you would not either so have bewailed that oversight of yours, in not asking for one, as now you have occasion to do. So all things work for good, and tend to make you more wary.

Chr. Shall we go back again to my Lord, and confess our folly, and ask one?

Rel. Your confession of your folly I will present him with. To go back again you need not; for in all places where you shall come, you shall find no want at all: for in every place of my Lord's lodgings, which he has prepared for the reception of his pilgrims, there is sufficient to furnish them against all attempts whatsoever. But as I said, "He will be inquired of by them to do it for them." (Ezek. xxxvi, 37.) And 'tis a poor thing that is not worth asking for.

[4] "Mark this!" observes Bunyan, in a marginal note.

When he had thus said, he went back to his place, and the pilgrims went on their way.

Then said Mercy, "What a sudden blank is here! made account that we had been past all danger, and that we should never see sorrow more."

"Thy innocency, my sister," said Christiana to Mercy, "may excuse thee much: but as for me, my fault is so much the greater, for that I saw this danger before I came out of the doors, and yet did not provide for it when provision might have been had. I am much to be blamed."

Then said Mercy, "How knew you this before you came from home? Pray open to me this riddle."

Chr. Why, I will tell you. Before I set foot out of doors, one night as I lay in my bed I had a dream about this; for methought I saw two men, as like these as ever any in the world could look, stand at my bed's feet, plotting how they might prevent my salvation. I will tell you their very words. They said, (it was when I was in my troubles,) "What shall we do with this woman? for she cries out waking and sleeping for forgiveness; if she be suffered to go on as she begins, we shall lose her as we have lost her husband." This you know might have made me take heed, and have provided when provision might have been had.

"Well," said Mercy, "as by this neglect we have occasion ministered unto us to behold our own imperfections, so our Lord has taken occasion thereby to make manifest the riches of his grace; for he, as we see, has followed us with unasked kindness, and has delivered us from their hands that were stronger than we, of his mere good pleasure."

Thus now when they had talked away a little more time, they drew near to a house which stood in the way, which house was built for the relief of pilgrims, as you will find more fully related in the First Part of these records of the Pilgrim's Progress. So they drew on toward the house, (the house of the Interpreter,) and when they came to the door they heard a great talk in the house. Then they gave ear, and heard, as they thought, Christiana mentioned by name; for you must know that there went along, even before her, a talk of her and her children's going on pilgrimage. And this was the more pleasing to them, because they had heard that she was Christian's wife, that woman who was some time ago so unwilling to hear of going on pilgrimage. Thus, therefore, they stood still, and heard the good people within commending her, who they little thought stood at the door. At last Christiana knocked, as she had done at the gate before. Now, when she had knocked, there came to the door a young damsel, and opened the door, and looked, and behold, two women were there.

Then said the damsel to them, "With whom would you speak in this place?"

Christiana answered, "We understand that this is a privileged place for those that are become pilgrims, and we now at this door are such; wherefore we pray that we may be partakers of that for which we at this time are come; for the day, as thou seest, is very far spent, and we are loth to-night to go any further."

Dam. Pray what may I call your name, that I may tell it to my Lord within?

Chr. My name is Christiana; I was the wife of that pilgrim that some years ago did travel this way, and these be his four children. This maiden is also my companion, and is going on pilgrimage too.

Then Innocent ran in, (for that was her name,) and said to those within, "Can you think who is at the door? There is Christiana and her children, and her companion, all waiting for entertainment here." Then they leaped for joy, and went and told their master. So he came to the door, and looking upon her, he said, "Art thou that Christiana whom Christian the good man left behind him when he betook himself to a pilgrim's life?"

Chr. I am that woman that was so hard-hearted as to slight my husband's troubles, and that left him to go on his journey alone, and these are his four children; but now also I am come, for I am convinced that no way is right but this.

Inter. Then is fulfilled that which is written of the man that said to his son, "Go work to-day in my vineyard; and he said to his father, I will not; but afterward repented and went." Matt. xxi, 29.

Then said Christiana, "So be it. Amen. God make it a true saying upon me, and grant that I may be found at the last of Him in peace, without spot, and blameless."

Inter. But why standest thou thus at the door? Come in, thou daughter of Abraham; we were talking of thee but now, for tidings have come to us before how thou art become a pilgrim. Come, children, come in · come, maiden, come in. (So he had them all into the house.)

So when they were within, they were bidden to sit down and rest them; the which when they had done, those that attended upon the pilgrims in the house,

Then said Christiana, "I persuade myself that I know somewhat the meaning of this; for this is the figure of a man of the world; is it not, good sir?"

came into the room to see them. And one smiled, and another smiled, and they all smiled for joy that Christiana was become a pilgrim. They also looked upon the boys, they stroked them over their faces with the hand in token of their kind reception of them: they also carried it lovingly to Mercy, and bid them all welcome into their master's house.

After a while, because supper was not ready, the Interpreter took them into his Significant Rooms, and showed them what Christian, Christiana's husband, had seen some time before. Here therefore they saw the man in the cage, the man and his dream, the man that cut his way through his enemies, and the picture of the biggest of them all, together with the rest of those things that were then so profitable to Christian.

This done, and after those things had been somewhat digested by Christiana and her company, the Interpreter takes them apart again, and has them first into a room where was a man that could look no way but downward, with a muck-rake in his hand. There stood also one over his head, with a celestial crown in his hand, and proffered him that crown for his muck-rake; but the man did neither look up nor regard, but raked to himself the straws, the small sticks, and dust of the floor.

Then said Christiana, "I persuade myself that I know somewhat the meaning of this: for this is the figure of a man of this world; is it not, good sir?"

"Thou hast said the right," said he; "and his muck-rake doth show his carnal mind. And whereas thou seest him rather give heed to rake up straws and sticks, and the dust of the floor, than to do what He says that calls to him from above with the celestial crown in his hand; it is to show, that heaven is but a fable to some, and that things here are counted the only things substantial. Now, whereas it was also showed thee that the man could look no way but downward, it is to let thee know that earthly things, when they are with power upon men's minds, quite carry their hearts away from God."

Then said Christiana, "O deliver me from this muck-rake!"

"That prayer," said the Interpreter, "has lain by till it is almost rusty. 'Give me not riches,' (Prov. xxx, 8, is scarce the prayer of one in ten thousand. Straws, and sticks, and dust, with most, are the great things now looked after."

With that Christiana and Mercy wept, and said, "It is, alas! too true."

When the Interpreter had showed them this, he had them into the very best room in the house; (a very brave room it was:) so he bid them look round about, and see if they could find anything profitable there. Then they looked round and round; for there was nothing to be seen but a very great spider on the wall, and that they overlooked.

Then said Mercy, "Sir, I see nothing." But Christiana held her peace.

"But," said the Interpreter, "look again." She therefore looked again, and said, "Here is not anything but an ugly spider, who hangs by her hands upon the wall." Then said he, "Is there but one spider in all this spacious room?" Then the water stood in Christiana's eyes, for she was a woman quick of apprehension: and she said, "Yea, Lord, there are more here than one; yea, and spiders whose venom is far more destructive than that which is in her." The Interpreter then looked pleasantly on her, and said, "Thou hast said the truth." This made Mercy to blush, and the boys to cover their faces; for they all began now to understand the riddle.

Then said the Interpreter again, "'The spider taketh hold with her hands, as you see, and is in king's palaces.' Prov. xxx, 28. And wherefore is this recorded, but to show you, that how full of the venom of sin soever you be, yet you may, by the hand of Faith, lay hold of and dwell in the best room that belongs to the King's house above."

"I thought," said Christiana, "of something of this; but I could not imagine it all. I thought that we were like spiders, and that we looked like ugly creatures, in what fine rooms soever we were; but that by this spider, that venomous and ill-favoured creature, we were to learn how to act faith, that came not into my thoughts; and yet she had taken hold with her hands, and, as I see, dwelleth in the best room in the house. God has made nothing in vain."[5]

[5] This emblem of the spider is founded on a mistranslated text of Scripture. The Hebrew word rendered "spider" in our version of Prov. xxx, 28, means properly the *lizard*, a harmless and inoffensive animal. The emblem is also defective in another particular: the "spider," retaining all its "venom," is represented as dwelling in the King's palace, yea, in "the very best room in the house." Now although the vilest and worst are invited to come to Christ, it is that they may be renewed in their hearts, and they can abide in him no longer than they continue to bear the fruit of righteousness; our author's emblem and interpretation *seem* to favour a very different doctrine; yet no man enforced more strenuously and constantly than he did, both in his preaching and his writings, the necessity of holiness of heart and life in the professed followers of Christ. The truth is, Bunyan's fondness for spiritualizing (a prevailing fault in his day, sometimes led him into absurdities.

Then they seemed all to be glad; but the water stood in their eyes: yet they looked one upon another, and also bowed before the Interpreter.

He had them then into another room, where were a hen and chickens, and bid them observe awhile. So one of the chickens went to the trough to drink; and every time she drank she lifted up her head and her eyes toward heaven. "See," said he, "what this little chick doth, and learn of her to acknowledge whence your mercies come, by receiving them with looking up. Yet again," said he, "observe and look." So they gave heed, and perceived that the hen did walk in a fourfold method toward her chickens: 1. She had a common call, and that she hath all day long; 2. She had a special call, and that she had but sometimes; 3. She had a brooding note; and 4. She had an outcry. Matthew xxiii, 37.

"Now," said he, "compare this hen to your King, and these chickens to his obedient ones; for, answerable to her, he himself hath his methods which he walketh in toward his people. By his common call, he gives nothing; by his special call, he always has something to give; he has also a brooding voice, for them that are under his wing; and he has an outcry, to give the alarm when he seeth the enemy come.[6] I chose, my darlings, to lead you into the room where such

[6] We think our author's fancy got the better of his judgment wher he was giving this account of the "calls" of the hen, and his explanations of them. "By the *common call* he probably intends the general invitations of the gospel; by the *special call*, the influences of the Spirit in conversion; by the *brooding note*, the consolatory influences which the believer derives from the 'communion of the Holy Ghost;' and by the *outcry*, those warnings and intimations of danger which the Lord gives his people, in his word and by his providence."

things are, because you are women, and they are easy for you."[7]

"And, sir," said Christiana, "pray let us see some more." So he had them into the slaughter-house, where was a butcher killing a sheep; and behold, the sheep was quiet, and took her death patiently. Then said the Interpreter, "You must learn of this sheep to suffer, and to put up with wrongs without murmurings and complaints. Behold how quietly she takes her death, and, without objecting, she suffereth her skin to be pulled over her ears. Your King doth call you his sheep."

After this he led them into his garden, where was

[7] From this and some other passages in Bunyan's writings it is plain that he entertained no very exalted opinion of the intellectual capacity of the other sex. In his Exposition of Genesis, he says, Women "are commanded to keep silence, and learn of their husbands; a command that is necessary enough for that simple and weak sex." The "causes of the judgment" pronounced upon Adam, he tells us, were "first, For that he hearkened to his wife; and also, for that he had eaten of the tree." The mere "hearkening to his wife" he considers to have been in itself a sin; "because therein he left his station and headship, and gave way for his wife to assume it; for God had made Adam lord and chief, who ought to have taught his wife, and not to have become her scholar." Nor does he much *mend* the matter in the qualifying sentences which occur in the next page to the above: "Although the Scripture doth lay a great blot upon women, and cautioneth man to beware of these fantastical and unstable spirits, yet it limiteth man in his censure. She is only to be rejected and rebuked when she doth things unworthy her place and calling. Such a thing *may* happen, as that the woman, not the man, may be in the right, but ordinarily it is otherwise." This depreciation of the female character, though quite in keeping with the spirit of the times in which he lived, we hardly expected to find in Bunyan, who, to his manifest profit, "hearkened" to his first wife, and whose second wife certainly showed, under most trying circumstances, a degree of sense and spirit that might have shamed many a one of the more favoured sex. See the Life of Bunyan, pp. 22, 23, 179–186.

great variety of flowers; and he said, "Do you see all these?" So Christiana said, "Yes." Then said he again, "Behold, the flowers are diverse in stature, in quality, and colour, and smell, and virtue; and some are better than others: also where the gardener hath set them, there they stand and quarrel not one with another."[8]

Again, he had them into his field, which he had sown with wheat and corn: but when they beheld, the tops of all were cut off, and only the straw remained, he said again, "This ground was dunged, and ploughed, and sowed, but what shall we do with the crop?" Then said Christiana, "Burn some, and make muck of the rest." Then said the Interpreter again, "Fruit, you see, is that thing you look for; and for want of that you condemn it to the fire, and to be trodden under foot of men: beware that in this you condemn not yourselves."[9]

[8] It is amiable and pleasant to God, when Christians keep their rank, relation, and station, doing all as becomes their quality and calling. When they stand every one in their places, and do the work of their relations, then they are like the flowers in the garden that stand and grow where the gardener hath planted them, and then they shall both honour the garden in which they are planted, and the gardener that hath so disposed of them.—*Bunyan's Christian Behaviour.*

[9] It is expected of all hands, that all the trees in the garden of God should be fruitful: *God* expects fruit, the *church* expects fruit, the *world*, even the world, concludes that professors should be fruitful in good works; I say, the very world expecteth that professors should be better than themselves: but, barren soul, thou disappointest all... How many showers of grace—how many dews from heaven—how many times have the golden streams of the city of God run gliding by thy roots, to cause thee to bring forth fruit! These showers and streams, and the drops that hang upon thy boughs, will all be accounted for; and will they not testify against thee that thou oughtest to be burned? Hear and tremble, O thou barren professor! Fruits that become thy profession of the gospel the God of heaven expect

Then, as they were coming in from abroad, they espied a little robin with a great spider in his mouth. So the Interpreter said, "Look here." So they looked, and Mercy wondered, but Christiana said, "What a disparagement is it to such a pretty little bird as the robin-redbreast is, he being also a bird above many, that loveth to maintain a kind of sociableness with men! I had thought they had lived upon crumbs of bread, or upon other such harmless matter; I like him worse than I did."

The Interpreter then replied, "This robin is an emblem, very apt to set forth some professors by; for to sight they are, as this robin, pretty of note, colour, and carriage. They seem also to have a very great love for professors that are sincere; and, above all others, to desire to associate with them, and to be in their company, as if they could live upon the good man's crumbs. They pretend also, that therefore it is that they frequent the house of the godly, and the appointments of the Lord: but when they are by themselves, as the robin, they can catch and gobble up spiders; they can change their diet, drink iniquity, and swallow down sin like water."

So when they were come again into the house, because supper as yet was not ready, Christiana again desired that the Interpreter would either show, or tell of, some other things that are profitable.

eth. The gospel hath in it the forgiveness of sins, the kingdom of heaven and eternal life; but what fruit hath thy profession of a belief of these things put forth in thy heart and life? Hast thou given thyself to the Lord; and is all that thou hast to be ventured for his name in this world? Dost thou walk like one that is bought with a price, even with the price of precious blood? O my brethren, "what manner of persons ought we to be!"—*Bunyan's Barren Fig-tree*

Then the Interpreter began and said: "The fatter the sow is, the more she desires the mire; the fatter the ox is, the more gamesomely he goes to the slaughter; and the more healthy the lustful man is, the more prone he is unto evil.

"There is a desire in women to go neat and fine; and it is a comely thing to be adorned with that which in God's sight is of great price. 1 Pet. iii, 3.

"'Tis easier watching a night or two, than to sit up a whole year together; so 'tis easier for one to begin to profess well, than to hold out as he should to the end.

"Every shipmaster, when in a storm, will willingly cast that overboard which is of the smallest value in the vessel; but who will throw the best out first? None but he that feareth not God.

"One leak will sink a ship, and one sin will destroy a sinner.

"He that forgets his friend, is ungrateful unto him; but he that forgets his Saviour, is unmerciful to himself.

"He that lives in sin, and looks for happiness hereafter, is like him that soweth cockle, and thinks to fill his barn with wheat or barley.

"If a man would live well, let him fetch his last day to him, and make it always his company-keeper.

"Whispering and change of thoughts, prove that sin is in the world.

"If the world, which God sets light by, is counted a thing of that worth with men, what is heaven that God commendeth?

"If the life that is attended with so many troubles, is so loth to be let go by us, what is the life above!

"Everybody will cry up the goodness of men; but who is there that is as he should be, affected with the goodness of God?

"We seldom sit down to meat, but we eat and leave. So there is in Jesus Christ more merit and righteousness than the whole world has need of."

When the Interpreter had done, he takes them out into his garden again, and had them to a tree whose inside was all rotten and gone, and yet it grew and had leaves. Then said Mercy, "What means this?" "This tree," said he, "whose outside is fair, and whose inside is rotten, is it to which many may be compared that are in the garden of God; who with their mouths speak high in behalf of God, but indeed will do nothing for him; whose leaves are fair, but their heart good for nothing but to be tinder for the devil's tinderbox."

Now supper was ready, the table spread, and all things set on the board; so they sat down, and did eat, when one had given thanks. And the Interpreter did usually entertain those that lodged with him with music at meals; so the minstrels played. There was also one that did sing, and a very fine voice he had. His song was this:—

"The Lord is only my support,
He that doth me feed;
How can I then want anything
Whereof I stand in need?"

When the song and music was ended the Interpreter asked Christiana, what it was that first did move her thus to betake herself to a pilgrim's life. Christiana answered, "First, the loss of my husband came into my mind, at which I was heartily grieved; but all that was but natural affection. Then after that came the troubles and pilgrimage of my husband into my mind, and also how like a churl I had carried it to him as to that. So guilt took hold of my mind, and would have drawn me into the pond, but that opportunely I had a dream of the well-being of my husband, and a letter sent me by the King of that country where my husband dwells, to come to him. The dream and the letter together so wrought upon my mind that they forced me to this way."

Inter. But met you with no opposition before you set out of doors?

Chr. Yes, a neighbour of mine, one Mrs. Timorous; (she was akin to him that would have persuaded my husband to go back for fear of the lions;) she also befooled me, for, as she called it, my intended desperate adventure; she also urged what she could to dishearten me from it, the hardship and troubles that my husband met with in the way: but all this I got over pretty well. But a dream that I had of two ill-looking ones, that I thought did plot how to make me miscarry in my journey, that hath troubled me much: yea, it still runs in my mind and makes me afraid of every one that I meet, lest they should meet me to do me a mischief, and turn me out of the way. Yea, I may tell my Lord, though I would not have every one know of it, that between this and the gate by which we got into the way, we were both so sorely assaulted, that we were made to cry out Murder! and the two that made this assault upon us were like the two that I saw in my dream.

Then said the Interpreter, "Thy beginning is good, thy latter end shall greatly increase."

So he addressed himself to Mercy, and said unto her, "And what moved thee to come hither, sweetheart?" Then Mercy blushed and trembled, and for a while continued silent. Then said he, "Be not afraid; only believe, and speak thy mind."

So she began and said, "Truly, sir, my want of experience is that which makes me covet to be in silence, and that also that fills me with fears of coming short at last. I cannot tell of visions and dreams, as my friend Christiana can; nor know I what it is to mourn for my refusing the counsel of those that were good relations."

Inter. What was it then, dear heart, that hath prevailed with thee to do as thou hast done?

Mer. Why, when our friend here was packing up to be gone from our town, I and another went accidentally to see her. So we knocked at the door and went in. When we were within, and seeing what she was doing, we asked her what was her meaning. She said she was sent for to go to her husband; and then she up and told us how she had seen him in a dream, dwelling in a curious place, among immortals, wearing a crown, playing upon a harp, eating and drinking at his Prince's table, and singing praises to him for bringing him thither, &c. Now methought, while she was telling these things unto us, my heart burned within me. And I said in my heart, If this be true I will leave my father and my mother, and the land of my nativity, and will, if I may, go along with Christiana. So I asked her further of the truth of these things, and if she would let me go with her; for I saw now there was no dwelling, but with the danger of ruin, any longer in our town. But yet I came away with a heavy heart; not for that I was unwilling to come away, but for that so many of my relations were left behind. And I am come with all the desire of my heart, and will go, if I may, with Christiana unto her husband and his King.

Inter. Thy setting out is good, for thou hast given credit to the truth; thou art a Ruth, who did, for the love she bare to Naomi, and to the Lord her God, leave father and mother, and the land of her nativity, to come out and go with a people that she knew not heretofore. The Lord recompense thy work, and a full reward be given thee of the Lord God of Israel, under whose wings thou art come to trust. Ruth ii, 11, 12.

Now supper was ended, and preparation was made for bed; the women were laid singly alone, the boys by themselves. Now when Mercy was in bed, she could not sleep for joy, for that now her doubts of missing at last were removed further from her than ever they were before. So she lay blessing and praising God, who had had such favour for her.

In the morning they arose with the sun, and prepared themselves for their departure: but the Interpreter would have them tarry awhile; "For," said he, "you must orderly go from hence." Then said he to the damsel that first opened unto them, "Take them and have them into the garden to the bath, and there wash them, and make them clean from the soil which they have gathered by traveling."[10]

Then Innocent, the damsel, took them and led them into the garden, and brought them to the bath; so she told them, that there they must wash and be clean, for so her Master would have the women to do that called at his house as they were going on pilgrimage. Then

[10] The bath in which the pilgrims washed, the author tells us in a marginal note, is "the bath of sanctification." In that day there shall be a fountain opened to the house of David and to the inhabitants of Jerusalem, for sin and for uncleanness. Zechariah xiii, 1. And he said unto me, These are they which have. . .washed their robes, and made them white in the blood of the Lamb. Revelation vii, 14

they went in and washed, yea, they and the boys, and all; and they came out of that bath, not only sweet and clean, but also much enlivened, and strengthened in their joints. So when they came in, they looked fairer a deal than when they went out to the washing.

When they were returned out of the garden from the bath, the Interpreter took them, and looked upon them, and said unto them, "Fair as the moon." Then he called for the seal wherewith they used to be sealed that were washed in his bath. So the seal was brought, and he set his mark upon them, that they might be known in the places whither they were yet to go. Now the seal was the contents and sum of the pass-over which the children of Israel did eat, when they came out of the land of Egypt, Exod. xiii, 8–10; and the mark was set between their eyes. This added greatly to their beauty, for it was an ornament to their faces. It also added to their gravity, and made their countenances more like those of angels.

Then said the Interpreter again to the damsel that waited upon these women, "Go into the vestry, and fetch out garments for these people." So she went and fetched out white raiment, and laid it down before him: so he commanded them to put it on: it was "fine linen, white and clean."[11] When the women were thus adorned, they seemed to be a terror one to the other; for that they could not see that glory each one had in herself, which they could see in each other. Now therefore they began to esteem each other better than themselves. For, "You are fairer than I am,' said

[11] And to her was granted that she should be arrayed in fine linen, clean and white: for the fine linen is the righteousness of the saints Revelation xix, 8. See also Isaiah lxi, 10

one; and, "You are more comely than I am," said another.[12] The children also stood amazed, to see into what fashion they were brought.

The Interpreter then called for a man-servant of his, one Great-Heart, and bid him take a sword, and helmet, and shield; and, "Take these my daughters,' said he, "conduct them to the house called Beautiful, at which place they will rest next." So he took his weapons, and went before them; and the Interpreter said, "God speed." Those also that belonged to the family sent them away with many a good wish. So they went on their way, and sang:—

"This place hath been our second stage;
  Here we have heard and seen
Those good things, that from age to age
  To others hid have been.
The dunghill-raker, spider, hen,
  The chicken, too, to me
Have taught a lesson: let me then
  Conformed to it be.
The butcher, garden, and the field,
  The robin and his bait,
Also the rotten tree doth yield
  Me argument of weight;
To move me for to watch and pray
  To strive to be sincere;
To take my cross up day by day,
  And serve the Lord with fear."

[12] Grace will make a man prize other men's graces and gracious actions above his own. As he thinks, every man's candle burns brighter than his, every man improves grace better than he, every good man does more sincerely his duty than he. And if these be not some of the effects of the renewings of grace, I will confess I have taken my mark amiss.—*Bunyan on the Righteous Man's Desires*

CHAPTER IV.

The pilgrims come to the cross—Discourse on being justified by Christ—They find Simple, Sloth, and Presumption hanged—They reach the Hill Difficulty, and are put to it in going up—They refresh themselves in the Arbour—Giant Grim backs the lions, and opposes the progress of the pilgrims—A fight between Grim and Greatheart—The giant is slain, and they pass by the lions without hurt.

Now I saw in my dream, that they went on, and Greatheart before them.[1] So they went, and came to the place where Christian's burden fell off his back, and tumbled into a sepulchre. Here then they made a pause; here also they blessed God.[2] "Now," said Christiana, "it comes to my mind what was said to us at the gate, to wit, that we should have pardon by word and deed; by word, that is, by the promise; by deed, to wit, in the way it was obtained. What the promise is, of that I know something; but what it is to have pardon by deed, or in the way that it was obtained, Mr. Greatheart, I suppose you know; wherefore, if you please, let us hear you discourse thereof."

Great. Pardon by the deed done, is pardon obtained by some one for another that hath need thereof; not by the person pardoned, but in the way, saith another, in which I have obtained it. So then to speak to the question more at large, the pardon that you, and Mercy, and these boys, have attained, was obtained by

[1] Greatheart represents a faithful and devoted pastor, who, under the direction of "the great Shepherd," takes charge of the little band of pilgrims, to conduct them to the Celestial City.

[2] There is no man that goeth to heaven but he must go by the *cross.* The cross is the standing way-mark by which all they that go to glory must pass by.—*Bunyan's Heavenly Footman*

another; to wit, by Him that let you in at the gate. And he hath obtained it in this double way; he hath performed righteousness to cover you, and spilt his blood to wash you in.

Chr. But if He parts with his righteousness to us, what will he have for himself?

Great. He has more righteousness than you have need of, or than he needeth himself.

Chr. Pray make that appear.

Great. With all my heart: but first I must premise that He of whom we are now about to speak, is one that has not his fellow. He has two natures in one person, plain to be distinguished, impossible to be divided. Unto each of these natures a righteousness belongeth, and each righteousness is essential to that nature; so that one may as easily cause the nature to be extinct as to separate its justice or righteousness from it. Of these righteousnesses therefore we are not made partakers, so as that they, or any of them, should be put upon us, that we might be made just, and live thereby. Besides these, there is a righteousness which this person has, as these two natures are joined in one. And this is not the righteousness of the Godhead, as distinguished from the manhood; nor the righteousness of the manhood as distinguished from the Godhead; but a righteousness which standeth in the union of both natures, and may properly be called the righteousness that is essential to his being prepared of God to the capacity of the mediatory office, which he was intrusted with. If he parts with his first righteousness, he parts with his Godhead; if he parts with his second righteousness, he parts with the purity of his manhood; if he parts with his third, he parts with that perfection which capacitates him for the office of mediation. He has therefore another righteousness, which standeth in performance, or obedience to a revealed will; and that is what he puts upon sinners, and that by which their sins are covered. Wherefore he saith, "As by one man's disobedience many were made sinners, so by the obedience of one shall many be made righteous." Romans v, 19.

Chr. But are the other righteousnesses of no use to us?

Great. Yes; for though they are essential to his natures and offices, and cannot be communicated unto another; yet it is by virtue of them that the righteousness that justifies is for that purpose efficacious. The righteousness of his Godhead gives virtue to his obedience; the righteousness of his manhood giveth capability to his obedience to justify; and the righteousness that standeth in the union of these two natures to his office, giveth authority to that righteousness to do the work for which it was ordained.

So then here is a righteousness that Christ, as God, has no need of; for he is God without it. Here is a righteousness that Christ, as man, has no need of to make him so; for he is perfect man without it. Again, here is a righteousness that Christ, as God-man, has no need of; for he is perfectly so without it. Here then is a righteousness that Christ, as God, and as God-man, has no need of with reference to himself, and therefore he can spare it; a justifying righteousness, that he for himself wanteth not, and therefore giveth it away: hence it is called "the gift of righteousness." Rom. v, 17. This righteousness, since Christ Jesus the Lord has made himself under the law, must be given away;

for the law doth not only bind him that is under it, to do justly, but to use charity. Wherefore he must, or ought, by the law, if he hath two coats, to give one to him that hath none. Now our Lord indeed hath two coats, one for himself, and one to spare; wherefore he freely bestows one upon those that have none. And thus, Christiana and Mercy, and the rest of you that are here, doth your pardon come by deed, or by the work of another man. Your Lord Christ is he that worked, and hath given away what he wrought for to the next poor beggar he meets.[3]

But again, in order to pardon by deed, there must something be paid to God as a price, as well as something prepared to cover us withal. Sin has delivered us up to the just curse of a righteous law: now from this curse we must be justified by way of redemption, a price being paid for the harms we have done; and this is by the blood of your Lord, who came and stood in your place and stead, and died your death for your transgressions. Thus has he ransomed you from your transgressions by blood, and covered your polluted and deformed souls with righteousness; for the sake of which, God passed by you, and will not hurt you when he comes to judge the world. Rom. viii, 34; Gal. iii, 13.

Chr. This is brave! Now I see that there was some thing to be learned by our being pardoned by word and deed. Good Mercy, let us labour to keep this in mind: and, my children, do you remember it also. But sir,

[3] The explanation which our author here gives of the "righteousnesses" of Christ, appears to us much more fanciful than either Scriptural or intelligible. "It is," says Mr. Scott, "needlessly systematic and obscure." We would, therefore, refer the reader to what is said on the same subject in the First Part of the Pilgrim, pages 237, 238

was not this it that made my good Christian's burden fall from off his shoulders, and that made him give three leaps for joy?

Great. Yes, it was the belief of this that cut those strings that could not be cut by other means; and it was to give him a proof of the virtue of this, that he was suffered to carry his burden to the cross.

Chr. I thought so; for though my heart was lightsome and joyous before, yet it is ten times more lightsome and joyous now. And I am persuaded by what I have felt, though I have felt but little as yet, that if the most burdened man in the world was here, and did see and believe as I now do, it would make his heart the more merry and blithe.

Great. There is not only comfort and the ease of a burden brought to us by the sight and consideration of these, but an endeared affection begot in us by it; for who can (if he doth but once think that pardon comes not only by promise, but thus) but be affected with the way and means of his redemption, and so with the man that hath wrought it for him?

Chr. True: methinks it makes my heart bleed, to think that he should bleed for me. O, thou loving One! O, thou blessed One! Thou deservest to have me; thou hast bought me: thou deservest to have me all; thou hast paid for me ten thousand times more than I am worth! No marvel that this made the tears stand in my husband's eyes and that it made him trudge so nimbly on. I am persuaded he wished me with him: but, vile wretch that I was, I let him come all alone. O Mercy, that thy father and mother were here! yea, and Mrs. Timorous also: nay, I wish now with all my heart that here was Madam Wanton too. Surely,

surely, their hearts would be affected; nor could the fear of the one, nor the powerful lusts of the other, prevail with them to go home again, and refuse to become good pilgrims.

Great. You speak now in the warmth of your affections; will it, think you, be always thus with you? Besides, this is not communicated to every one, nor to every one that did see your Jesus bleed. There were that stood by, and that saw the blood run from his heart to the ground, and yet were so far off this, that, instead of lamenting, they laughed at him, and, instead of becoming his disciples, did harden their hearts against him. So that all that you have, my daughters, you have by peculiar impression made by a divine contemplating upon what I have spoken to you. Remember that 'twas told you, that the hen, by her common call, gives no meat to her chickens. This you have therefore by a special grace.[4]

Now I saw in my dream, that they went on until they were come to the place that Simple, and Sloth, and Presumption lay and slept in, when Christian went by on pilgrimage: and behold, they were hanged up in irons a little way off on the other side.

Then said Mercy to him that was their guide and conductor, "What are these three men? and for what are they hanged there?"

Great. These three men were men of bad qualities: they had no mind to be pilgrims themselves, and whomsoever they could they hindered. They were for sloth and folly themselves, and whomsoever they

[4] The gospel is no good news to them that refuse to receive it; nor will the atonement of Christ be of any avail except to such as believe on him with the heart unto righteousness. See John iii, 16–18.

could persuade they made so too, and withal taught them to presume that they should do well at last. They were asleep when Christian went by, and now you go by they are hanged.

Mer. But could they persuade any to be of their opinion?

Great. Yes, they turned several out of the way. There was Slow-pace that they persuaded to do as they. They also prevailed with one Short-wind, with one No-heart, with one Linger-after-lust, and with one Sleepy-head, and with a young woman, her name was Dull, to turn out of the way and become as they. Besides they brought up an ill report of your Lord, persuading others that he was a hard taskmaster. They also brought up an evil report of the good land, saying it was not half so good as some pretended it was. They also began to vilify his servants, and to count the very best of them meddlesome, troublesome, busy-bodies. Further, they would call the bread of God husks; the comforts of his children fancies; the travail and labour of pilgrims, things to no purpose.

"Nay," said Christiana, "if they were such, they shall never be bewailed by me: they have but what they deserve; and I think it is well that they stand so near the highway, that others may see and take warning. But had it not been well if their crimes had been engraven in some plate of iron or brass, and left here where they did their mischiefs, for a caution to other bad men?"

Great. So it is, as you may well perceive, if you will go a little to the wall.

Mer. No, no; let them hang, and their names rot, and their crimes live for ever against them. I think it a high favour that they were hanged afore we came hither: who knows else what they might have done to such poor women as we are?

Then she turned it into a song, saying,—

"Now then you three hang there, and be a sign
To all that shall against the truth combine.
And let him that comes after, fear this end,
If unto pilgrims he is not a friend.
And thou, my soul, of all such men beware,
That unto holiness opposers are."

Thus they went on till they came at the foot of the hill Difficulty, where again the good Mr. Greatheart took an occasion to tell them what happened there when Christian himself went by. So he had them first to the spring. "Lo," said he, "this is the spring that Christian drank of before he went up this hill: and then it was clear and good; but now it is dirty with the feet of some that are not desirous that pilgrims here should quench their thirst." Ezek. xxxiv, 18, 19.[5]

Thereat Mercy said, "And why so envious, trow?" But, said the guide, "It will do, if taken up and put into a vessel that is sweet and good; for then the dirt will sink to the bottom, and the water come out by itself more clear." Thus therefore Christiana and her companions were compelled to do. They took it up, and put it into an earthen pot, and so let it stand till the dirt was gone to the bottom, and then they drank thereof.[6]

[5] By the fouling of the spring is meant the corrupting of the pure doctrine of the gospel by dangerous and unscriptural opinions, which were very rife at the time this book was written. "Indeed," says Bunyan, in another of his works, "this is an age of errors, if ever there was an age of errors in this world."

[6] "It is difficult getting good doctrine in erroneous times," says the author in a marginal note. We must not hastily receive every opinion that may be presented to us, however plausible it may appear; but

Next he showed them the two by-ways that were at the foot of the hill, where Formality and Hypocrisy lost themselves. And said he, "These are dangerous paths. Two were here cast away when Christian came by · and although, as you see, these ways are since stopped up with chains, posts, and a ditch, yet there are those that will choose to adventure here rather than take the pains to go up this hill."

Chr. "The way of transgressors is hard." Prov. xiii, 15. It is a wonder that they can get into these ways without danger of breaking their necks.

Great. They will venture; yea, if at any time any of the King's servants doth happen to see them, and doth call upon them, and tell them that they are in the wrong way, and do bid them beware of the danger, then they will railingly return them answer, and say, "As for the word that thou hast spoken unto us in the name of the King, we will not hearken unto thee; but we will certainly do whatsoever thing goeth out of our mouth." Jer. xliv, 16, 17. Nay, if you look a little further, you will see that these ways are made cautionary enough, not only by these posts, and ditch, and chain, but also by being hedged up: yet they will choose to go there.

Chr. They are idle; they love not to take pains: up-hill way is unpleasant to them. So it is fulfilled unto them as it is written, "The way of the slothful man is as a hedge of thorns." Prov. xv, 19. Yea, they will rather choose to walk upon a snare, than to go up this hill, and the rest of this way to the City.

'ake time to consider, and compare it with the word of God. "To he law and to the testimony; if they speak not according to this word, it is because there is no light in them." Isaiah viii, 20.

Then they set forward, and began to go up the hill, and up the hill they went. But before they got to the top, Christiana began to pant, and said, "I dare say this is a breathing hill; no marvel if they that love their ease more than their souls choose to themselves a smoother way." Then said Mercy, "I must sit down:" also the least of the children began to cry. "Come, come," said Greatheart, "sit not down here; for a little above is the Prince's arbour." Then he took the little boy by the hand, and led him up thereto.

When they were come to the arbour they were very willing to sit down, for they were all in a pelting heat. Then said Mercy, "'How sweet is rest to them that labour!' (Matt. xi, 28;) and how good is the Prince of pilgrims to provide such resting places for them! Of this arbour I have heard much; but I never saw it before. But here let us beware of sleeping; for, as I have heard, it cost poor Christian dear."

Then said Mr. Greatheart to the little ones, "Come, my pretty boys, how do you do? what think you now of going on pilgrimage?"

"Sir," said the least, "I was almost beat out of heart; but I thank you for lending me a hand, at my need, and I remember now what my mother hath told me, namely, that the way to heaven is as a ladder, and the way to hell is as down a hill. But I had rather go up the ladder to life, than down the hill to death."

Then said Mercy, "But the proverb is, To go down the hill is easy." But James said, (for that was his name,) "The day is coming when, in my opinion, going down the hill will be the hardest of all."* "'Tis a good boy," said his master; "thou hast given her a righ: answer." Then Mercy smiled, but the little boy did blush.

"Come," said Christiana, "will you eat a bit, a little to sweeten your mouths while you sit here to rest your legs? for I have here a piece of pomegranate, which Mr. Interpreter put into my hand just when I came out of his door: he gave me also a piece of a honeycomb, and a little bottle of spirits." "I thought he gave you something," said Mercy, "because he called you aside." "Yes, so he did," said the other; "but," said Christiana, "it shall be still as I said it should, when at firs we came from home; thou shalt be a sharer in all the good that I have, because thou so willingly didst become my companion." Then she gave to them and they did eat, both Mercy and the boys. "And," said Christiana to Mr. Greatheart, "sir, will you do as we?" But he answered, "You are going on pilgrimage, and presently I shall return; much good may what you have do you: at home I eat the same every day."

Now when they had eaten and drank, and had chatted a little longer, their guide said to them, "The day wears away; if you think good, let us prepare to be going." So they got up to go, and the little boys went before; but Christiana forgot to take her bottle of spirits with her, so she sent her little boy back to fetch it. Then said Mercy, "I think this is a losing place; here Christian lost his roll, and here Christiana left her bottle behind her: sir, what is the cause of this?" So their guide made answer, and said, "The cause is sleep, or forgetfulness: some sleep when they should keep awake, and some forget when they should remember; and this is the very cause why often at the resting-places some pilgrims, in some things, come off losers.

Pilgrims should watch, and remember what they have already received, under their greatest enjoyments; but for want of doing so, oftentimes their rejoicing ends in tears, and their sunshine in a cloud; witness the story of Christian at this place."

When they were come to the place where Mistrust and Timorous met Christian, to persuade him to go back for fear of the lions, they perceived as it were a stage, and before it, toward the road, a broad plate with a copy of verses written thereon, and underneath, the reason of raising up of that stage in that place rendered. The verses were these:—

> "Let him that sees this stage, take heed
> Unto his heart and tongue;
> Lest, if he do not, here he speed
> As some have long agone."

The words underneath the verses were, "This stage was built to punish those upon, who, through timorousness or mistrust, shall be afraid to go further on pilgrimage. Also, on this stage both Mistrust and Timorous were burned through the tongue with a hot iron, for endeavouring to hinder Christian on his journey."

Then said Mercy, "This is much like to the saying of the Beloved, 'What shall be given unto thee, or what shall be done unto thee, thou false tongue? Sharp arrows of the mighty, with coals of juniper.'" Psalm cxx, 3, 4.

So they went on till they came within sight of the lions. Now Mr. Greatheart was a strong man, so he was not afraid of a lion. But yet when they were come up to the place where the lions were, the boys, that went before, were now glad to cringe behind, for they were afraid of the lions; so they stepped back, and went behind.[7] At this their guide smiled, and said, "How now, my boys, do you love to go before when no danger doth approach, and love to come behind so soon as the lions appear?"

Now as they went on Mr. Greatheart drew his sword, with intent to make a way for the pilgrims in spite of the lions. Then there appeared one that, it seems, had taken upon him to back the lions; and he said to the pilgrims' guide, "What is the cause of your coming hither?" Now the name of that man was Grim, or Bloodyman, because of his slaying of pilgrims; and he was of the race of the giants.[8]

Then said the pilgrims' guide, "These women and children are going on pilgrimage, and this is the way they must go; and go it they shall, in spite of thee and the lions."

Grim. This is not their way, neither shall they go therein. I am come forth to withstand them, and to that end will back the lions.

Now, to say truth, by reason of the fierceness of the lions, and of the grim carriage of him that did back them, this way had of late lain much unoccupied, and was almost grown over with grass.

Then said Christiana, "Though the highways have been unoccupied heretofore, and though the travellers have been made in times past to walk through by-paths, it must not be so now I am risen, now I am arisen a mother in Israel." Judges v, 6, 7.

[7] An emblem of those that go on bravely when there is no danger, but shrink when trouble comes.—*Bunyan's Marginal Note.*

[8] Giant Grim, (who was not seen by Christian when he came this way,) now "backs the lions" in opposing the progress of the pilgrims; an indication, probably, that the spirit of persecution now raged more violently than when the First Part of the Pilgrim was written.

Then he swore by the lions that it should, and therefore bid them turn aside, for they should not have passage there.

But Greatheart their guide made first his approach unto Grim, and laid so heavily at him with his sword that he forced him to retreat.

Then said he that attempted to back the lions, "Will you slay me on my own ground?"

Great. It is the King's highway that we are in, and in his way it is that thou hast placed the lions; but these women, and these children, though weak, shall hold on their way in spite of thy lions.

And with that he gave him again a downright blow, and brought him upon his knees. With this blow also he broke his helmet, and with the next he cut off an arm. Then did the giant roar so hideously that his voice frightened the women, and yet they were glad to see him lie sprawling upon the ground. Now the lions were chained, and so of themselves could do nothing. Wherefore, when old Grim, that intended to back them, was dead, Mr. Greatheart said to the pilgrims, "Come now, and follow me, and no hurt shall happen to you from the lions." They therefore went on, but the women trembled as they passed by them; the boys also looked as if they would die; but they all got by without further hurt.

CHAPTER V.

The pilgrims come to the Porter's lodge, where Greatheart leaves them—They are welcomed to the House Beautiful—Joy in the house on their arrival—Mercy's dream—Prudence catechises the children—Mr. Brisk addresses Mercy—Matthew falls sick—He is restored by taking Mr. Skill's pills—Various emblems—Greatheart comes again to conduct them—They proceed on their journey.

Now when they were within sight of the Porter's lodge, they soon came up unto it, but they made the more haste after this to go thither, because it is dangerous travelling there in the night. So when they were come to the gate the guide knocked, and the Porter cried, "Who is there?" But as soon as the guide had said, "It is I," he knew his voice, and came down, for the guide had oft before that come thither as a conductor of pilgrims. When he was come down he opened the gate; and seeing the guide standing just before it, (for he saw not the women, for they were behind him,) he said unto him, "How now, Mr. Greatheart, what is your business here so late to-night?" "I have brought," said he, "some pilgrims hither, where, by my Lord's commandment, they must lodge: I had been here some time ago, had I not been opposed by the giant that did use to back the lions. But I, after a long and tedious combat with him, have cut him off, and have brought the pilgrims hither in safety."

Por. Will you not go in, and stay till morning?

Great. No, I will return to my Lord to-night.

Chr. O, sir, I know not how to be willing you should leave us in our pilgrimage, you have been so faithful and so loving to us; you have fought so stoutly for us, you have been so hearty in counselling of us, that I shall never forget your favour toward us.

Then said Mercy, "O that we might have thy company to our journey's end! How can such poor women as we hold out in a way so full of troubles as this way is without a friend and defender?"

Then said James, the youngest of the boys, "Pray, sir, be persuaded to go with us, and help us, because we are so weak, and the way so dangerous as it is."

Great. I am at my Lord's commandment; if he shall allot me to be your guide quite through, I will willingly wait upon you. But here you failed at first; for when he bid me come thus far with you, then you should have begged me of him to go quite through with you, and he would have granted your request.[1] However, at present I must withdraw; and so, good Christiana, Mercy, and my brave children, adieu.

Then the Porter, Mr. Watchful, asked Christiana of her country, and of her kindred. And she said, "I come from the City of Destruction. I am a widow woman, and my husband is dead; his name was Christian, the pilgrim." "How!" said the Porter, "was he your husband?" "Yes," said she, "and these are his children; and this (pointing to Mercy) is one of my townswomen." Then the Porter rang his bell, as at such times he is wont, and there came to the door one of the damsels, whose name was Humble-mind; and to her the Porter said, "Go tell it within that Christiana, the wife of Christian, and her children, are come hither on pilgrimage." She went in therefore, and told it. But O, what noise for gladness was there within when the damsel did but drop that word out of her mouth!

[1] Help is lost for want of asking for it.—*Bunyan's Marginal Note.*

So they came with haste to the Porter, for Christiana stood still at the door. Then some of the most grave said unto her, "Come in, Christiana, come in, thou wife of that good man; come in, thou blessed woman, come in, with all that are with thee." So she went in, and they followed her that were her children and companions. Now when they were gone in, they were had into a very large room, where they were bidden to sit down: so they sat down, and the chief of the house were called to see and welcome the guests. Then they came in, and understanding who they were, did salute each one with a kiss, and said, "Welcome, ye vessels of the grace of God! welcome to us your friends!"

Now, because it was somewhat late, and because the pilgrims were weary with their journey, and also made faint with the sight of the fight, and of the terrible lions, therefore they desired, as soon as might be, to prepare to go to rest. "Nay," said those of the family, "refresh yourselves first with a morsel of meat;" for they had prepared for them a lamb, with the accustomed sauce belonging thereto, (Exod. xii, 21; John i, 29;) for the Porter had heard before of their coming, and had told it to them within. So when they had supped, and ended their prayer with a psalm, they desired they might go to rest. "But let us," said Christiana, "if we may be so bold as to choose, be in that chamber that was my husband's when he was here." So they had them up thither, and they lay all in a room. When they were at rest, Christiana and Mercy entered into discourse about things that were convenient.

Chr. Little did I think once, when my husband went on pilgrimage, that I should ever have followed.

Mer. And you as little thought of lying in his bed, and in his chamber to rest, as you do now.

Chr. And much less did I ever think of seeing his face with comfort, and of worshipping the Lord, the King, with him; and yet now I believe I shall.

Mer. Hark! don't you hear a noise?

Chr. Yes; it is, as I believe, a noise of music, for joy that we are here.

Mer. Wonderful! Music in the house, music in the heart, and music also in heaven, for joy that we are here!

Thus they talked awhile, and then betook themselves to sleep.

So in the morning when they were awake, Christiana said to Mercy, "What was the matter that you did laugh in your sleep to-night? I suppose you were in a dream."

Mer. So I was, and a sweet dream it was; but are you sure I laughed?

Chr. Yes, you laughed heartily; but prithee, Mercy, tell me thy dream.

Mer. I was dreaming that I sat all alone in a solitary place, and was bemoaning of the hardness of my heart. Now I had not sat there long, but methought many were gathered about me to see me, and to hear what it was that I said. So they hearkened, and I went on bemoaning the hardness of my heart. At this some of them laughed at me, some called me fool, and some began to thrust me about. With that, methought I looked up and saw one coming with wings toward me. So he came directly to me, and said, "Mercy, what aileth thee?" Now when he had heard me make my complaint, he said, "Peace be to thee;" he also wiped my eyes with his handkerchief, and clad me in silver and gold. He put a chain about my neck, and ear-rings in my ears, and a beautiful crown upon my head. Ezek. xvi, 8–12. Then he took me by the hand, and said, "Mercy, come after me." So he went up, and I followed till we came at a golden gate. Then he knocked; and when they within had opened, the man went in, and I followed him up to a throne, upon which one sat; and he said to me, "Welcome, daughter." The place looked bright and twinkling, like the stars, or rather like the sun, and I thought that I saw your husband there: so I awoke from my dream. But did I laugh?

Chr. Laugh! ay, and well you might to see yourself so well. For you must give me leave to tell you that I believe it was a good dream; and that as you have begun to find the first part true, so you shall find the second at last. "God speaks once, yea twice, yet man perceiveth it not; in a dream, in a vision of the night, when deep sleep falleth upon men, in slumberings upon the bed." Job xxxiii, 14, 15. We need not, when a-bed, to lie awake to talk with God; he can visit us while we sleep, and cause us then to hear his voice. Our heart oftentimes wakes when we sleep, and God can speak to that, either by words, by proverbs, by signs and similitudes, as well as if one was awake.

Mer. Well, I am glad of my dream; for I hope ere long to see it fulfilled, to the making of me laugh again.

Chr. I think it is now high time to rise, and to know what we must do.

Mer. Pray, if they invite us to stay awhile, let us willingly accept of the proffer. I am the willinger to stay awhile here, to grow better acquainted with these maids: methinks Prudence, Piety, and Charity, have very comely and sober countenances.

Chr. We shall see what they will do.

So when they were up and ready, they came down and they asked one another of their rest, and if it was comfortable or not.

"Very good," said Mercy, "it was one of the best night's lodgings that ever I had in my life."

Then said Prudence and Piety, "If you will be persuaded to stay here awhile, you shall have what the house will afford."

"Ay, and that with a very good will," said Charity. So they consented, and stayed there about a month, or above, and became very profitable one to another. And because Prudence would see how Christiana had brought up her children, she asked leave of her to catechise them. So she gave her free consent.

Then she began with the youngest, whose name was James. And she said, "Come, James, canst thou tell me who made thee?"

James. God the Father, God the Son, and God the Holy Ghost.

Prud. Good boy. And canst thou tell who saves thee?

James. God the Father, God the Son, and God the Holy Ghost.

Prud. Good boy still. But how doth God the Father save thee?

James. By his grace.

Prud. How doth God the Son save thee?

James. By his righteousness, death and blood, and life.

Prud. And how doth God the Holy Ghost save thee?

James. By his illumination, his renovation, and his preservation.

Then said Prudence to Christiana, "You are to be commended for thus bringing up your children. I suppose I need not ask the rest these questions, since the youngest of them can answer them so well. I will therefore now apply myself to the next youngest."

Then she said, "Come, Joseph, (for his name was Joseph,) will you let me catechise you?"

Joseph. With all my heart.

Prud. What is man?

Joseph. A reasonable creature, so made by God, as my brother said.

Prud. What is supposed by this word, saved?

Joseph. That man, by sin, has brought himself into a state of captivity and misery.

Prud. What is supposed by his being saved by the Trinity?

Joseph. That sin is so great and mighty a tyrant that none can pull us out of its clutches but God; and that God is so good and loving to man, as to pull him indeed out of this miserable state.

Prud. What is God's design in saving poor men?

Joseph. The glorifying of his name, of his grace, and justice, &c., and the everlasting happiness of his creatures.

Prud. Who are they that must be saved?

Joseph. Those that accept of his salvation.

Prud. Good boy, Joseph; thy mother hath taught thee well, and thou hast hearkened unto what she has said unto thee.

Then said Prudence to Samuel, who was the eldest

son but one, "Come, Samuel, are you willing that I should catechise you?"

Sam. Yes, forsooth, if you please.

Prud. What is heaven?

Sam. A place and state most blessed, because God dwelleth there.

Prud. What is hell?

Sam. A place and state most woful, because it is the dwelling place of sin, the devil, and death.

Prud. Why wouldst thou go to heaven?

Sam. That I may see God, and serve him without weariness; that I may see Christ, and love him everlastingly; that I may have that fulness of the Holy Spirit in me which I can by no means here enjoy.

Prud. A very good boy also, and one that has learned well.

Then she addressed herself to the eldest, whose name was Matthew; and she said to him, "Come, Matthew, shall I also catechise you?"

Matt. With a very good will.

Prud. I ask then, if there was ever anything that had a being antecedent to, or before God?

Matt. No, for God is eternal; nor is there anything, excepting himself, that had a being, until the beginning of the first day.[2] "For in six days the Lord made heaven and earth, the sea, and all that in them is." Exodus xx, 11.

Prud. What do you think of the Bible?

Matt. It is the holy word of God.

Prud. Is there nothing written therein but what you understand?

Matt. Yes, a great deal.

[2] That is, nothing in this world; angels existed before. Job xxxviii

Prud. What do you do when you meet with such places therein that you do not understand?

Matt. I think God is wiser than I. I pray also that he will please to let me know all therein that he knows will be for my good.

Prud. How believe you as touching the resurrection of the dead?

Matt. I believe they shall rise the same that was buried; the same in nature, though not in corruption. And I believe this upon a double account: first, because God has promised it; secondly, because he is able to perform it.

Then said Prudence to the boys, "You must still hearken to your mother; for she can learn you more. You must also diligently give ear to what good talk you shall hear from others; for, for your sakes do they speak good things. Observe also, and that with carefulness, what the heavens and the earth do teach you; but especially be much in the meditation of that book which was the cause of your father's becoming a pilgrim. I, for my part, my children, will teach you what I can while you are here, and shall be glad if you will ask me questions that tend to godly edifying."

Now by that these pilgrims had been at this place a week, Mercy had a visiter that pretended some good will unto her, and his name was Mr. Brisk: a man of some breeding, and that pretended to religion, but a man that stuck very close to the world. So he came once, or twice, or more, to Mercy, and offered love unto her. Now Mercy was of a fair countenance, and therefore the more alluring. Her mind also was to be always busying of herself in doing; for when she had nothing to do for herself, she would be making hose and garments for others, and would bestow them upon them that had need.[3] And Mr. Brisk not knowing where or how she disposed of what she made, seemed to be greatly taken, for that he found her never idle. "I will warrant her a good housewife," quoth he to himself.

Mercy then revealed the business to the maidens that were of the house, and inquired of them concerning him, for they did know him better than she. So they told her that he was a very busy young man, and one who pretended to religion, but was, as they feared, a stranger to the power of that which is good.

"Nay then," said Mercy, "I will look no more on him; for I purpose never to have a clog to my soul."

Prudence then replied, that there needed no great matter of discouragement to be given to him; for continuing so as she had begun to do for the poor would quickly cool his courage.

So the next time he came he finds her at her old work, a-making things for the poor. Then said he, "What! always at it?" "Yes," said she, "either for myself or for others." "And what canst thou earn a day?" said he. "I do these things," replied she, "that I may be rich in good works, laying a good foundation against the time to come, that I may lay hold on eternal life." 1 Timothy vi, 18, 19. "Why, prithee, what dost thou do with them?" said he. "Clothe the naked," said she. With that his countenance fell. So he forbore to come at her again. And when he was asked the reason why, he said, that Mercy was a pretty lass, but troubled with ill conditions.

[3] The heart that is fullest of "good works," hath in it the least room for Satan's temptations.—*Bunyan's Christian Behaviour.*

When he had left her, Prudence said, "Did I not ell thee that Mr. Brisk would soon forsake thee? yea, he will raise up an ill report of thee; for, notwithstanding his pretence to religion, and his seeming love to Mercy, yet Mercy and he are of tempers so different that I believe they will never come together."

Mer. I might have had husbands before now, though I spoke not of it to any; but they were such as did not like my conditions, though never did any of them find fault with my person. So they and I could not agree.

Prud. Mercy in our days is little set by any further than as to its name; the practice, which is set forth by thy conditions, there are but few that can abide.

"Well," said Mercy, "if nobody will have me, I will die a maid, or my conditions shall be to me as a husband; for I cannot change my nature: and to have one who lies cross to me in this, that I purpose never to admit of as long as I live. I had a sister named Bountiful, that was married to one of these churls, but he and she could never agree; but because my sister was resolved to do as she had begun, that is, to show kindness to the poor, therefore her husband first cried her down at the Cross,[4] and then turned her out of his doors.

Prud. And yet he was a professor, I warrant you?

Mer. Yes, such a one as he was, and of such as he the world is now full: but I am for none of them all.

Now Matthew, the eldest son of Christiana, fell sick, and his sickness was sore upon him, for he was much

[4] In Roman Catholic countries it is common to erect large crosses in the open air, in markets, and other places of public resort. Some of these monuments of superstition still remain in England, and the places where they stand are commonly called "the Cross"

pained in his bowels, so that he was with it at times pulled, as it were, both ends together. There dwelt also not far from thence one Mr. Skill, an ancient and well-approved physician. So Christiana desired it, and they sent for him, and he came. When he was entered the room, and had a little observed the boy, he concluded he was sick of the gripes.[5] Then he said to his mother, "What diet has Matthew of late fed upon?" "Diet!" said Christiana, "nothing but what is wholesome." The physician answered, "This boy has been tampering with something that lies in his maw undigested, and that will not away without means. And I tell you he must be purged or else he will die."

Then said Samuel, "Mother, what was that which my brother did gather up and eat as soon as we were come from the gate that is at the head of this way? You know that there was an orchard on the left hand, on the other side of the wall, and some of the trees hung over the wall, and my brother did pluck and eat."

"True, my child," said Christiana, "he did take thereof and did eat; naughty boy as he was; I chid him, and yet he would eat thereof."

Skill. I knew he had eaten something that was not wholesome food; and that food, to wit, that fruit, is even the most hurtful of all. It is fruit of Beelzebub's orchard. I do marvel that none did warn you of it; many have died thereof.

Then Christiana began to cry; and she said, "O naughty boy! and O careless mother! what shall I do for my son?"

Skill. Come, do not be too much dejected; the boy may do well again, but he must purge and vomit.

[5] Gripes of conscience.—*Bunyan's Marginal Note*

Chr. Pray, sir, try the utmost of your skill with him, whatever it costs.

Skill. Nay, I hope I shall be reasonable.

So he made him a purge, but it was too weak; 'twas said it was made of the blood of a goat, the ashes of a heifer, and some of the juice of hyssop, &c. Heb. ix, 13; x, 4. When Mr. Skill had seen that that purge was too weak, he made him one to the purpose. It was made *ex carne et sanguine Christi*,[6] John vi, 54–57; Heb. ix, 1–4; (you know physicians give strange medicines to their patients;) and it was made into pills, with a promise or two, and a proportionable quantity of salt. Now he was to take them three at a time, fasting, in half a quarter of a pint of the tears of repentance. Zech. xii, 10.

When this potion was prepared, and brought to the boy, he was loath to take it, though torn with the gripes as if he should be pulled in pieces. "Come, come," said the physician, "you must take it." "It goes against my stomach," said the boy. "I must have you take it," said his mother. "I shall vomit it up again," said the boy. "Pray, sir," said Christiana to Mr. Skill, "how does it taste?" "It has no ill taste," said the doctor; and with that she touched one of the pills with the tip of her tongue. "O, Matthew," said she, "this potion is sweeter than honey. If thou lovest thy mother, if thou lovest thy brothers, if thou lovest Mercy, if thou lovest thy life, take it." So with much ado, after a short prayer for the blessing of God upon it, he took it, and it wrought kindly with him. It caused him to purge; it caused him to sleep and rest quietly; it put him into a fine heat and breathing sweat, and did

[6] "Of the flesh and blood of Christ." The Latin I borrow.—*Bunyan.*

quite rid him of his gripes. So in a little time he got up, and walked about with a staff,[7] and would go from room to room, and talked with Prudence, Piety, and Charity, of his distemper, and how he was healed.

So when the boy was healed, Christiana asked Mr. Skill, saying, "Sir, what will content you for your pains and care to and of my child?" And he said, "You must pay the Master of the College of Physicians, according to rules made in that case and provided." Heb. xiii, 11–15.

"But, sir," said she, "what is this pill good for else?"

Skill. It is a universal pill; it is good against all the diseases that pilgrims are incident to; and when it is well prepared it will keep good time out of mind.

Chr. Pray, sir, make me up twelve boxes of them; for, if I can get these, I will never take other physic.

Skill. These pills are good to prevent diseases, as well as to cure when one is sick. Yea, I dare say it, and stand to it, that if a man will but use this physic as he should, it will make him live for ever. John vi, 56–58. But good Christiana, thou must give these pills no other way than as I have prescribed; for if you do they will do no good.

So he gave unto Christiana physic for herself, and her boys, and for Mercy: and bid Matthew take heed how he ate any more green plums, and kissed them and went his way.

It was told you before, that Prudence bid the boys, that if at any time they would, they should ask her some questions that might be profitable, and she would say something to them.

Then Matthew, who had been sick, asked her,

[7] A word of God in the hand of faith.—*Bunyan's Marginal Note.*

why for the most part physic should be bitter to our palates.

Prud. To show how unwelcome the word of God and the effects thereof are to the carnal heart.

Matt. Why does physic, if it does good, purge, and cause to vomit?

Prud. To show that the word, when it works effectually, cleanseth the heart and mind. For look, what the one doth to the body, the other doth to the soul.

Matt. What should we learn by seeing the flame of our fire go upward, and by seeing the beams and sweet influences of the sun strike downward?

Prud. By the going up of the fire we are taught to ascend to heaven by fervent and hot desires. And by the sun's sending his heat, beams, and sweet influences downward, we are taught that the Saviour of the world though high, reaches down with his grace and love to us below.

Matt. Where have the clouds their water?

Prud. Out of the sea.

Matt. What may we learn from that?

Prud. That ministers should fetch their doctrine from God.

Matt. Why do they empty themselves upon the earth?

Prud. To show that ministers should give out what they know of God to the world.

Matt. Why is the rainbow caused by the sun?

Prud. To show that the covenant of God's grace is confirmed to us in Christ.

Matt. Why do the springs come from the sea to us through the earth?

Prud. To show that the grace of God comes to us through the body of Christ.

Matt. Why do some of the springs rise out of the tops of high hills?

Prud. To show that the Spirit of grace shall spring up in some that are great and mighty, as well as in many that are poor and low.

Matt. Why doth the fire fasten upon the candle-wick?

Prud. To show that unless grace doth kindle upon the heart, there will be no true light of life in us.

Matt. Why are the wick, and tallow, and all spent to maintain the light of the candle?

Prud. To show that body, and soul, and all should be at the service of, and spend themselves to maintain in good condition, that grace of God that is in us.

Matt. Why doth the pelican pierce her own breast with her bill?

Prud. To nourish her young ones with her blood;[8] and thereby to show that Christ the blessed so loved his young, his people, as to save them from death by his blood.

Matt. What may one learn by hearing the cock to crow?

Prud. Learn to remember Peter's sin, and Peter's repentance. The cock's crowing shows also, that day is coming on: let then the crowing of the cock put thee in mind of that last and terrible day of judgment.

[8] In feeding its young, the pelican disgorges the contents of its capacious pouch by pressing it with its bill against the neck and breast; during this action the point of the upper mandible would appear to come in contact with the breast, which doubtless gave rise to the once popular error that this bird nourished her young with her own blood. In former years we have often seen pictures representing the pelican lacerating her breast with her beak, and the blood spirting from the wounds into the gaping mouths of her offspring.

Now about this time their month was out; wherefore they signified to those of the house, that 'twas convenient for them to up and be going. Then said Joseph to his mother, "It is proper that you forget not to send to the house of Mr. Interpreter, to pray him to grant that Mr. Greatheart should be sent unto us, that he may be our conductor the rest of our way." "Good boy," said she, "I had almost forgot."[9] So she drew up a petition, and prayed Mr. Watchful, the Porter, to send it by some fit man to her good friend Mr. Interpreter; who, when it was come, and he had seen the contents of the petition, said to the messenger, "Go, tell them that I will send him."

When the family where Christiana was saw that they had a purpose to go forward, they called the whole house together, to give thanks to their King for sending of them such profitable guests as these. Which done, they said unto Christiana, "And shall we not show thee something as our custom is to do to pilgrims, on which thou mayest meditate when thou art upon the way?" So they took Christiana, her children, and Mercy, into the closet, and showed them one of the apples that Eve ate of, and that she also did give to her husband, and that for the eating of which they were both turned out of paradise, and asked her what she thought that was. Then Christiana said, "It is food or poison, I know not which." So they opened the matter to her, and she held up her hands and wondered. Gen. iii, 6; Rom. vii, 24.

Then they had her to a place and showed her Jacob's ladder. Now at that time there were some angels as-

The weak may sometimes call the strong to prayers.—*Bunyan.*

cending upon it. Gen. xxviii, 12. So Christiana looked and looked to see the angels go up; so did the rest of the company. Then they were going into another place, to show them something else; but James said to his mother, "Pray bid them stay here a little longer, for this is a curious sight." So they turned again, and stood feeding their eyes with this so pleasing a prospect.[10]

After this they had them into a place where did hang up a golden anchor. So they bid Christiana take it down; "for," said they, "you shall have it with you, for 'tis of absolute necessity, that you may lay hold of that within the veil, and stand steadfast in case you should meet with turbulent weather." Hebrews vi, 19; Joel iii, 16. So they were glad thereof.

Then they took them, and had them to the mount upon which Abraham our father offered up Isaac his son, and showed them the altar, the wood, the fire, and the knife, for they remain to be seen to this very day. Gen. xxii, 9. When they had seen it, they held up their hands, and blessed themselves, and said, "O! what a man for love to his Master, and for denial to himself, was Abraham!"

After they had showed them all these things, Prudence took them into a dining-room, where stood a pair

10 We read of Jacob's ladder: Christ is Jacob's ladder that reacheth up to heaven, and he that refuseth to go by this ladder thither, will scarce by other means get up so high. There is none other name given whereby we must be saved.—*Bunyan's Jerusalem Sinner Saved.* All the rounds of this ladder are sound, and fitly placed; not one of them is set further than that by faith thou mayest ascend step by step unto, even until thou shalt come to the highest step thereof, from whence thou mayest step in at the celestial gate, where thy soul desireth to dwell.—*Bunyan's Saint's Knowledge of Christ's Love*

of excellent virginals;[11] so she played upon them, and turned what she had showed them into this excellent song, saying,—

"Eve's apple we have show'd you;
Of that be you aware:
You have seen Jacob's ladder too,
Upon which angels are.

"An anchor you received have;
But let not these suffice,
Until with Abra'm you have gave
Your best a sacrifice."

Now about this time one knocked at the door. So the Porter opened, and behold Mr. Greatheart was there: but when he was come in, what joy was there! For it came now afresh again into their minds how but a little while ago he had slain old Grim Bloodyman, the giant, and had delivered them from the lions.

Then said Mr. Greatheart to Christiana and to Mercy, "My Lord has sent each of you a bottle of wine, and also some parched corn, together with a couple of pomegranates: he has also sent the boys some figs and raisins, to refresh you in your way."

Then they addressed themselves to their journey, and Prudence and Piety went along with them. When they came to the gate, Christiana asked the Porter if any of late went by. He said, "No; only one some time since, who also told me, that of late there had been a great robbery committed on the King's highway as you go: but," said he, "the thieves are taken, and will shortly be tried for their lives." Then Christiana and Mercy were afraid; but Matthew said, "Mother,

[11] "Virginals"—a musical instrument which was so called because it was commonly used by young ladies.

fear nothing as long as Mr. Greatheart is to go with us, and to be our conductor."

Then said Christiana to the Porter, "Sir, I am much obliged to you for all the kindnesses that you have showed me since I came hither; and also for that you have been so loving and kind to my children. I know not how to gratify your kindness; wherefore, pray, as a token of my respect to you, accept of this small mite." So she put a gold angel[11] in his hand; and he made her a low obeisance, and said, "'Let thy garments be always white; and let thy head want no ointment.' (Eccles. ix, 8.) Let Mercy live and not die, and let not her works be few." Deut. xxxiii, 6. And to the boys he said, "Do you fly youthful lusts, and follow after godliness with them that are grave and wise, (2 Tim. ii, 22;) so shall you put gladness into your mother's heart, and obtain praise of all that are sober-minded." So they thanked the Porter, and departed.

[11] An old English coin valued at ten shillings sterling. It derived its name from its being impressed with the figure of an angel, in memory of the observation of Pope Gregory, who, seeing some beautiful youths in the market at Rome, and being told that they were *Angli*, English, said, They ought rather to have been called *angeli*, angels.

CHAPTER VI.

They go down into the Valley of Humiliation—Why Christian there was so beset—Many thrive in this valley—The contented shepherd boy—Forgetful Green—A monument of Christian's victory—Valley of the Shadow of Death—Maul, a giant, quarrels with Greatheart—The giant struck down—He is slain, and his head disposed of.

Now I saw in my dream that they went forward until they were come to the brow of the hill; where Piety bethinking herself, cried out, "Alas! I have forgot what I intended to bestow upon Christiana and her companions: I will go back and fetch it." So she ran and fetched it. While she was gone, Christiana thought she heard in a grove, a little way off on the right hand, a most curious melodious note, with words much like these:—

"Through all my life Thy favour is
So frankly show'd to me,
That in Thy house for evermore
My dwelling-place shall be."

And listening still, she thought she heard another answer it, saying,—

"For why? The Lord our God is good;
His mercy is for ever sure;
His truth at all times firmly stood,
And shall from age to age endure."

So Christiana asked Prudence who it was that made those curious notes. "They are," said she, "our country birds; they sing these notes but seldom, except it be at the spring, when the flowers appear, and the sun shines warm, and then you may hear them all day long. I often," said she, "go out to hear them;

we also ofttimes keep them tame in our house. They are very fine company for us when we are melancholy: also they make the woods, and groves, and solitary places, places desirous to be in." Sol. Song ii, 11, 12.

By this time Piety was come again. So she said to Christiana, "Look here, I have brought thee a scheme of all those things that thou hast seen at our house, upon which thou mayest look when thou findest thyself forgetful, and call those things again to remembrance for thy edification and comfort."

Now they began to go down the hill into the Valley of Humiliation. It was a steep hill, and the way was slippery; but they were very careful; so they got down pretty well. When they were down in the valley, Piety said to Christiana, "This is the place where Christian, your husband, met with the foul fiend Apollyon, and where they had that dreadful fight that they had: I know you cannot but have heard thereof. But be of good courage; as long as you have here Mr. Greatheart to be your guide and conductor, we hope you will fare the better." So when these two had committed the pilgrims unto the conduct of their guide, he went forward, and they went after.

Then said Mr. Greatheart, "We need not be so afraid of this valley, for here is nothing to hurt us, unless we procure it to ourselves. 'Tis true that Christian did here meet with Apollyon, with whom he had also a sore combat: but that fray was the fruit of those slips that he got in his going down the hill; for they that get slips there, must look for combats here. And hence it is that this valley has got so hard a name. For the common people, when they hear that some frightful thing has befallen such a one in such a place are of opinion that that place is haunted with some foul fiend or evil spirit; when, alas! it is for the fruit of their own doing that such things do befall them there. This Valley of Humiliation is of itself as fruitful a place as any the crow flies over; and I am persuaded, if we could hit upon it, we might find somewhere hereabouts something that might give us an account why Christian was so hardly beset in this place."

Then James said to his mother, "Lo, yonder stands a pillar, and it looks as if something was written thereon; let us go and see what it is." So they went, and found there written, "Let Christian's slips before he came hither, and the battles that he met with in this place, be a warning to those that come after." "Lo," said their guide, "did not I tell you that there was something hereabouts that would give intimation of the reason why Christian was so hard beset in this place?" Then turning himself to Christiana, he said, "No disparagement to Christian more than to many others whose hap and lot it was. For it is easier going up than down this hill, and that can be said but of few hills in all these parts of the world. But we will leave the good man; he is at rest: he also had a brave victory over his enemy: let Him grant that dwelleth above, that we fare not worse, when we come to be tried, than he.

"But we will come again to this Valley of Humiliation. It is the best and most fruitful piece of ground in all these parts. It is fat ground, and, as you see, consisteth much in meadows; and if a man was to come here in summer-time, as we do now, if he knew not anything before thereof, and if he also delighted himself in the sight of his eyes, he might see that which would be delightful to him. Behold how green this

I will dare to say this boy leads a merrier life and wears more of that herb called heart's-ease in his bosom, than he that is clad in silk and velvet.

valley is, also how beautiful with lilies.[1] Sol. Song ii, 1. I have also known many labouring men that have got good estates in this Valley of Humiliation; for God resisteth the proud, but giveth grace to the humble. (Jas. iv, 6; 1 Pet. v, 5.) Indeed it is a very fruitful soil, and doth bring forth by handfuls. Some also have wished that the next way to their Father's house were here, that they might be troubled no more with either hills or mountains to go over; but the way is the way, and there's an end."

Now as they were going along and talking, they spied a boy feeding his father's sheep. The boy was in very mean clothes, but of a fresh and well-favoured countenance; and as he sat by himself he sung. "Hark," said Mr. Greatheart, "to what the shepherd's boy saith." So they hearkened, and he said,—

"He that is down, needs fear no fall;
He that is low, no pride;
He that is humble, ever shall
Have God to be his guide.

"I am content with what I have,
Little be it or much;
And, Lord, contentment still I crave,
Because thou savest such.

"Fulness to such a burden is,
That go on pilgrimage;
Here little, and hereafter bliss
Is best from age to age."
Heb. xiii, 5; Phil. iv, 11-13.

Then said their guide, "Do you hear him? I will dare to say this boy lives a merrier life, and wears more of that herb called heart's-ease in his bosom, than he that is clad in silk and velvet. But we will proceed in our discourse.

[1] Christians adorning an humble station with a holy life.

"In this valley our Lord formerly had his country-house: he loved much to be here: he loved also to walk these meadows, for he found the air was pleasant. Besides, here a man shall be free from the noise, and from the hurryings of this life: all states are full of noise and confusion; only the Valley of Humiliation is that empty and solitary place. Here a man shall not be so let and hindered in his contemplation as in other places he is apt to be. This is a valley that nobody walks in but those that love a pilgrim's life. And though Christian had the hard hap to meet here with Apollyon, and to enter with him in a brisk encounter, yet I must tell you, that in former times men have met with angels here, have found pearls here, and have in this place found the words of life.

"Did I say our Lord had here in former days his country-house, and that he loved here to walk? I will add, in this place, and to the people that love and trace these grounds, he has left a yearly revenue, to be faithfully paid them at certain seasons, for their maintenance by the way, and for their further encouragement to go on in their pilgrimage."

Now, as they went on, Samuel said to Mr. Great-heart, "Sir, I perceive that in this valley my father and Apollyon had their battle; but whereabout was the fight? for I perceive this valley is large."

Great. Your father had the battle with Apollyon a a place yonder before us, in a narrow passage, just beyond Forgetful Green. And indeed that place is the most dangerous place in all these parts. For if at any time pilgrims meet with any brunt, it is when they forget what favours they have received, and how unworthy they are of them. This is the place also where others have been hard put to it. But more of the place when we are come to it; for I persuade myself, that to this day there remains either some sign of the battle, or some monument to testify that such a battle there was fought."

Then said Mercy, "I think I am as well in this valley as I have been anywhere else in all our journey: the place, methinks, suits with my spirits. I love to be in such places, where there is no rattling with coaches, nor rumbling with wheels. Methinks, here one may, without much molestation, be thinking what he is, whence he came, what he has done, and to what the King has called him. Here one may think, and break at heart, and melt in one's spirit, until one's eyes become as 'the fishpools of Heshbon.' They that go rightly through this 'valley of Baca, make it a well; the rain' that God sends down from heaven upon them that are here 'also filleth the pools.' (Psa. lxxxiv, 5–7.) This valley is that from whence also the King will give to his their vineyards, (Hos. ii, 15,) and they that go through it shall sing, as Christian did, for all he met with Apollyon."

"'Tis true," said their guide; "I have gone through this valley many a time, and never was better than when here. I have also been a conductor to several pilgrims, and they have confessed the same. 'To this man will I look,' saith the King, 'even to him that is poor and of a contrite spirit, and that trembleth at my word.'" Isa. lxvi, 2.

Now they were come to the place where the aforementioned battle was fought. Then said the guide to Christiana, her children, and Mercy, "This is the place: on this ground Christian stood, and up there came Apollyon against him. And, look, did not I tell you? here is some of your husband's blood upon these stones to this day. Behold, also, how here and there are yet to be seen upon the place some of the shivers of Apollyon's broken darts. See also how they did beat the ground with their feet as they fought, to make good their places against each other, how also with their by-blows they did split the very stones in pieces. Verily, Christian did here play the man, and showed himself as stout as Hercules could, had he been here, even he himself. When Apollyon was beat, he made his retreat to the next valley, that is called the Valley of the Shadow of Death, unto which we shall come anon. Lo, yonder also stands a monument on which is engraven this battle, and Christian's victory, to his fame throughout all ages."[2]

So because it stood just on the way-side before them, they stepped to it, and read the writing, which word for word was this :—

"Hard by here was a battle fought,
 Most strange, and yet most true ;
Christian and Apollyon sought
 Each other to subdue.

"The man so bravely play'd the man,
 He made the fiend to fly ;
Of which a monument I stand,
 The same to testify."

When they had passed by this place, they came upon the borders of the Shadow of Death ; and this valley was longer than the other ; a place also most

[2] The records of the trials and triumphs of those that have gone before are a great help and encouragement to the church. There is scarce any reading, except the Holy Scriptures, more profitable to Christians than the biographies of eminent saints, "who through faith subdued" their enemies, and now "inherit the promises."

strangely haunted with evil things, as many are able to testify; but these women and children went the better through it, because they had daylight, and because Mr. Greatheart was their conductor.

When they were entered upon this valley, they thought they heard a groaning as of dying men; a very great groaning. They thought also that they did hear words of lamentation, spoken as of some in extreme torment. These things made the boys to quake; the women also looked pale and wan; but their guide bid them be of good comfort.

So they went on a little further, and they thought that they felt the ground begin to shake under them, as if some hollow place was there: they heard also a kind of hissing, as of serpents, but nothing as yet appeared. Then said the boys, "Are we not yet at the end of this doleful place?" But the guide also bid them be of good courage, and look well to their feet; "lest haply," said he, "you be taken in some snare."

Now James began to be sick; but I think the cause thereof was fear: so his mother gave him some of that glass of spirits that had been given her at the Interpreter's house, and three of the pills that Mr. Skill had prepared, and the boy began to revive. Thus they went on till they came to about the middle of the valley; and then Christiana said, "Methinks I see something yonder upon the road before us, a thing of a shape such as I have not seen." Then said Joseph, "Mother, what is it?" "An ugly thing, child; an ugly thing," said she. "But, mother, what was it like?" said he. "'Tis like I cannot tell what," said she; "and now it is but a little way off." Then said she, "It is nigh." "Well, well," said Mr. Greatheart, "let them that are most afraid keep close to me." So the fiend came on, and the conductor met it; but when it was just come to him it vanished to all their sights. Then remembered they what had been said some time ago, "Resist the devil, and he will flee from you." James iv, 7.

They went therefore on, as being a little refreshed. But they had not gone far before Mercy, looking behind her, saw, as she thought, something most like a lion, and it came a great padding pace after; and it had a hollow voice of roaring; and at every roar it gave, it made all the valley echo, and all their hearts to ache, save the heart of him that was their guide. So it came up, and Mr. Greatheart went behind, and put the pilgrims all before him. The lion also came on apace, and Mr. Greatheart addressed himself to give him battle. But when he saw that it was determined that resistance should be made, he also drew back, and came no further. 1 Peter v, 8, 9.

Then they went on again, and their conductor went before them, till they came to a place where was cast up a pit the whole breadth of the way; and before they could be prepared to go over that, a great mist and a darkness fell upon them, so that they could not see. Then said the pilgrims, "Alas! what now shall we do?" But their guide made answer, "Fear not, stand still, and see what an end will be put to this also." So they stayed there, because their path was marred. They then also thought that they did hear more apparently the noise and rushing of the enemies; the fire also, and smoke of the pit, was much easier to be discerned. Then said Christiana to Mercy, "Now I see what my poor husband went through. I have heard much of this place, but I never was here afore now. Poor man:

he went here all alone in the night; he had night almost quite through the way; also these fiends were busy about him, as if they would have torn him in pieces. Many have spoken of it; but none can tell what the Valley of the Shadow of Death should mean until they come in it themselves. 'The heart knoweth its own bitterness; and a stranger intermeddleth not with its joy.' (Prov. xiv, 10.) To be here is a fearful thing."

Great. This is like doing business in great waters, or like going down into the deep. This is like being in the heart of the sea, and like going down to the bottoms of the mountains. Now it seems as if the earth, with its bars, were about us for ever. But let them that walk in darkness, and have no light, trust in the name of the Lord, and stay upon their God. (Isa. l, 10.) For my part, as I have told you already, I have gone often through this valley, and have been much harder put to it than now I am; and yet you see I am alive. I would not boast, for that I am not my own saviour; but I trust we shall have a good deliverance. Come, let us pray for light to Him that can lighten our darkness, and that can rebuke not only these, but all the Satans in hell.

So they cried and prayed, and God sent light and deliverance, for there was now no let in their way: no, not there where but now they were stopped with a pit. Yet they were not got through the valley. So they went on still, and behold, great stinks and loathsome smells, to the great annoyance of them. Then said Mercy to Christiana, "There is not such pleasant being here as at the gate, or at the Interpreter's, or at the house where we lay last."

"O but," said one of the boys, "it is not so bad to go

through here as it is to abide here always; and for aught I know, one reason why we must go this way to the house prepared for us is, that our home might be made the sweeter to us."

"Well said, Samuel," quoth the guide; "thou hast now spoke like a man." "Why, if ever I get out here again," said the boy, "I think I shall prize light and good way better than ever I did in all my life." Then said the guide, "We shall be out by and by."

So on they went, and Joseph said, "Cannot we see to the end of this valley as yet?" Then said the guide, "Look to your feet, for we shall presently be among the snares:" so they looked to their feet, and went on; but they were troubled much with the snares. Now when they were come among the snares they spied a man cast into the ditch on the left hand, with his flesh all rent and torn. Then said the guide, "That is one Heedless, that was going this way; he has lain there a great while. There was one Takeheed with him when he was taken and slain; but he escaped their hands. You cannot imagine how many are killed hereabouts, and yet men are so foolishly venturous as to set out lightly on pilgrimage, and to come without a guide. Poor Christian! It was a wonder that he here escaped; but he was beloved of his God: also he had a good heart of his own, or else he could never have done it."

Now they drew toward the end of this way; and just there where Christian had seen the cave when he went by, out thence came forth Maul, a giant. This Maul did use to spoil young pilgrims with sophistry; and he called Greatheart by his name, and said unto him, "How many times have you been forbidden to do these things?" Then said Mr. Greatheart, "What things?" "What things?" quoth the giant; "you know what things: but I will put an end to your trade."

"But pray," said Mr. Greatheart, "before we fall to it, let us understand wherefore we must fight." (Now the women and children stood trembling, and knew not what to do.) Quoth the giant, "You rob the country, and rob it with the worst of thefts." "These are but generals," said Mr. Greatheart; "come to particulars, man."

Then said the giant, "Thou practisest the craft of a kidnapper; thou gatherest up women and children, and carriest them into a strange country, to the weakening of my master's kingdom." But now Greatheart replied, "I am a servant of the God of heaven; my business is to persuade sinners to repentance. I am commanded to do my endeavour to turn men, women, and children, 'from darkness to light, and from the power of Satan unto God;' and if this be indeed the ground of thy quarrel, let us fall to it as soon as thou wilt."

Then the giant came up, and Mr. Greatheart went to meet him; and as he went he drew his sword, but the giant had a club. So without more ado they fell to it, and at the first blow the giant struck Mr. Greatheart down upon one of his knees. With that the women and children cried out.[3] So Mr. Greatheart recovering himself, laid about him in full lusty manner, and gave the giant a wound in his arm. Thus he fought for the space of an hour, to that height of heat, that the breath came out of the giant's nostrils as the heat doth out of a boiling caldron.

Then they sat down to rest them; but Mr. Greatheart betook himself to prayer. Also the women and

[3] Weak folks' prayers sometimes help strong folks' cries.—*Bunyan.*

children did nothing but sigh and cry all the time that the battle did last.

When they had rested them, and taken breath, they both fell to it again, and Mr. Greatheart, with a blow, fetched the giant down to the ground. "Nay, hold, let me recover," quoth he. So Mr. Greatheart fairly let him get up; so to it they went again; and the giant missed but little of all-to-breaking Mr. Greatheart's skull with his club.

Mr. Greatheart seeing that, runs to him in the full heat of his spirit, and pierceth him under the fifth rib. With that the giant began to faint, and could hold up his club no longer. Then Mr. Greatheart seconded his blow, and smote the head of the giant from his shoulders. Then the women and children rejoiced, and Mr. Greatheart also praised God for the deliverance he had wrought.[4]

When this was done, they amongst them erected a pillar, and fastened the giant's head thereon, and wrote under it, in letters that passengers might read,—

"He that did wear this head was one
That pilgrims did misuse;
He stopt their way, he spared none,
But did them all abuse:
Until that I, Greatheart, arose,
The pilgrims' guide to be;
Until that I did him oppose
That was their enemy."

[4] Giant Maul is represented as coming out of the cave in which Pagan and Pope once dwelt; probably to show that though Pagan had long been dead, and Pope had (in England) lost his power to harm the pilgrims, yet the then dominant priesthood were not less slow to wield the "club" of secular power to beat down those who would not conform to the practice of "the church as by law established."

CHAPTER VII.

Discourse of the fight—They find old Honest asleep under an oak—Talk of Mr. Fearing and his troublesome pilgrimage—His behaviour at the Slough, at the Gate, and at the Interpreter's house—He is cheery at the Cross, and pleasant in the Valley of Humiliation, but perplexed in the Valley of the Shadow of Death—His behaviour at Vanity Fair—His boldness at the last—About Mr. Self-will.

Now I saw that they went on to the ascent that was a little way off, cast up to be a prospect for pilgrims. That was the place from whence Christian had the first sight of Faithful his brother. Wherefore, here they sat down and rested. They also here did eat and drink, and make merry, for that they had gotten deliverance from this so dangerous an enemy. As they sat thus and did eat, Christiana asked the guide if he had caught no hurt in the battle. Then said Mr. Greatheart, "No, save a little on my flesh; yet that also shall be so far from being to my detriment, that it is at present a proof of my love to my Master and you, and shall be a means, by grace, to increase my reward at last." 2 Cor. iv, 10, 11.

Chr. But was you not afraid, good sir, when you saw him come with his club?

"It is my duty," said he, "to mistrust my own ability, that I may have reliance on Him that is stronger than all." Rom. viii, 37.

Chr. But what did you think when he fetched you down to the ground at the first blow?

"Why, I thought," replied he, "that so my Master himself was served, and yet he it was that conquered at last." Heb. ii, 9, 14; Col. ii, 15.

Matt. When you all have thought what you please, I think God has been wonderful good unto us, both in bringing us out of this valley, and in delivering us out of the hand of this enemy. For my part I see no reason why we should distrust our God any more, since he has now, and in such a place as this, given us such testimony of his love.

Then they got up, and went forward. Now a little before them stood an oak, and under it, when they came to it, they found an old pilgrim fast asleep. They knew that he was a pilgrim, by his clothes, and his staff, and his girdle.

So the guide, Mr. Greatheart, awaked him; and the old gentleman, as he lifted up his eyes, cried out, "What's the matter? who are you? and what is your business here?"

Great. Come, man, be not so hot; here are none but friends.

Yet the old man gets up, and stands upon his guard, and will know of them what they are. Then said the guide, "My name is Greatheart; I am the guide of these pilgrims that are going to the Celestial Country."

Then said Mr. Honest, "I cry you mercy; I feared that you had been of the company of those that some time ago did rob Little-faith of his money; but now I look better about me, I perceive you are honester people."

Great. Why, what would or could you have done to have helped yourself, if indeed we had been of that company?

Hon. Done! Why, I would have fought as long as breath had been in me; and had I so done, I am sure you could never have given me the worst on't; for a

Christian can never be overcome unless he shall yield of himself.

"Well said, father Honest," quoth the guide; "for by this I know that thou art a cock of the right kind, for thou hast said the truth."

Hon. And by this also I know that thou knowest what true pilgrimage is: for all others do think that we are the soonest overcome of any.

Great. Well, now we are so happily met, pray let me crave your name, and the name of the place you came from.

Hon. My name I cannot; but I came from the town of Stupidity; it lieth about four degrees beyond the City of Destruction.

Great. O! Are you that countryman? Then I deem I have half a guess of you; your name is old Honesty, is it not?

So the old gentleman blushed, and said, "Not Honesty in the abstract, but Honest is my name; and I wish that my nature may agree to what I am called. But, sir," said the old gentleman, "how could you guess that I am such a man, since I came from such a place?"

Great. I had heard of you before by my Master, for he knows all things that are done on the earth. But I have often wondered that any should come from your place; for your town is worse than is the City of Destruction itself.

Hon. Yes, we lie more off from the sun, and so are more cold and senseless: but was a man in a mountain of ice, yet if the Sun of Righteousness will arise upon him, his frozen heart shall feel a thaw; and thus it has been with me.

Great. I believe it, father Honest, I believe it; for I know the thing is true.

Then the old gentleman saluted all the pilgrims with a holy kiss of charity, and asked them of their names, and how they had fared since they set out on their pilgrimage.

Then said Christiana, "My name I suppose you have heard of; good Christian was my husband, and these four are his children." But can you think how the old gentleman was taken when she told him who she was? He skipped, he smiled, he blessed them with a thousand good wishes, saying, "I have heard much of your husband, and of his travels and wars which he underwent in his days. Be it spoken to your comfort, the name of your husband rings all over these parts of the world: his faith, his courage, his enduring, and his sincerity under all, have made his name famous."

Then he turned him to the boys, and asked them of their names, which they told him; and then said he unto them, "Matthew, be thou like Matthew the publican, not in vice, but in virtue. (Matt. x, 3.) Samuel," said he, "be thou like Samuel the prophet, a man of faith and prayer. (Psalm xcix, 6.) Joseph," said he, "be thou like Joseph in Potiphar's house, chaste, and one that flies from temptation. (Gen. xxxix.) And James, be thou like James the just, and like James the brother of our Lord." Acts i, 13.

Then they told him of Mercy, and how she had left her town and her kindred to come along with Christiana, and with her sons. At that the old honest man said, "Mercy is thy name; by mercy shalt thou be sustained and carried through all those difficulties that shall assault thee in thy way, till thou shalt come thither where thou shalt look the Fountain of mercy in the face with comfort."

All this while the guide, Mr. Greatheart, was very well pleased, and smiled upon his companions.

Now, as they walked along together, the guide asked the old gentleman, if he did not know one Mr. Fearing, that came on pilgrimage out of his parts.

"Yes, very well," said he. "He was a man that had the root of the matter in him; but he was one of the most troublesome pilgrims that ever I met with in all my days."

Great. I perceive you knew him, for you have given a very right character of him.

Hon. Knew him! I was a great companion of his; I was with him most an end; when he first began to think upon what would come upon us hereafter, I was with him.

Great. I was his guide from my Master's house to the gates of the Celestial City.

Hon. Then you knew him to be a troublesome one.

Great. I did so; but I could very well bear it; for men of my calling are oftentimes intrusted with the conduct of such as he was.[1]

Hon. Why, then, pray let us hear a little of him, and how he managed himself under your conduct.

[1] The character of Mr. Fearing is one of the most finished and skilfully drawn in the whole book. "The peculiarity of this description of Christians," says Mr. Scott, "must be traced back to constitution, habit, first impressions, disproportionate and partial views of truth, and improper instructions; these, concurring with weakness of faith, and the common infirmities of human nature, give a cast to the experience and character which renders them uncomfortable to themselves and troublesome to others. Yet no competent judges doubt that they have the root of the matter in them; and none are more entitled to the patient, sympathizing, and tender attentions of ministers and Christians."—*Notes on Pilgrim's Progress.*

Great. Why, he was always afraid that he should come short of whither he had a desire to go. Everything frightened him that he heard anybody speak of, if it had but the least appearance of opposition in it. I heard that he lay roaring at the Slough of Despond for above a month together; nor durst he, for all he saw several go over before him, venture, though they many of them offered to lend him their hands. He would not go back again neither. The Celestial City,—he said he should die if he came not to it; and yet he was dejected at every difficulty, and stumbled at every straw that anybody cast in his way. Well, after he had lain at the Slough of Despond a great while, as I have told you, one sunshiny morning, I don't know how, he ventured, and so got over; but when he was over, he would scarce believe it. He had, I think, a Slough of Despond in his mind, a slough that he carried everywhere with him, or else he could never have been as he was.

So he came up to the Gate (you know what I mean) that stands at the head of this way, and there also he stood a good while before he would venture to knock. When the Gate was opened, he would give back, and give place to others, and say that he was not worthy. For, for all he got before some to the Gate, yet many of them went in before him. There the poor man would stand shaking and shrinking; I dare say it would have pitied one's heart to have seen him. Nor would he go back again. At last he took the hammer that hanged on the Gate in his hand, and gave a small rap or two; then one opened to him, but he shrunk back as before. He that opened, stepped out after him, and said, "Thou trembling one, what wantest thou?" With that he fell down to the ground. He that spoke to him wondered to see him so faint, so he said to him, "Peace be to thee; up, for I have set open the door to thee; come in, for thou art blessed." With that he got up, and went in trembling; and when that he was in, he was ashamed to show his face. Well, after he had been entertained there awhile, as you know how the manner is, he was bid go on his way, and also told the way he should take. So he went on till he came to our house; but as he behaved himself at the Gate, so he did at my Master the Interpreter's door. He lay thereabout in the cold a good while, before he would adventure to call; yet he would not go back; and the nights were long and cold then. Nay, he had a note of necessity in his bosom to my Master to receive him, and grant him the comfort of his house, and also to allow him a stout and valiant conductor, because he was himself so chicken-hearted a man; and yet for all that he was afraid to call at the door. So he lay up and down thereabouts, till, poor man, he was almost starved; yea, so great was his dejection, that though he saw several others for knocking get in, yet he was afraid to venture. At last, I think I looked out of the window, and perceiving a man to be up and down about the door, I went out to him, and asked what he was; but, poor man, the water stood in his eyes; so I perceived what he wanted. I went therefore in, and told it in the house, and we showed the thing to our Lord: so he sent me out again, to entreat him to come in; but I dare say, I had hard work to do it. At last he came in: and I will say that for my Lord, he carried it wonderful lovingly to him. There were but a few good bits at the table but some of it was laid upon his trencher. Then he presented the note; and my Lord looked thereon, and said his desire should be granted. So when he had been there a good while, he seemed to get some heart, and to be a little more comfortable; for my Master, you must know, is one of tender bowels, especially to them that are afraid; wherefore he carried it so toward him as might tend most to his encouragement. Well, when he had had a sight of the things of the place, and was ready to take his journey to go to the City, my Lord, as he did to Christian before, gave him a bottle of spirits, and some comfortable things to eat. Thus we set forward, and I went before him; but the man was of but few words, only he would sigh aloud.

When we were come to the place where the three fellows were hanged, he said that he doubted that that would be his end also. Only he seemed glad when he saw the Cross and the Sepulchre. There I confess he desired to stay a little to look; and he seemed for awhile after to be a little cheery. When he came to the hill Difficulty, he made no stick at that, nor did he much fear the lions: for you must know that his trouble was not about such things as these; his fear was about his acceptance at last.

I got him in at the house Beautiful, I think, before he was willing: also when he was in, I brought him acquainted with the damsels of the place; but he was ashamed to make himself much in company. He desired much to be alone; yet he always loved good talk, and often would get behind the screen to hear it. He also loved much to see ancient things, and to be pondering them in his mind. He told me afterward, that he loved to be in those two houses from which he came last, to wit, at the Gate, and that of the Interpreter, but that he durst not be so bold as to ask.

When we went also from the house Beautiful, down the hill, into the Valley of Humiliation, he went down as well as ever I saw a man in my life; for he cared not how mean he was, so he might be happy at last. Yea, I think there was a kind of sympathy betwixt that valley and him; for I never saw him better in all his pilgrimage than he was in that valley. Here he would lie down, embrace the ground, and kiss the very flowers that grew in this valley. He would now be up every morning by break of day, tracing and walking to and fro in the valley.[2]

But when he was come to the entrance of the Valley of the Shadow of Death, I thought I should have lost my man: not for that he had any inclination to go back; that he always abhorred; but he was ready to die for fear. "O, the hobgoblins will have me! the hobgoblins will have me!" cried he; and I could not beat him out on't. He made such a noise, and such an outcry here, that had they but heard him, it was enough to encourage them to come and fall upon us.

But this I took very great notice of, that this valley was as quiet when we went through it as ever I knew it before or since. I suppose those enemies here had now a special check from our Lord, and a command not to meddle until Mr. Fearing had passed over it.

[2] A low and obscure situation suits the dispositions of the persons here described; they do not object to the most humiliating views of their own hearts, of human nature, or of the way of salvation; they are little tempted to covet eminence among their brethren, and find it easier to esteem others better than themselves than persons of different frame can conceive.—*Rev. T. Scott.*

It would be too tedious to tell you of all: we will therefore only mention a passage or two more. When he was come to Vanity Fair, I thought he would have fought with all the men in the fair. I feared there we should have been both knocked on the head, so hot was he against their fooleries. Upon the Enchanted Ground he was very wakeful. But when he was come at the river where was no bridge, there again he was in a heavy case. Now, now, he said, he should be drowned for ever, and so never see that face with comfort that he had come so many miles to behold.

And here also I took notice of what was very remarkable: the water of that river was lower at this time than ever I saw it in all my life; so he went over at last, not much above wetshod. When he was going up to the gate I began to take leave of him, and to wish him a good reception above. So he said, "I shall, I shall." Then parted we asunder, and I saw him no more.

Hon. Then it seems he was well at last.

Great. Yes, yes, I never had doubt about him. He was a man of a choice spirit, only he was always kept very low, and that made his life so burdensome to himself, and so troublesome to others. Psa. lxxxviii. He was, above many, tender of sin: he was so afraid of doing injuries to others, that he often would deny himself of that which was lawful, because he would not offend. Rom. xiv, 21; 1 Cor. viii, 13.

Hon. But what should be the reason that such a good man should be all his days so much in the dark?

Great. There are two sorts of reasons for it. One is, the wise God will have it so: some must pipe, and some must weep. Matt. xi, 16. Now Mr. Fearing was one that played upon the bass. He and his fellows sound the sackbut, whose notes are more doleful than the notes of other music are: though indeed, some say, the bass is the ground of music. And for my part, I care not at all for that profession that begins not in heaviness of mind. The first string that the musician usually touches is the bass, when he intends to put all in tune. God also plays upon this string first, when he sets the soul in tune for himself. Only there was the imperfection of Mr. Fearing; he could play upon no other music but this, till toward his latter end.

(I make bold to talk thus metaphorically for the ripening of the wits of young readers, and because, in the book of the Revelation, the saved are compared to a company of musicians that play upon their trumpets and harps, and sing their songs before the throne. Revelation v, 8; xiv, 2, 3.)

Hon. He was a very zealous man, as one may see by that relation which you have given of him. Difficulties, lions, or Vanity Fair, he feared not at all; it was only sin, death, and hell, that were to him a terror, because he had some doubts about his interest in that Celestial Country.

Great. You say right, those were the things that were his troublers; and they, as you have well observed, arose from the weakness of his mind thereabout, not from weakness of spirit as to the practical part of a pilgrim's life. I dare believe that, as the proverb is, he could have bit a firebrand, had it stood in his way; but the things with which he was oppressed, no man ever yet could shake off with ease.

Then said Christiana, " This relation of Mr. Fearing has done me good: I thought nobody had been like me; but I see there was some semblance betwixt this good man and me; only we differed in two things. His troubles were so great that they broke out; but mine I kept within: his also lay so hard upon him, they made him that he could not knock at the houses provided for entertainment; but my trouble was always such as made me knock the louder."

Mer. If I might also speak my heart, I must say that something of him has also dwelt in me. For I have ever been more afraid of the lake, and the loss of a place in paradise, than I have been of a loss of other things. O, thought I, may I have the happiness to have a habitation there! 'Tis enough, though I part with all the world to win it.

Then said Matthew, "Fear was one thing that made me think that I was far from having that within me that accompanies salvation. But if it was so with such a good man as he, why may it not also go well with me?"

"No fears, no grace," said James. "Though there is not always grace where there is the fear of hell; yet, to be sure, there is no grace where there is no fear of God."

Great. Well said, James, thou hast hit the mark; for the fear of God is the beginning of wisdom; and to be sure, they that want the beginning have neither middle nor end. But we will here conclude our discourse of Mr. Fearing, after we have sent after him this farewell:—

"Well, Master Fearing, thou didst fear
Thy God, and wast afraid
Of doing anything, while here,
That would have thee betray'd.

"And didst thou fear the lake and pit?
Would others do so too!
For, as for them that want thy wit,
They do themselves undo."[3]

Now I saw that they still went on in their talk. For after Mr. Greatheart had made an end with Mr. Fearing, Mr. Honest began to tell them of another, but his name was Mr. Self-will. "He pretended himself to be a pilgrim," said Mr. Honest; "but I persuade myself he never came in at the Gate that stands at the head of the way."

Great. Had you ever any talk with him about it?

Hon. Yes, more than once or twice; but he would always be like himself, self-willed. He neither cared for man, nor argument, nor yet for example; what his mind prompted him to, that he would do, and nothing else could he be got to do.

Great. Pray what principles did he hold? for I suppose you can tell.

Hon. He held that a man might follow the vices as well as the virtues of the pilgrims; and that if he did both, he should be certainly saved.

Great. How! If he had said, it is possible for the best to be guilty of the vices, as well as partake of the virtues of pilgrims, he could not much have been blamed; for indeed we are exempted from no vice absolutely, but on condition that we watch and strive.

[3] Few ministers who have had an opportunity of carefully observing the people intrusted to their pastoral care, can help thinking of some individual who might seem to have been the original of this admirable portrait, which is full of instruction both to them and the timid but conscientious part of their congregations. Indeed, numbers who are not characteristically Fearings, have something of the same disposition in many particulars.—*Rev. T. Scott.*

But this I perceive is not the thing; but, if I understand you right, your meaning is, that he was of opinion that it was allowable so to be.

Hon. Ay, ay, so I mean, and so he believed and practised.

Great. But what grounds had he for his so saying?

Hon. Why, he said he had the Scripture for his warrant.

Great. Prithee, Mr. Honest, present us with a few particulars.

Hon. So I will. He said, to have to do with other men's wives had been practised by David, God's beloved; and therefore he could do it. He said, to have more women than one was a thing that Solomon practised, and therefore he could do it. He said that Sarah and the godly midwives of Egypt lied, and so did saved Rahab, and therefore he could do it. He said that the disciples went at the bidding of their Master, and took away the owner's ass, and therefore he could do so too. He said that Jacob got the inheritance of his father in a way of guile and dissimulation, and therefore he could do so too.

Great. High base indeed! And are you sure he was of this opinion?

Hon. I have heard him plead for it, bring Scripture for it, bring arguments for it, &c.

Great. An opinion that is not fit to be with any allowance in the world!

Hon. You must understand me rightly; he did not say that any man might do this; but that they who had the virtues of those that did such things, might also do the same.

Great. But what more false than such a conclusion?

For this is as much as to say, that because good men heretofore have sinned of infirmity, therefore he had allowance to do it of a presumptuous mind; or that if, because a child, by the blast of the wind, or for that it stumbled at a stone, fell down and defiled itself in the mire, therefore he might wilfully lie down and wallow like a boar therein. Who could have thought any one could so far have been blinded by the power of lust? But what is written must be true; they "stumble at the word, being disobedient, whereunto they also were appointed." 1 Peter ii, 8.[4] His supposing that such may have the godly men's virtues, who addict themselves to their vices, is also a delusion as strong as the other. To eat up the sin of God's people (Hos. iv, 8) is no sign of one that is possessed of their virtues. Nor can I believe that one who is of this opinion can at present have faith or love in him. But I know you have made some strong objections against him: prithee what can he say for himself?

Hon. Why, he says, to do this by way of opinion seems abundantly more honest than to do it, and yet hold contrary to it in opinion.

Great. A very wicked answer. For though to let loose the bridle of lusts, while our opinions are against such things, is bad, yet to sin, and plead a toleration so to do, is worse: the one stumbles beholders accidentally, the other leads them into the snare.

Hon. There are many of this man's mind, that have not this man's mouth; and that makes going on pilgrimage of so little esteem as it is.

[4] They were not appointed to be "disobedient;" but *because* they were disobedient they were appointed to stumble and fall: and this will be the fate of all those who "obey not the truth." Rom. ii, 8.

Great. You have said the truth, and it is to be a-mented: but he that feareth the King of paradise sh come out of them all.

Chr. There are strange opinions in the world. I know one that said, it was time enough to repent when we come to die.

Great. Such are not over-wise; that man would have been loth, might he have had a week to run twenty miles in his life, to have deferred his journey to the last hour of that week.

Hon. You say right; and yet the generality of them who count themselves pilgrims do indeed do thus. I am, as you see, an old man, and have been a traveller in this road many a day; and I have taken notice of many things. I have seen some that have set out as if they would drive all the world before them, who yet have, in a few days, died as they in the wilderness, and so never got sight of the promised land. I have seen some that have promised nothing at first setting out to be pilgrims, and that one would have thought could not have lived a day, that have yet proved very good pilgrims. I have seen some who have run hastily forward, that again have, after a little time, run just as fast back again. I have seen some who have spoken very well of a pilgrim's life at first, that after awhile have spoken as much against it. I have heard some, when they first set out for paradise, say positively, There is such a place, who, when they have been almost there, have come back again, and said, There is none. I have heard some vaunt what they would do in case they should be opposed, that have, even at a false alarm, fled faith, the pilgrim's way, and all.

CHAPTER VIII.

Fresh news of trouble—Christiana wishes for an inn—Gaius entertains them—Talk between Gaius and his guests—Of Christiana's ancestors—A match between Mercy and Matthew—The supper—Old Honest's riddle—Greatheart's riddle—A story and a question—Giant Slay-good found with one Feeble-mind in his hand—The giant is assaulted and slain—How Feeble-mind came to be a pilgrim—James and Matthew married—The pilgrims prepare to go forward.

Now as they were thus on their way, there came one running to meet them, and said, "Gentlemen, and you of the weaker sort, if you love life, shift for yourselves, for the robbers are before you."

Then said Mr. Greatheart, "They be the three that set upon Little-faith heretofore. Well," said he, "we are ready for them:" so they went on their way. Now they looked at every turning when they should have met with the villains; but whether they heard of Mr. Greatheart, or whether they had some other game, they came not up with the pilgrims.

Christiana then wished for an inn to refresh herself and her children, because they were weary. Then said Mr. Honest, "There is one a little before us, where a very honourable disciple, one Gaius, dwells." Romans xvi, 23. So they all concluded to turn in thither; and the rather, because the old gentleman gave him so good a report. When they came to the door they went in, not knocking, for folks use not to knock at the door of an inn. Then they called for the master of the house, and he came to them. So they asked if they might lie there that night.

Gaius. Yes, gentlemen, if you be true men; for my house is for none but pilgrims.

Then were Christiana, Mercy, and the boys, the more glad, for that the innkeeper was a lover of pilgrims. So they called for rooms, and he showed them one for Christiana and her children, and Mercy, and another for Mr. Greatheart and the old gentleman.

Then said Mr. Greatheart, "Good Gaius, what hast thou for supper? for these pilgrims have come far today, and are weary."

"It is late," said Gaius, "so we cannot conveniently go out to seek food; but such as we have you shall be welcome to, if that will content."

Great. We will be content with what thou hast in the house; for as much as I have proved thee, thou art never destitute of that which is convenient.

Then he went down and spake to the cook, whose name was Taste-that-which-is-good, to get ready supper for so many pilgrims. This done, he came up again, saying, "Come, my good friends, you are welcome to me, and I am glad that I have a house to entertain you in; and while supper is making ready, if you please, let us entertain one another with some good discourse;" so they all said, "Content."[1]

[1] It is the ordinance of God, that Christians should be often asserting the things of God each to others; and that by their so doing they should edify one another. Christians are like the several flowers in a garden, that have upon each of them the dew of heaven, which being shaken with the wind, they let fall their dew at each other's roots, whereby they are jointly nourished, and become nourishers of one another. For Christians to commune savourly of God's matters one with another, it is as if they opened to each other's nostrils boxes of perfume.—*Bunyan's Christian Behaviour: or Fruits of Christianity*

Then said Gaius, "Whose wife is this aged matron? and whose daughter is this young damsel?"

Great. This woman is the wife of one Christian, a pilgrim of former times; and these are his four children. The maid is one of her acquaintance, one that she hath persuaded to come with her on pilgrimage. The boys take all after their father, and covet to tread in his steps: yea, if they do but see any place where the old pilgrim hath lain, or any print of his foot, it ministereth joy to their hearts, and they covet to lie or tread in the same.[2]

Then said Gaius, "Is this Christian's wife, and are these Christian's children? I knew your husband's father, yea, also his father's father. Many have been good of this stock; their ancestors dwelt first at Antioch. (Acts xi, 26.) Christian's progenitors (I suppose you have heard your husband talk of them) were very worthy men. They have, above any that I know, showed themselves men of great virtue and courage for the Lord of the pilgrims, his ways, and them that loved him. I have heard of many of your husband's relations that have stood all trials for the sake of the truth. Stephen, that was one of the first of the family from whence your husband sprang, was knocked on the head with stones. (Acts vii, 59, 60.) James, another of this generation, was slain with the edge of the sword. (Acts xii, 2.) To say nothing of Paul and Peter, men anciently of the family from whence your husband came, there was Ignatius, who was cast to the lions; Roma-

[2] And we desire that every one of you do show the same diligence to the full assurance of hope unto the end: that ye be not slothful, but followers of them who through faith and patience inherit the promises. Hebrews vi, 11, 12.

nus, whose flesh was cut by pieces from his bones; and Polycarp, that played the man in the fire. There was he that was hanged up in a basket in the sun for the wasps to eat; and he whom they put into a sack and cast into the sea to be drowned. It would be impossible utterly to count up all of that family that have suffered injuries and death for the love of a pilgrim's life. Nor can I but be glad to see that thy husband has left behind him four such boys as these. I hope they will bear up their father's name, and tread in their father's steps, and come to their father's end."

Great. Indeed, sir, they are likely lads: they seem to choose heartily their father's ways.

Gaius. That is it that I said. Wherefor Christian's family is like still to spread abroad upon the face of the ground, and yet to be numerous upon the face of the earth; let Christiana look out some damsels for her sons, to whom they may be betrothed, &c., that the name of their father, and the house of his progenitors, may never be forgotten in the world.

Hon. 'Tis pity his family should fall and be extinct.

Gaius. Fall it cannot, but be diminished it may; but let Christiana take my advice, and that's the way to uphold it. And Christiana, (said this inn-keeper,) I am glad to see thee and thy friend Mercy together here, a lovely couple. And if I may advise, take Mercy into a nearer relation to thee: if she will, let her be given to Matthew, thy eldest son. It is the way to preserve a posterity in the earth. (So this match was concluded, and in process of time they were married: but more of that hereafter.)

Gaius also proceeded, and said, "I will now speak on the behalf of women, to take away their reproach

For as death and the curse came into the world by a woman, (Gen. iii,) so also did life and health: God sent forth his Son, made of a woman. (Gal. iv, 4.) Yea, to show how much they that came after did abhor the act of the mother, this sex in the Old Testament coveted children, if happily this or that woman might be the mother of the Saviour of the world. I will say again, that when the Saviour was come, women rejoiced in him, before either man or angel. (Luke i, 42–46.) I read not that ever any man gave unto Christ so much as one groat; but the women followed him, and ministered to him of their substance. (Luke viii, 2, 3.) 'Twas a woman that washed his feet with tears, (Luke vi, 37–50;) and a woman that anointed his body to the burial. (John xi, 2; xii, 3.) They were women that wept when he was going to the cross, (Luke xxiii, 27;) and women that followed him from the cross, (Matt. xxvii, 55, 56; Luke xxiii, 54;) and that sat over against his sepulchre when he was buried. (Matthew xxvii, 61.) They were women that were first with him at his resurrection-morn, (Luke xxiv, 1;) and women that brought tidings first to his disciples that he was risen from the dead. (Luke xxiv, 22, 23.) Women therefore are highly favoured, and show by these things that they are sharers with us in the grace of life."

Now the cook sent up to signify that supper was almost ready, and sent one to lay the cloth, and the trenchers, and to set the salt and bread in order.

Then said Matthew, "The sight of this cloth, and of this forerunner of the supper, begetteth in me a greater appetite to my food than I had before."

Gaius. So let all ministering doctrines to thee in this life beget in thee a greater desire to sit at the supper of the great King in his kingdom; for all preaching, books, and ordinances here, are but as the laying of the trenchers, and the setting of salt upon the board, when compared with the feast that our Lord will make for us when we come to his house.

So supper came up.[3] And first a heave-shoulder and a wave-breast were set on the table before them; to show that they must begin the meal with prayer and praise to God. The heave-shoulder David lifted up his heart to God with; and with the wave-breast, where his heart lay, he used to lean upon his harp when he played. These two dishes were very fresh and good, and they all ate heartily thereof. Lev. vii, 30–34; x, 15.

The next they brought up was a bottle of wine, as red as blood.[4] So Gaius said to them, "Drink freely; this is the true juice of the vine, that makes glad the heart of God and man." So they drank and were merry.

The next was a dish of milk well crumbed; Gaius said, "Let the boys have that, that they may grow thereby." 1 Peter ii, 1, 2.[5]

[3] The "supper" may be taken as a figurative representation of the spiritual refreshment which believers derive from the services of the sanctuary, and from a right enjoyment of communion and fellowship with each other. The spirit and temper of the pilgrims at supper are such as should always characterize Christians in their social intercourse: they are cheerful but not light, serious but not sad; and their discourse such as tends to edification.

[4] The remembrance of Christ's love in shedding for us his blood, of which "wine" is the appointed emblem. "And he took the cup, and when he had given thanks, he gave it to them; and they all drank of it. And he said unto them, 'This is my blood of the new testament, which is shed for many.'" Mark xiv, 23, 24.

[5] "The sincere milk of the word"—the pure and unadulterated doctrines of the Bible, which should be early and faithfully inculcated in the minds of children and young converts. Deut. vi, 7; xi, 18, 19

Then they brought up in course a dish of butter and honey. Then said Gaius, "Eat freely of this, for this is good to cheer up and strengthen your judgments and understandings. This was our Lord's dish when he was a child; 'Butter and honey shall he eat, that he may know how to refuse the evil, and choose the good.'" Isa. vii, 15.

Then they brought them up a dish of apples, and they were very good-tasted fruit. Then said Matthew, "May we eat apples, since they were such by and with which the serpent beguiled our first mother?"

Then said Gaius:—

"Apples were they with which we were beguiled,
Yet sin, not apples, hath our souls defiled:
Apples forbid, if ate, corrupt the blood;
To each such, when commanded, does us good:
Drink of his flagons then, thou church his dove,
And eat his apples, who art sick of love."

Then said Matthew, "I made the scruple, because I awhile since was sick with the eating of fruit."

Gaius. Forbidden fruit will make you sick; but not what our Lord has tolerated.

While they were thus talking, they were presented with another dish, and it was a dish of nuts. Sol. Song vi, 11. Then said some at the table, "Nuts spoil tender teeth, especially the teeth of children:" which when Gaius heard, he said:—

"Hard texts are nuts, (I will not call them cheaters,[6])
Whose shells do keep their kernels from the eaters;
Open the shells, and you shall have the meat;
They here are brought for you to crack and eat."

Then were they very merry, and sat at the table a ng time, talking of many things. Then said the old

[6] Nuts which when cracked are found to have no kernels.

gentleman, "My good landlord, while we are cracking your nuts, if you please, do you open this riddle :—

> 'A man there was, though some did count him mad,
> The more he cast away, the more he had.'"

Then they all gave good heed, wondering what good Gaius would say; so he sat still awhile, and then thus replied :—

> "He who bestows his goods upon the poor,
> Shall have as much again, and ten times more."

Then said Joseph, "I dare say, sir, I did not think you could have found it out."

"O!" said Gaius, "I have been trained up in this way a great while: nothing teaches like experience. I have learned of my Lord to be kind, and have found by experience that I have gained thereby. 'There is that scattereth, and yet increaseth; and there is that withholdeth more than is meet, but it tendeth to poverty. There is that maketh himself rich, yet hath nothing: there is that maketh himself poor, yet hath great riches.'" Prov. xi, 24; xiii, 7.

Then Samuel whispered to Christiana, his mother, and said, "Mother, this is a very good man's house: let us stay here a good while, and let my brother Matthew be married here to Mercy, before we go any further." The which Gaius, the host, overhearing, said, "With a very good will, my child." So they staid there more than a month, and Mercy was given to Matthew to wife. While they staid here, Mercy, as her custom was, made coats and garments to give to the poor, by which she brought a very good report upon pilgrims.

But to return again to our story. After supper the lads desired a bed, for they were weary with travelling. Then Gaius called to show them their chamber; but said Mercy, "I will have them to bed." So she had them to bed, and they slept well: but the rest sat up all night; for Gaius and they were such suitable company, that they could not tell how to part.[7] Then after much talk of their Lord, themselves, and their journey, old Mr. Honest, he that put forth the riddle to Gaius, began to nod. Then said Greatheart, "What, sir, you begin to be drowsy; come, rub up, here is a riddle for you." Then said Mr. Honest, "Let us hear it." Then said Mr. Greatheart:—

> "He that would kill, must first be overcome:
> Who live abroad would, first must die at home."

"Ha!" said Mr. Honest, "it is a hard one; hard to

[7] The ancient Christians were accustomed to spend, sometimes whole nights in religious exercises, which were called *vigils*. This practice was also adopted by the early Methodists, its origin among whom is thus related by Mr. Wesley:—"I was informed that several persons in Kingswood frequently met together at the school, and when they could spare the time, spent the greater part of the night in prayer, and praise, and thanksgiving. Some advised me to put an end to this; but upon weighing the thing thoroughly, and comparing it with the practice of the ancient Christians, I could see no cause to forbid it. Rather I believed it might be made of more general use. So I sent them word I designed to watch with them on the Friday nearest the full moon, that we might have light thither and back again. I gave public notice of this the Sunday before, and, withal, that I intended to preach; desiring that they, and they only, would meet me there, who could do it without prejudice to their business or families. On Friday abundance of people came. I began preaching between eight and nine; and we continued a little beyond the noon of night, singing, praying, and praising God. This we have continued to do once a month ever since, in Bristol, London, and Newcastle, as well as Kingswood; and exceeding great are the blessings we have found therein: it has generally been an extremely solemn season; when the word of God sunk deep into the heart even of those who till then knew him not." These meetings, which are called *watch-nights*, are not now held so frequently as they formerly were, being, in most places, confined to the last night in the year.

expound, and harder to practise. But, come, landlord," said he, "I will, if you please, leave my part to you: do you expound it, and I will hear what you say."

"No," said Gaius, "it was put to you, and 'tis expected you should answer it."

Then said the old gentleman:—

"He first by grace must conquer'd be,
That sin would mortify:
Who that he lives would convince me
Unto himself must die."

"It is right," said Gaius; "good doctrine and experience teach this. For first, Until grace displays itself, and overcomes the soul with its glory, it is altogether without heart to oppose sin. Besides, if sin is Satan's cords, by which the soul lies bound, how should it make resistance before it is loosed from that infirmity? Secondly, Nor will any that knows either reason or grace believe that such a man can be a living monument of grace that is a slave to his own corruptions. And now it comes into my mind, I will tell you a story worth the hearing. There were two men that went on pilgrimage; the one began when he was young, the other when he was old. The young man had strong corruptions to grapple with; the old man's were weak with the decays of nature. The young man trod his steps as even as did the old one, and was every way as light as he. Who now, or which of them, had their graces shining clearest, since both seemed to be alike?"

Hon. The young man's, doubtless: for that which heads it against the greatest opposition, gives best demonstration that it is strongest; especially when it also holdeth pace with that which meets not with half so much, as to be sure old age does not. Besides, I have observed that old men have blessed themselves with this mistake; namely, taking the decays of nature for a gracious conquest over corruptions, and so have been apt to beguile themselves. Indeed, old men that are gracious are best able to give advice to them that are young, because they have seen most of the emptiness of things: but yet, for an old and a young man to set out both together, the young one has the advantage of the fairest discovery of a work of grace within him, though the old man's corruptions are naturally the weakest. (Thus they sat talking till break of day.[8])

Now when the family was up, Christiana bid her son James that he should read a chapter; so he read the fifty-third of Isaiah. When he had done, Mr. Honest asked why it was said that the Saviour is said to "come out of a dry ground;" and also that "he had no form or comeliness in him."

Then said Mr. Greatheart, "To the first I answer, Because the church of the Jews, of which Christ came, had then lost almost all the sap and spirit of religion. To the second I say, The words are spoken in the per-

[8] We must here be allowed to question somewhat the correctness of our author's position; for though it be true that in the case of an old man and a young one setting out together, the former, owing to the "decays of nature," and that incapacity for worldly pleasures which age commonly induces, may feel less sensibly the corruptions of his nature, yet this seeming advantage is more than counterbalanced by the force of sinful habits indulged through a long series of years, and that deadness of heart to spiritual things which is the result of a long course of resistance to the strivings of the Holy Ghost. "'Tis easier work," says the poet, "if we begin to serve the Lord betimes;" and the sinner who is converted in advanced life, will find that he needs at least as much grace to "keep him from falling," as does the man who learned to "remember his Creator in the days of his youth."

son of unbelievers, who, because they want the eye that can see into our Prince's heart, therefore they judge of him by the meanness of his outside, just like those that know not that precious stones are covered over with a homely crust, who, when they have found one, because they know not what they have found, cast it away again, as men do a common stone."

"Well," said Gaius, "now you are here, and since, as I know, Mr. Greatheart is good at his weapons, if you please, after we have refreshed ourselves, we will walk into the fields to see if we can do any good. About a mile from hence there is one Slay-good, a giant, that doth much annoy the King's highway in these parts; and I know whereabout his haunt is. He is master of a number of thieves: 'twould be well if we could clear these parts of him." So they consented and went; Mr. Greatheart with his sword, helmet, and shield; and the rest with spears and staves.

When they were come to the place where he was, they found him with one Feeble-mind in his hand, whom his servants had brought unto him, having taken him in the way. Now the giant was rifling him with a purpose after that to pick his bones; for he was of the nature of flesh-eaters.

Well, so soon as he saw Mr. Greatheart and his friends, at the mouth of his cave, with their weapons, he demanded what they wanted.

Great. We want thee; for we are come to revenge the quarrels of the many that thou hast slain of the pilgrims when thou hast dragged them out of the King's highway: wherefore come out of thy cave. (So he armed himself and came out; and to battle they went, and fought for above an hour, and then stood still to take wind.)

Then said the giant, "Why are you here on my ground?"

Great. To revenge the blood of pilgrims, as I told thee before.

So they went to it again, and the giant made Mr. Greatheart give back: but he came up again, and in the greatness of his mind he let fly with such stoutness at the giant's head and sides, that he made him let his weapon fall out of his hand. So he smote him, and slew him, and cut off his head, and brought it away to the inn. He also took Feeble-mind, the pilgrim, and brought him with him to his lodgings. When they were come home, they showed his head to the family, and set it up, as they had done others before, for a terror to those that should attempt to do as he hereafter.

Then they asked Mr. Feeble-mind how he fell into his hands.

Then said the poor man, "I am a sickly man, as you see; and because death did usually once a day knock at my door, I thought I should never be well at home; so I betook myself to a pilgrim's life, and have travelled hither from the town of Uncertain, where I and my father were born. I am a man of no strength at all of body, nor yet of mind, but would, if I could, though I can but crawl, spend my life in the pilgrim's way. When I came at the Gate that is at the head of the way, the Lord of that place did entertain me freely; neither objected he against my weakly looks, nor against my feeble mind; but gave me such things as were necessary for my journey, and bid me hope to the end. When I came to the house of the Interpreter I received much kindness there: and because the hill of Difficulty was judged too hard for me, I was carried up that by one of his servants. Indeed I have found much relief from pilgrims, though none was willing to go so softly as I am forced to do: yet still as they came on, they bid me be of good cheer, and said, that it was the will of their Lord that comfort should be given to the feeble minded, (1 Thess. v, 14;) and so went on their own pace. When I was come to Assault-lane, then this giant met with me, and bid me prepare for an encounter. But, alas! feeble one that I was, I had more need of a cordial; so he came up and took me. I conceited he should not kill me. Also when he had got me into his den, since I went not with him willingly, I believed I should come out alive again; for I have heard, that not any pilgrim that is taken captive by violent hands, if he keeps heart whole toward his Master, is, by the laws of Providence, to die by the hand of the enemy. Robbed I looked to be, and robbed to be sure I am; but I am, as you see, escaped with life, for the which I thank my King as the author, and you as the means. Other brunts I also look for; but this I have resolved on, to wit, to run when I can, to go when I cannot run, and to creep when I cannot go. As to the main, I thank Him that loved me, I am fixed; my way is before me, my mind is beyond the river that has no bridge, though I am, as you see, but of a feeble mind."

Then said old Mr. Honest, "Have not you, some time ago, been acquainted with one Mr. Fearing, a pilgrim?"

Feeble. Acquainted with him! Yes, he came from the town of Stupidity, which lieth four degrees to the northward of the City of Destruction, and as many off of where I was born: yet we were well acquainted, for indeed he was my uncle, my father's brother. He and I have been much of a temper: he was a little shorter than I, but yet we were much of a complexion.

Hon. I perceive you knew him, and I am apt to believe also that you were related one to another; for you have his whitely look, a cast like his with your eye, and your speech is much alike.

Feeble. Most have said so that have known us both: and, besides, what I have read in him I have for the most part found in myself.[9]

"Come, sir," said good Gaius, "be of good cheer; you are welcome to me and to my house. What thou hast a mind to, call for freely; and what thou wouldst have my servants do for thee, they will do it with a ready mind."

Then said Mr. Feeble-mind, "This is an unexpected favour, and as the sun shining out of a very dark cloud. Did giant Slay-good intend me this favour when he stopped me, and resolved to let me go no further? Did he intend, that after he had rifled my pockets I should go to Gaius mine host? Yet so it is.

Now just as Mr. Feeble-mind and Gaius were thus in talk, there came one running, and called at the door, and said, that about a mile and a half off there was one Mr. Not-right, a pilgrim, struck dead upon the place where he was, with a thunderbolt.

"Alas!" said Mr. Feeble-mind, "is he slain? He overtook me some days before I came so far as hither,

[9] Fearing and Feeble-mind, though of the same family, have their distinctive shades of character. The discouragements of the former arose from within; he cared little for persecution or opposition, his great fear being that he should not be received at last: while the latter is more disturbed by outward opposition, but appears not to have much fear as to the result of his pilgrimage.

and would be my company-keeper. He was also with me when Slay-good the giant took me, but he was nimble of his heels, and escaped; but it seems he escaped to die, and I was taken to live.

"What one would think doth seek to slay outright,
Ofttimes delivers from the saddest plight.
That very Providence whose face is death,
Doth ofttimes to the lowly life bequeath.
I taken was, he did escape and flee;
Hands cross'd gave death to him and life to me."

Now about this time Matthew and Mercy were married; also Gaius gave his daughter Phebe to James, Matthew's brother, to wife; after which time, they yet stayed about ten days at Gaius's house, spending their time, and the seasons, like as pilgrims used to do.

When they were to depart, Gaius made them a feast, and they did eat and drink, and were merry. Now the hour was come that they must be gone; wherefore Mr. Greatheart called for a reckoning. But Gaius told him that at his house it was not the custom for pilgrims to pay for their entertainment. He boarded them by the year, but looked for his pay from the good Samaritan, who had promised him, at his return, whatsoever charge he was at with them, faithfully to repay him.[10]

Then said Mr. Greatheart to him: "Beloved, thou doest faithfully whatsoever thou doest to the brethren, and to strangers which have borne witness of thy charity before the church, whom if thou yet bring forward on their journey, after a godly sort, thou shalt do well."[11]

Then Gaius took his leave of them all, and his children, and particularly of Mr. Feeble-mind. He also gave him something to drink by the way.

[10] Luke x, 34, 35. [11] 3 John 5, 6.

CHAPTER IX.

Mr. Feeble-mind is for going behind—He is glad to see Ready-to-halt come—The pilgrims enter the town of Vanity, and lodge in one Mr. Mnason's house—They desire to see some of the good people of the town—Some are sent for—Talk between Mr. Honest and Mr. Contrite—Persecution not so hot at Vanity Fair as formerly—A monster.

Now Mr. Feeble-mind, when they were going out of the door, made as if he intended to linger. The which, when Mr. Greatheart espied, he said, "Come, Mr. Feeble-mind, pray do you go along with us; I will be your conductor, and you shall fare as the rest."

Feeble. Alas! I want a suitable companion. You are all lusty and strong, but I, as you see, am weak; I choose therefore rather to come behind, lest, by reason of my many infirmities, I should be both a burden to myself and to you. I am, as I said, a man of a weak and feeble mind, and shall be offended and made weak at that which others can bear I shall like no laughing; I shall like no gay attire; I shall like no unprofitable questions. Nay, I am so weak a man as to be offended with that which others have a liberty to do. I do not know all the truth: I am a very ignorant Christian man. Sometimes if I hear some rejoice in the Lord, it troublés me, because I cannot do so too. It is with me as it is with a weak man among the strong, or as with a sick man among the healthy, or as a lamp despised; so that I know not what to do. ("He that is ready to slip with his feet is as a lamp despised in the thought of him that is at ease." Job xii, 5.)

"But, brother," said Mr. Greatheart, "I have it in commission to 'comfort the feeble-minded,' and to 'support the weak.' (1 Thess. v, 14.) You must needs go along with us; we will wait for you; we will lend you our help; we will deny ourselves of some things, both opinionative and practical, for your sake; (1 Cor. viii, 9–13;) we will not enter into doubtful disputations before you; (Rom. xiv, 1;) we will be made all things to you, (1 Cor. ix, 22,) rather than you shall be left behind."[1]

Now all this while they were at Gaius's door; and behold, as they were thus in the heat of their discourse, Mr. Ready-to-halt came by, with his crutches in his hand, and he also was going on pilgrimage.

Then said Mr. Feeble-mind to him, "Man, how camest thou hither? I was but now complaining that I had not a suitable companion, but thou art according to my wish. Welcome, welcome, good Mr. Ready-to-halt, I hope thou and I may be some help."

"I shall be glad of thy company," said the other; "and good Mr. Feeble-mind, rather than we will part, since we are thus happily met, I will lend thee one of my crutches."[2]

"Nay," said he, "though I thank thee for thy good will, I am not inclined to halt before I am lame. Howbeit, I think, when occasion is, it may help me against a dog."

Ready. If either myself or my crutches can do thee

[1] O that this were more practised among Christians of different standing, degrees, and judgment! If they who are strong were thus to bear the infirmities of the weak as they ought, (Rom. xv, 1,) how much more love, peace, and unanimity would prevail!—*Mason's Notes.*

[2] They that truly love God will also love the children of God, (1 John v, 2,) and, like the apostle, seek not their own profit, but the profit of others that they may be saved. 1 Cor. x, 33. How finely is this characteristic exhibited in the conduct of Ready-to-halt, who is willing to spare to his brother that which he himself has occasion for! From this we may learn that even the weaker members may

a pleasure, we are both at thy command, good Mr. Feeble-mind.

Thus therefore they went on: Mr. Greatheart and Mr. Honest went before, Christiana and her children went next, and Mr. Feeble-mind, and Mr. Ready-to-halt, came behind, with his crutches.

Then said Mr. Honest, "Pray, sir, now we are upon the road, tell us some profitable things of some that have gone on pilgrimage before us."

Great. With a good will. I suppose you have heard how Christian of old did meet with Apollyon in the Valley of Humiliation, and also what hard work he had to go through the Valley of the Shadow of Death. Also I think you cannot but have heard how Faithful was put to it by Madam Wanton, with Adam the First, with one Discontent, and Shame; four as deceitful villains as a man can meet with upon the road.

Hon. I have heard of all this; but indeed good Faithful was hardest put to it with Shame: he was an unwearied one.

Great. Ay; for, as the pilgrim well said, he of all men had the wrong name.

Hon. But pray, sir, where was it that Christian and

be mutually helpful, and by bearing each other's burdens, fulfil the law of Christ. Galatians vi, 2.

"Didst Thou not make us one, That we might one remain,
Together travel on, And bear each other's pain;
Till all thy utmost goodness prove, And rise renew'd in perfect *love*!

"Surely thou didst unite Our kindred spirits here;
That all hereafter might Before thy throne appear;
Meet at the marriage of the Lamb, And all thy glorious love proclaim.

"Then let us ever bear The blessed end in view,
And join with mutual care, To fight our passage through;
And kindly help each other on, Till all receive a starry crown"

Faithful met Talkative? That same was also a notable one.

Great. He was a confident fool; yet many follow his ways.

Hon. He had liked to have beguiled Faithful.

Great. Ay, but Christian put him into a way quickly to find him out.

Thus they went on till they came to the place where Evangelist met with Christian and Faithful, and prophesied to them what should befall them at Vanity Fair. Then said the guide, "Hereabouts did Christian and Faithful meet with Evangelist, who prophesied to them of what troubles they should meet with at Vanity Fair.

Hon. Say you so? I dare say it was a hard chapter that then he did read unto them.

Great. 'Twas so; but he gave them encouragement withal. But what do we talk of them? They were a couple of lion-like men; they had set their faces like flint. Do not you remember how undaunted they were when they stood before the judge?

Hon. Well; Faithful bravely suffered.

Great. So he did, and as brave things came o'nt; for Hopeful and some others, as the story relates it, were converted by his death.

Hon. Well, but pray go on; for you are well acquainted with things.

Great. Above all that Christian met with after he had passed through Vanity Fair, one By-ends was the arch one.

Hon. By-ends! what was he?

Great. A very arch fellow, a downright hypocrite; one that would be religious, which ever way the world went; but so cunning, that he would be sure never to lose or suffer for it. He had his mode of religion for every fresh occasion, and his wife was as good at it as he. He would turn from opinion to opinion; yea, and plead for so doing too. But so far as I could learn, he came to an ill end with his by-ends; nor did I ever hear that any of his children were ever of any esteem with any that truly feared God.

Now by this time they were come within sight of the town of Vanity, where Vanity Fair is kept. So when they saw that they were so near the town, they consulted with one another how they should pass through the town; and some said one thing, and some another. At last Mr. Greatheart said, "I have, as you may understand, often been a conductor of pilgrims through this town. Now I am acquainted with one Mr. Mnason, (Acts xxi, 16,) a Cyprusian by nation, an old disciple, at whose house we may lodge. If you think good, (said he,) we will turn in there."

"Content," said old Honest; "Content," said Chris tiana; "Content," said Mr. Feeble-mind; and so they said all. Now you must think that it was even-tide by that they got to the outside of the town; but Mr. Greatheart knew the way to the old man's house. So thither they came; and he called at the door, and the old man within knew his tongue so soon as ever he heard it; so he opened the door, and they all came in. Then said Mnason their host, "How far have ye come to-day?" So they said, "From the house of Gaius, our friend." "I promise you," said he, "you have gone a good stitch; you may well be weary; sit down." So they sat down.

Then said their guide, "Come, what cheer, good sirs? I dare say you are welcome to my friend."

"I also," said Mr. Mnason, "do bid you welcome, and whatever you want, do but say, and we will do what we can to get it for you."

Hon. Our great want, awhile since, was harbour and good company, and now I hope we have both.

Mnas. For harbour, you see what it is; but for good company, that will appear in the trial.

"Well," said Mr. Greatheart, "will you have the pilgrims up into their lodging?"

"I will," said Mr. Mnason. (So he had them to their respective places; and also showed them a very fair dining-room, where they might be, and sup together until the time was come to go to rest.)

Now, when they were seated in their places, and were a little cheery after their journey, Mr. Honest asked his landlord if there were any store of good people in the town.

Mnas. We have a few; for indeed they are but a few when compared with them on the other side.

Hon. But how shall we do to see some of them? for the sight of good men to them that are going on pilgrimage is like the appearing of the moon and stars to them that are sailing upon the seas.

Then Mr. Mnason stamped with his foot, and his daughter Grace came up. So he said unto her, "Grace, go you, tell my friends, Mr. Contrite, Mr. Holy-man, Mr. Love-saints, Mr. Dare-not-lie, and Mr. Penitent, that I have a friend or two at my house that have a mind to see them." So Grace went to call them, and they came; and after salutation made, they sat down together at the table.

Then said Mr. Mnason their landlord, "My neighbours, I have, as you see, a company of strangers come to my house; they are pilgrims: they come from afar, and are going to Mount Zion. But who, (quoth he,) do you think this is? (pointing his finger to Christiana.) It is Christiana, the wife of Christian, the famous pilgrim, who, with Faithful his brother, was so shamefully handled in our town." At that they stood amazed, saying, "We little thought to see Christiana when Grace came to call us; wherefore this is a very comfortable surprise." They then asked her of her welfare, and if these young men were her husband's sons. And when she had told them they were, they said, "The King whom you love and serve make you as your father, and bring you where he is in peace."

Then Mr. Honest (when they had all sat down) asked Mr. Contrite and the rest, in what posture their town was at present.

Contr. You may be sure we are full of hurry in fair-time. 'Tis hard keeping our hearts and spirits in good order when we are in a cumbered condition. He that lives in such a place as this, and has to do with such as we have, has need of an item to caution him to take heed every moment of the day.[3]

Hon. But how are your neighbours now for quietness?

Contr. They are much more moderate now than formerly. You know how Christian and Faithful were used at our town; but of late, I say, they have been

[3] This shows the reason of all those dreadful falls and miscarriages that many of the saints sustain; they make it not their business to watch to see what is coming, and to pray for a supply of grace to uphold them; they, with David, are too careless, or with Peter, too confident, or with the disciples, too sleepy, and so the temptation comes upon them, and their want like an armed man. A new temptation, a sudden temptation, an unexpected temptation, usually foils those that are not upon their watch.—*Bunyan's Saint's Privilege.*

far more moderate. I think the blood of Faithful lieth with a load upon them till now; for since they burned him, they have been ashamed to burn any more. In those days we were afraid to walk the streets; but now we can show our heads. Then the name of a professor was odious; now, especially in some parts of our town, (for you know our town is large,) religion is counted honourable.[4]

Then said Mr. Contrite to them, "Pray how fared it with you in your pilgrimage? how stands the country affected toward you?"

Hon. It happens to us as it happeneth to wayfaring men; sometimes our way is clean, sometimes foul; sometimes up hill, sometimes down hill; we are seldom at a certainty. The wind is not always on our backs, nor is every one a friend that we meet with in the way. We have met with some notable rubs already, and what are yet behind we know not; but for the most part we find it true that has been talked of old, "A good man must suffer trouble."

Contr. You talk of rubs; what rubs have you met withal?

Hon. Nay, ask Mr. Greatheart, our guide; for he can give the best account of that.

[4] This favourable state of public opinion is an encouraging circumstance, when it has not been the result of any degeneracy in discipline or practice on the part of the church; but at the same time it is not without cause of apprehension to the followers of Christ, who have now more cause than ever to "watch with godly jealousy over their evil hearts." "The smiles of the town of Vanity," as one observes, "often prove more injurious than its frowns." When the profession of religion is attended with no reproach, but is rather accounted reputable than otherwise, there is great danger of professors being seduced into some degree of conformity to the maxims and practices of the world: therefore at such times let them beware.

Great. We have been beset three or four times already. First, Christiana and her children were beset by two ruffians, that they feared would have taken away their lives. We were beset with Giant Bloody-man, Giant Maul, and Giant Slay-good. Indeed, we did rather beset the last than were beset of him. And thus it was: after we had been some time at the house of Gaius mine host, and of the whole church, we were minded upon a time to take our weapons with us, and go see if we could light upon any of those that are enemies to pilgrims; for we heard that there was a notable one thereabouts. Now Gaius knew his haunt better than I, because he dwelt thereabout. So we looked, and looked, till at last we discerned the mouth of his cave: then we were glad, and plucked up our spirits. So we approached up to his den; and lo, when we came there, he had dragged, by mere force, into his net, this poor man, Mr. Feeble-mind, and was about to bring him to his end. But when he saw us, supposing, as we thought, he had had another prey, he left the poor man in his hole, and came out. So we fell to it full sore, and he lustily laid about him; but, in conclusion, he was brought down to the ground, and his head cut off, and set up by the way-side, for a terror to such as should after practise such ungodliness. That I tell you the truth, here is the man himself to affirm it, who was as a lamb taken out of the mouth of the lion.

Then said Mr. Feeble-mind, "I found this true to my cost and comfort: to my cost, when he threatened to pick my bones every moment; and to my comfort, when I saw Mr. Greatheart and his friends, with their weapons, approach so near for my deliverance."

Then said Mr. Holy-man, "There are two things that they have need to be possessed with who go on pilgrimage; courage, and an unspotted life. If they have not courage, they can never hold on their way; and if their lives be loose, they will make the very name of a pilgrim to stink."

Then said Mr. Love-saints, "I hope this caution is not needful among you: but truly there are many that go upon the road, that rather declare themselves strangers to pilgrimage than strangers and pilgrims on the earth."

Then said Mr. Dare-not-lie, "'Tis true. They have neither the pilgrim's weed, nor the pilgrim's courage; they go not uprightly, but all awry with their feet; one shoe goes inward, another outward; and their hosen out behind; here a rag, and there a rent, to the disparagement of their Lord."

"These things," said Mr. Penitent, "they ought to be troubled for; nor are the pilgrims like to have that grace put upon them and their pilgrim's progress as they desire, until the way is cleared of such spots and blemishes."

Thus they sat talking and spending the time until supper was set upon the table, unto which they went, and refreshed their weary bodies: so they were to rest.

Now they stayed in the fair a great while, at the house of this Mr. Mnason, who in process of time gave his daughter Grace unto Samuel, Christiana's son, to wife, and his daughter Martha to Joseph.

The time as I said, that they stayed here, was long for it was not now as in former times. Wherefore the pilgrims grew acquainted with many of the good people of the town, and did them what service they could Mercy, as she was wont, laboured much for tho poor:

wherefore their bellies and backs blessed her, and she was there an ornament to her profession. And, to say the truth for Grace, Phebe, and Martha, they were all of a very good nature, and did much good in their places. They were also all of them very fruitful; so that Christian's name, as was said before, was like to live in the world.

While they lay here there came a monster out of the woods, and slew many of the people of the town. It would also carry away their children, and teach them to suck its whelps.[5] Now no man in the town durst so much as face this monster; but all fled when they heard the noise of his coming.

The monster was like unto no one beast on the earth. Its body was like a dragon, and it had seven heads and ten horns. Rev. xii, 3. It made great havoc of children, and yet it was governed by a woman. Rev. xvii, 3. This monster propounded conditions to men, and such men as loved their lives more than their souls accepted of those conditions. So they came under.

Now Mr. Greatheart, together with those who came to visit the pilgrims at Mr. Mnason's house, entered into a covenant to go and engage this beast, if perhaps they might deliver the people of this town from the paws and mouths of this so devouring a serpent.

Then did Mr. Greatheart, Mr. Contrite, Mr. Holyman, Mr. Dare-not-lie, and Mr. Penitent, with their

[5] It is the policy of the Romish Church in those countries where they have not full sway, to establish schools, or obtain the control of schools already established, and use every influence to get children placed under their care, when they sedulously instil into their young and unsuspecting minds the dogmas of the Romish faith. This game they have often played with but too much success, as many Protestant parents who have been so inconsiderate as to place their children in such institutions have found to their cost and sorrow.

weapons, go forth to meet him. Now the monster at first was very rampant, and looked upon these enemies with great disdain; but they so belabored him, being sturdy men at arms, that they made him make a retreat; so they came home to Mr. Mnason's house again.

The monster, you must know, had his certain seasons to come out in, and to make his attempts upon the children of the people of the town. At these seasons did these valiant worthies watch him in, and did still continually assault him; insomuch that in process of time he became not only wounded, but lame. Also he has not made that havoc of the townsmen's children as formerly he had done; and it is verily believed by some, that this beast will die of his wounds.[6]

This, therefore, made Mr. Greatheart and his fellows of great fame in this town; so that many of the people that wanted their taste of things, yet had a reverent esteem and respect for them. Upon this account, therefore, it was, that these pilgrims got not much hurt here. True, there were some of the baser sort that could see no more than a mole, nor understand no more than a beast; these had no reverence for these men, nor took they notice of their valour and adventures.

[6] This whole passage doubtless refers, as Mr. Scott observes, to the increase of Popish influence in England for some time previous to the revolution of 1688. Encouraged by the countenance of the king, (James II.,) who was himself a Papist, and aimed at the re-establishment of Popery, the emissaries of Rome exerted every influence in their power to make proselytes, and many weak-minded and time-serving persons were drawn aside by their sophistries, or seduced by hopes of favour when Popery should again wield the civil power. But through the blessing of God upon the zealous labours of the friends of religion, both in the pulpit and through the press, the "man of sin" was disappointed of his expectation, and the Popish monarch compelled to abdicate his throne.

CHAPTER X.

Departure from Vanity Fair—House for lambs by the side of the river of the Water of Life—The pilgrims assault Doubting Castle, which they demolish, and slay the Giant and his wife—They come to the Delectable Mountains—Their entertainment by the Shepherds.

WELL, the time grew on that the pilgrims must go on their way; wherefore they prepared for their journey. They sent for their friends; they conferred with them; they had some time set apart therein to commit each other to the protection of their Prince. There were again that brought them of such things as they had, that were fit for the weak and the strong, for the women and the men, and so laded them with such things as were necessary. Acts xxviii, 10. Then they set forward on their way, and their friends accompanying them so far as was convenient, they again committed each other to the protection of their King, and departed.

They therefore that were of the pilgrims' company went on, and Mr. Greatheart went before them. Now the women and children being weakly, they were forced to go as they could bear; by this means Mr. Ready-to-halt and Mr. Feeble-mind had more to sym pathize with their condition.

When they were gone from the townsmen, and when their friends had bid them farewell, they quickly came to the place where Faithful was put to death. There fore they made a stand, and thanked Him that had enabled him to bear his cross so well; and the rather, because they now found they had a benefit by such a manly suffering as his was. They went on therefore after this a good way further, talking of Christian and

Faithful, and how Hopeful joined himself to Christian after that Faithful was dead.

Now they were come up with the hill Lucre, where the silver mine was which took Demas off from his pilgrimage, and into which, as some think, By-ends fell and perished; wherefore they considered that. But when they were come to the old monument that stood over against the hill Lucre, to wit, to the pillar of salt, that stood also within view of Sodom and its stinking lake, they marvelled, as did Christian before, that men of that knowledge and ripeness of wit as they were, should be so blinded as to turn aside here. Only they considered again, that nature is not affected with the harms that others have met with, especially if that thing upon which they look has an attracting virtue upon the foolish eye.

I saw now that they went on till they came to the river that was on this side of the Delectable Mountains; to the river where the fine trees grow on both sides, and whose leaves, if taken inwardly, are good against surfeits: where the meadows are green all the year long; and where they might lie down safely. Psalm xxiii, 2.

By this river-side, in the meadows, there were cotes and folds for sheep, a house built for the nourishing and bringing up of those lambs, the babes of those women that go on pilgrimage.[1] Also there was here one

[1] In an index prefixed to one edition of the Pilgrim, this account of the house built by the "*river* side" for the "*babes*" of pilgrims, is referred to as setting forth the advantages of which children are made partakers through being early admitted by baptism into the visible church. The phraseology of the passage would certainly justify such an interpretation; but the well-known principles of the author on the subject of infant baptism preclude the possibility of his having so intended it. His object was doubtless merely to point out to parents

that was intrusted with them, who could have compassion; (Heb. v, 2;) and that could "gather these lambs with his arm, and carry them in his bosom," and that could "gently lead those that were with young." Isa. xl, 11. Now to the care of this man Christiana admonished her four daughters to commit their little ones, that by these waters they might be housed, harboured, succoured, and nourished, and that none of them might be lacking in time to come. This man, if any of them go astray, or be lost, he will bring them again; he will also bind up that which was broken, and will strengthen them that are sick. Jer. xxiii, 4; Ezek. xxxiv, 11–16. Here they will never want meat, drink, and clothing; here they will be kept from thieves and robbers; for this man will die before one of those committed to his trust shall be lost. Besides, here they shall be sure to have good nurture and admonition, and shall be taught to walk in right paths, and that you know is a favour of no small account. Also, here, as you see, are delicate waters, pleasant meadows, dainty flowers, variety of trees, and such as bear wholesome fruit; fruit, not like that which Matthew ate of, that fell over the wall out of Beelzebub's garden; but fruit that procureth health where there is none, and that continueth and increaseth it where it is. So they were content to commit their little ones to him; and that which was also an encouragement to them so to do, was, for that all this was to be at the charge of the King, and so was as an hospital for young children and orphans.

the duty of inculcating the principles of religion on the tender minds of their children, and bringing them up in the fear of the Lord: but we know not how they can better begin this work than by presenting them in the house of God, and solemnly dedicating them in holy baptism.

Now they went on. And when they were come to By-path meadow, to the stile over which Christian went with his fellow Hopeful, when they were taken by Giant Despair and put into Doubting Castle, they sat down, and consulted what was best to be done: to wit, now that they were so strong, and had got such a man as Mr. Greatheart for their conductor, whether they had not best to make an attempt upon the giant, demolish his castle, and if there were any pilgrims in it, to set them at liberty before they went any further. So one said one thing, and another said the contrary. One questioned if it was lawful to go upon unconsecrated ground; another said they might, provided their end was good; but Mr. Greatheart said, "Though that assertion offered last cannot be universally true, yet I have a commandment to resist sin, to overcome evil, to fight the good fight of faith: and I pray, with whom should I fight this good fight, if not with Giant Despair? I will therefore attempt the taking away of his life, and the demolishing of Doubting Castle." Then said he, "Who will go with me?" Then said old Honest, "I will." "And so will we too," said Christiana's four sons, Matthew, Samuel, Joseph, and James; for they were young men and strong. 1 John ii, 13, 14. So they left the women in the road, and with them Mr. Feeble-mind, and Mr. Ready-to-halt with his crutches, to be their guard, until they came back; for in that place the Giant Despair dwelt so near, they keeping in the road, a little child might lead them.[2] Isaiah xi, 6. So Mr. Greatheart, old Honest, and the four young

[2] The enemy cannot harm us so long as we keep in the narrow way. "In the way of righteousness," says the wise man, "is life and in the pathway thereof there is no death." Proverbs [illegible], 28.

men, went to go up to Doubting Castle, to look for Giant Despair. When they came at the castle gate, they knocked for entrance with an unusual noise. At that the old giant comes to the gate, and Diffidence his wife follows. Then said he, "Who and what is he that is so hardy, as after this manner to molest the Giant Despair?" Mr. Greatheart replied, "It is I, Greatheart, one of the King of the Celestial Country's conductors of pilgrims to their place; and I demand of thee that thou open thy gates for my entrance: prepare thyself also to fight, for I am come to take away thy head, and to demolish Doubting Castle."

Now Giant Despair, because he was a giant, thought no man could overcome him: and again thought he, "Since heretofore I have made a conquest of angels, shall Greatheart make me afraid?" So he harnessed himself and went out. He had a cap of steel upon his head, a breast-plate of fire girded to him, and he came out in iron shoes, with a great club in his hand. Then these six men made up to him, and beset him behind and before: also when Diffidence the giantess came up to help him, old Mr. Honest cut her down at one blow. Then they fought for their lives, and Giant Despair was brought down to the ground, but was very loath to die. He struggled hard, and had, as they say, as many lives as a cat; but Greatheart was his death; for he left him not till he had severed his head from his shoulders.

Then they fell to demolishing Doubting Castle, and that you know might with ease be done, since Giant Despair was dead. They were seven days in destroying of that; and in it of pilgrims they found one Mr. Despondency, almost starved to death, and one Much-afraid, his daughter: these two they saved alive. But

Though Doubting Castle be demolished,
And Giant Despair too has lost his head,
Sin can rebuild the castle, make't remain,
And make Despair, the giant, live again.

it would have made you a-wondered to have seen the dead bodies that lay here and there in the castle yard, and how full of dead men's bones the dungeon was.[3]

When Mr. Greatheart and his companions had performed this exploit, they took Mr. Despondency, and his daughter Much-afraid, into their protection; for they were honest people, though they were prisoners in Doubting Castle to that tyrant Giant Despair. They, therefore, I say, took with them the head of the giant, (for his body they had buried under a heap of stones,) and down to the road and to their companions they came, and showed them what they had done. Now when Feeble-mind and Ready-to-halt saw that it was the head of Giant Despair indeed, they were very jocund and merry. Now Christiana, if need was, could play upon the viol, and her daughter Mercy upon the lute: so since they were so merry disposed, she played them a lesson, and Ready-to-halt would dance. So he took Despondency's daughter, Much-afraid, by the hand, and to dancing they went in the road. True, he could not dance without one crutch in his hand, but I promise you he footed it well: also the girl was to be commended, for she answered the music handsomely.

As for Mr. Despondency, the music was not so much to him; he was for feeding, rather than dancing, for that he was almost starved. So Christiana gave him

[3] The killing of Despair, and the demolishing of his castle, have by some been objected to as a defect, on the ground that "the giant is still alive, and many poor captives are often immured within the walls of his dreary castle." This objection, however, was anticipated and removed by Bunyan in the lines appended to the cut, wherein he admonished the reader that "sin" would "make the giant live again," and therefore the unwary, and those that wander out of the way, would still be in danger of falling into his hands.

some of her bottle of spirits for present relief, and then prepared him something to eat; and in a little time the old gentleman came to himself, and began to be finely revived.

Now I saw in my dream, when all these things were finished, Mr. Greatheart took the head of Giant Despair, and set it upon a pole by the highway side, right over against the pillar that Christian erected for a caution to pilgrims that came after, to take heed of entering into his ground. Then he writ under it upon a marble stone these verses following:—

"This is the head of him whose name only
In former times did pilgrims terrify.
His castle's down, and Diffidence his wife
Brave Mr. Greatheart has bereft of life.[4]
Despondency, his daughter Much-afraid,
Greatheart for them also the man has play'd.
Who hereof doubts, if he'll but cast his eye
Up hither, may his scruples satisfy.
This head also, when doubting cripples dance,
Doth show from fears they have deliverance."

When these men had thus bravely showed themselves against Doubting Castle, and had slain Giant Despair, they went forward, and went on till they came to the Delectable Mountains, where Christian and Hopeful refreshed themselves with the varieties of the place. They also acquainted themselves with the Shepherds there, who welcomed them, as they had done Christian before, unto the Delectable Mountains.

Now the Shepherds seeing so great a train follow Mr. Greatheart, (for with him they were well acquainted,) they said unto him, "Good sir, you have got a goodly company here; pray where did you find all these?"

[4] This line should read "Brave Mr. *Honest*," &c., as it was by his hands that Mrs. Diffidence was "bereft of life." See on page 427.

Then Mr. Greatheart replied :—

"First, here is Christiana and her train,
Her sons, and her sons' wives, who like the wain,
Keep by the pole, and do by compass steer
From sin to grace, else they had not been here
Next here's old Honest come on pilgrimage,
Ready-to-halt too, who I dare engage
True-hearted is, and so is Feeble-mind,
Who willing was not to be left behind.
Despondency, good man, is coming after,
And so also is Much-afraid, his daughter.
May we have entertainment here, or must
We further go? Let's know whereon to trust"

Then said the Shepherds, "This is a comfortable company. You are welcome to us; for we have for the feeble, as well as for the strong. Our Prince has an eye to what is done to the least of these; (Matt. xxv, 40;) therefore infirmity must not be a block to our entertainment." So they had them to the palace door and then said unto them, "Come in, Mr. Feeble-mind; come in Mr. Ready-to-halt; come in, Mr. Desponden cy, and Mrs. Much-afraid his daughter. These, Mr. Greatheart," said the Shepherds to the guide, "we call in by name, for that they are most subject to draw back; but as for you, and the rest that are strong, we leave you to your wonted liberty." Then said Mr. Greatheart, "This day I see that grace doth shine in your faces, and that you are my Lord's Shepherds indeed: for that you have not pushed these diseased neither with side nor shoulder, but have rather strewed their way into the palace with flowers, as you should." Ezekiel xxxiv, 21.

So the feeble and weak went in, and Mr. Greatheart and the rest did follow. When they were also set down, the Shepherds said to those of the weaker sort

"What is it that you would have? for, (said they,) all things must be managed here to the supporting of the weak, as well as to the warning of the unruly." So they made them a feast of things easy of digestion, and that were pleasant to the palate, and nourishing; the which when they had received, they went to their rest, each one respectively unto his proper place.

When morning was come, because the mountains were high and the day clear, and because it was the custom of the Shepherds to show the pilgrims before their departure some rarities, therefore after they were ready, and had refreshed themselves, the Shepherds took them out into the fields, and showed them first what they had shown to Christian before.

Then they had them to some new places. The first was Mount Marvel, where they looked, and beheld a man at a distance that tumbled the hills about with words. Then they asked the Shepherds what that should mean. So they told them, that that man was the son of one Mr. Great-grace, of whom you read in the first part of the records of the Pilgrim's Progress; and he is set there to teach pilgrims how to believe down, or to tumble out of their ways, what difficulties they should meet with, by faith. Mark xi, 23, 24. Then said Mr. Great-heart, "I know him, he is a man above many."

Then they had them to another place called Mount Innocence. And there they saw a man clothed all in white; and two men, Prejudice and Ill-will, continually casting dirt upon him. Now behold, the dirt, whatsoever they cast at him, would in a little time fall off again, and his garment would look as clear as if no dirt had been cast thereat. Then said the pilgrims, "What means this?" The Shepherds answered, "This man is named Godly-man, and this garment is to show the innocency of his life. Now those that throw dirt at him are such as hate his well-doing; but, as you see, the dirt will not stick upon his clothes, so it shall be with him that liveth innocently in the world. Whoever they be that would make such men dirty, they labour all in vain; for God, by that a little time is spent, will cause that their innocence shall break forth as the light, and their righteousness as the noon-day."

Then they took them, and had them to Mount Charity, where they showed them a man that had a bundle of cloth lying before him, out of which he cut coats and garments for the poor that stood about him; yet his bundle or roll of cloth was never the less. Then said they, "What should this be?" "This is," said the Shepherds, "to show you, that he who has a heart to give of his labour to the poor, shall never want wherewithal. He that watereth shall be watered himself. And the cake that the widow gave to the prophet did not cause that she had the less in her barrel."

They had them also to the place where they saw one Fool, and one Want-wit, washing an Ethiopian, with intention to make him white; but the more they washed him the blacker he was. Then they asked the Shepherds what that should mean. So they told them, saying, "Thus it is with the vile person; all means used to get such a one a good name, shall, in conclusion, tend but to make him more abominable. Thus it was with the Pharisees; and so it shall be with all hypocrites."

Then said Mercy, the wife of Matthew, to Christiana her mother, "Mother, I would, if it might be, see the hole in the hill, or that commonly called the by-way to hell." So her mother brake her mind to the Shepherds. Then they went to the door; it was on the side of a hill; and they opened it, and bid Mercy hearken awhile. So she hearkened, and heard one saying, "Cursed be my father for holding of my feet back from the way of peace and life." Another said, "O, that I had been torn in pieces before I had, to save my life, lost my soul!" And another said, "If I were to live again, how would I deny myself rather than come to this place!" Then there was as if the very earth had groaned and quaked under the feet of this young woman for fear; so she looked white, and came trembling away, saying, "Blessed be he and she that is delivered from this place!"[5]

Now when the Shepherds had shown them all these things, then they had them back to the palace, and entertained them with what the house would afford. But Mercy, being a young and married woman, longed for something that she saw there, but was ashamed to ask. Her mother-in-law then asked her what she ailed, for she looked as one not well. Then said Mercy, "There is a looking-glass hangs up in the dining-room, off which I cannot take my mind; if, therefore, I have it not, I think I shall miscarry." Then said her mother, "I will mention thy wants to the Shepherds, and they will not deny it thee." But she said, "I am ashamed that these men should know that I longed." "Nay my daughter," said she, "it is no shame, but a virtue to long for such a thing as that." So Mercy said,

[5] Friend, I have given you but a short touch of the torments of hell. O! I am set, I am *set*, and am not able to utter what my mind conceives of the torments of hell! Yet this let me say to thee, "Accept of God's mercy through our Lord Jesus Christ, lest thou feel that with thy conscience which I cannot express with my tongue, and 'I am sorely tormented in this flame.'"—*Bunyan's Jerus. Sinner.*

"Then, mother, if you please, ask the Shepherds if they are willing to sell it."

Now the glass was one of a thousand.[6] It would present a man, one way, with his own features exactly; and turn it but another way, and it would show one the very face and similitude of the Prince of pilgrims himself. Yes, I have talked with them that can tell, and they have said that they have seen the very crown of thorns upon his head by looking in that glass; they have therein also seen the holes in his hands, his feet, and his side. Yea, such an excellency is there in this glass, that it will show him to one where they have a mind to see him; whether living or dead; whether in earth or in heaven; whether in a state of humiliation or in his exaltation; whether coming to suffer or coming to reign. James i, 23; 1 Cor. xiii, 12; 2 Cor. iii, 18.

Christiana therefore went to the Shepherds apart, (now the names of the Shepherds were Knowledge, Experience, Watchful, and Sincere,) and said unto them, "There is one of my daughters a married woman, that I think doth long for something that she hath seen in this house; and she thinks that she shall miscarry if she should by you be denied."

Experience. Call her, call her, she shall assuredly have what we can help her to.

So they called her, and said to her, "Mercy, what is that thing thou wouldst have?" Then she blushed, and said, "The great glass that hangs up in the dining-room." So Sincere ran and fetched it, and with a joyful consent it was given her. Then she bowed her head, and gave thanks, and said, "By this I know that I have obtained favour in your eyes."

[6] This glass "was the word of God."—*Bunyan's Marginal Note*

They also gave to the other young women such things as they desired, and to their husbands great commendations, for that they had joined with Mr. Greatheart in the slaying of Giant Despair, and the demolishing of Doubting Castle.

About Christiana's neck the Shepherds put a bracelet, and so did they about the necks of her four daughters; also they put ear-rings in their ears, and jewels on their foreheads.[7]

When they were minded to go hence, they let them go in peace, but gave not to them those certain cautions which before were given to Christian and his companion. The reason was, for that these had Greatheart to be their guide, who was one that was well acquainted with things, and so could give them their cautions more seasonably, to wit, even when the danger was nigh the approaching. What cautions Christian and his companion had received of the Shepherds, they had also lost by that the time was come that they had need to put them in practice. Wherefore here was the advantage that this company had over the other.[8]

From thence they went on singing, and they said,—

"Behold how fitly are the stages set
For their relief that pilgrims are become,
And how they us receive without one let,
That make the other life our mark and home!

"What novelties they have to us they give,
That we, though pilgrims, joyful lives may live:
They do upon us, too, such things bestow,
That show we pilgrims are where'er we go."

[7] These ornaments represent those Christian graces with which professors should be adorned. 1 Peter iii, 3; Colossians iii, 12.

[8] Here observe the advantage which Christians derive from the admonition, instruction, and care of a judicious and faithful pastor

CHAPTER XI.

How Turn-away managed his apostacy—One Valiant-for-truth beset with thieves—How Mr. Valiant came to go on pilgrimage—He begins right—He is much rejoiced to see Christian's wife—The great stumbling-blocks that by Mr. Valiant's friends were laid in his way—How he got over these stumbling-blocks—A song.

When they were gone from the Shepherds, they quickly came to the place where Christian met with one Turn-away that dwelt in the town of Apostacy. Wherefore of him Mr. Greatheart their guide did now put them in mind, saying, "This is the place where Christian met with one Turn-away, who carried with him the character of his rebellion at his back. And this I have to say concerning this man; he would hearken to no counsel, but once a-falling, persuasion could not stop him. When he came to the place where the cross and sepulchre were, he did meet with one that bid him look there: but he gnashed with his teeth, and stamped, and said he was resolved to go back to his own town. Before he came to the gate he met with Evangelist, who offered to lay hands on him, to turn him into the way again; but this Turn-away resisted him, and having done much despite unto him, he got away over the wall, and so escaped his hand."

Then they went on; and just at the place where Little-faith formerly was robbed, there stood a man with his sword drawn, and his face all over with blood. Then said Mr. Greatheart, "Who art thou?" The man made answer, saying, "I am one whose name is Valiant-for-truth. I am a pilgrim, and am going to the Celestial City. Now, as I was in my way, there were three men did beset me, and propounded unto me these three things: 1. Whether I would become one of them. 2. Or go back from whence I came. 3. Or die upon the place. To the first I answered, I had been a true man for a long season, and therefore it could not be expected that I should now cast in my lot with thieves. (Prov. i, 10–16.) Then they demanded what I would say to the second. So I told them, the place from whence I came, had I not found incommodity there, I had not forsaken it at all; but finding it altogether unsuitable to me, and very unprofitable for me, I forsook it for this way. Then they asked me what I said to the third. And I told them my life cost far more dear than that I should lightly give it away. Besides, you have nothing to do thus to put things to my choice; wherefore at your peril be it if you meddle. Then these three, to wit, Wild-head, Inconsiderate, and Pragmatic, drew upon me, and I also drew upon them. So we fell to it, one against three, for the space of above three hours. They have left upon me, as you see, some of the marks of their valour, and have also carried away with them some of mine. They are but just now gone: I suppose they might, as the saying is, hear your horse dash, and so they betook themselves to flight!"

Great. But here was great odds, three against one.

Valiant. 'Tis true; but little or more are nothing to him that has the truth on his side: "Though a host should encamp against me, (said one,) my heart shall not fear: though war should rise against me, in this will I be confident," &c. Psa. xxvii, 3. Besides, (said he,) I have read in some records that one man has fought an army: and how many did Samson slay with the jaw-bone of an ass! (1 Chr. xi, 11, 20; Judg. xv, 15.)

Then said the guide, "Why did you not cry out, that some might have come in for your succour?"

Valiant. So I did to my King, who I knew could hear me and afford invisible help, and that was sufficient for me.

Then said Mr. Greatheart to Mr. Valiant-for-truth, "Thou hast worthily behaved thyself; let me see thy sword." So he showed it him.

When he had taken it in his hand, and looked thereon awhile, he said, "Ha! it is a right Jerusalem blade."

Valiant. It is so. Let a man have one of these blades, with a hand to wield it, and skill to use it, and he may venture upon an angel with it. He need not fear its holding, if he can but tell how to lay on. Its edge will never blunt. It will cut flesh and bones, and soul and spirit, and all. Heb. iv, 12.

Great. But you fought a great while; I wonder you was not weary.

Valiant. I fought till my sword did cleave to my hand; and then they were joined together as if a sword grew out of my arm; and when the blood ran through my fingers, then I fought with most courage.

Great. Thou hast done well; thou hast resisted unto blood, striving against sin. Thou shalt abide by us, come in and go out with us; for we are thy companions.

Then took they him and washed his wounds, and gave him of what they had, to refresh him: and so they went on together. Now as they went on, because Mr. Greatheart was delighted in him, (for he loved one greatly that he found to be a man of his hands,) and because there were in company them that were feeble and weak, therefore he questioned with him about many things; as first, what countryman he was.

Valiant. I am of Dark-land; for there was I born and there my father and mother are still.

"Dark-land!" said the guide, "doth not that lie on the same coast with the city of Destruction?"

Valiant. Yes it doth. Now that which caused me to come on pilgrimage was this. We had one Mr. Tell-true come into our parts, and he told it about what Christian had done, that went from the City of Destruction; namely, how he had forsaken his wife and children, and had betaken himself to a pilgrim's life. It was also confidently reported how he had killed a serpent that did come out to resist him in his journey; and how he got through to whither he intended. It was also told what welcome he had at all his Lord's lodgings, especially when he came to the gates of the Celestial City; for there, said the man, he was received with sound of trumpet by a company of shining ones. He told also how all the bells in the city did ring for joy at his reception, and what golden garments he was clothed with; with many other things that now I shall forbear to relate. In a word, that man so told the story of Christian and his travels that my heart fell into a burning haste to be gone after him; nor could father or mother stay me. So I got from them, and am come thus far on my way.

Great. You came in at the Gate, did you not?

Valiant. Yes, yes; for the same man also told us, that all would be nothing if we did not begin to enter this way at the Gate.

"Look you," said the guide to Christiana, "the pilgrimage of your husband, and what he has gotten thereby, is spread abroad far and near."

Valiant. Why, is this Christian's wife?

Great. Yes, that it is; and these also are his four sons.

Valiant. What, and going on pilgrimage too?

Great. Yes, verily, they are following after.

Valiant. It glads me at the heart. Good man, how joyful will he be when he shall see them that would not go with him, yet to enter after him in at the gates into the Celestial City!

Great. Without doubt it will be a comfort to him; for next to the joy of seeing himself there, it will be a joy to meet there his wife and children.

Valiant. But now you are upon that, pray let me see your opinion about it. Some make a question whether we shall know one another when we are there.

Great. Do you think they shall know themselves then, or that they shall rejoice to see themselves in that bliss? and if they think they shall know and do this, why not know others, and rejoice in their welfare also? Again, since relations are our second self, though that state will be dissolved there, yet why may it not be rationally concluded that we shall be more glad to see them there than to see they are wanting?

Valiant. Well, I perceive whereabouts you are as to this. Have you any more things to ask me about my beginning to come on pilgrimage?

Great. Yes; were your father and mother willing that you should become a pilgrim?

Valiant. O no; they used all means imaginable to persuade me to stay at home.

Great. Why, what could they say against it?

Valiant. They said it was an idle life; and if I myself were not inclined to sloth and laziness, I would never countenance a pilgrim's condition.

Great. And what did they say else?

Valiant. Why, they told me that it was a dangerous way; yea, the most dangerous way in the world, said they, is that which the pilgrims go.

Great. Did they show you wherein this way is so dangerous?

Valiant. Yes; and that in many particulars.

Great. Name some of them.

Valiant. They told me of the Slough of Despond, where Christian was well nigh smothered. They told me that there were archers standing ready in Beelzebub Castle to shoot them who should knock at the Wicket-gate for entrance. They told me also of the wood and dark mountains; of the hill Difficulty; of the lions; and also of the three giants, Bloody-man, Maul, and Slay-good. They said, moreover, that there was a foul fiend haunted the Valley of Humiliation; and that Christian was by him almost bereft of life. Besides, said they, you must go over the Valley of the Shadow of Death, where the hobgoblins are, where the light is darkness, where the way is full of snares, pits, traps, and gins. They told me also of Giant Despair, of Doubting Castle, and of the ruin that the pilgrims met with there. Further, they said I must go over the Enchanted Ground, which was dangerous; and that after all this I should find a river, over which there was no bridge; and that that river did lie betwixt me and the Celestial Country.

Great. And was this all?

Valiant. No. They also told me that this way was full of deceivers, and of persons that lay in wait there to turn good men out of the path.

Great. But how did they make that out?

Valiant. They told me that Mr. Worldly-wiseman did lie there in wait to deceive. They said also, that there were Formality and Hypocrisy continually on the road. They said also, that By-ends, Talkative, or Demas, would go near to gather me up ; that the Flatterer would catch me in his net; or that with green-headed Ignorance, I would presume to go on to the gate, from whence he was sent back to the hole that was in the side of the hill, and made to go the by-way to hell.

Great. I promise you this was enough to discourage you ; but did they make an end here?

Valiant. No, stay. They told me also of many that had tried that way of old, and that had gone a great way therein, to see if they could find something of the glory there that so many had so much talked of from time to time, and how they came back again, and befooled themselves for setting a foot out of doors in that path, to the satisfaction of all the country. And they named several that did so, as Obstinate and Pliable, Mistrust and Timorous, Turn-away and old Atheist, with several more ; who, they said, had some of them gone far to see what they could find, but not one of them had found so much advantage by going as amounted to the weight of a feather.

Great. Said they anything more to discourage you?

Valiant. Yes. They told me of one Mr. Fearing, who was a pilgrim, and how he found his way so solitary that he never had a comfortable hour therein; also, that Mr. Despondency had liked to have been starved therein : yea, and also (which I had almost forgot) that Christian himself, about whom there has been such a noise, after all his ventures for a celestial crown, was certainly drowned in the Black River, and never went a foot further, however it was smothered up.

Great. And did none of these things discourage you?

Valiant. No, they seemed but as so many nothings to me.

Great. How came that about?

Valiant. Why, I still believed what Mr. Tell-true had said; and that carried me beyond them all.

Great. Then this was your victory, even your faith.

Valiant. It was so. I believed, and therefore came out, got into the way, fought all that set themselves against me, and, by believing, am come to this place.

Who would true valour see,
Let him come hither;
One here will constant be,
Come wind, come weather;
There's no discouragement
Shall make him once relent
His first avow'd intent
To be a pilgrim

Who so beset him round
With dismal stories,
Do but themselves confound
His strength the more is.
No lion can him fright,
He'll with a giant fight,
But he will have a right
To be a pilgrim

Hobgoblin nor foul fiend
Can daunt his spirit;
He knows he at the end
Shall life inherit.
Then fancies fly away,
He'll not fear what men say;
He'll labour night and day
To be a pilgrim.

CHAPTER XII.

The pilgrims get to the Enchanted Ground—An arbour, and two asleep therein—They try to awake them—Their endeavour is fruitless—The children cry for weariness—The pilgrims find Standfast on his knees—Why he was so found—Talk between him and Honest.

By this time they were got to the Enchanted Ground, where the air naturally tended to make one drowsy. And that place was all grown over with briers and thorns, excepting here and there, where was an enchanted arbour, upon which if a man sits, or in which if a man sleeps, it is a question, some say, whether ever he shall rise or wake again in this world. Over this forest, therefore, they went both one and another, and Mr. Greatheart went before, for that he was the guide; and Mr. Valiant-for-truth came behind, being rear-guard, for fear lest peradventure some fiend, or dragon, or giant, or thief, should fall upon their rear, and so do mischief. They went on here, each man with his sword drawn in his hand; for they knew it was a dangerous place. Also they cheered up one another as well as they could. Feeble-mind, Mr. Greatheart commanded should come up after him; and Mr. Despondency was under the eye of Mr. Valiant.

Now they had not gone far, but a great mist and darkness fell upon them all; so that they could scarce, for a great while, see the one the other. Wherefore they were forced, for some time, to feel for one another by words; for they walked not by sight. But any one must think, that here was but sorry going for the best of them all; but how much worse for the women and children, who both of feet and heart were but tender!

Yet so it was, that through the encouraging words of him that led in the front, and of him that brought them up behind, they made a pretty good shift to wag along.

The way was also here very wearisome, through dirt and slabbiness. Nor was there, on all this ground, so much as one inn or victualing-house wherein to refresh the feebler sort. Here, therefore, was grunting, and puffing, and sighing; while one tumbleth over a bush, another sticks fast in the dirt, and the children, some of them, lost their shoes in the mire; while one cries out, "I am down;" and another, "Ho, where are you?" and a third, "The bushes have got such fast hold on me, I think I cannot get away from them."[1]

Then they came at an arbour, warm, and promising much refreshing to the pilgrims; for it was finely wrought above head, beautified with greens, furnished with benches and settles. It also had in it a soft couch, whereon the weary might lean. This, you must think, all things considered, was tempting; for the pilgrims already began to be foiled with the badness of the way: but there was not one of them that made so much as a motion to stop there. Yea, for aught I could perceive, they continually gave such good heed to the advice of their guide, and he did so faithfully tell them of dangers, and of the nature of dangers when they were at them, that usually when they were nearest to them, they did

[1] The "briers and thorns" which grew upon the Enchanted Ground, and obstructed the passage of the pilgrims, represent the perplexities and entanglements to which those professors are exposed who are much engaged in worldly business. Such persons, if they be not exceedingly watchful and circumspect, are in great danger of suffering "the cares of this world and the deceitfulness of riches," (which in Scripture are figured by "thorns,") to "choke the word" so that "it becometh unfruitful." Matthew xiii, 22; Mark iv, 18, 19.

most pluck up their spirits, and hearten one another to deny the flesh. . This arbour was called The Slothful's Friend, on purpose to allure, if it might be, some of the pilgrims there to take up their rest when weary.

I saw them in my dream, that they went on in this their solitary ground till they came to a place at which a man is apt to lose his way. Now, though when it was light their guide could well enough tell how to miss those ways that led wrong, yet in the dark he was put to a stand. But he had in his pocket a map of all ways leading to or from the Celestial City; wherefore he struck a light, (for he never goes without his tinder-box also,) and takes a view of his book or map, which bids him to be careful in that place to turn to the right hand. And had he not been careful here to look in his map, they had all, in probability, been smothered in the mud; for just a little before them, and that at the end of the cleanest way too, was a pit, none knows how deep, full of nothing but mud, there made on purpose to destroy the pilgrims in.

Then thought I with myself, Who that goeth on pilgrimage but would have one of these maps about him, that he may look, when he is at a stand, which is the way he must take?

Then they went on in this Enchanted Ground till they came to where there was another arbour, and it was built by the highway-side. And in that arbour there lay two men, whose names were Heedless and Too-bold. These two went thus far on pilgrimage; but here, being wearied with their journey, sat down to rest themselves, and so fell fast asleep. When the pilgrims saw them, they stood still and shook their heads; for they knew that the sleepers were in a pitiful case.

Then they consulted what to do, whether to go on and leave them in their sleep, or to step to them and try to awake them; so they concluded to go to them and awake them; that is, if they could; but with this caution, namely, to take heed that they themselves did not sit down nor embrace the offered benefit of that arbour.

So they went in, and spake to the men, and called each by his name, for the guide, it seems, did know them; but there was no voice nor answer. Then the guide did shake them, and do what he could to disturb them. Then said one of them, "I will pay you when I take my money." At which the guide shook his head. "I will fight so long as I can hold my sword in my hand," said the other. At that one of the children laughed.

Then said Christiana, "What is the meaning of this?" The guide said, "They talk in their sleep. If you strike them, beat them, or whatever else you do to them, they will answer you after this fashion; or as one of them said in old time, when the waves of the sea did beat upon him, and he slept as one upon the mast of a ship, 'When I awake I will seek it again.' (Prov. xxiii, 34, 35.) You know when men talk in their sleep they say anything; but their words are not governed either by faith or reason. There is an incoherency in their words now as there was before betwixt their going on pilgrimage and sitting down here. This, then, is the mischief of it: when heedless ones go on pilgrimage 'tis twenty to one but they are served thus. For this Enchanted Ground is one of the last refuges that the enemy to pilgrims has; wherefore it is, as you see, placed almost at the end of the way, and so it standeth against us with the more advantage. For when, thinks the enemy, will these fools be so desirous to sit down as when they are weary? and when so like to be weary as when almost at their journey's end? Therefore it is, I say, that the Enchanted Ground is placed so nigh to the land Beulah, and so near the end of their race. Wherefore let pilgrims look to themselves, lest it happen to them as it has done to these that, as you see, are fallen asleep, and none can awake them.

Then the pilgrims desired, with trembling, to go forward; only they prayed their guide to strike a light, that they might go the rest of their way by the help of the light of a lantern.[2] So he struck a light, and they went by the help of that through the rest of this way, though the darkness was very great. 2 Pet. i, 19. But the children began to be sorely weary, and they cried out unto Him that loveth pilgrims to make their way more comfortable. So by that they had gone a little further a wind arose that drove away the fog, so the air became more clear. Yet they were not off (by much) of the Enchanted Ground; only now they could see one another better, and the way wherein they should walk.

Now, when they were almost at the end of this ground, they perceived that a little before them was a solemn noise as of one that was much concerned. So they went on, and looked before them: and behold they saw, as they thought, a man upon his knees, with hands and eyes lifted up, and speaking, as they thought, earnestly to one that was above. They drew nigh, but could not tell what he said; so they went softly till he had done. When he had done he got up, and began to

[2] The light of the word.—*Bunyan's Marginal Note.* Thy word is a lamp to my feet, and a light unto my path. Psalm cxix, 105.

run toward the Celestial City. Then Mr. Greatheart called after him, saying, "Soho, friend! let us have your company, if you go, as I suppose you do, to the Celestial City." So the man stopped, and they came up to him. But as soon as Mr. Honest saw him he said, "I know this man." Then said Mr. Valiant-for-truth, "Prithee, who is it?" "It is one," said he, "that comes from whereabout I dwelt. His name is Standfast; he is certainly a right good pilgrim."

So they came up one to another; and presently Standfast said to old Honest, "Ho, father Honest, are you there?" "Ay, (said he,) that I am, as sure as you are there." "Right glad am I, (said Mr. Standfast,) that I have found you on this road." "And as glad am I, (said the other,) that I espied you on your knees." Then Mr. Standfast blushed, and said, "But why, did you see me?" "Yes, that I did, (quoth the other,) and with my heart was glad at the sight." "Why, what did you think?" said Standfast. "Think! (said old Honest,) what could I think? I thought we had an honest man upon the road, and therefore should have his company by and by." "If you thought not amiss, (said Standfast,) how happy am I! But if I be not as I should, 'tis I alone must bear it." "That is true, (said the other,) but your fear doth further confirm me that things are right betwixt the Prince of pilgrims and your soul; for he saith, 'Blessed is the man that feareth always.'" Prov. xxviii, 14.

Valiant. Well but, brother, I pray thee tell us what was it that was the cause of thy being upon thy knees even now; was it for that some special mercy laid obligations upon thee, or how?

Stand. Why, we are, as you see, upon the Enchanted

Ground; and as I was coming along, I was musing with myself of what a dangerous nature the road in this place was, and how many that had come even thus far on pilgrimage had here been stopped and been destroyed. I thought also of the manner of the death with which this place destroyeth men. Those that die here, die of no violent distemper; the death which such die is not grievous to them. For he that goeth away in a sleep, begins that journey with desire and pleasure Yea, such acquiesce in the will of that disease.

Then Mr. Honest, interrupting him, said, "Did you see the two men asleep in the arbour?"

Stand. Ay, ay, I saw Heedless and Too-bold there; and for aught I know, there they will lie till they rot. (Prov. x, 7.) But let me go on with my tale. As I was thus musing, as I said, there was one in very pleasant attire, but old, who presented herself to me, and offered me three things, to wit, her body, her purse, and her bed. Now the truth is, I was both weary and sleepy. I am also as poor as an owlet, and that perhaps the witch knew. Well, I repulsed her once and again, but she put by my repulses, and smiled. Then I began to be angry; but she mattered that nothing at all. Then she made offers again, and said if I would be ruled by her, she would make me great and happy; for said she, "I am the mistress of the world, and men are made happy by me." Then I asked her name, and she told me it was Madam Bubble.[3] This set me further from her; but she still followed me with enticements. Then I betook me, as you saw, to my knees, and with hands lifted up, and cries, I prayed to Him that had said he would help. So just as you came up

[3] Madam Bubble, or this vain world.—*Bunyan's Marginal Note.*

the gentlewoman went away.[4] Then I continued to give thanks for this my great deliverance; for I verily believe she intended no good, but rather sought to make stop of me in my journey.

Hon. Without doubt her designs were bad. But, stay, now you talk of her, methinks I either have seen her, or have read some story of her.

Stand. Perhaps you have done both.

Hon. Madam Bubble! Is she not a tall, comely dame, something of a swarthy complexion?

Stand. Right, you hit it: she is just such a one.

Hon. Doth she not speak very smoothly, and give you a smile at the end of a sentence.

Stand. You fall right upon it again, for these are her very actions.

Hon. Doth she not wear a great purse by her side, and is not her hand often in it, fingering her money, as if that was her heart's delight?

Stand. 'Tis just so; had she stood by all this while you could not more amply have set her forth before me, and have better described her features.

Hon. Then he that drew her picture was a good limner, and he that wrote of her said true.

Great. This woman is a witch, and it is by virtue

[4] The Christian can best resist temptation when upon his knees; for then is he strongest, when, distrusting his own strength, he "takes hold of the strength" of the Most High. When, therefore, the world smiles, and seeks to allure thee from the pilgrims' way, follow the example of Standfast, and call upon thy God, and he who "knoweth how to deliver the godly out of temptations," (2 Peter ii, 9,) will

"Save thee in the prosperous hour
From the flattering tempter's power;
From his unsuspected wiles,
From the world's pernicious smiles

of her sorceries that this ground is enchanted. Whoever doth lay his head down in her lap, had as good lay it down on that block over which the axe doth hang; and whoever lay their eyes upon her beauty are counted the enemies of God.[5] This is she that maintaineth in their splendour all those that are the enemies of pilgrims. Yea, this is she that hath bought off many a man from a pilgrim's life. She is a great gossiper; she is always, both she and her daughters, at one pilgrim's heels or another, now commending, and then preferring the excellences of this life. She is a bold and impudent slut: she will talk with any man. She always laugheth poor pilgrims to scorn, but highly commends the rich. If there be one cunning to get money in a place, she will speak well of him from house to house. She loveth banqueting and feasting mainly well; she is always at one full table or another. She has given it out in some places that she is a goddess, and therefore some do worship her. She has her time and open places of cheating; and she will say and avow it, that none can show a good comparable to hers. She promiseth to dwell with children's children, if they will but love her and make much of her. She will cast out of her purse gold like dust in some places and to some persons. She loves to be sought after, spoken well of, and to lie in the bosoms of men. She is never weary of commending her commodities, and she loves them most that think best of her. She will promise to some crowns and kingdoms if they will but take her advice; yet many hath she brought to the halter, and ten thousand times more to hell.

[5] The friendship of the world is enmity with God. Jas. iv, 4. If any man love the world, the love of the Father is not in him. 1 John ii, 15

"O!" said Standfast, "what a mercy is it that I did resist her; for whither might she have drawn me!"

Great. Whither! nay, none but God knows whither. But in general, to be sure, she would have drawn thee into many foolish and hurtful lusts, which drown men in destruction and perdition. (1 Tim. vi, 9.) 'Twas she that set Absalom against his father, and Jeroboam against his master. 'Twas she that persuaded Judas to sell his Lord; and that prevailed with Demas to forsake the godly pilgrim's life. None can tell of the mischief that she doth. She makes variance betwixt rulers and subjects, betwixt parents and children, betwixt neighbour and neighbour, betwixt a man and his wife, betwixt a man and himself, betwixt the flesh and the spirit. Wherefore, good Mr. Standfast, be as your name is, and when you have done all, stand.

At this discourse there was among the pilgrims a mixture of joy and trembling; but at length they broke out and sang:—

"What danger is the pilgrim in!
How many are his foes!
How many ways there are to sin
No living mortal knows.

"Some in the ditch are spoil'd, yea can
Lie tumbling in the mire:
Some, though they shun the frying-pan
Do lea into the fire."

CHAPTER XIII.

They come to the land of Beulah—A messenger of death sent to Chiistiana—Her speech to the guide, to her children, and to hei companions—Her last day, and manner of departure—Mr. Ready to-halt summoned—His will—Mr. Feeble-mind summoned—His will—Mr. Despondency summoned—His will—His daughter goes too—Mr. Honest is summoned—He makes no will—A summons comes for Mr. Valiant-for-truth—His will—Mr. Standfast is summoned—His errand to his family—His last words—Conclusion.

After this I beheld until they were come into the land of Beulah, where the sun shineth night and day. Here, because they were weary, they betook themselves awhile to rest. And because this country was common for pilgrims, and because the orchards and vineyards that were here belonged to the King of the Celestial Country, therefore they were licensed to make bold with any of his things. But a little while soon refreshed them here ; for the bells did so ring, and the trumpets continually sounded so melodiously, that they could not sleep, and yet they received as much refreshing as if they slept their sleep ever so soundly. Here also all the noise of them that walked the streets was, "More pilgrims are come to town!" And another would answer, saying, "And so many went over the water, and were let in at the golden gates to-day!" They would cry again, "There is now a legion of shining ones just come to town, by which we know that there are more pilgrims upon the road for here they come to wait for them, and to comfort them after all their sorrow!" Then the pilgrims got up, and walked to and fro. But how were their ears now filled with heavenly noises, and their eyes delighted with celestial visions! In this land they heard nothing, saw nothing, felt nothing, smelt nothing, tasted nothing, that was offensive to their stomach or mind; only when they tasted of the water of the river over which they were to go, they thought that it tasted a little bitterish to the palate; but it proved sweeter when it was down.

In this place there was a record kept of the names of them that had been pilgrims of old, and a history of all the famous acts that they had done. It was here also much discoursed, how the river to some had had its flowings, and what ebbings it has had while others have gone over. It has been in a manner dry for some, while it has overflowed its banks for others.

In this place the children of the town would go into the King's gardens, and gather nosegays for the pilgrims, and bring them to them with much affection. Here also grew camphire, with spikenard and saffron, calamus and cinnamon, with all the trees of frankincense, myrrh, and aloes, with all chief spices. With these the pilgrims' chambers were perfumed while they stayed here; and with these are their bodies anointed, to prepare them to go over the river, when the time appointed was come.

Now while they lay here, and waited for the good hour, there was a noise in the town that there was a post come from the Celestial City, with matter of great importance to one Christiana, the wife of Christian the pilgrim. So inquiry was made for her, and the house was found out where she was. So the post presented her with a letter. The contents were, "Hail, good woman; I bring thee tidings that the Master calleth for thee, and expecteth that thou shouldst stand in his presence in clothes of immortality within these ten days."

When he had read this letter to her he gave her therewith a sure token that he was a true messenger and was come to bid her make haste to be gone. The token was an arrow with a point sharpened with love, let easily into her heart, which by degrees wrought so effectually with her, that at the time appointed she must be gone.

When Christiana saw that her time was come, and that she was the first of this company that was to go over, she called for Mr. Greatheart her guide, and told him how matters were. So he told her he was heartily glad of the news, and could have been glad had the post come for him.[1] Then she bid him that he should give advice how all things should be prepared for her journey. So he told her, saying, "Thus and thus it must be, and we that survive will accompany you to the river-side."

Then she called for her children, and gave them her blessing, and told them that she had read with comfort the mark that was set in their foreheads, and was glad to see them with her there, and that they had kept their garments so white. Lastly, she bequeathed to the poor that little she had, and commanded her sons and

[1] How welcome death is to them that have nothing to do but to die!—*Bunyan's Marginal Note*. Let dissolution come when it will, it can do thee no harm, that hast gotten the faith of the Lord Jesus into thy soul; (but be sure thou have it;) for it will be only a passage out of prison into a palace; out of a sea of troubles into a haven of rest; out of a cloud of enemies to an innumerable company of true, loving, and faithful friends; out of shame, reproach, and contempt, into exceeding great and eternal glory. For death shall not hurt thee with his sting, nor bite thee with his soul-murdering teeth, but shall be a welcome guest to thee, even to thy soul, in that it is sent to free thee from thy troubles which thou art in whilst here in this world, dwelling in the tabernacle of clay.—*Bunyan's Sighs from Hell.*

daughters to be ready against the messenger should come for them.

When she had spoken these words to her guide, and to her children, she called for Mr. Valiant-for-truth, and said unto him, "Sir, you have in all places showed yourself true-hearted; be faithful unto death, and my King will give you a crown of life. (Rev. ii, 10.) I would also entreat you to have an eye to my children; and if at any time you see them faint, speak comfortably to them. For my daughters, my sons' wives, they have been faithful, and a fulfilling of the promise upon them will be their end." But she gave Mr. Standfast a ring.

Then she called for old Mr. Honest, and said of him, "Behold an Israelite indeed, in whom is no guile!" John i, 47. Then said he, "I wish you a fair day when you set out for Mount Zion, and shall be glad to see that you go over the river dry-shod." But she answered, "Come wet, come dry, I long to be gone; for however the weather is in my journey, I shall have time enough when I come there to sit down and rest me and dry me."[2]

[2] Rest! how sweet the sound! It is melody to my ears! It lies as a reviving cordial at my heart, and from thence sends forth lively spirits which beat through all the pulses of my soul! Rest—not as the stone that rests on the earth, nor as this flesh shall rest in the grave, nor such a rest as the carnal world desires. O blessed rest! when we "rest not day nor night, saying, Holy, holy, holy, Lord God Almighty!" When we shall rest from sin, but not from worship; from suffering and sorrow, but not from joy! O blessed day! When I shall rest with God! When I shall rest in the bosom of my Lord! When I shall rest in knowing, loving, rejoicing, and praising! When my perfect soul and body shall together perfectly enjoy the most perfect God! When God, who is love itself, shall perfectly love me, and rest in his love to me, as I shall rest in my love to him; and rejoice over me with joy, and joy over me with singing, as I shall rejoice in him! There shall I be encircled with eternity, and ever, ever, praise the Lord. My

Then came in that good man, Mr. Ready-to-halt, to see her. So she said to him, "Thy travel hitherto has been with difficulty; but that will make thy rest the sweeter. Watch and be ready; for at an hour when ye think not, the messenger may come."

After him came Mr. Despondency and his daughter Much-afraid, to whom she said, "You ought with thankfulness for ever to remember your deliverance from the hands of Giant Despair, and out of Doubting Castle. The effect of that mercy is that you are brought with safety hither. Be ye watchful, and cast away fear; be sober, and hope to the end."

Then she said to Mr. Feeble-mind, "Thou wast delivered from the mouth of Giant Slay-good, that thou mightest live in the light of the living, and see thy King with comfort. Only I advise thee to repent of thine aptness to fear and doubt of his goodness, before he sends for thee; lest thou shouldst, when he comes, be forced to stand before him for that fault with blushing."

Now the day drew on that Christiana must be gone. So the road was full of people to see her take her journey. But behold, all the banks beyond the river were full of horses and chariots, which were come down from above to accompany her to the city gate. So she came forth, and entered the river, with a beckon of farewell to those that followed her. The last words that she was

face will not wrinkle, nor my hair be gray, for this corruptible shall have put on incorruption, and this mortal immortality, and death shall be swallowed up in victory. The date of my lease shall no more expire, nor shall I more trouble myself with thoughts of death, nor lose my joys through fear of losing them. When millions of ages are passed, my glory is but beginning; and when millions more are passed, it is no nearer ending Every day is all noon, every month is harvest, every year is a jubilee, every age is full manhood, and all this is one eternity —*Baxter's Saints' Everlasting Rest.*

heard to say were, "I come, Lord, to be with thee and bless thee!" So her children and friends returned to their place, for those that waited for Christiana had carried her out of their sight. So she went, and called, and entered in at the gate with all the ceremonies of joy that her husband Christian had entered with before her. At her departure the children wept. But Mr. Greatheart and Mr. Valiant played upon the well-tuned cymbal and harp for joy. So all departed to their respective places.

In process of time, there came a post to the town again, and his business was with Mr. Ready-to-halt. So he inquired him out, and said, "I am come from Him whom thou hast loved and followed, though upon crutches; and my message is to tell thee that he expects thee at his table to sup with him in his kingdom, the next day after Easter; wherefore prepare thyself for this journey." Then he also gave him a token that he was a true messenger, saying, "I have broken thy golden bowl, and loosed thy silver cord." Eccles. xii, 6.

After this Mr. Ready-to-halt called for his fellow-pilgrims, and told them, saying, "I am sent for, and God shall surely visit you also." So he desired Mr. Valiant to make his will. And because he had nothing to bequeath to them that should survive him but his crutches, and his good wishes, therefore thus he said, "These crutches I bequeath to my son, that shall tread in my steps, with a hundred warm wishes that he may prove better than I have been." Then he thanked Mr. Greatheart for his conduct and kindness, and so addressed himself to his journey. When he came to the brink of the river he said, "Now I shall have no more need of these crutches, since yonder are chariots and horses for me to ride on." The last words he was heard to say were, "Welcome life!" So he went his way.

After this Mr. Feeble-mind had tidings brought him that the post sounded his horn at his chamber door. Then he came in and told him, saying, "I am come to tell thee that thy Master hath need of thee, and that in a very little time thou must behold his face in brightness. And take this as a token of the truth of my message: 'Those that look out at the windows shall be darkened.'" Eccles. xii, 3. Then Mr. Feeble-mind called for his friends, and told them what errand had been brought unto him, and what token he had received of the truth of the message. Then he said, "Since I have nothing to bequeath to any, to what purpose should I make a will? As for my feeble mind, that I will leave behind me, for that I shall have no need of in the place whither I go, nor is it worth bestowing upon the poorest pilgrims; wherefore, when I am gone, I desire that you, Mr. Valiant, would bury it in a dunghill." This done, and the day being come on which he was to depart, he entered the river as the rest. His last words were, "Hold out, faith and patience!" So he went over to the other side.

When days had many of them passed away, Mr. Despondency was sent for; for a post was come, and brought this message to him: "Trembling man! these are to summon thee to be ready with the King by the next Lord's day, to shout for joy for thy deliverance from all thy doubtings. And, (said the messenger,) that my message is true, take this for a proof:" so he gave him a grasshopper to be a burden unto him. Eccl. xii, 5.

Now Mr. Despondency's daughter, whose name was Much-afraid, said, when she heard what was done, that she would go with her father. Then Mr. Despondency said to his friends, "Myself and my daughter, you know what we have been, and how troublesomely we have behaved ourselves in every company. My will and my daughter's is, that our desponds and slavish fears be by no man ever received, from the day of our departure, for ever; for I know that after my death they will offer themselves to others. For to be plain with you, they are ghosts which we entertained when we first began to be pilgrims, and could never shake them off after; and they will walk about, and seek entertainment of the pilgrims; but for our sakes, shut the doors upon them." When the time was come for them to depart, they went up to the brink of the river. The last words of Mr. Despondency were, "Farewell, night! welcome, day!" His daughter went through the river singing, but none could understand what she said.

Then it came to pass awhile after, that there was a post in the town that inquired for Mr. Honest. So he came to the house where he was, and delivered to his hand these lines: "Thou art commanded to be ready against this day seven-night, to present thyself before thy Lord, at his Father's house. And for a token that my message is true, 'All the daughters of music shall be brought low.'" Eccles. xii, 4. Then Mr. Honest called for his friends, and said unto them, "I die, but shall make no will. As for my honesty, it shall go with me; let him that comes after be told of this." When the day that he was to be gone was come, he addressed himself to go over the river. Now the river at that time overflowed its banks in some places; but Mr. Honest, in his life-time, had spoken to one Good-conscience to meet him there, the which he also did, and lent him his hand, and so helped him over.[3] The last words of Mr. Honest were, "Grace reigns!" So he left the world.

After this it was noised abroad that Mr. Valiant-for truth was taken with a summons, by the same post as the other, and had this for a token that the summons was true, "That his pitcher was broken at the fountain." Eccles. xii, 6. When he understood it, he called for his friends, and told them of it. Then said he, "I am going to my Father's; and though with great difficulty I have got hither, yet now I do not repent me of all the trouble I have been at to arrive where I am. My sword I give to him that shall succeed me in my pilgrimage, and my courage and skill to him that can get it. My marks and scars I carry with me, to be a witness for me that I have fought His battles who will now be my rewarder." When the day that he must go hence was come, many accompanied him to the river-side, into which as he went, he said, "Death, where is thy sting?" And as he went down deeper, he said, "Grave, where is thy victory?" Sohe passed over, and all the trumpets sounded for him on the other side.

Then there came forth a summons for Mr. Standfast. This Mr. Standfast was he that the pilgrims found upon his knees in the Enchanted Ground. And the post brought it him open in his hands; the contents whereof were, that he must prepare for a change of life, for his Master was not willing that he should be so far from him any longer. At this Mr. Standfast was put in a muse. "Nay," said the messenger, "you need not doubt of the truth of my message: for here is

[3] A dying bed is made easy by those good works that men have done in their life for the name of God.—*Bunyan's Paul's Departure.*

a token of the truth thereof: 'Thy wheel is broken at the cistern.'" Eccles. xii, 6. Then he called to him Mr. Greatheart, who was their guide, and said unto him, "Sir, although it was not my hap to be much in your good company during the days of my pilgrimage, yet, since the time I knew you, you have been profitable to me. When I came from home, I left behind me a wife and five small children; let me entreat you, at your return, (for I know that you go and return to your Master's house, in hopes that you may yet be a conductor to more of the holy pilgrims,) that you send to my family, and let them be acquainted with all that hath and shall happen unto me. Tell them moreover of my happy arrival at this place, and of the present and late blessed condition I am in. Tell them also of Christian and Christiana his wife, and how she and her children came after her husband. Tell them also what a happy end she made, and whither she has gone. I have little or nothing to send to my family, unless it be prayers and tears for them; of which it will suffice that you acquaint them, if peradventure they may prevail."

When Mr. Standfast had thus set things in order, and the time being come for him to haste him away, he also went down to the river. Now there was a great calm at that time in the river; wherefore Mr. Standfast, when he was about half way in, stood awhile, and talked to his companions that had waited upon him thither. And he said, "This river has been a terror to many; yea, the thoughts of it also have often frightened me; but now methinks I stand easy; my foot is fixed upon that on which the feet of the priests that bare the ark of the covenant stood while Israel went over Jordan. (Josh. iii, 17.) The waters indeed are to the palate bitter, and to the stomach cold; yet the thoughts of what I am going to, and of the conduct that waits for me on the other side, doth lie as a glowing coal at my heart. I see myself now at the end of my journey; my toilsome days are ended. I am going to see that head that was crowned with thorns, and that face that was spit upon for me. I have formerly lived by hearsay and faith; but now I go where I shall live by sight, and shall be with Him in whose company I delight myself. I have loved to hear my Lord spoken of; and wherever I have seen the print of his shoe in the earth, there I have coveted to set my foot too. His name has been to me a civet-box; yea, sweeter than all perfumes. His voice to me has been most sweet, and his countenance I have more desired than they that have most desired the light of the sun. His words I did use to gather for my food, and for antidotes against my faintings. He has held me, and hath kept me from mine iniquities; yea, my steps hath he strengthened in his way."

Now while he was thus in discourse his countenance changed; his strong man bowed under him: and after he had said, "Take me, for I come unto thee," he ceased to be seen of them.

But glorious it was to see how the open region was filled with horses and chariots, with trumpeters and pipers, with singers and players on stringed instruments, to welcome the pilgrims as they went up, and followed one another in at the Beautiful Gate of the City.

As for Christiana's children, the four boys that Christiana brought, with their wives and children, I did not stay where I was till they were gone over. Also since I came away, I heard one say that they were yet alive, and so would be for the increase of the church in that place where they were, for a time.

Should it be my lot to go that way again, I may give those that desire it an account of what I here am silent about. Meantime I bid my reader

FAREWELL.[4]

[4] Thus have I done with directing thee how to run to the kingdom; be sure thou keep in memory what I have said unto thee, lest thou lose thy way. But because I would have thee think of them, take all in short in this little bit of paper:—

1. Get into the way. 2. Then stand in it. 3. Then strip and lay aside everything that would hinder. 4. Beware of by-paths. 5. Do not gaze and stare too much about thee, but be sure to ponder the path of thy feet. 6. Do not stop for any that call after thee, whether it be the world, the flesh, or the devil; for all these will hinder thy journey if possible. 7. Be not daunted with any discouragements thou meetest with as thou goest. 8. Take heed of stumbling at the cross. 9. Cry hard to God for an enlightened heart and willing mind: and God give thee a prosperous journey.—*Bunyan's Heavenly Footman*

A new and enlarged edition of

THE LIFE OF JOHN BUNYAN,

AUTHOR OF THE PILGRIM'S PROGRESS, HOLY WAR, ETC.

BY STEPHEN B. WICKENS.

Large 18*mo*. *Pages* 344. *Price* 25 *cents*.

This volume embraces the substance of Bunyan's remarkable autobiography, entitled, "Grace Abounding to the Chief of Sinners;" together with what else is known with certainty respecting his life, labours, writings, and character. It is embellished with a portrait and several wood-cuts.

This is a precious little volume, in which all who sincerely desire to be Christians, in heart and in life, will find instruction and comfort. Bunyan's life gives both precept and example to guide the spiritual traveler. His religious exercises, both as a seeker and a professor of religion, are given with remarkable clearness and point, and his whole experience is in the highest degree edifying. The author evidently aims to be useful, and has adapted his style as happily to his purpose as to his subject. This should be a standard book, and found in every family and Sunday-school library, close beside the Pilgrim's Progress, and the Holy War.—*Christian Advocate and Journal.*

We have read this Life of Bunyan with uncommon interest and pleasure, and regard it, for several reasons, as the best and most satisfactory that we have seen. Bunyan was one of the most remarkable men of that remarkable age in which he lived, and this excellent and judicious account of his parentage, conversion, trials, life, doings, and death, is such as we can cordially and conscientiously recommend.—*Lutheran Observer.*

Everybody who reads the Pilgrim's Progress (and almost everybody does read it over and over again) will surely like to read under what circumstances it was written. The Life of the author of the Pilgrim, which is full of interest, has not lost any of its attractions in the hands of this writer: on the contrary, he has in this work imbodied many interesting facts only heretofore found in detached parts. The volume is particularly adapted to family and Sabbath-school libraries.—*Christian Repository.*

What more interesting biography could appear than one, well-written, having for its subject the author of the Pilgrim's Progress? Such is the book before us. It contains a handsome engraved likeness of the celebrated *dreamer*, (who, though incarcerated in the darkness of a prison, was truly "a burning and a shining light,") and is well worth reading.—*Pittsburg Christian Advocate.*

This is one of the most judicious biographies of Bunyan that we have seen. The author evidently appreciates the genius and character of that extraordinary man, and has an accurate knowledge of cotemporaneous events and personages, and with much industry has collected a great number of facts connected directly or indirectly with his subject. We have been especially pleased with the minute analysis of Bunyan's character, both as to his natural abilities and those all-powerful impulses which, after his conversion, forced him to the defense of the truth. The work is embellished with a well-engraved portrait of Bunyan and several excellent wood-cuts representing his birth-place, residence, burial-place, &c.—*Columbian Magazine.*

This little volume is altogether creditable to the author's pen. It is well digested, well written, and illustrated by some half a dozen engravings.—*Zion's Herald.*

Decidedly the best Life of "good old Bunyan" we have yet seen. The author has brought to his task every requisite for such a work, admiration of the subject of his memoir, a thorough acquaintance with his writings, a unison of sentiment and an experimental knowledge of those religious feelings and spiritual conflicts of which Bunyan was the subject, and has produced a more original work on the life and character of Bunyan than we expected, at this late day, to have the pleasure of perusing. Added to these, the work is distinguished by sound criticism, impartial judgment, and a clear and nervous style.—*New-York Spectator.*

This small volume gives a more complete and connected account of Bunyan than is elsewhere to be found. It is a very neat and interesting piece of biography, and shows in the construction a pen not unused to literary work. Whoever has the "Pilgrim's Progress," should have the Life of its lowly but immortal author; and no family or Sunday school should be without them both. It has several interesting wood-cuts: a view of Bunyan's cottage at Elstow; a fac-simile of his writing; the London pulpit in which he preached; and his tomb in Bunhill Fields, the burial-place of Dissenters in London. There is also an engraved portrait of Bunyan. We are very much pleased with the work, and cannot but highly recommend it to our readers.—*Canada Christian Guardian.*

INDEX.

ENGRAVINGS.

THE END.

www.ingramcontent.com/pod-product-compliance
Lightning Source LLC
LaVergne TN
LVHW020924110826
845150LV00004B/766

* 9 7 8 1 4 2 5 5 5 4 1 8 7 *